Review

Once again we find Terrllss-rr, up to his ears in trouble. *With Shadow and Thunder* plunges the reader into the corrupt world of diplomatic manoeuvring. This book is an astonishing display of craftsmanship, a must read. Stefan Vučak weaves a science fiction world of mystery and suspense. The numerous plots of the story are intricately woven together to make for a smooth and entertaining read.

Serial Science Fiction Reviews

2002 EPIC finalist

I0592619

Books by Stefan Vučak

General Fiction:
Cry of Eagles
All the Evils
Towers of Darkness
Strike for Honor
Proportional Response
Legitimate Power
Autumn Leaves
All My Sunsets
F/X-26
28th Amendment
Night Sirens
Broken Rose

Shadow Gods Saga:
In the Shadow of Death
Against the Gods of Shadow
A Whisper from Shadow
Shadow Masters
Immortal in Shadow
With Shadow and Thunder
Through the Valley of Shadow
Guardians of Shadow

Science Fiction:
Fulfillment
Lifeliners

Non-Fiction:
Writing Tips for Authors

Contact at:
www.stefanvucak.com

WITH SHADOW AND THUNDER

By

Stefan Vučak

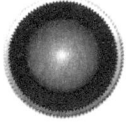

Stefan Vučak ©2000
ISBN-10: 0648473171
ISBN-13: 9780648473176

Dedication

To my mother ... and her own life in shadow

Acknowledgments

Omega Swan Nebula (M17) – Credit: NASA, ESA, and J. Hester (ASU).

Cover art by Laura Shinn.
http://laurashinn.yolasite.com

Map of the Serrll Combine

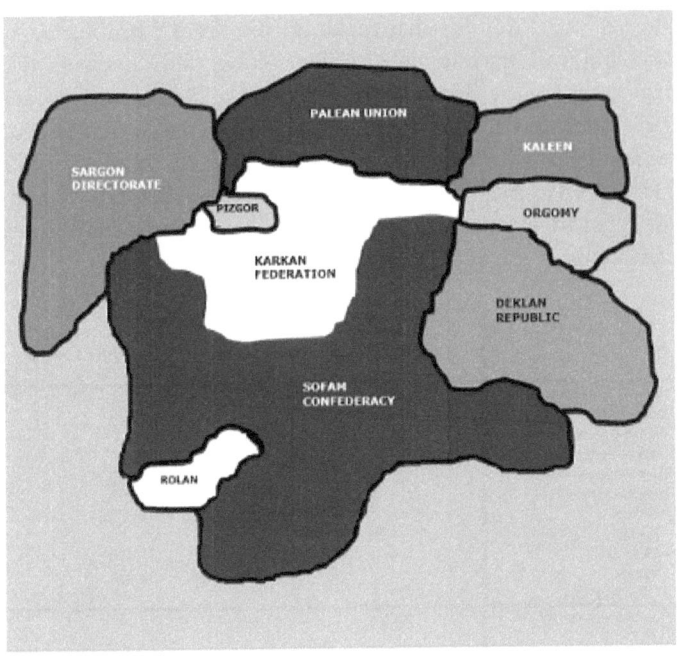

Composition of the Serrll Combine

The 247 star systems that make up the Serrll Combine is an association of six interstellar power blocks, split between two rival camps—the Servatory Party and the Revisionists. Each star system has a single representative in Captal's General Assembly from which members are elected to the ruling ten-seat Executive Council. Seats are based on a percentage of systems occupied by each power block in relation to the total number of systems in the Serrll Combine.

Name	No of Star Systems	Percentage of Total	Executive Council Seats
Sofam Confederacy	83	34	4
Deklan Republic	19	8	1
Palean Union	28	11	1
Karkan Federation	46	19	2
Sargon Directorate	32	12	1
Independents:		15	1
- Kaleen	8		
- Rolan	5		
- Orgomy	6		
- Pizgor	3		
- Other systems	17		
General Assembly	**247**	**100**	**10**
Outposts	40		
Protectorates	34		

Principal political blocks:

Revisionist Party:	Palean Union
	Deklan Republic
	Sofam Confederacy
Servatory Party:	Karkan Federation
	Sargon Directorate
	Nonaligned Independents

Composition of the Executive Council:

Security Council	Bureau of Colonial and Protectorate Affairs
	Bureau of Defense
	Bureau of Cultural Affairs
Administrative Council	Bureau of Administrative Affairs
	Bureau of Justice
Economics Council	Bureau of Economic Affairs
	Bureau of Technology and Development
Central Planning Council	Bureau of Central Planning and Development

Chapter One

At the Field, the shuttle waited.

Official gatherings always gave Terr a pain, and this one was no exception. He attached himself to a tight little group, staked out a bit of floor space and tried to appear attentive. It wasn't working. Surrounded by a throng of beribboned uniforms, thinly clad female forms, friendly chatter and lots of laughter, he suddenly felt alone.

Ornate chandeliers hung from heavy chains beneath a sculptured dome. Frescos of past deeds and valor helped fill the ceiling spaces. Tall black-veined marble columns hugged the walls. They provided a measure of relative seclusion from prying eyes. Each small group, hands waving and ample bellies heaving, claimed one. Intruders were discouraged. A surprising amount of business got done behind such pillars. Terr should know, about to conclude a deal of his own.

At the far end of the hall a band toiled gamely on strands of reedy music, thin and scratchy. It drifted forlornly above the noise of the party and did little to perk him up, but that was the kind of stuff they went for around here. He nodded sagely at some witty crack and made the usual crappy responses that went with small talk on occasions such as these. Things could have been worse. He'd had his choice; this or fill out reports.

There were all kinds of uniforms on display: dark green of the assault forces, dress blacks of the Scout Fleet, and a sprinkling of parade whites. Terr noted with a nod the conspicuous absence of any working grays. Its appearance would probably have earned the unfortunate a terminal career gasper. The brass knobs from Captal wore what they damn well pleased. The local female community added color—in eye-popping fashion. For the occasion, Terr squeezed himself into a full-decked white Scout uniform. His left breast held a bordered gold oval full of little colored pins—decorations fruit salad. A thin yellow stripe ran down the seam of his trousers, denoting a field grade officer. He looked the part, but it made him uncomfortable—a dressed-up cadet!

After an urbane smile and a mumbled excuse, he disengaged himself from the tableau and pushed his way through clearly defined demarcation lines that marked flag officer territories, senior diplomats and the rest, trying to hang some enthusiasm on his face and not making it. He figured this whole job was a case of Anabb's twisted sense of humor, a way of getting even for past sins. Dirty, rotten old fart.

Well, the only way to beat the game, he could slosh his brain or go cruising for some female action. On this occasion, he couldn't do either. He owed it to Teena not to mess around, not that he would ever betray her trust. Which was a damned shame, for there were enough willing ladies on the prowl to add interest to the hunt. He shook his head and grunted. Time to do some paid work.

He snagged a frosted tumbler off a passing tray wielded by one of the unobtrusive drifting waiters and took a sip. The stuff burned on its way down and his eyes unfocused a bit. He blinked at the cloying yellow liquid and shrugged.

Life in the Diplomatic Branch was hell.

He'd been told this was a small gathering as functions usually go. The cavernous Trillian Assembly reception hall had seen bigger. Then again, this was supposed to be a formal occasion, strictly by invitation only. Looking around, he couldn't really tell the difference. Only a speck in Sargon space, the Trillian locals figured any excuse to hold a blowout should not be missed. Tonight, the political knives were sheathed and the vitriol forgotten. Probably diluted by a drink or two, he thought moodily.

Trillian's diplomatic community were toasting the Controller's first year in office. Seen as a rising star, the local Servatory Party branch went all out. Terr got picked, among other things, to represent Captal's Bureau of Cultural Affairs. After all, the Controller being one of government's own, nobody could say afterward the government didn't take care of its own.

He swallowed the last of his drink and concluded that Anabb would have fitted right in with all the other starched shirts. This would definitely be his macabre idea of a good time.

He absently touched a ragged scar above his left eyebrow, a close encounter with a raider. Not quite bored, he looked around, counting the gun handlers. Easy to spot, they were guys wearing wooden smiles, cold eyes and suspicious stares. The Controller they were guarding chatted busily with a demurely provocative female dressed in a shimmering wisp of blue nothing. She wore a sultry destructive look that always meant trouble for someone. In a moment, the Controller would have more trouble than he could handle. Around them, hovering like a cloud, clustered the usual swarm of foreign dignitaries and hangers-on.

Gashkarali, Controller of Trillian, looked ordinary enough. Terr wondered what he did to deserve Death's wrath. A year in office didn't seem long enough to screw things up that much. He must have pissed off somebody real bad, though. During the mission brief, Anabb had given Terr the usual glib worm crap about factional plots and Captal secrets, that kind of stuff. The way he said it, the fate of the Serrll hung in the balance. Terr admitted it sounded good at the time. It almost got him all choked up and patriotic, but he managed to contain himself.

Still, Anabb's fancy tirade could not hide the blunt orders.

Gashkarali had to die.

Normally, that would have been enough for Terr. So far, he was happy leaving the whys to Anabb. That gambit had worked for almost two years—until his last mission, a General

Assembly rep in her first term. She spoiled it all and got him thinking. Always a bad sign in his line of work. Her Servatory Party cell managed to execute a level two penetration of the Diplomatic Branch's comms center and compromised two of Anabb's best operatives. What he said to the security people hadn't been pretty, but nonetheless effective. The ensuing stink resulted in another operative suddenly enjoying an extended vacation on Cantor—counting rocks on the penal planet. She was returning to Captal when Terr caught up with her. The fact that the target was a female didn't faze him at all. There were as many bitches around as there were traitorous bastards.

Something she said before the lightnings struck her, looking at him with fierce defiance, challenging him, got him thinking. She died believing in the conviction of her cause. Where was the conviction of *his* cause, she demanded scornfully. Technically, he executed an untraceable termination mission, but could not get her words out of his mind. The rot had set in.

Afterward, he kept seeing the wrinkled features of his old master set in stern disapproval. He was not exactly using his gift for self-enlightenment. He remembered drinking quite a lot while waiting for the liner to touch down on the transit port to Taltair.

Looking around now at the glitter and pomp of the hall, his master did not have to tell him the gods would not exactly approve the abuse of their gift. Terr allowed himself a brief frown of uncertainty. The last thing he needed right now was his conscience giving him a hard time. Anabb paid him to do a job, not to like it.

Rit!

As he studied the hired stiffs, he clicked his tongue and shook his head. The security here was lousy. Lousy or not, he wasn't about to rush in and fumble it. There were plenty of other beginner's tricks he could fall for.

On a job, he always worked under his official persona. That precaution saved him more than once from a compromisingly sticky predicament. As Anabb pointed out the obvious on many occasions: any cover, no matter how elaborate, can be blown. A diplomatic attaché, Terr could move around without attracting more than his usual quota of hostile stares. If some dignitary should suddenly fade out of sight while he chanced to be around…well, it happened to the best of them.

Still, a possibility existed that some smart computer somewhere could build a correlation between his movements and a few untimely deaths. The result would undoubtedly cause someone in the Servatory Party machine to raise a speculative eyebrow. Not that he handled a body job every time he went out. He *did* do legitimate work on occasions, enough to keep below the statistical threshold. Nevertheless, he knew if he kept this up long enough, he was bound to fall for some terminal gag. Anabb didn't have to tell him that one. He sort of figured it out by himself.

Time perhaps for him to go into a new line of business. Like conning a ship again. Right now, he reflected wistfully, he would be quite happy herding his old M-3, anything that would take him away from Anabb. The craggy old face and grating humor had started to get on his nerves. *Psandra* had been a good ship to him…

The party getting kind of boring, people were beginning to drift away. The hall was too hot and the atmosphere cloying. The chatter a constant wash of noise, Terr longed for a moment of silence. Getting restless, he looked for an excuse to do a fade himself.

But if he wanted to catch that shuttle, he better finish with Gashkarali. He leaned against a convenient pillar, twirled his tumbler of cloying booze, and allowed the images to come. The sounds of the party faded around him, the figures blurred, and he merged with the reality in his mind. Arms raised, cape fluttering behind him, he contemplated the rolling dunes and the shifting sands beneath a hot amber sky. He could almost feel the heat and the smells of desert sands wash over him. The words came to him easily. When Death settled on his shoulders, he found the burden heavy. The images faded and he felt a sharp pang of loss. He badly needed the solitude and vastness of the open sands to heal himself. Someone bumped into him and mumbled an apology. Terr didn't even notice him.

He gritted his teeth, primed the Death Messenger and moved in. The security guys never reacted when he approached Gashkarali. To them, he was only another minor flunkey. That was all right with him. Walking past the Controller, Terr hesitated, tempted to let him live, then brushed his arm as he went. A small blue spark jumped between them. Gashkarali merely twitched, not breaking his gushing tirade to the pretty thing hanging onto his every word. In eighteen hours, the hand of Death would collect him and no one would be able to connect it to this party, or to Terr.

He melted into the crowd, suddenly soured of the whole thing, but a bit late for second thoughts or regrets. Once loosed, Death had to feed. He pushed his way through the grouped guests, just wanting to get out of the damned place.

Outside, the air had a clean washed smell that comes after a shower and he breathed it in deeply. It helped to clean the stale odor he had picked up inside. The guard, crisp and regulation, his phase rifle vertical by his side, snapped to attention when Terr appeared in the doorway. The communal driver, looking bored and sleepy, brightened as Terr descended down polished stone steps. He quickly raised the bubble canopy and climbed out. He beamed as though Terr was his long lost son returned, sketched a brief salute and opened the door. Terr settled into the upholstery with a stifled grunt. He felt Death linger, then the power faded, leaving him empty and hollow.

"The Ambassador, sir?" the driver asked, rich with experience, used to carrying the movers and the powerful. The bubble snicked shut around them. Terr thumbed the mike pad and the driver's face glowed in the plate.

"Yeah," he said impatiently. He touched another pad and

the bubble became opaque. A thin ribbon of green, softly glowing around the bubble boundary, remained. The communal rose with a faint hum of power and he felt himself sag.

He must have dozed off, for the next thing he heard was the incessant buzz from the mike. Through the transparent bubble, he saw the combie approaching one of the landing ramps of the Ambassador hotel. The ramp protruded like a rude tongue near the top of the glittering column of ceramic and color-reactive panels. The communal hovered briefly, then settled to the spooling down sound of the power plant.

The charge pad glowed brown, pulsing gently as it waited. Terr pressed his palm against it and it changed to dull yellow. The door opened. The driver stood beside it, still beaming. Terr climbed out and the driver gave him another one of his home-made salutes. Terr nodded as the driver wished him a pleasant night. He waited while the communal took off, then followed it with his eyes as it disappeared into the traffic stream. Shoulders drooping, he walked slowly toward the entrance. Reaction had set in and he was beginning to feel fragile and moody. This job got him thinking again, and he didn't want to do any thinking just then.

He didn't have much to pack. The hotel management was sorry to see him go—at least they pretended. A chorus of 'Have a good flight, sir.', and 'We hope you will visit the Ambassador again, sir.', and crap like that followed him to the cable-tube. He hated goodbyes!

The tube deposited him at the civilian end of the Field inter-star terminus. His footsteps echoed faintly on the hard polished floor as he strode through the crowded departure lounge toward the security gate. Trillian was not exactly on the beaten tourist path, but locals still traveled within the system. With his Diplomatic Branch ID, he cleared customs without having to wade through packed queues, snarling children and harassed parents. He gave silent thanks for that. Twenty minutes later the shuttle punched through the atmosphere bound for Karmal, where he would change flights for Taltair.

* * *

Anatol Keller simmered, his attention focused on the main holoview plot as it followed the trace of the Orieli ship slowly moving toward him. Thick stubby fingers tapped the armrest of his command couch, the only evidence of his restlessness. Unconsciously, he pulled back his purple-red lips into a silent snarl of frustration.

Perdition on the aliens!

His skin deepest black, head perfectly round, covered by a faint oily sheen. Normally thin and pinched, his nostrils now flared as they tended to do in moments of tension. His thick heavy-set form shifted restlessly as he clutched the armrest.

Unwelcome or not, he had to deal with them.

"Plot? Talk to me," he demanded without turning his head. His deep throaty voice reflected his heaviness.

"Target now showing two point-eight million talans indicated. No course deviations. No anomalous power emissions. Detecting primary interceptor net configuration only. Scan matches previously recorded ident curve. Profile confirmed," the tactical plot officer announced briskly. His eyes flicked briefly at Anatol, not wishing to draw further attention from his irascible commander.

Profile confirmed. As though there was any doubt, Anatol mused bitterly.

In the plot display, the image of the Orieli cruiser rotated through various multi-dimensional position schematics. Columns of figures flashed and faded beside each image. The images and the figures did not tell Anatol anything he didn't already know. His eyes probed the plot officer.

"The other two M-4s maintaining relativity?"

"In position. Tandem link established and in standby

mode. All systems read nominal. Tactical available on command."

"Mmm." Anatol gave a noncommittal grunt. At least the crew were with it.

The M-4 6/A Sofam-built main battle cruiser was the mainstay of the Serrll Scout Fleet, and a front-line presence of the General Assembly's authority. It had a better part of nine tetalans grade C composite armor on top of the four-tetalan-thick polymer hull construct. Even without the secondary shield grid, it could withstand several twenty-four-millisecond bursts of up to one hundred and twenty-eight TeV at close range. Hopefully, it gave it enough time to get away or press an attack.

It mounted two Koyami 3/C phased array generators; their power channeled through a single projector dome beneath its belly. Capable of pouring almost continuous twenty-four-millisecond, 128 TeV bursts to a maximum range of 140,000 talans, an M-4 carried a crew of 240. Formed into a triad with two other ships, their fire control systems slaved to the command unit, the M-4 represented a formidable weapons platform.

Sofam Industries built them well, but they didn't have the Orieli in mind when they did it.

Unable to contain his irritation, Anatol slapped the armrest with the flat of his hand and sprang out of the formchair. Everyone suddenly found themselves preoccupied, conscious of Anatol's discomfort. He started pacing along the raised tactical platform overlooking the main control stations two steps down. He shot a withering glance at his executive officer, standing apparently unconcerned behind the tactical station console, hands clasped casually behind his back. It irritated him that the exec could be so unmoved by the irony of the situation. Then again, it wasn't *his* ass on the line. Anatol paced up and down, his eyes flicking from time to time at the main plot.

Beneath the transparent navigation bubble the darkened command deck was deceptively quiet. The silence distracted by the muted whisper of status reports, inter-deck comms and tactical computer readiness notices. Blocking a full quarter of the bubble, the Moon was a brilliant wedge of grays, whites and blacks; a smooth sickle that bordered a circle of darkness drilled through the stars. Above it, almost within touching distance, hung the blue and white of Earth.

The nav dome ringed the deck above them. Beneath it, display plates, sensor stations and touch-sensitive, color-reactive control panels arrayed the inward-sloping frame. A full-dimensional holograph node occupied the center of the deck. If necessary the tactical plot it now showed could be replicated on the bubble above them. Officers and crew unobtrusively monitored the largely automated operation of the warship.

Anatol paused in his stride and glowered at his executive officer.

"And what are you so damned smug about? Never mind, I don't want to know," he growled and jerked his head at the plot. "What do you make of all this?"

Used to these bursts of vitriolic behavior from Anatol, the exec ignored them. He raised a quizzical eyebrow and pointed at the repeater plate beside them.

"They're already in the inner system. Doctrine calls for a standard defensive posture."

"A standard defensive posture, eh?" Anatol pierced his exec with eyes of ebony, expressionless buttons that reflected no light or the individual within. "Is that your recommendation?"

Sensitive to his commander's frustration the exec shrugged. "Tactically, there is nothing to be gained by going farther out."

Anatol planted his hands on his hips. "Who said this was a tactical situation, anyway?"

"It isn't? Five years ago—"

"One of those damned things from the pit almost put three of my ships in the junkyard. I haven't forgotten."

"I didn't mean it that way—"

"Hah!"

Anatol shook his head in disgust and stomped away. With a surly glance at the plot, he lowered himself stiffly into the command couch.

Silent rage kept his tall two-katalan-high frame coiled in his seat. The alien ship out there represented everything that had gone wrong with his career. With the precision of a well-planned campaign, he had positioned himself on track for Prima Scout rank and a coveted post at CAPFLTCOM, Cap-tal's Fleet Command headquarters. Tactical command never appealed to him. He saw himself as a strategist, a thinker, above the mundane minutiae of ship routine. With the cultivation of a few carefully chosen Servatory Party luminaries, his future seemed assured.

Like a cup from which he was about to drink, that future was dashed by a single encounter with a ship just like the one at whose plot he stared now. It might even be the very one. Even now the memory of that brief exchange made him cringe.

It all started innocently enough. After a routine mission on Earth to destroy an old C-32 scoutship the locals managed to dig up in a Mayan ruin, First Scout Terrllss-rr was returning to Taltair when he encountered the enigmatic Orieli. The alien survey ship came through the Moanar Nebula, some two thousand light-years beyond Serrll space. They were about to head home when leakage from the Serrll Moon Base power core attracted them to Sol. The aliens invited Terr aboard their ship and, after a brief exchange of information, the Orieli proceeded to do a quick survey of Earth. Twenty days later, they made another unexpected appearance. With only an M-1, Terr was in no position to stop the Orieli, but with three M-4s around him, Anatol was not about to let them into the Sol system that easily. When the Orieli ship began to move, he fired at it.

Refusing to withdraw, the Orieli ship simply stood there, taking everything Anatol could throw at it. Confident in his ability to interdict the alien, he hadn't bothered to slave in the firepower of his two supporting M-4s. That turned out to be a serious tactical mistake. When the alien finally tired of his game and fired back, its single burst crashed through his shield grids as though they were not there. It took the Orieli ship two more shots to disable his other ships. Three bursts, that is all it took to take out three front-line Serrll ships. That kind of firepower chilled him.

With the ships of his triad crippled, shields down, Anatol waited for the fire that would have reduced his M-4s to slag. It might have been better that way, but the Orieli ship did not fire. It just moved past his wallowing M-4s.

He survived the ensuing political furrow, but even his powerful Captal friends could not remove an official reprimand now blotting his record. CAPFLTCOM cited his action as an exemplary lack of command judgment. No matter what they called it, it was a career stopper. The reprimand ensured he would never make Prima Scout.

The knowledge galled him.

What in perdition was he supposed to do? Allow those Orieli sons of bitches to breach Serrll's territorial integrity? The Rules of Engagement left him little option. If he hadn't stood his ground, those bureaucratic bastards on Captal would've had him on charges of dereliction of duty, conduct unbecoming, even cowardice. To cover their embarrassment at having three line warships dismissed so easily, CAPFLTCOM looked around for someone to carry the fallout. It was his bad luck they decided to pick him.

Since then, he'd had a series of dead-end assed commands. His current tour as commander of the Serrll Moon Base a case in point. The Sol system was considered the crappy end of nowhere. A posting for losers who could not otherwise make it. Still, no matter what the worm shitters at CAPFLTCOM might otherwise think, he executed his duty as he saw it.

To the pit with them all!

But his exec was right, of course. Whether he liked it or

not, and he didn't, he must face the oncoming ship—and his nightmare.

And if the Orieli demurred?

Fuckers!

Against the backdrop of two worlds the alien ship slowed and stopped…and waited. Energy discharge lines barely flickered within the contours of its primary interceptor net.

"Better start telling me what's going on, Plot," Anatol growled.

"Target is outside our firing envelope, sir. Range now showing one-point six-three million talans," the plot operator said hastily. "No relative momentum. No weapons status indicated. Our secondary shield grid is still down. Their interceptor net is extended to twenty-two talans."

Not taking any chances with warm Serrll hospitality, eh? Anatol's features twisted into a grim smile.

Cloaked in black, running at half secondary boost, his M-4 blotted out the stars as it closed to intercept. The covering M-4s maintained relativity. One of them took a high port, the other a starboard low position in a classic triad maneuver, for all the good it did.

The exec strode up from the comms station, his round features grim. "We have a priority three message from Serrll Moon Base."

"Not now! Close to six hundred thousand talans and stop."

"Six hundred thousand talans indicated. Relativity in two point-three minutes."

"You need to look at this one," the exec insisted and Anatol bit off an angry retort.

"What in perdition do they want? Can't it wait—"

"They reported cascade failure on all distortion screens—"

"So?"

"That new survey bird Earth sent up the other day? It just happened to be overhead at the time."

Anatol took a few seconds to digest the information, then his face contorted in weary resignation.

"Oh great! That's all we need now."

"SMB thinks they might be compromised."

The comms officer looked up. "Sir, the Orieli have opened a channel."

"Just hold your water!" Torn between two problems, Anatol pulled at his chin. "That satellite. What kind of TLM has it got? Real-time or passive?"

"Real-time," the exec said.

"That tears it, then. The damned thing probably dumped its data bank as soon as it got out of the Moon's LOS zone. We should have vaporized that piece of junk before it achieved orbital insertion. Another example of Captal's idiotic policy to pander to Earth's primitive space efforts. Well, there is little we can do about it from here. Tell SMB to advise COMSAROPS. Let them deal with it. You know the form. Let's go to tactical."

"Full alert?" the exec queried, his face impassive, but his eyes twinkled.

"What's the matter? You anxious to see the Orieli in action?" Anatol rasped, ignoring the implied impertinence.

Under increased readiness some of the sensitized control panels immediately changed from soft yellow to pulsing amber. Previously inactive action contact pads rippled to life in arrays of colored strips and squares. The cable-tube doors opened and two additional watch officers quietly took up their control stations.

In the engineering spaces below, almost directly above the projector dome, there wasn't much to do except monitor procedures as the computer increased the level of energy management readiness. Stripped helium nuclei plasma powered the primary fusion chamber that fed the artificial antimatter convergence point and kept it from collapsing. The energy surge from particle annihilation then channeled through the containment field directly into the shield grid.

With Shadow and Thunder

The M-4's secondary shield grid extended to eight talans beyond the primary along almost spherical lines of force. With both shield grids in place, a cocoon of energy extending sixteen talans enclosed the M-4.

In a separate reaction chamber, energy flooded the twin Koyami 3/C generators. Coils fully powered up, the computer waited for the command to synchronize the firing pulses with the shield management system and the ship would be ready to do business.

The M-4 slid to a stop. At six hundred thousand talans, sensors could just make out the flowing rectangular shape of the Orieli ship. Its edges curved down, tapered like drooping wings. The obsidian shape did not show any lights. Nothing about it suggested menace, but Anatol felt its palpable power.

He had forgotten the huge size of the bastard. According to plot the ship was over 800 katalans long—almost twice the size and mass of the M-4.

Anatol stared at the deceptive simplicity of the alien ship's design and slowly clenched his fists. This time, he wasn't about to repeat the mistake he made years ago. If the Orieli wanted Earth, they could have the damned place.

"Comms? Let's see what they have to say," he said, unaware his teeth were grinding.

* * *

READ ALL ABOUT IT! MOON AN ALIEN SPY STATION
NASA PROBE DISCOVERS EXTRATERRESTRIAL BASE
EXTRA! EARTH SCRUTINIZED BY LITTLE GREEN MEN
DO WE FACE AN INVASION FROM SPACE, PEOPLE ASK
MOON STORY A VIRTUAL REALITY GAME HOAX

"Jack Willison reporting from the CNN center in New York. This afternoon in building two-sixty-four of NASA's Jet Propulsion Laboratory in Pasadena, a routine press conference erupted into several minutes of total confusion, excitement, fear and disbelief. A live data feed from one of the two SIR-E, Spaceborne Imaging Radar satellites, revealed what appeared to be artificial structures nestled deep in the permanent shadow of the Moon's northern pole. From its almost circular twenty-six-kilometer orbit the satellite provided a definitive topographical and mineralogical survey of the Moon. One of a series of steps undertaken to define the site for the UN-sponsored permanently manned base.

"Even as the sensational images were being flashed around the world, the White House spokesman refused to offer a comment. He said the President would be making a measured statement once the implications of a possible extraterrestrial presence on the Moon have been fully evaluated. Asked whether the administration will consider sending a manned mission to the Moon to further investigate the sighting, the response was a flat 'No comment'. Meanwhile, NASA officials emphatically denied the transmission was nothing more than an elaborately staged publicity stunt, as has already been suggested by some commentators. Someone pointed out that the White House may get more than a 'No comment' from its Area 51 facility at Groom Lake in Nevada and the MJ-12 program. The remark earned the unfortunate a withering glance. We'll flash you the latest developments in this electrifying event as they occur. Stay tuned."

* * *

"In New York today, Archbishop Waller stated calmly that if extraterrestrials do exist, and he wasn't postulating they didn't, they too must be creatures of God. After all, He created the universe and everything in it. Asked whether that meant the aliens must look like us since God created man in his image, the cardinal paused and said he saw the image of God reflected in the soul and not necessarily in the physical vessel it inhabits.

The remark, I'm sure, will raise a few theological eyebrows in the Vatican tonight.

"There is one question that all Christian denominations will have to come to grips with. If Christ is seen as man's redeemer, has He repeated the passion, in all its unpleasant variations, on every alien world? In this respect the other major world religions feel comfortable with the notion of spreading their faith to the stars. On the other hand, what if the aliens sitting nonchalantly on our Moon are missionaries? Are our beliefs as outmoded as the ones held by the Africans or the great South American civilizations before the Europeans brought them enlightenment with fire and sword? This is Mark Rown for NBC news."

Chapter Two

"It's not a request," Enllss-rr corrected firmly, allowing a touch of irritation to creep into his voice.

"Then I assume, sir, this has been cleared by Commissioner Sill-Anais?" Dharaklin inquired gravely, his voice cavernous, rumbling like dying thunder.

"Assume? Now you listen to me." Enllss pierced Dhar with eyes that suddenly turned frigid. "I'm having a real lousy day and it's only morning. I've had junior Assemblymen jerking me off with their endless petitions and world-saving schemes. They mean well, and who knows? One of them just might have a germ of an idea that will make sense. So I've got to listen to them. Illeran has been pissing in my ear wanting to know what the blazes I'm doing about that damned Orieli ship hanging off Sol. He is an Executive Director and my boss, so I got to explain myself to him. Son, the only good thing about this day is that I don't have to explain myself to junior Scout Fleet officers. While you're detached to my Bureau, you take your orders from me. Without question. Do I make myself clear?"

Dhar held his sinewy two point-three katalan frame at attention. The vertical red slits of his large orange eyes betrayed nothing. The thin membranes, designed to protect the eyes from fine sand, were now slid shut in pique. His yellow skin dry, drawn tight over the bony ridges of his long face. His nose, broad and flat with flared nostrils, added to his skeletal appearance.

He felt the Commissioner's intimidating presence crush his spirit and his righteous protest died stillborn. Enllss radiated an almost visible aura of authority and self-assurance. It may not have been the strength of the Discipline, but nonetheless, it emitted a force he could not ignore. Breathing deeply, he summoned the words from the *Saftara* that would calm him. In adversity, the spirit grows, he reminded himself.

He studied the bulky figure framed against a floor-to-ceiling window screen. The Captal sky dark and threatening, lit by an ugly furnace glow from the west. Muscular and powerful, with a hint of a bulge around his middle, Enllss thrust out a square jaw, used to command and instant obedience. Dark gray eyes flared with opaque anger. Beneath the almost pure white hair, the aquiline nose stood out sharp above a firm, full mouth.

"It wasn't a statement of personal concern, sir," Dhar said without expression, betraying nothing of his inner turmoil.

Enllss gave an impatient flick of his hand. "I don't give a crap about your concern, son. Personal or otherwise. The only thing I want from you is compliance."

"When I exposed Gashkarali's clandestine activities, I didn't envisage that he would be sanctioned—"

"I wouldn't be so damned sympathetic, if I were you. His antics have caused us a lot of grief…and lives. You better than anyone should know that."

Dhar took a deep breath. "I still submit the Bureau of Administrative Affairs should have stripped him of his authority. He would have been neutralized just as effectively."

Enllss slammed his fist against the desk. "Enough! I'm not here to debate this with you."

"I meant no disrespect, Mr. Commissioner."

"The blazes you didn't. Parading your moral outrage may give you a measure of personal satisfaction, but don't let your indignation blind you to the job at hand. Clear?"

Dhar could not keep his resentment bottled up any longer. "I would suggest, Mr. Commissioner, the job at hand has more to do with the one vote the Unified Independent Front will hold in the Executive Council than the threat posed by Gashkarali's activities, or Sargon's vision of another empire."

Enllss looked startled, then laughed outright. "By damn, if you're not right there. But I never doubted your capability, or your intelligence. You should know then why it's so important that you continue to maintain your cover as a Servatory Party operative. Terchran already suspects your loyalty—"

"As you do, sir," Dhar said flatly, his eyes impenetrable.

Enllss snorted and shook his head. Was the boy deliberately goading him? Dhar would be playing an extremely dangerous game if he were. It would only take a word and Dhar would be counting worm fuzz for the rest of his career. No, the Wanderer wanted an out of a messy assignment.

Well, it's not going to be that easy. You started this, and now you've got to finish it.

Looking at him, Enllss could easily imagine Dhar clad in brown robes, cape flying behind him, standing on a dune with the desert as his only friend. He sensed power held in check behind those eyes. Eyes that could rip through a soul. He shuddered at the thought of Wanderers bursting from Anar'on, flooding the Serrll with death in one hand and their hellish Discipline in another. He was not ready to submit to that kind of justice.

"As a Scout Fleet officer, your loyalty to the Serrll is not in question," he said harshly. "However, as a Wanderer, I would be less than wise to ignore your allegiance to Anar'on and its formative influence on the Unified Independent Front. The Captal government supports the objectives of the UIF, and your actions will further its interests, however unclear that may seem to you at the moment."

"What is clear to me, sir, through my actions, my brother took a life and I have violated the teachings of the Discipline."

Enllss nodded, his eyes suddenly bleak. "Before this is over, my boy, more than one life will be taken. If that presents you with a problem, take your damned whining and get the blazes out of my sight!" he roared and pointed at the door.

Dhar blanched, shaken by the strength of emotions churning around Enllss like coiled lightning. Confused, he sought comfort in the words of his master, and found them strangely unhelpful. Everything he knew, everything his master taught him, protested at the taking of any life; even one of his enemy.

That, however, framed a two-dimensional perspective.

Faced with the multi-faceted environment of Serrll politics, his precepts were taking a severe beating. He saw himself drawn inexorably into a web of action whose end offered no clarity. No, that wasn't quite true. He frowned, not prepared to face the brutal reality.

He knew all too well where his actions would lead. Back on Anar'on, did the Rahtir Council count the cost of shattered lives while they coldly plotted the formation of the Unified Independent Front? Could they afford to care? The cause had no room for an individual's feelings. He did not believe it. The Rahtir and the UIF faced that very dilemma five years ago when they tried to recruit Terr. The individual always mattered, but he had to be prepared to bury his misgivings for the greater goal. Right then, he could not say he could.

He set his mouth and lifted his head. He tensed, forcing himself to say the words.

"I apologize, sir."

"Humph! Then shut your mouth and stop pissing in my ear," Enllss said gruffly and shifted in the formchair. "As I was saying, Terchran suspects your loyalty. You're going to allay his suspicions by revealing to him Terr's mission."

Dhar stared, taken completely by surprise. "Has Sankri completed it?"

"He should be on his way to Taltair right now."

"But…Terchran will retaliate!"

"I'm counting on it."

"He will want Sankri killed. And it's probable that he will order me to do it."

"If he doesn't, suggest it. Report to Terchran, then take an

21

M-1 to Taltair. I have one waiting for you at Sal Field. Get the details from my assistant."

"Sankri is my bond brother!" Dhar protested in outrage.

"Do you want someone else to get the job, and possibly succeed? This way, you can control the situation. One more thing," Enllss went on remorselessly. "Whatever your relationship with Terr, you're not to discuss any of this with him. Is that clearly understood?"

Dhar looked helplessly at Enllss, realizing how cleverly he'd been manipulated.

"For my actions to be credible, Sankri will have to believe that I really intend to kill him. Mr. Commissioner, you are asking me to deliberately destroy his trust in me. I urge you to reconsider."

Enllss thrust out his jaw. "You have your orders. Carry them out."

Left with few choices, Dhar seemed to sag. His soul heavy, he walked out. The translucent panels closed behind him with a soft click.

Enllss stared at the panels, swore, pushed back the form-chair, and stood up. He clasped his hands behind his back and turned. Dark, bleak clouds smeared the sky, matching his mood. The rain fell heavily. Lightning strikes ripped the sky into jagged tears. A watery haze obscured the towers of the Center. Endless lines of communals, combies, and private sled-pads crossed above the city in controlled patterns. The tubeways linking the towers were blurred outlines of pearly light. Far below, the avenues were alive with the throng from nameless worlds of the Serrll Combine.

He stood there and watched the rain.

Raw power radiated from the city, almost tangible in its substance. After more than two decades learning how to wield that power, Enllss harbored few illusions as to its use. Power got things done. To hold it, he needed to dominate. In comparison, Dhar's moral misgivings hardly merited consideration.

Or did they?

He sighed and sank back into the formchair. With the smooth leather molded around him, he rubbed the ache behind his eyes. He needed to get away for a while. He needed to get back to Kaplan and touch base with some of the more influential constituency groups and the Party machinery. He badly needed some quiet time with his partner. His job consumed too much of his time. Could it be that he did not have a strong enough reason to spend more time at home? No, Rhea had been the only woman he had ever deeply loved. Without her quiet, uncomplaining support, he would have given up long ago. The simple truth, he liked his work too much. It...*consumed* him.

In the gathering gloom the ceiling automatically compensated, turning brighter blue. The walls of his spacious office glowed subdued orange. Before him, a full-dimensional holographic Wall communications extension took up a whole wall, cycling through random color gyrations, pooling into each other in complex patterns. On his right, in a little L-shaped alcove, stood an oval table. Its patterned wooden surface lovingly hand-polished into hues of deep reds. Elaborately carved matching padded chairs were arranged around the table with mathematical precision.

A thin-necked rock vase occupied the center of the table. Dry flowers arched from its neck. They gave off a subtle mixture of redolent scents, reminding him of deep forests and rolling fields of his native Kaplan.

He leaned back and ordered his special blend of herbal tea. Waiting, he told the computer to dim the lights. A panel slid away in his desk from which rose the tea set. Steam snaked lazily from the fragile delicacy of the porcelain. He inhaled deeply of the aroma and closed his eyes. After a moment, he poured himself a cup and sipped, savoring the tangy flavor. He held the cup in both hands, allowing its warmth to seep through his hands.

The comms alert beeped, flashing for attention. The lighting flared to full intensity. Muttering, he laid the cup down with a click. He reached across the desk and touched a pad on the inlaid console array.

"Yes, what is it?" he demanded as the image of his personal aide cleared in the Wall.

"Commissioner Sill-Anais is here to see you, sir," she said breathlessly in a low contralto deliberately designed to disturb. Now, it only irritated.

His previous aide had lasted three years, something of a record. With his backing, she now held a director's post of one of the branches in the Bureau of Administrative Affairs. This one, on the other hand, if she didn't stop her amorous advances, would probably end up as Warden on Cantor. He knew his office staff were running a pool on how long she would last. Absently, he wondered what the odds were.

"Very well, show him in, will you?"

The door panels slid away with a hiss and Sill walked through. He carried himself with ease, moving with quick short strides. Tall and thin, Sill wore a dry, pinched face beneath an olive complexion traced with lines of age and responsibility. Wiry white eyebrows outlined large, liquid wide-set eyes, now dark with hidden humor.

Sill managed an easy grin and slid one hand quickly down the side of his head, hair streaked with twin bands of dark gray of a mature male, worn in traditional Deklan fashion. Running the Bureau of Cultural Affairs under Bakral, Sofam's senior Executive Director, Sill had grown into power and carried it well.

He bowed quickly and inclined his head at the door. "I saw agent Dharaklin a moment ago," he piped in high treble and thrust out a massive barrel chest. "He looked very unhappy. Your doing?"

"Being happy is not part of his job description," Enllss said callously. He raised his cup and took a sip. "Want some?"

Sill twisted his face into a grimace. "Ach! I cannot stand

watching you drink those dried lawn clippings."

Enllss shrugged. "Suit yourself." He stood and extended his hand at the soft cushions. Sill sprawled down with a grunt and cast a speculative eye over the office. The trappings of power may appear flashy to the uninitiated, but in their respective positions neither he nor Enllss had time to wallow in the luxury. Responsibility far outweighed the privileges.

On his left the wall was lined with uneven shelves crowded with memorabilia, data cubes, hand-tooled leather books and oddly carved objects; probably gifts from innumerable diplomatic missions. Battle honors, he mused. Beneath his feet, etched into the carpet, lay a yellow-orange circle containing the crest of the Bureau for Colonial and Protectorate Affairs, symbol of Enllss' bureaucratic empire.

For a moment, Sill contemplated the storm clouds outside.

"Winter is early in Captal and I miss the still, drowsy days of Deklan," he said musingly. "It's been over a year since I last set foot there. Can you believe it?"

"There is nothing there you want to see, anyway," Enllss quipped. "I heard that one of your boys made Second Scout grade three."

"Ach! Off on an M-4 somewhere in the Sargon Directorate."

"And the other one? Still in the Diplomatic Corps?"

Sill's eyes lit up. "He is a Senior Councilor in Anall-Marr's administrative department."

"Not bad for someone so young."

"Sinful, but you will allow some father's pride. Pride in both of them, despite the fact my eldest chose the Fleet. He tells me I don't understand him," Sill added plaintively.

"Truncated and out of sync," Enllss agreed.

Sill shook a finger at him. "Ach! Just be glad you don't have my problems."

"I'm sympathizing, not criticizing. And who says I don't?"

"Ah, your nephew. I heard the funeral made quite a spectacle. Got everybody on Trillian all sentimental."

"Gashkarali was a fool," Enllss said and snorted. "With Terchran as his mentor, his career in the Servatory Party made, he wanted more. He got involved with Sargon's grand unification scheme."

"So why is Dhar pissed? I would have thought he'd be glad to see Gashkarali gone. The man gave all of us enough grief."

Enllss took a sip, eyeing Sill above the rim of the cup. "I ordered him to expose Terr."

Sill's thin eyebrows converged in a frown and his eyes turned cold. "I don't like this operation, Enllss. And I like it less the longer it continues. You're not running the Bureau of Cultural Affairs anymore, you know. And I don't like your interference in my department or my men," he said, annoyed the situation threatened to get out of hand.

"Bit late for second thoughts, isn't it?" Enllss said easily, looking at his friend with amusement.

Sill pursed his lips and glared. "Ach! Your preoccupation with the Unified Independent Front is turning into a fixation."

"You sanctimonious son of a bitch! You're actually enjoying this, aren't you?"

"If you mean whether it would be nice to see the Servatory Party and the Revisionists come crawling cap in hand to the UIF for support, then you can say that I'm enjoying this."

"Enjoy yourself, then," Enllss grunted and sipped his tea.

"Face it, Enllss. Ach! In two short years, come the next elections, the Unified Independent Front will hold more than five percent of all systems in the Serrll Combine, allowing them to take a seat in the Executive. The irony is that we've only ourselves to blame for this mess. We always treated the independent nonaligned systems with irritation and indifference. The only reason why we haven't absorbed them is that neither major block is prepared to make the first move for fear what the other would do in retaliation."

"Maybe. But the UIF will never hold that seat if Sargon and the Paleans pull off their merger," Enllss pointed out meditatively.

Sill shrugged. "Oh, I don't know. The Paleans were seriously embarrassed five years ago when the raider bases on Lemos and Italan were uncovered. The illegal Alikan Union Party operation at Khiman-ra three years ago has not helped their cause either. Ach! But the reason I think the merger *might* succeed now is that under Karkan dominance, the Servatory Party has been more preoccupied with gaining the government majority than meeting the coalition's needs. Sargon is getting more than a little impatient."

"You don't know how much I appreciate your in-depth analysis of the situation," Enllss said with heavy irony.

"Ach! Screw yourself, Mr. Commissioner."

"It's been tried."

"The problem with you and me, my friend, we've been fighting the same old weary battles for too long. Our political enemies are now almost friends. It is time for new challenges."

"I have enough challenges, thank you. Until I know what the UIF will do, I'll sleep better knowing that every Wanderer has been removed from an intelligence-sensitive area."

"Like Dhar and your nephew?"

"Damn right."

Sill stood up and walked to the window screen. The rain still drove hard under a sullen, heavy sky. He turned and folded his hands before his chest.

"I hate it when it rains. Ach! But I didn't come here to talk about the cursed Unified Independent Front or your grand policy schemes."

"Then why the blazes *did* you come?"

"Temper. It's about that infernal Orieli ship."

Enllss nodded, looking glum. "Don't tell me Anatol has jumped them again?"

Sill smiled. "The last I heard, he got orders to escort them to Salina with his M-4s. They should arrive in eight days."

"Hah! Fat lot of good that'll do him if the Orieli decide to simply brush him aside. I presume someone updated Trianon? Who is heading the formal Mission?"

"Anabb."

Enllss nodded. "Good enough," he said and pointed a finger at Sill. "If Trianon even *thinks* of talking to them, I'll have his butt."

"Don't worry. He's been given the word. There is something else, though. The cover on our Moon Base may have been compromised," Sill said and Enllss looked at him sharply.

"Compromised? How?"

"Its distortion screens collapsed for about six minutes just as one of Earth's survey birds happened to be overhead."

"How could they collapse? The system is supposed to be foolproof, layered backups."

"Just one of those unpleasant coincidences, I guess. Bound to happen sooner or later."

"By damn! And you think the base was scanned?"

"The satellite was over twenty-three talans high and carried no direct imaging hardware. At least we don't think it did. There is no way it could have seen the base."

"Unless that probe held a payload of packed sensor arrays," Enllss mused.

"Count on it. Still, even if they detected anomalous energy readings, their imaging would need to be pretty fancy to generate a visible resolution. The point is; what are you going to do about it? Earth is a protectorate and this falls under your jurisdiction."

Enllss winced as if in pain. "Nothing much that I *can* do. If they've seen us, they've seen us."

"Any word from the American government?"

"Nothing. The PLATO and SIGMA channels are silent. They're probably resigned to the situation as we are. I would expect them to send up a special bird and do a low orbital to get a visual to make sure. Maybe even a manned mission. Despite the screens, they'll see the surface installations. No way to hide that. After all the centuries…"

"Ach! That means we may have to go down to Earth and formally reveal ourselves. It would cause hell. Here *and* on Earth."

Enllss spent a few seconds in silent musing. When he looked up, his eyes were mischievous.

"Maybe not. Not for a while, at least."

"Enllss, you know as well as I do, no matter what kind of government Earth's got, they won't be able to keep the lid on a thing like this. We were lucky five years ago with that C-32 at Comalcalco. This time, we'll have Earth crawling all over that base within a year, and we'll blow our clandestine deals with them."

"Can't see how we can avoid it."

"From unfounded speculation, the general population will be faced with hard evidence of alien presence. It could cause massive cultural dislocation."

"They've had enough time to get used to the idea of extra-terrestrials. On the other hand, why not let the Orieli take the heat for us?" Enllss mused and pulled at his chin.

* * *

Low in the sky, the sun painted torn clouds with fire. Bathed in an eerie orange glow the towers of the Center stood cold and tall.

Diplomatic Branch Director Anabb Karr squared his powerful shoulders and moved away from the window screen. The comms alert beeped. He reached across the polished expanse of his desk and touched a pad in the inlaid console.

"Commissioner Enllss-rr, sir," his aide announced.

Anabb's unruly white eyebrows climbed and the amber flecks in his brown eyes suddenly brightened. He wondered what the old devil wanted now.

"Thank you, Ariane. Hold all calls."

He eased himself into the formchair with a grunt, tapped another pad and turned toward the Wall as the image in it began to form. The square face staring at him from the full-dimensional display projected power, a face used to authority and command. Dark gray eyes looked at him intently through the Wall.

"Anabb, you old space pirate! Haven't heard from you for some time," Enllss boomed, all smiles. Anabb did not share his good humor.

"Ever since Sill-Anais called, I've had chills running down my spine, Commissioner. When you get involved with the Bureau of Cultural Affairs, my orderly peaceful life gets shot to hell."

Enllss smiled and pointed a long finger at him. "You've been too long in the Diplomatic Branch, that's your problem. You should be back here on Captal where things happen."

"Then I'd be just another nut in that fruitcake," Anabb grumbled and Enllss laughed.

"With that disrespectful attitude, maybe it's better that you remain on Taltair. You tend to rub people the wrong way. Captal isn't used to straight shooters; tends to throw them off."

"What you mean to say is, I'm not polished enough for Captal's high society."

Enllss shrugged and grinned disarmingly. "It's better this way. Anyway, as much as I would love to chat, this is not a social call."

"I knew that."

"Did you get the latest update on the Orieli?"

"Couple of hours ago. I was all set to leave for Salina when Sill called. I figured you wouldn't be far behind. What is going on, Enllss?"

"I want you to suspend the formal Mission until Terr gets back from Trillian."

"Suspend the Mission?"

"Your other protégé, Second Scout Dharaklin, will shortly be on his way to Taltair. He has specific orders relating to Terr's Trillian assignment. He will accompany you to Salina."

Anabb stared at him. "You can't be serious. I won't do it. For one thing, Terr is not a diplomat and neither is that young pup Dhar. More importantly, I cannot hang around waiting for Terr to show up. Delaying the Mission and keeping the Orieli waiting on a couple of amateurs is not my idea of good diplomacy. And besides, who knows what Trianon might decide to do in the meantime. He could screw up everything."

"Trianon won't be screwing up anything. He has been straightened out," Enllss said icily and thrust out his jaw. "This is important, you know."

Anabb snorted in disgust. "I don't care how important it is. You cannot order me to suspend a formal Mission. This matter doesn't fall under the jurisdiction of the Bureau of Colonial and Protectorate Affairs."

Enllss tsked and shook a finger at him. "That's treasonous talk, Anabb. Earth is a protectorate, or have you forgotten?"

"But Salina is not!" Anabb retorted in triumph.

"This is still an alien contact, Anabb."

"Thunderation! Just for once, you could keep things simple."

"A matter of perspective, wouldn't you say?"

"Screw you."

"Funny, you're the second one today to tell me that."

"I'm not surprised."

Enllss laughed as he watched Anabb's internal struggle. Anabb could be hardnosed and an obstinate son of a bitch. As a former Fleet Prima Scout, he brought with him years of experience navigating through Captal's labyrinthine corridors of power. Anabb would make a bad enemy if he were ever turned.

"Tell me one thing. Why?" Anabb demanded at length, resigning himself to the inevitable.

"To maintain his cover with the Servatory Party, I ordered Dhar to expose Terr's Trillian mission to Terchran."

"All this simply to keep Terchran from finding out that Gashkarali was working for the AUP Provisional Committee and those Palean worms?"

"More or less."

"Terchran knows that already."

Enllss shook his head. "He suspects. There is a big difference."

"So?"

Enllss smiled thinly. "Let me say that although the Revisionists cannot stand idly by while Sargon indulges in fantasies of conquest and empire building, it's another thing to extricate the Servatory Party from its political troubles. They'll have to do that themselves."

"Sounds convenient, but I don't believe it. I'll tell you what I *do* believe. You're hatching all this to remove Dhar from the Bureau of Cultural Affairs on Captal where he won't be nosing around for the Unified Independent Front," Anabb said, his voice gravelly and thick with disapproval.

"And Terr from the Diplomatic Branch," Enllss finished for him.

"I haven't forgotten. Nephew or not, ever since he returned from that crash on Anar'on, you've looked at Terr as a Wanderer and you suspect his allegiance, which is idiotic. I don't like it, Enllss. You're spinning a complicated web and I'd hate to see those two get hurt."

"If it's a web, Anabb, I'm certainly not the one who is spinning it. But I cannot ignore the opportunity. Just send the request. One other thing. Don't make any promises to the Orieli we cannot keep." The Wall dissolved into shifting pools of color.

Anabb leaned back in the formchair and rubbed his temples. This he did not need. Bad enough having to worry about the Orieli and the possible compromise of the Serrll Moon Base without getting tangled up in one of Enllss' grand schemes. With a snarl of frustration, he crashed his fist against the desk that sent the stationery jumping.

Stefan Vučak

Chapter Three

It was third on his list of visited establishments.

Terr pushed the door open with a stiff hand and walked through. It creaked as it swung shut behind him. No attendant waited for him. It was that type of hole. Blaring music washed past him mixed with inane babble, hearty shouting, and clinking of drinking hardware. The gloomy place, filled with smoke, stank of spilled booze, and stale sweat. His nose crinkled with distaste. He figured it was due to the low class of clientele the dive favored. Razzo ought to clean up the place and attract a better class of patrons.

Most of the tables were filled. The odd empty chair looked out of place. A harried waiter nimbly sidestepped flailing arms and outstretched feet as he carried a tray of drinkables. Someone yelled an obscenity after the retreating figure, causing an outburst of hilarity from his companions. In the pairs ring tucked away in one of the shadowy corners, two couples clutched each other for moral support. The Wall colors clashed in jagged patterns as couples tried to sync their movements to the music. They weren't making it.

Ignoring the buzzing in his ears, Terr stood there, surveying his fellow connoisseurs with disgust. He hated the sight of closely packed humanity. Their cloying, gushing familiarity made him restless. Better the clean emptiness of desert sands beneath the sweep of an amber sky.

He was getting moody, always a bad sign.

Too many drinks, he guessed. Then again, not enough. On the flight from Trillian, he should have spent more time drinking instead of thinking, not a fatal oversight. After landing, he'd been sampling the dives along the Beltway: bars, restaurants, and other attractions lining the road ring approach to Tal Field spaceport. Nothing unusual about that in itself. Lately, he took to tanking up with fortified support after one of his body jobs.

Must be a moral in it somewhere, he figured absently.

He saw Razzo standing negligently behind the bar, pulling at his flattened nose. His bald head shone a mottled pink, all knobby and scarred, evidence of an evil past. Terr glowered as he pushed his way between the tables. He picked a spot against the bar and settled down for business. A merchant pilot swiveled his rheumy eyes at him, but the effort seemed too much. Still clutching his glass, his head sagged gently against his chest. The bar kept him upright.

Razzo walked up wearing a dark scowl.

"I kinda hoped you'd be taking your business someplace else," he said, glaring at Terr with moist, innocent-looking blue eyes.

"Now, Razzo," Terr said with a pained expression. "That kind of talk does not exactly make me feel welcome. Not after all we've been through."

"It wasn't supposed to. Last time you visited cost me nearly five thousand Serrlls to get the joint back into shape. I'm tired of cleaning up the messes after you."

Terr looked around and made a face. "You've wasted your money, if you asked me."

Somewhere behind him a chair fell with a crash, followed by raucous laughter. Razzo ignored it.

"Nobody asked you. I just don't want the kinda excitement that seems to follow you around, that's all."

"What's ruined *your* day?" Terr demanded, slightly miffed.

Someone farther down the bar smashed a glass against the wall, causing a ripple of angry shouts. No one paid any attention.

"You not in some kind of trouble, are you?" Razzo asked, barely glancing at the commotion at the other end of the bar.

He hadn't come by those pretty scars falling out of bed.

"Not that I know of," Terr said, if he didn't count the man he'd killed a few days ago. He could see Razzo chewing that one over.

"Wish I could believe you. Cuppla heavies been cruising around looking for you. They both wore that standard government-issue look. You know the type."

Rit!

Nobody was supposed to know he landed on Taltair. Except Anabb, of course. If somebody had blown his cover, he couldn't do much about it, or wanted to. Not right now anyway.

"They didn't happen to say what they wanted, did they?"

"Didn't ask."

"Could have."

"Do I look like some kind of message service or something?"

To hell with it.

"Never mind. How about that drink?"

"Seems to me you already tanked a few."

"You counting or just worried about my health?"

Razzo shrugged. "No skin off my nose if you kill yourself."

"That's what I like about you, Razzo. Despite the crusty exterior, you cannot disguise genuine warmth and care."

"Shove it up your pipe."

"Just bring me something with a bit of bite this time, okay? And I don't mean the colored piss you usually serve to innocent merchant pilots," Terr said and hooked a thumb at the sprawled form beside him.

Razzo walked away muttering and Terr smiled after him. Razzo might be grumpy and evil-tempered, but Terr wouldn't want anyone else to cover his back in an awkward situation. Five years ago, Razzo did just that, throwing himself in front of a needler beam meant for Terr. They cornered Kai Tanard, a renegade Palean Scout Fleet officer, who organized raids against Pizgor commerce from a secret base on Lemos. Trying to kill Terr was Tanard's way of getting even for discovering the base. The medics patched up the crusty assault forces chief, but his Fleet days were over. Terr made it up to him by helping him settle into this joint.

Waiting for the drink, he watched the action in the pairs ring. The two couples were still in their deadly embrace. When the drink arrived, he turned and eyed the heavy gray liquid with suspicion.

Razzo smirked as Terr picked up the frosted tumbler. Terr tossed back the stuff and the buzzing in his ears suddenly got louder. He exhaled the pungent fumes with a shudder and slammed the tumbler on the bar. The pilot beside him rolled up his bloodshot eyes and slowly crumpled to the floor.

"You've been watering it!" Terr croaked.

"In your ass," Razzo grated and leaned across the bar, playing with his rag. "If those goons show up, I don't want you messing up my furniture," he said, the warning in his voice clear.

"I only came in for a peaceful drink, in case anyone asks," Terr added, blinking back tears.

Razzo's scowl deepened. "No need to pull that naive routine with me, hero. I kinda keep things close to my chest, but I wasn't born in an alley. Everybody knows about you and Anabb's dirty tricks department."

"Ugly rumors spread around by Servatory Party subversives," Terr suggested breezily.

"Sure, but don't come around lots," Razzo growled, gave Terr a refill and walked down the bar.

The thrill of getting back had truly worn off. Right now, Terr needed Teena's sympathy and warmth. He needed to feel her sweet breath, feel her touch, hear her soothing whispers. She would understand and smooth away the hurt. The thought of her arms cradling him against her soft breasts gave him a warm fuzzy all over. He spent a few moments wallowing in pleasant anticipation.

He didn't know how long he clutched the edge of the bar before deciding to see the next item on the list. Avoiding the credit pad, he threw a couple of Serrll fivers on the counter and gulped back the last of the drink. He knew Razzo hated cash—screws up his accounting. Blinking, he pushed his way toward the door. The floor felt a bit unsteady, but that was all right. He wondered if he would make it before he threw up.

Outside, fine drizzle shrouded the towers of Tal Field's inter-star terminus. A thin wind keened mournfully and he grimaced at its impersonal bite. Combies and public communals crowded against the landing ramps, filling a murky sky. He didn't like civilian ports, and this one was no exception.

He did not much care for the cold, the rain, or the wind either.

He worked his mouth, tasting all the lived-in smells of Razzo's Corner and made a face. He'd reached that stage where things were pleasantly buzzing, but not quite there, where he could forget, for a while at least. Standing there, the wind tugging at him, he wondered which bar to hit next.

"First Scout Terrllss-rr?" a restrained voice demanded behind him.

He tensed and turned slowly, keeping his arms still. There were two of them, heavy-set, dressed in mufti, but both had that aware look. He could tell. They held their hands in bulging overcoat pockets trying to appear casual in a strained sort of way. Terr allowed himself a faint smile.

"I'm trying to forget that for the day, boys," he said and waited for them to come up to him.

But they were professionals. They just stood there, eyeing him.

"We have a message from Director Anabb Karr, sir," one of them said in a dry clipped voice, not sure how to deliver an unwelcome message to a superior officer. "You're to meet him at the Field Dispatcher's office immediately."

"Field Dispatcher? But I just got in!" Terr protested in dismay.

"Sorry about that, sir," the dry voice said, not looking at all sorry. "Just carrying out orders."

Terr stood there watching them, thinking dark and evil thoughts. After spending a better part of three weeks on an assignment, he did not want more of Anabb's official crap.

What the hell could the old fart want that couldn't wait until tomorrow? If it was all that damn important, Anabb could have sent a message to Terr's shuttle while still in transit.

Could this be a pinch? He fingered a ragged scar above his left eyebrow.

"You wouldn't mind showing me some ID, huh?"

The guy with the dry voice reached into his jacket, his eyes never leaving Terr. He pulled out his hand and held out an ID tag. Terr glanced at the insignia of the Diplomatic Branch. It could have been a fake, but he didn't think so.

"Okay. What's this all about, anyway?"

"Wouldn't know about that, sir. Just—"

"Yeah, I know. Carrying out orders," Terr said in disgust, the day ruined.

The stiffs hesitated, looking uncomfortable. The dry voice cleared his throat.

"Ah, the Director—"

"Shove off!" Terr rasped savagely, the buzzing in his ears really loud. "I got your message."

"Sir, if you don't come with us, we'll have to take you in," the dry voice said, real unhappy now.

Terr blinked. "I suppose you got orders for that too?"

The other didn't say anything.

Rit!

* * *

The two stickup artists made sure Terr did not get distracted along the way. They marched him to a cable-tube landing bay like they knew what they were doing. At least they had the grace to take the seat behind him, leaving him to his thoughts. Resigned, Terr watched the Field Administration building grow before him. The tower reared above the terminus complex like a giant mushroom, with two caps supported by a flared base. The lower larger cap acted as a landing platform for communals, combies and such. The upper level handled the business end of Taltair's SC&C traffic control.

The cable-tube seemed to pause before disappearing into the tunnel beneath the building. Terr didn't feel anything as it whisked them up one of the shafts.

The tube door opened and they found themselves in a circular observation lounge. Tal Field lay spread around them like a kid's toy set. Misty drizzle shrouded the main civilian and military terminus buildings. Liners from nameless worlds hovered above the landing rings, connected to the terminus by access tubes. Not far off stood the ugly shape of an M-4, a silent triangular hulk showing no lights. A mixture of civilian and military craft squatted on the wide expanse of the apron. They were probably up for maintenance or just hanging around with nowhere to go. In the background the thin towers of the Center poked into low clouds.

One of the floor-to-ceiling window screen panels was polarized a smoky brown. Before it stood a broad polished desk occupied by a dour individual who eyed them with thinly veiled disdain. He was guarding a railed stairway leading down to the main office. Terr's two buddies ignored the individual and made directly for the stairs.

Anabb stood beside a large curved console staring at the Field complex through floor-to-ceiling window screens, hands clasped behind him at parade rest. The console bristled with more inlaid displays and control pads than a starship. Behind it, an entire wall displayed a Field schematic: run-up ramps, parking aprons, military and civilian sections, glowing lines everywhere. Depending on its status a colored light represented a ship. It all looked pretty damn impressive.

Terr wondered what Anabb said to make the dispatcher part with all these nice toys. Nominally, Field Administration could thumb its nose at the military. But the Diplomatic Branch was not exactly a military organization and the dispatcher wasn't exactly a civilian.

Anabb turned, pulled back his shoulders and gave Terr a measured look. Of medium height, same as Terr, but that's where the similarity ended. Terr had a conscience, Anabb didn't. Looking at him, he wondered how Anabb managed to sleep at night.

Anabb's eyes flickered at the two security types.

"You can leave him to me," he commanded, his voice deep, devoid of humor, although rumors hinted he had one. Terr knew he did. He just returned from one of Anabb's practical gags.

"Sir!" the dry voice said and they faded. Terr waited. The buzzing in his ears seemed awfully loud in the artificial silence of the office.

Without a word, Anabb pushed back the formchair and grunted as he lowered his stocky bulk into the yielding frame. He crossed his hands over the desk and looked up. A disapproving frown clouded his close-set oval eyes. The olive skin of his chiseled narrow face was a wrinkled parchment marred by a ragged blue-veined burn on his left cheek.

Terr didn't know Anabb's age. In the five years he'd been working for him, he never bothered to find out. Whatever his age, Anabb carried it well. After a successful career in the Scout Fleet, he turned his considerable talents to fighting Capital bureaucrats from the inside. His nomination to a seat and subsequent entry to the General Assembly in a by-election done without fuss.

Through Enlss' influence, becoming Director of the Diplomatic Branch in his first ten-year term generated a lot of fuss.

On active Fleet service then, Terr remembered well the ripple of consternation the appointment caused in the upper echelons. Some of the high military brass saw it as selling out. In the eyes of the old Fleet protective association, Anabb was a traitor. He had turned. More calculating heads saw his appointment as a stepping-stone to a possible commissioner post, which could not be all bad for the Fleet. After all, it never hurt to have a knowing ear in Captal.

The only knowing ear Terr wanted right now was Teena's.

"Sit down." Anabb pointed at one of the spare chairs.

"I hope this isn't a debriefing," Terr said unsteadily, ignoring the offer.

"You've been drinking," Anabb growled sharply in rebuke, his nose wrinkling with distaste. The waiting obviously hadn't helped his mood either.

"Just washing out a bad taste I picked up on Trillian. Besides, I'm not on duty now."

"An officer of the Serrll is always on duty."

Terr let that one ride. "I've had a long, hard day. Couldn't this wait until morning? Teena hasn't seen me in weeks. I land and the place is crawling with beefy guys looking for me."

"Sorry about that, it couldn't be helped."

"Did you have to have them *drag* me here?"

"If I didn't, you'd still be boozing."

"You're a cold, callous bastard," Terr told him with relish.

"I said I was sorry!" Anabb bellowed and sent his fist crashing against the desk. "By the beard of the canal worm. I don't explain myself to you. Who the thunderation do you think you are, anyway?"

Terr clamped his mouth and glared. After a few moments, Anabb relented.

"Do you have time to sit down or were you planning to make a break for it?" he said, wide-eyed and innocent.

Terr didn't trust him, crafty old devil.

"Rit!" he said.

Anabb leaned forward. The amber flecks in his eyes suddenly took on a cold glitter. The burn on his cheek started to color, but Terr was too far gone to notice the warning signs.

"Now, you listen to me. The Diplomatic Branch is not run for my personal convenience, or yours, for that matter. I also take orders. It doesn't always mean I like them. You're not the only one who is pissed off, even though the reasons may be different."

Terr clutched the edge of the formchair. "I wouldn't know about the reasons. And who cares anyway? Will the Revisionist majority fall if one lousy Controller in the Sargon Directorate happens to be double-crossing us? Hardly a sin worthy a life, is it? Besides, aren't those Servatory thugs supposed to be our political enemies? I seem to remember that from somewhere. We should be celebrating. Score one for our side. And you know? That's exactly what I've been doing, drinking to a successful mission."

"You finished?"

"Not quite. The thrill of being your hatchet man, Anabb, has kind of worn off. You'll have to get yourself another wide-eyed trusting innocent to screw over. Maybe one of those smooth-talking mealy-mouthed Captal hacks would care for it. Let them clean up their own messes, I say. Either way, you can all go and screw yourselves!"

Terr didn't realize he was shouting or close to pasting him one.

"If you don't play by my rules, I'll take home my marbles and you can shove it. Right?" Anabb said, ignoring the boy's outburst. A tight little smile played at the corner of his mouth.

"I don't give a damn," Terr muttered.

"Feeling kind of used, are you? It's no longer fun, right?"

Terr hated him then, evil old scheming...

"Oh, cut the philosophy crap, okay? If this isn't a debriefing, I want to know why you sent those goons after me."

"When you're finished feeling sorry for yourself, we're leaving."

"Leaving? Leaving where?"

"Salina. I have an M-3 sweeper waiting for us at the landing ramp."

Terr found himself sobering up real fast. After three weeks on a mission, his boss wanted to send him out again?

"Don't say it. I'm not in the mood for it," Anabb growled and raised a finger in warning.

Terr ignored him. "Damn it all, Anabb! Salina is a round trip of twelve days, not counting whatever time we'll be spending in that hole. What do I tell Teena?"

"Enough!" Anabb slapped his palm against the desk. "I've had a bellyful of your bitching already. I'm sick and tired of your self-righteous indignation. Your attack of conscience has a hypocritical ring to it. Accept the implications of your job and the consequence of using your power, or get the damnation out of my face!"

Like a landed fish, Terr stood there, mouth agape, dismayed at the transparency of his internal conflict. He should have known. Anabb had spent years working with men and reading them.

In the heavy quiet, the office noises were suddenly loud. He wondered what skeletons Anabb kept around that rattled in his sleep.

"I can live with the job," he said the lie evenly. "It's your methods that stink."

"*My* methods?" Anabb said mockingly, amused. "No, not mine, my boy. Yours! You were so full of idealism and impatience to right all the wrongs, I couldn't stop you from wading in, lightning blazing. Your disdain for Captal bureaucracy is well known, but you're ready enough to implement their decisions as long as you can play the avenger. So don't stand there wearing your cloak of acrimony asking whether someone deserved to die."

Anabb's words slammed into him like physical blows. A flicker of reality and the dunes were all around him. In the distance the cliffs of Athal Than swam and danced in the heat of the desert, beckoning him.

He felt its pull and growing fear. This was the second time he'd felt the call. He would be compelled to answer it sometime, but not now, not with the burden of guilt riding him. He did not figure the gods would look kindly at their power being used as a tool for political expediency. Sooner or later, though, he would have to stand in the shadow of Athal Than and await the god's judgment.

He stared vacantly at the mist hiding the Field. Morality and honor were merely cheap commodities traded in the sleazy world of Captal's infighting and intrigue. He apparently sold his lightly.

No wonder he found the burden of Death heavy.

"I don't care how you do it, just deal with it." Anabb's eyes were hard. "But if you want to feel sorry for yourself, don't do it here. I don't have time for it. Right now, both of us have a job to do and I need you."

Terr looked for some sympathy behind those eyes and didn't find any. Not that he had expected it. He set his mouth and nodded.

"Deal with it, right," he said, feeling hollow and wrung out. He groped for the formchair and sank into its folds, too dejected to fight. His fingers unconsciously brushed the scar on his temple.

"Terr—"

"I don't want to hear it, Anabb. Not now. I'm here and leave it at that. So what's the big deal with Salina, anyway?" Terr demanded querulously. "It's just a dump."

Anabb stared at his operative with a mixture of fondness

and concern. He'd watched Terr wrestle with his conscience for the last four months, not daring to meddle. This was something the boy would have to work out for himself. Terr's belligerency only proved the struggle may have been won, but evidently not necessarily on terms Terr liked. He'd long waited for the boy to emerge out of his comfortable chrysalis into harsh reality. Like any change, the process had its share of pain.

"A dump it is, but the Orieli Technic Union thinks it's a nice place to visit," he said and smiled with satisfaction at Terr's confusion.

"Orieli? Here?"

"That's what I've been trying to tell you. They appeared outside the Sol system, just like the last time. COMSAROPS alerted SMB and three M-4s met them above the planetary plane."

"Anatol still commanding the Serrll Moon Base?"

Anabb nodded and his lips curled in distaste. "This time, there was none of that interdiction nonsense that happened five years ago. They're being escorted to Salina—"

"Trianon is Controller there, isn't he? I thought he was counting rocks on Cantor after that appropriation scandal," Terr said.

"He supposed to be. At any rate, he's not only Controller of Salina, but Prime Director of the Rolan group as well."

"Great. Nice to have pull like that. When did all this Orieli stuff happen?"

"Four days ago."

"Four days ago? What the hell were we doing sitting on our hands here?"

"Waiting for you."

"Me?"

"Don't look so shocked. After all, you made the first contact."

"Sure, but—"

46

"You're our resident expert on the Orieli. That's sufficient."

"You think I've got a brick between my ears to believe that crap?"

"I haven't been waiting here just to see your ugly face," Anabb countered.

Terr smelled a con job. Still, unlikely as it seemed, it *could* be true. Coming from Anabb, he had to be flexible, and there was always room for doubt.

"Okay, so I'm an expert and you've been waiting for me. What brings the Orieli out here again? And to Sol in particular? That's a long way from the Moanar Nebula. They could have landed on any number of outer Palean systems."

"That's what we're going to find out," Anabb said briskly and his eyes softened. "To sweeten this, I have an old friend of yours from Captal making fourth in a formal Mission. He is due to land in two hours."

"Old friend?" Terr frowned. He didn't have any friends, old or new. In his job even Teena was a liability, which Anabb never tired of telling him, and she one of his own analysts!

Anabb shook his head sadly. "Poor Terr. This job has finally got to you when you can't remember old shipmates."

"Dhar? You've got him here?"

Nightwings, my brother of the night…

Anabb grinned at him like a father at a well-meaning, but stupid child.

"A lucky break for us that you returned from Trillian when you did. You were almost left behind."

"Yeah. I seem to be getting all the breaks, all right," Terr mumbled sullenly.

* * *

Dharaklin, sometimes called Nightwings, the shadow who walks at night, sat cross-legged on the carpeted deck of the M-

47

3. He gazed at the images in the Wall, composing his mind, stilling the turmoil of his thoughts. Beneath an amber sky, rusty dunes stretched toward a line of brown hills vanishing into a shimmering haze. The relentless dry heat of the desert came palpably through the Wall. The smell of burnt rock, sand, and tarad grass permeated the air.

Clad in a traditional brown surtaf robe of a Saddish-aa Wanderer, his eyes took in the vastness of the open sands. A loose red hood covered his head, signifying he had twice walked in the shadow of the god of Death, and lived. One final time would the gods call him. If he survived the trial, he would be entitled to wear a purple hood. After ten years, immersed in the contemplation of the forces checked in his hands, he would discard the need for external symbolism and once again don the plain brown hood. By then, his power would be such that any outward display of its manifestation would be superfluous. He would, externally at least, live the life of a simple Wanderer.

However, having the power was not the same as having the judgment to exercise it. In essence these were the opposing forces that ruled every initiated Wanderer's life, and burdened him. As his master often said, the mere presence of power is an influence.

Unmoving, Dhar contemplated those words.

The small cabin, deep in shadow, proved adequate for his modest needs. Many of the conveniences were folded into the bulkheads, giving the impression of extra space. On his right, the transparent wall showed the thin drizzle of Tal Field. At his command, the computer could make the wall fade to dull gray of its polymer hull. A small worktable stood on his left. Two formchairs added variety. The ceiling frame glowed pale yellow.

Sitting there, hands resting on his knees, he longed to take a step into the image in the Wall and feel the dunes sigh beneath his feet. He wanted to reach out and feel the hot sand run between his fingers. He wanted to merge with the desert and be one with the Saffal, but it was only an image conjured by his mind.

His thoughts were troubled, jumping between his loyalty to Anar'on and his obligation as a serving officer of the Serrll Scout Fleet. His duty there was clear, and his commitment to the Unified Independent Front. A seemingly impossible conflict. Yet if he wanted to maintain his honor as a Saddish-aa Wanderer, he needed to resolve that conflict.

He wished he could unburden himself to his master. He realized he was avoiding a problem that ultimately he must solve himself. That is how the spirit grows, he reminded himself. He stilled his thoughts, willing himself to embrace the peace that came from the desert.

Tah, the gods will tell. It will come of itself.

He did not know how long he sat there gazing at the sands. Imperceptibly the dunes dissolved and gave way to a face. Dark gray eyes haunted him. A hint of laughter lurked in their depths. They were hard, unforgiving eyes, eyes that didn't miss much and did not lie. Broad brown eyebrows kept them in shadow, mocking above an aquiline nose. A strong face, not angular, topped by a shock of brown-black hair, with a small cleft in the chin.

Sankri, the strange one, his master named him. Sidhara had named him well. Dhar stared impassively at the face, embracing the features of his alien brother. So reckless and brave, unaware of the terrible power he wielded so casually. Yet, Terr's affinity with Anar'on was powerful. That troubled him. In a flash of premonition, he saw the shadows around Terr gather and lightnings danced in his hands.

They were lightnings of revenge.

Beside a dark pool of still water, Dhar saw a body, and it was his. Around him, the sand lay fused into glass as Terr hurled bolts of light into the sky, and thunder shook the ground at their feet.

The vision shifted and faded, leaving Dhar with a memory of a dark future.

The cabin dissolved around him and he remembered. Four days ago, he rode a cable-tube suspended high among the towers of Captal's Center. Rain fell steadily, spattering against the transparent tubeway linking the buildings of the Bureau of Colonial and Protectorate Affairs with the main Economics Council tower. The drops glittered like ice from the defused light outside. Moving silently toward the looming tower, the otherwise empty tube gave Dhar a moment in which to compose his thoughts. Enllss' words still echoed in his mind. He pursed his lips with resentment and uncertainty what he was about to do. The wall of the tower rushed at him and the tube slid to a stop in the brightly lit landing bay.

He walked into an office much like the one from which he just came. Perhaps a touch larger, befitting a director and a member of the Executive Council. The muddy-gray carpet held an elaborate crest woven in the red and yellow of the Serrll within which stood an overlay of technological symbols.

Dhar's eyes remained fixed on the figure sitting behind the wide expanse of an empty desk…Terchran, Executive Director for the Bureau of Technology and Development, native of Karkan. Next to Illeran, a driving force behind the Servatory Party machine on Captal. He was also Dhar's undercover control.

He waited as Terchran turned his wide, slightly flattened head away from one of the inlaid display plates in the desk. The long, slender neck made his every movement very graceful. Broad scales covered a pale green head. They glistened and changed color as Terchran turned. Beneath a thin ridge of darker green scales, fishy black eyes stared from horizontal slits.

Terchran always kept his offices at high humidity. Many of his visitors found the heavy atmosphere oppressive. It drained energy and will. Dhar often toyed with the idea that it was nothing but a ploy, a psychological gambit to put people on the defensive. Patiently, he endured his discomfort.

The sky outside looked like a sheet of crumpled lead. Thunder occasionally rolled among the unsettled clouds. He knew

Terchran hated the cold drizzle which Captal's fickle wintry weather sometimes produced. Karkan's hot, swampy climate had never known the whip of a cold wind. The rain outside apparently did nothing to improve Terchran's temper. For that matter, he didn't care much for Captal's weather himself, preferring the hot open sands of the Saffal.

When the fishy black eyes turned fully on him, they gave no sign of the thoughts behind them. They were something to look out with, not to provide a window in. Terchran listened as Dhar gave his report, his thin tongue flicking delicately from his mouth. An occasional hiss was the only sign of smoldering anger.

In the ensuing silence, Dhar watched Terchran's delicate tongue flick in and out. Finally, Terchran shook his head and sighed.

"This First Scout, Terrllss-rr. How well do you know him?"

Dhar checked his surprise. His service record wasn't restricted, certain that Terchran would have made himself aware of all relevant facts regarding his operatives. Men like Terchran always took care of details first. A question of character then, past loyalties, or future ones, perhaps?

"Before joining the Diplomatic Branch, sir, he was my commanding officer on an M-3," Dhar said carefully.

The fishy black eyes did not blink as they stared at him. Dhar knew what the Karkan was thinking, dislike written all over the scaled face.

"Fa'sure," Terchran muttered at length. "Your motives are your own, as long as they don't interfere with my objectives. Do I make myself perfectly clear?" Hiss.

"We both have our objectives, Mr. Director. At the moment they happen to coincide. They don't require that you like me, but you must trust me."

"As long as we understand one another. You know what you have to do, then. Yes, of course, you do. You're not like some, having to be told everything."

"Mr. Director, is this really necessary? It is a life you are asking me to take."

"It's more than a mere gesture. I cannot allow the Revisionists to offhandedly liquidate someone without an appropriately measured response. But why Gashkarali?" Hiss. "It's something to look into. Since I cannot get at Enllss, this will have to do. On the other hand," Terchran mused and tilted his head, "I find the incident puzzling. Enllss doesn't normally resort to something so crass. The implication is that he must be up to something. Your analysis?"

From a different perspective, Dhar had spent a lot of time pondering that very question himself.

"Sanctions at that level are carried out for two reasons only, sir. Controller Gashkarali must have either compromised himself, or—"

"Compromised someone else." The eyes turned cold and Dhar felt a moment of unease. "Fa'sure. This First Scout dies. Is that understood?" The tongue flickered in a blur.

The words were still echoing in Dhar's mind as the memory of that meeting faded. The desert felt hot and the amber sky clear of cloud.

Sitting there, aware the course of action imposed on him by Enllss placed him in the path of Sankri's wrath. Terr may be his bonded brother, he was still an alien before he became a Wanderer. He could not predict how Sankri would react to what Dhar was about to do. No, that was not exactly true.

The warning from the gods all too clear, and the image of his body beside a still pool.

"Whatever the fates decide, my brother," he said softly.

When he rose, the image of the desert faded.

* * *

Hands clasped behind his back, Terr watched as the M-3 surged through the thin film of the atmosphere. It did not take long to turn the sky from washed blue to deep violet. When the stars emerged, cold and hard, he clamped his mouth into a sulky scowl. Taltair fell away and shifted as the M-3 paused, hunting. Then the stars rushed together and flared blue-white as the ship transited into subspace.

Among the faint orange and brown patterns of gravity waves, he stood alone in the silence of his cabin. Anabb hadn't said much as the sled-pad glided toward the looming shape of the M-3. Terr did not feel like talking either, preferring to brood, still sore at Anabb for hijacking him like this.

He was also confused.

Things used to be simple when he first started working for Anabb. He believed in the right of the government to defend the implementation of its policies, any government, no matter what its political persuasion. As a government organ the Diplomatic Branch was not supposed to care whether the Revisionists or the Servatory Party thugs ruled.

It wasn't supposed to.

Anabb was right about one thing. Terr didn't really give a fart who held the General Assembly majority on Captal, as long as he could wield the hand of Death. If he wanted to be honest with himself, he couldn't blame Anabb for pointing that out, but he did. Anabb's cutting words had shattered the comfortable facade behind which he'd been so conveniently hiding. Now, he could either face the breeze or build another wall.

Anabb had merely brought into the open what Terr wanted hard to avoid facing. Maybe he should deal honestly with what and who he was. He realized he wasn't going to have any peace until he did, but he did not feel ready. Five years ago, he made a resolution to test the limits of his power. He had done that, and in the process, perhaps pushed those limits too far.

The M-3 steadied on its course as it left the influence of Taltair's sun. The density of gravity waves thinned and spread into long, flowing filaments. He felt them coiling around him, pulling him toward Anar'on and the escarpment of Athal Than.

As he stood there, he doubted his resolve to face the gods right now, let alone accept their judgment.

In the end, it didn't actually matter. It would come with the waiting. Staring at the backdrop of stars, he called her name.

The words came unbidden and he stood in the shadow of the god of Death. He only had to reach out and thunder and lightning would come forth. Strong with the power coursing through him, he gave a shuddering groan. With a grimace of anguish and desire, he placed the palm of his right hand against the warmth of the transparent polymer hull and reached for her. Blue sparks crackled around his hand. They coiled and twisted and spread along the hull. From the depths of his mind, she came to him.

She lay sprawled in the lounge of their house, supporting herself with an outstretched hand. Her long hair, spread in soft curls across her shoulders, shone with black fire. Her slender legs curled sinuously beneath her body. Small fingers twisted strands of carpet. She looked fragile and delicate, merely an illusion, of course. His Teena could be as hard and uncompromisingly ruthless as any field agent. Anabb did not pick softies to work for him. Holding her image, he hurt with longing for her.

Before her, the Wall showed a scene from some nameless city. Crowded streets, bustling traffic, slender towers of ceramic and transparent polymer panels that reached toward a pale sky.

"Teena?" he whispered and held his breath.

He saw her stiffen and look around in puzzlement. Her eyes, pale green and slightly too far apart, were large enough to wade in. The fine lines of her oval face, the high cheekbones, and pert little nose made his breath catch, her small, delicate mouth open. Generous red lips revealed even white teeth, the top two showing a slight gap. She turned and settled back to watch the Wall.

It all faded, leaving him staring at the brittle stars. His power can do much, but it could not bring her to him. He felt guilt at not being with her, and he'd been away from her for too long. His missions never ended, and left precious little time to renew what they had. He feared they might be drifting apart. The thought chilled him.

"I'm sorry, Teena," he murmured. He pulled back his shoulders and strode out of the cabin, leaving her and the god of Death behind.

He didn't meet anyone in the corridors. Perhaps it was just as well. Waiting for the cable-tube, his thoughts turned to his Anar'on Wanderer brother. A long year since Dhar's transfer to Captal. A lot of things happened since then—most of them bad. Terr didn't exactly lead the exemplary life of a Wanderer and he didn't know how Dhar would react. Terr wanted approval and dreaded that Dhar might find him unworthy.

It would only be the truth.

Dhar waited for him in the darkness of the recreation lounge, gazing into nothing. The stars stared white through the transparent hull. He turned as Terr stepped out of the tube. The background lighting brightened and chased the shadows away.

Terr took it all at a glance: the long orange hair, thin wiry build, narrow head, and towering height, a bit thinner than he remembered. Then again, it had been a while between visits. The yellow skin lacked some of its sheen, drawn tight over the bony ridges of his face. The orange eyes with their vertical red slits were bright and searching. The wide mouth with its drawn dry lips pulled back into a thin smile that revealed even brown teeth.

There was something else…an aura of power hung about him like a cloak. He could only have come by it one way. Terr doubted that a mere mortal would have noticed. Then again, he was not exactly a mortal. Despite the power, Dhar seemed like he needed a long stretch of leave. Terr felt a bit like that himself.

"Sankri," Dhar rumbled warmly, his voice coming from the deeps of the desert. It sent a shiver down Terr's back, no judgment in those eyes and voice, only acceptance. Dhar took the few hurried steps separating them.

Looking up at him, Terr broke into a huge smile and his cares dropped away. He felt Dhar's strength and a measure of peace. Grinning, he punched him on the shoulder.

"It is good to see you again, Nightwings, my brother," he gushed and felt the emotions crowding him.

"Someone has to look after you, Sankri," Dhar said with a straight face and Terr laughed.

"It's the evil life I lead."

"I always knew your holier-than-thou look was only a facade."

Terr's smile faded. "Truer than you think," he said and slowly extended his left palm. Dhar brought up his hand. "Nightwings, in your shadow, I am filled with the joy of your presence, my brother," he said and their palms touched.

"Sankri," Dhar said, his eyes gentle and forgiving. "I am enriched as always when I stand with you."

Small blue lightnings crackled between them. Terr felt a tingling and stared. The sparks softened and pulsed around their hands, growing quickly into a ball of blue radiance. It expanded and flared and twined around them.

They stood there, warm in each other's company, surrounded by the light of Death. There was no need for words, for they were one. Dhar's love radiated from him and Terr felt comforted. Nothing had changed between them, and he felt foolish to doubt it. After a time the light faded.

Terr gripped Dhar's arms. "How I missed you, Nightwings, and you're renewed," he said gruffly and sank down on one knee in supplication.

Dhar touched his shoulder as ritual demanded. "You have my blessing, my brother."

They were nursing some shipboard slop and Terr apologized for the lack of Anar'on prana water. Dhar shrugged and thanked him for the consideration.

"The thought is as good as the object desired," he said, his eyes large. "Besides, that stuff is good for you."

Terr lifted his glass of bug juice and made a face. "Tastes like sump oil," he said, playing with his tumbler. "You want to tell me about it?"

Dhar hesitated, not sure how to express a very personal and intimate experience, facing the gods for the second time and being reborn. It was one of the few things the Saddish-aa did not speak about among themselves, not even with a brother. Then again, Terr was not *exactly* a blood brother.

"Our master told me once that hell existed for people with no imagination," he said quietly, feeling his way through a jumble of images. "The rest of us, we create our own. For me the prospect of damnation was just as terrifying as anything I experienced during my first trial. Worse, for I didn't know what I faced then. This time, I knew.

"You can imagine my apprehension and uncertainty. I thought Sidhara would accompany me, but he said I had to face this alone." Dhar smiled wryly. "That didn't help. I took an oark mount and used the journey to prepare myself, as much as anyone can for something like that. I camped in the shadow of Athal Than. When the first rays of dawn struck the escarpment, I went in."

He hung his head and Terr could see him reliving every torturous moment. He reached out with his hand.

"Nightwings—"

"I'm all right. The memories, they tend to crowd me sometimes. You know the Litany of Preparation?"

Terr frowned, remembering. "And you shall walk through the valley of shadow with my hand as your only guide." He felt his voice deepen as though the god spoke through him. The hairs on the back of his neck prickled. "There, you will face my judgment, your soul as the price for absolution. Before me shall you answer for your deeds."

Their eyes locked as the words from the *Saftara* echoed between them. Dhar did not say anything else. He didn't have to.

Terr knew exactly what waited for him when he faced his second trial.

"Sorry I asked," he mumbled and Dhar nodded once.

"You have felt the call yourself, Sankri. I can sense the web of tension around you even now."

Terr chuckled. "It will have to wait."

"This mission, you mean?"

Terr nodded. "And other things. There is something wrong with this mission. I cannot pin it down; it's only a feeling. Have you wondered why we're here?"

"You and me? As a matter of fact, I have."

"And?"

"I am still thinking about it."

"Then think about this. By the time we get to Salina, the Orieli would have been cooling themselves for two days. A long time to wait on Serrll pleasure, don't you think? Anabb should have left the minute COMSAROPS had them detected, or at least arranged a Wall hookup."

Dhar looked thoughtful. "I don't get the connection."

"Don't you see? Someone told him to wait."

"You mean us? He was told to wait for us?"

"Anabb said as much."

"I cannot believe Enllss would hold up a formal Mission on our account."

"We're here, aren't we?"

"I cannot argue with that. Anabb will surely brief us before we get to Salina."

Terr took a pull at his juice and grimaced. "Don't count on it. We'll have our noses pressed against the Wall, told only what we need to know while he and Enllss spin the big picture. Hell, I wouldn't mind seeing the Orieli again. Remember when their cruiser jumped out of subspace? Right on top of us, eight hundred katalans of black, flowing cliff. Gods, I nearly wet myself. There is something compelling about them, my brother, overpowering. It's almost an arrogance, as though they knew everything."

"They've simply had millennia more practice, Sankri. Don't let their technology fool you. They are still groping around in the dark like the rest of us. If they knew it all, that ship would not have been there."

"Perhaps you're right. It seems like a lifetime ago when we were herding *Ramora* all over Sargon space."

"Much to their relief that we're not anymore," Dhar said and his eyes glowed. Terr grinned.

"We raised some hell, eh? How did we ever let it go?"

"We became heroes, remember?"

"That crap has kind of worn off."

"I should imagine. Let's face it, my brother. After Lemos, we were suckers for a high visibility profile gag Anabb pulled on us."

"I'm still chuckling, but you cannot say it's been dull."

"That it hasn't," Dhar agreed dryly. "When the gods want to punish us they grant us our wishes."

Terr laughed. "I wonder what they will grant me when I face them," he pondered. Dhar did not say anything. "Your parents, they all right?"

"They are both well. Thank you for your concern."

"It's what, fall there? The village would have returned from its summer pastures then."

"The Rahtir delayed the migration because of the marrakan storms, particularly heavy this year. They caused a lot of damage to the encampment. Not only ours. Two of the villages along the Katai Than range were almost obliterated. I spent part of my leave mending huts."

Dhar's mask of stern self-discipline momentarily slipped and they talked freely. Terr felt close to him, then. It reminded him of the long walks they used to take to the Katai Than escarpment. They would camp in some deep gorge with only the stars and the hissing crackle of their fire for company. They talked into the small hours, each learning about the other. They pontificated on the stupidity of high command, solving the problems of the Serrll with sweeping one-liners, grappling with the heritage of the Discipline and the power coiled in their hands. They were both more than a little innocent then, Terr decided.

"I wish I was on Anar'on now," he said urgently. "I need to lose myself in the silence of the desert. I need to replenish something that has slipped away. Somewhere along the way, I seem to have lost the meaning of it all. If I keep this up, I shall lose Teena as well." He twirled the mess in his tumbler and stared moodily at the table.

"Adversity tests us all," Dhar said softly and Terr frowned.

"You don't have to make any excuses for me. I guess I'm not a very good disciple of the Discipline. The burden is heavy, my brother, and I'm weary. As a part-time executioner, I no longer believe in the cause. As a Fleet officer, I no longer believe in the need. As a Wanderer, I feel the burden of my guilt."

"Humility heals all," Dhar said, reflecting that he too happened to be caught in a web of his own making. "Your soul yearns for the distances between the stars, the feel of a deck beneath your feet, and the sight of strange skies. My poor brother, fates are cruel to those who dream."

"Yeah," Terr said.

Chapter Four

Salina did not look much from orbit, a fat blotchy green crescent. Thick clouds covered the high northern latitudes. A cool, watery world, sunshine came feebly from a bloated red primary. Terr didn't have a chance to admire the scenery. SC&C, Surface Command and Control, shuffled them quickly out of the approach pattern. The M-3 hardly paused before it slanted down toward the atmosphere.

High, wispy clouds streaked the sky above Cel Field. Sullen white from above, fog hung low over the Field. Brown smog smeared the city. Tall towers rose out of the mist like lost ghosts.

Ships dragged wispy streamers of fog as they rose or sank into the white oblivion without a ripple. Like carelessly strewn jewels the navigation bubbles of larger craft poked through the fog into weak sunshine.

They came down quickly without maneuvering to hover beside the landing ring's access tube. Waiting for it to connect, Terr studied the Orieli lander hanging above the wet apron. The elegant pebble form, its trailing edges sloping down, stood dwarfed by the ugly gray shape of a towering M-4. Terr grinned, comforted by the thought the Scout Fleet were protecting the local citizenry from an alien menace.

The news snoops were waiting for them even as the cable-tube slid into the Executive Lounge of the military terminus. Reporters, axe grinders, friends of this, and enemies of that, ambushed them at the exit. Recorders and mikes bristling, they surged around them, gabbling, held in check by burly unsmiling MPs with phase rifles held at port arms.

"Mister Director! Can you comment on the Orieli—"

"What is the government doing about this threat—"

"Those aliens have been sitting out there for days! Why hasn't—"

Terr winced inwardly at the barrage, wondering who allowed civilians into a restricted area. Anabb scowled angrily at the spectacle, the burn on his cheek slowly coloring.

A young Third Scout, his face lined with worry, appeared out of a side entrance. He glanced at the media and hurried toward Anabb. Decked out in crisp parade grays with black trouser seams, he stopped, pulled his shoulders back and stood to attention.

"Welcome to Salina, sir."

Anabb tore him apart with his eyes. "What is all this, Mister?" he grated and waved at the crowd.

"Sorry about that, sir," the unfortunate said, faltering. "I'm supposed to be running interference for your team, sir. Things have just gotten out of hand a bit."

"You're not kidding."

"Last minute changes. It always happens."

"Hah! You stop this nonsense. I'm not in the mood for it."

"But Prime Director Trianon—"

"He's only polishing his image, is all."

"You *have* to make a statement, sir," the youngster insisted in panic.

"No, I don't. Let's go, son."

"But—"

"Now!"

They moved off, leaving behind the unhappy media. Angry invective followed in their wake. Anabb obviously did not give a damn as they plowed through.

They spent the combie flight to the executive offices of the Center in silence. Two APCs, Armored Personnel Carriers, paced them on either side. Terr tried to ignore them. The Third Scout beside him kept clenching his fists, no doubt wondering how he was going to explain the whole thing to the PR boys. His hard luck.

Terr didn't have anything particularly witty to say. He wasted time gawking at the scenery, although he couldn't see much. There was nothing to distinguish this urban sprawl from the countless ones on other worlds. After a while they all blended into anonymous invisibility. Maybe he would have time to walk around later and see it from the inside. Given their schedule, he doubted it.

An honor guard waited for them at the landing ramp of the executive building. This high up they were above the fog and the city towers sprouted around them from a sea of white. Streaming traffic of communals, combies, sled-pads and assorted heaps filled the pink sky, buzzing above them like swarms of disturbed insects.

They filed into the cable-tube without ceremony. Formal speeches and such crap were dispensed with, which Terr appreciated. Either the Orieli visit did not warrant a high profile, or the whole thing meant to be handled low-key, also okay with him. Pomp and stuff always made him uncomfortable. Had he gotten too used to slinking around dark alleys? Now *that* was a disturbing thought.

The executive offices took an entire floor. They went through two reception barriers before escorted to the inner sanctum. Administrative staff looked at them with undisguised curiosity. A whispered buzz followed in their wake. Feet sinking into thick, cream pile, gawking at the open luxury of the layout, Terr told himself he could get used to this kind of lifestyle.

Dark red solid wood doors slid back with a hiss and they were there.

"Diplomatic Branch Mission, sir," the Third Scout announced and left hurriedly. The doors clicked shut behind him.

Terr looked around and nodded in appreciation. It was an immense office. The floor-to-ceiling glazed window took a substantial part of the curved wall, opening to a sweeping view of the Center and the surrounding city. On his left the Wall plate pooled in neutral pastels. On either side of it stood a line of staggered shelves crowded with mineral specimens, trophies, an odd potted plant, and an assortment of memorabilia affected by senior politicos.

A distinguished older person sat behind a long oval black table. Terr figured it was Trianon. On one side, shoved against the window in a loose crescent, lay several modular formchairs. Standing beside one of them stood a Master Scout: tall, trim, serious, and black as midnight.

Terr looked him over. The guy looked like he had all his shit in one bag. The head perfectly round with no hair, lips purple and full, unable to hide a cruel mouth. Terr decided they were not going to get along.

The old politico planted both hands on the desk and heaved up his bulk.

"Prima Scout, always a pleasure, I'm sure," he said, smooth, suave, and sophisticated.

"Terr, my boy," Anabb boomed and seated himself unceremoniously into one of the formchairs. "Meet Trianon, Controller of Salina and Prime Director of the Rolan group."

Terr nodded and gave the old geezer what could generously be called a smile.

Trianon wore a conservative dull white suit, a bit tight around the middle. His white hair matched a gray complexion. His black eyes were little bright buttons, darting as they sized Terr up. He behaved as though Salina was a distasteful distraction to be borne stoically until something better turned up. A polished and dangerous character, Terr figured

From what he'd heard, Trianon's climb to the General Assembly was as spectacular as his fall. His high-profile activities for the nonaligned independent systems earned him a nomination from Salina to the Assembly during the previous elections. The Rolan group saw him as a comer and potential Commissioner material, an absurd proposition for someone from a nonaligned system. Had he behaved, the coming elections would have assured him a senior position, a directorship of some branch at least.

Unfortunately, Captal had its own ideas on how interstellar politics should be played. Trianon bought his sophistication dearly. He might have been a high mover in the Rolan group, but his voice as a single independent rep didn't count for much in Captal's factional byplays. The ponderous bureaucratic machinery chewed him up. All it took was one unwise policy move. Tangling with Sargon's dream of merger with the Paleans, Terr easily saw how he made it.

The idea of ceding Rolan's five systems to Sargon in exchange for a new Fleet base to be sited on Salina appeared an attractive one. After the Lemos debacle, Sargon saw an opportunity to secure five systems with little cost to itself, the main reason for raiding Pizgor, and what got Lemos derailed. Then the Orieli showed up and the Paleans ended up getting the Fleet base. The ensuing fallout made Trianon's position in the Assembly untenable, but the wily politico seemed to have made the best of it, Terr mused.

Trianon waved casually at the master scout and Terr locked eyes with him.

"Anatol Keller, commanding the M-4 at Cel Field." Trianon smiled and showed a mouthful of white, crowded teeth.

Then it dawned on Terr. He turned to Anabb. "Is that the guy who—"

Anabb grunted and Terr laughed silently. He reminded himself to ask Anatol sometime how it felt going up against the Orieli ship five years ago.

"You should stand to First Scout, when addressing the Controller." Anatol's voice sounded like ripping steel, his small eyes bulged as they lashed at Terr.

"Sorry about that," Terr said easily, not giving a damn.

Anatol stiffened and Terr watched the working of his face

Stefan Vučak

with amusement. If Anatol wasn't careful, he could break something.

"At ease, Mister," Anabb said coldly.

"But, sir—"

"Quiet. And you show respect toward a superior officer," he snapped at Terr.

Anatol glared. Before he could sit down, Anabb pointed a finger at him. "Don't bother. You'll not be around long enough to relax," he said and turned to Trianon who wisely refrained from interfering.

"Did you order that M-4 down?"

"Yes. So what?"

"Why?"

"An obvious precaution, of course. What is this anyway, Anabb?"

"No wonder they had you dumped in this backwater. You're a fool."

"Now just a minute! You cannot talk to me like that. As Prime Director, I rank you. One word to the Executive Council—"

"And?"

They locked eyes. After a moment, Trianon grunted and sat down. "Why all this fuss over a lousy M-4, anyway?"

Anabb ignored him and turned to Anatol. "Mister, get your ship off the Field and into orbit. Maintain neutral status on the Orieli cruiser until further notice. Copy?"

"Aye, sir!" Anatol snapped, stood to, and his eyes were cups of poison as he stomped past Terr. Anabb looked at Trianon with distaste.

"Leave diplomacy to someone who knows what's it all about, which includes Fleet tactics. Instead of maintaining a watch on the Orieli mother ship, you split the M-4s to babysit a lone landing craft. Bah!"

"The other M-4 *is* with the Orieli ship. And while we're talking about diplomacy, Mr. Director, you didn't go out of

66

your way to display any," Trianon said waspishly.

"You're referring to that media fiasco, are you?"

Trianon managed a brittle grin. "I couldn't have put it better myself. I watched the whole thing in the Wall. And you head the *Diplomatic* Branch. Really, Anabb! Answering a few harmless questions for the media would have been politically expedient for both of us. Instead of exploiting the situation, you merely raised unwarranted speculation."

"Unwarranted speculation? Trianon, if it hasn't crossed your mind already, that's all we happen to have at the moment. As for harmless questions, there is no such thing. Inform the Orieli that I'll open shop at fifteen hundred. Now, we should talk about the meeting."

* * *

They were all seated on one side of a wide oval table exchanging small talk. Fine lines of dark red grain flowed through the almost black wood. Bathed in diffused light streaming through the ceiling-high windows, the conference room was otherwise unadorned, made for business. A large Wall station cycled through twisted patterns of blue hues, offsetting the azure of the walls. An elaborate crest of the Serrll Combine hung behind the table.

Anabb pressed a pad on the inlaid console and black heavy doors separated, sliding into the wall with a pained rasp. When the three members of the Orieli delegation moved in, Terr felt the hair on the back of his neck rise. They looked like they owned the place. Two of them were native Zaronians and just short of average height, but they seemed to dominate all the space around them. Their skin was a beautiful shade of blue-green, growing black around the eyes and powerful mouth. Large brown eyes shone with scornful intelligence, their hair short, black and thick.

On the left side of their chest, they wore a small Cluster-

and-Circle emblem, a densely packed conglomeration of yellow stars representing the Orieli globular cluster. From Terr's previous encounter, he knew the variable color of the circle represented rank. The perfectly cut dark indigo one-piece uniforms were unadorned by extraneous gold braid.

An elegant statement of total authority, and what made his hair stand on end.

The other thing that made his skin crawl was the chilling enormity of the culture the aliens represented. The Orieli cluster was more than twelve thousand light-years above the galactic plane and had some nineteen hundred inhabited systems. It did not end there. Reaching into the local arm of The Arch, the Orieli Technic Union as a whole held some three thousand two hundred systems; a colossal sprawl of disparate cultures.

Terr hoped Anabb did not lose sight of that harsh reality.

The Cetan towered over the others, two katalans of muscle and power. Terr figured him to be the karhide, equivalent in rank to a master scout. His straight red hair spilled to his shoulders. Dark brown skin covered a very reasonable solid, angular human face. His red eyes were cold and impersonal, eyes that had seen everything. Terr glanced at Dhar. The resemblance was close, but superficial.

Anabb waved casually at the formchairs around the table.

"I don't stand much on ceremony. We can save that for later," he said, his gravelly voice impatient.

The Cetan nodded and his pale pink tongue ran quickly around black fleshy lips.

"Thank you, Da Director," he said in firm flawless Serrll interlingua without a trace of accent. He lowered himself gingerly into the chair and allowed the thing to mold itself around him.

His two offsiders followed suit and suddenly, the atmosphere seemed to lighten. It wasn't anything Terr could put his finger on, just an impression the ice had been broken somehow.

"On behalf of the Serrll, welcome to Salina, gentlemen,"

Trianon said smoothly, looking every bit the polished states-man.

"With your permission, Da." The Cetan nodded and shifted his eyes to Anabb. "Please allow me to introduce myself. I am Karhide Arlon Dee. My officers, Opturkarh Tavac and Taroptur Farly." The pale tongue paused, then went around the lips. "The Orieli Technic Union extends cordial greetings to the worlds of the Serrll Combine."

Introductions were returned all around, formal and stilted. Arlon glanced at Terr at the mention of his name, but Terr did not try to look dignified or some such crap. If the Orieli could not read their facial expressions, he was wasting his breath. If they could, whom was he trying to fool?

"Please allow me to extend an apology on behalf of the Serrll government for the delay of my arrival, Karhide," Anabb said affably.

Arlon, ultimately tactful, smiled briefly in acknowledgment. "Even today, Da, it takes time to bridge the distances between the stars."

"And disparate cultures," Anabb added wryly.

Terr watched the byplay with interest, hoping Anabb re-membered what he told him about the Orieli. Engage them in mind games, Anabb was likely to wind up in a mental sling.

"Indeed, Da. I would like to suggest, though, distance does not always guarantee isolation, and passage of time does not necessarily represent protection."

Anabb broke into a broad grin and chuckled. "The lan-guage of diplomacy, Karhide, you speak it well. It's a language I understand and appreciate. However, plain speaking has its value at times. Are you trying to tell me that your presence rep-resents a threat to the Serrll?"

"A possible threat, Da," Arlon corrected mildly.

"All by yourself, Karhide?" Trianon said and glanced defi-antly at Anabb.

Anabb shot a flicker of irritation at Trianon, then stared

thoughtfully at the alien.

"If I understand you correctly, your appearance on this side of the Moanar Nebula has attracted hostile attention. This could complicate my life, you know, when I already have enough problems."

Arlon's mouth twitched into a reluctant smile of admiration. Terr didn't have to pretend. He just gaped at Anabb. If true, it was a fantastic leap of understanding.

Arlon folded his arms across his lap and settled himself more comfortably into the formchair.

"Da Director, what makes you think the Orieli have third-party problems?"

"Come, Karhide. I didn't always drive a desk," Anabb said dryly. "I see here a classic military maneuver: power projection, extend lines of communication, and securing fleet integrity. Despite the incident five years ago, the Orieli have not displayed any belligerency toward the Serrll. It's highly unlikely then your visit here is now a prelude to hostilities. The logical conclusion is that you must be having difficulties with someone else. Difficulties that might extend in our direction."

"Your analysis, of course, is quite correct," Arlon acknowledged with barely a trace of irony.

"If I may, Da," Tavac put in, his voice strong and resonant. "It has taken us many years to break through what you call the Moanar Nebula, and it only became possible after we discovered a natural breach in the cloud, enabling us to survey this side for the first time. Once through, we encountered alien ships of advanced design. Ignoring all attempts at communication, they attacked without warning. When Karhide Zor-Ell made the initial contact with Agent Terrllss-rr five years ago, he was on one of those survey missions. Studying captured units—"

"Captured units?" Trianon demanded.

Arlon's eyes turned hard. "The occupants of these ships, Da, are not organic. They're artificially constructed lifeforms

70

calling themselves the Celi-Kran."

Trianon leaned over the table and palmed his chin. "Artificial lifeforms?"

"I would be happy to show you one, Da."

Anabb sighed and shook his head. "Karhide, I should have you thrown out of here. With your quantum point singularity drives and direct field transfer screens, you must realize that alien ships capable of presenting *you* with difficulties will undoubtedly give us even *greater* problems. Problems which *you* have caused by your presence on this side of the Moanar. You have not told me directly, but these artificial things could not be from around here or we would have detected them long ago. They're explorers, aren't they, just like you?"

Arlon inclined his head slightly. "Well, not quite like us."

"Thunderation!" The burn on Anabb's cheek had begun to color. "If those monstrosities aren't from here—"

"Pattern analysis of their movements suggests they come from the inner arm of The Arch, as you call the galaxy," Tavac said. "Since our initial contact with them, we have detected a marked increase in the disposition of their ships. We believe the Krans have been scouting this arm of the galaxy…searching for us."

"You understand, Da," Arlon added firmly, "the mere presence of our ships implies a sophisticated social and economic infrastructure capable of supporting many star systems. The Krans would also have determined that transitioning the Moanar was impossible. As a consequence, they reached an obvious, albeit a mistaken conclusion."

"Searching for you, they'll find *us*," Anabb said in disgust.

"I'm afraid so."

"Wait a minute!" Trianon pointed a manicured finger at the Cetan. "These Kran things should have been able to pick up your comms bands from the other side of the Moanar, identifying the presence of your worlds."

"Have the Serrll picked up anything?" Arlon queried

mildly. Anabb glared at Trianon.

"The plasma lines of the Moanar make an effective interference field, and as you're aware, the very nature of subspace communication makes tracing difficult," he rasped and turned to Arlon. "In time the Krans will undoubtedly detect you." Arlon didn't say anything. Perhaps the answer was obvious. "Let me guess, Karhide. You are here to warn us of the potential threat represented by these Krans?"

Terr didn't believe it. From what he knew of the Orieli, their technology was at least nine to eleven thousand years ahead of the Serrll, a staggering timeframe. He could not even begin to guess at their cultural and moral development. Why would they bother warning the Serrll? Unless, he figured, they were after something.

"Karhide, the Moanar Nebula isn't over the next hill," Trianon said. "From the extremities of the Palean Union, it's about two thousand light-years. I would have thought this would make a formidable enough barrier to most intruders. Besides, all of our enemies are now friends. The rest are no longer around," he quipped and flashed Anabb a triumphant glare.

Arlon's expression was bleak. "Believe me, Da, there is no making friends of these enemies. To them, all organic life represents a focus for destruction. I admit the threat to the Serrll might be a remote one, but it's only a matter of time before they reach your sphere of influence. You're unlikely to appreciate the encounter."

Anabb cleared his throat. "Your presence here, Karhide, suggests to me the threat is manageable. Otherwise, you would have retreated beyond the Moanar and collapsed the breach, if that's possible. Tell me. Why would the Orieli, after five years of total silence, suddenly develop a concern for our well-being?"

"We're not concerned with the Serrll Combine, Da Director. At least not directly."

"And what *is* your concern, Karhide?" Trianon demanded.

"Our own security," Arlon said simply. "We're not altruistic, but as Da Karr pointed out, the Celi-Kran threat is manageable, for now. However unintentionally, our activities will invariably lead them to you. We are here to make amends."

The silence hung heavy in the room. Anabb's forehead creased in concentration.

"Karhide, if you're concerned that your activities may lead the Krans to us, suspend them."

Arlon almost looked embarrassed. He shifted and cleared his throat.

"Unfortunately, that's not possible, Da. The Krans have already initiated a search process for reasons which I have previously mentioned."

Anabb shook his head. "I don't like it, but I appreciate your warning. The Serrll government has much to think about and prepare."

Terr brought his hands over the table and set his fingertips into a triangle.

"But that isn't all, is it, Karhide? Your visit here represents more than a warning or a desire to extend cultural contact and make amends. The Kran threat has forced you to extend your lines of communication and logistics beyond the Moanar. There is something you want from us, isn't there?"

"Thunderation, you're right there!" Anabb boomed and pounded the table with the palm of his hand.

From Arlon's look, Terr figured the Orieli were having second thoughts about Serrll provincials.

"Agent Terrllss-rr is perfectly correct, Da Karr," Arlon said heavily. "I am here to request nominal approval from your Executive Council to construct a final link in a chain of observatories designed to detect, track and monitor Kran activities on this side of the Moanar. Our preferred site is the Sol system. Specifically the Earth's satellite, the Moon."

Terr took time to digest that. A chain of observatories over three thousand light-years long? It didn't seem likely or possible, but the Serrll knew very little about the Orieli.

"Nominal approval?" Anabb asked in disbelief.

"That is correct."

"This is an outrage, sir!" Trianon exploded and jumped to his feet, unable to contain himself. "We don't usually parcel out Serrll space simply for the asking, no matter what the threat."

"Please elaborate, Karhide," Anabb said sternly. "But stand warned. The Serrll will not be pushed around to suit casual passersby. We've been confronted with muscle before. As you can see, we're still around."

Arlon bowed in acknowledgment. "If you will permit me to clarify. We intrude out of necessity; we do not invade. The critical nature of the threat facing all of us means that we're forced to maintain a presence on the periphery of your space. The time we spend here cannot be devoted to settling political technicalities arising out of mutual differences. Therefore, our contact must be sufficiently peaceful in order for us to carry out our mission."

Anabb pursed his lips. "Your corollary is clear, Karhide. You could have kept away and left us to face the consequence of your encounter alone."

Terr could see what Anabb was getting at. In case of Kran incursion, and given its location, the Palean Union would be first to fall under any attack. Faced with such a threat, it could be the final push that could consolidate its merger with Sargon. The merger would also wrest control of the Servatory Party coalition from the Karkan Federation, dashing its hopes of a ruling majority on Captal, and could send the Serrll into internal turmoil.

Terr almost felt sorry for Anabb.

"Karhide, I doubt very much whether the Serrll would be prepared to relinquish territory to anyone, Kran threat or not," Anabb said briskly, the burn on his cheek quite red. Arlon was going to catch it if he wasn't careful.

"May I proceed?" Arlon asked.

Anabb nodded and waved him on.

"We understand that Sol is a protectorate. It is not our intention to annex the system. The space between Sol and the Moanar represents an interdiction line beyond which Kran incursion will not be permitted. We'll see to that. I don't need to point out the obvious strategic implication to the Serrll Combine in maintaining such a line."

"You're not telling me everything Karhide," Anabb said bluntly. "Why Sol? Why not something at the edge of the Palean Union? A more logical choice, wouldn't you say? And it would be much closer to your existing facilities. What does Sol mean to you that you must build a base there when your lines of supply, communication and support are so far away? Tell me. What did your initial survey mission five years ago reveal about Earth to make you go to all this trouble? And what brought you back a year later?"

"Sol is a strategically convenient location," Arlon replied and gave his lips a quick lick. "The Palean/Sargon line is an exposed flank, Da."

"I don't buy it. As I have said before, Karhide, we don't usually relinquish territory just for the asking. And I'm not in a position to preempt decisions by the Executive Council. However, I can state government policy. The Council is not likely to favor the Moon for real estate development with Earth over the horizon. Even if they did approve Sol as your site, they'll point out the numerous asteroids and Jovian satellites more suitable for your needs while removing you from the prying eyes of Earth. All this, of course, if you can convince them why a site in the Palean Union wouldn't be better suited, which seems to me a much more logical choice."

"I am afraid the Moon is the only piece of real estate, as you put it, Da, that *is* suitable." Arlon raised his hand to forestall Anabb's protest. "Please hear me out. Your points are no longer valid and don't apply."

"I'd be interested to know why," Anabb said grimly.

"Even though Earth is a protectorate, the Serrll maintains a base of its own on the Moon," Arlon pointed out candidly. "By your own argument, it will be discovered as soon as Earth begins systematic topographical surveys of the far side, as has already happened. Also, your patrol ships have been under objective observation for more than eighty years. Earth knows there is someone prowling through its system. They have concrete evidence from ships that have crashed or been shot down, and positive identification of your personnel. With respect, I would be extremely surprised if the Serrll has not already established informal contact with at least one major Earth government."

"Mmm. You seem to know a confounded lot about Earth, Karhide. Especially for someone who has never been to the place."

"We learned a lot from our first survey, Da Director." Arlon smiled, showing even white teeth. "And Agent Terr's data pack to Karhide Zor-Ell was very comprehensive."

"To be sure," Anabb growled and glared at Terr.

Arlon stood up and looked straight at Anabb. "Da Director, I have been instructed by the Orieli government to advise you that we will have an operational base on the Moon in sixty days. You have five days in which to reach a decision. On the sixth day, I will be forced to lift for Sol."

"Sir!" Trianon jumped up. "That sounds dangerously like an ultimatum."

"That is regrettable," Arlon said.

Anabb didn't say anything. He just sat there frowning. The burn on his cheek had already turned a mottled purple.

* * *

Enllss sat behind a wide polished desk, his lined face split in a toothy grin. In the background, Captal's wintry blue-green sky lay smeared with puffy clouds.

"It's been a long day, Enllss, and I'm not relishing the prospect of a weary debriefing session. This could wait until we were off Salina at least before pouncing on me," Anabb complained petulantly. The words seemed to have a familiar ring to them and he spent a moment trying to remember from where the memory came.

"My day isn't about to end anytime soon either, Anabb," Enllss said callously. "But I do need a summary and I won't keep you long."

"Humph!"

"The Orieli put you through the wringer, did they?" Enllss asked, eyes twinkling.

"Hardly that. I don't really think they were trying. For what it's worth, it felt more like a come-on session."

"Now isn't that interesting? Keep feeding you problems just to see how you'll react, eh? Well, two can play that game. Okay, what's this nonsense about a base on the Moon?"

"It's not nonsense. They're serious, Enllss."

"By damn! We've got outposts in Sargon which I would have thought would be better suited for their purpose, provided the Executive buys into their story. A big ask. It would also keep them out of our hair. Artificial lifeforms you said? Crock! At any rate, if I remember correctly, we also have an ecoforming planet, Devon 3-VL4, I think, somewhere at the edge of the Palean Union. It has a large moon, uninhabited, and it's out of everybody's way. We could let them use it. Much better than getting ourselves entangled with Earth and all its historical baggage."

"You make it sound like a retirement resort," Anabb retorted.

"And you could be the first to go there!" Enllss snapped and thrust out his jaw.

"Look, Enllss. I don't believe this is a question of real estate. During their survey of Earth, the Orieli managed to dig up something which has got them curious, and now they're back to scratch the itch."

"Crap. We've had the place under observation for millennia and came up with nothing. It's just another backward planet."

"Backward enough to leap from sailing ships to spaceships in a century?"

"You call those flimsy rocket things ships?" Enllss laughed derisively. "Now, if you listen to Katan at the Bureau of Defense, his theory is that the Orieli want to interdict our expansion. What do you think of that?"

"An interdiction line over two thousand light-years long? And that's only to Palean space, remember. Add another thousand or so to Sol. Come on! If that was their objective, they'd just set it up without telling anyone about it. It's something we would do. We wouldn't know of it until we bumped into it. Take it from me, Enllss. From a military point of view a string of observatories covering such a distance would be a logistical nightmare. You would never set up such a thing without a damn good reason."

"Like the one they came up with?" Enllss suggested.

Anabb shrugged. "At least it's plausible and makes more sense than Katan's interdiction line. Although once they've got it up, it could be used as such, but I don't believe it. In my opinion, this Celi-Kran business has forced them to cover their back door and they've seized an opportunity to achieve two objectives."

"And these would be…"

"Establish closer relations with us, and since they were in the neighborhood, satisfy their curiosity about Earth."

"I can accept the first part, Anabb, but your fixation with Earth is a load of crock."

Anabb chuckled. "It might be a load of crock, but it's not my fixation. You'll have to credit Terr with the idea."

Enllss snorted. "You've been a bad influence on that boy, Anabb."

"You forget that Terr knows Earth very well, having served a stint at the Moon Base," Anabb countered. "And he knows the Orieli, at least better than any of us do."

"Something to think about then, isn't it? I understand you have confirmation why it took the Orieli this long to break through the Moanar?"

"It's technical, but our own observations confirm it. The Moanar, as you might know, is one of nine super gas filaments girthing the inner and outer galactic core. It makes a 6,800 light-year-long barrier. Normally, transiting through any nebula is not a problem, being basically vacuum; but given Moanar's thickness of almost four hundred light-years, the mass profile invariably begins to interfere with the ship's shield grid, causing the field precursor to decay and collapse. Once a ship drops normal, the surrounding mass prevents transition into faster than lightspeed and you're stuck. We lost ships there like that, and I suspect the Orieli have not fared better. You can understand why they haven't made an appearance earlier."

"I will let the Bureau of Technology mull it over. You know, this situation could be just what I have been looking for," Enllss mused and pulled at his chin.

"What are you talking about?"

"The Serrll Moon Base. If we've been compromised by Earth's survey, we may have to reveal ourselves formally to them. There are powerful factions in the General Assembly who would oppose any such move. Now, if the Orieli were to set up camp on the Moon, they could take the heat for whatever happens."

Anabb stared at the Wall. "You're amazing, Enllss. In the interest of interstellar expediency the Executive will bow to the Orieli. Is that it?"

"Something like that."

"You sound like the request of theirs is approved already."

"Look at it this way, Anabb. While they're studying us, we can be studying them, as long as we're going to be neighbors.

And Terr will have a chance to explain his theories to me personally after you and I have our debriefing on Taltair."

"You're coming there?"

"I don't have much of a choice. This deadline of theirs is a pain and I suspect deliberately designed to get us swarming. By the way, Terchran will be coming with me," he said and watched Anabb's confusion with amusement.

"It's an unwarranted risk," Anabb growled and shook his head.

"Terchran is an Executive Director, Anabb, and a senior member of the government. He is also a maluran of the Karkan Kapu legislature. This Orieli business is too important for partisan byplays."

"What about Dhar's covert assignment? Having Terchran on Taltair will only serve to bring additional pressure on Dhar. It could force him to do something hasty."

"Let's not lose sight of our objective," Enllss said sternly. "We cannot be too obvious, particularly where Dhar is concerned. His cover is too valuable to be thrown away by him doing anything hasty. As far as Terchran is concerned, Dhar is carrying out his orders."

"I told you before. I don't like this."

"You don't have to like it, Prima Scout. You just have to do it. Do I make myself clear?"

"What is clear to me, Mr. Commissioner, you seem to have forgotten that behind your big picture and grand strategy stand people whose lives you so casually manage. If you had to clean up some of your own mistakes, I imagine you would see things differently."

Enllss set his mouth. "I'm sure I would, but that's why I have professionals like you to see to it that mistakes aren't made," he flashed then held up his hand. "Sorry. That was uncalled for, but I don't have too many options, Anabb. Until the Unified Independent Front decides whether or not they're going to support the Revisionist Party, I want every Wanderer out of the Bureaus."

"It's a poor way to show trust in our own people," Anabb bridled.

"Maybe. Just have Terr report to me after we've had our debriefing."

Anabb waited until the Wall faded then muttered an obscenity.

Chapter Five

The communal descended in a leisurely sweep. Terr sat back in the upholstery and watched the sky and the ground beneath. Far in the west bunched clouds clad themselves in gold and fire, hovering above the city. In the east a rolling front of darkness obscured everything. In its depths needles of light flickered impatiently. A low muted rumble made the communal shiver. Black shadows covered the wooded hills like a blight. Slanting columns of gray indicated an advancing rain front. A flock of camalrens made a wavering V as they drifted westward.

Sprawling villas dotted the hills, hiding among the trees. The communal slowed and headed toward a house jutting out the side of a steep hill. The domed top level overhung a railed balcony. At the main level below, a broad landing apron began to glow pale blue in response to the communal's interrogative. They hovered briefly and then sagged toward the apron. Once down, the bubble opened and Terr breathed deeply of the cold, moist air. Scents chased themselves in familiar assault.

The driver opened the door for him. Terr climbed out, looked up at the clouds, and frowned.

"Gonna be a mean one," the driver agreed and shook his head resignedly. "And I just started my shift."

Terr mumbled something sympathetic.

The communal took off quickly, its navigation lights blinking. Terr watched it fade into the gathering gloom and wondered where Teena was. Usually when he came home, she swarmed all over him, a little game they played. Then again, she could be at the Center, or visiting or shopping...or anything. He felt a moment of keen loneliness.

At the entrance, he told the house to open up. The door cycled and there was a delighted squeal. She rushed him and clamped her arms around his neck.

"Oh, Terr!" she murmured breathlessly and pressed herself against him. He gathered her about the waist and swung her around him. She gasped and tightened her grip on him. When he put her down, he mussed her hair and glared at her.

"You imp, I thought you weren't home."

"No way, buster. I've waited too long for this. Besides, Anabb tipped me off. But forget that. Have I got a special deal for you tonight," she murmured and rubbed herself provocatively against him. He felt all prickly then.

His smile faded and he stared hungrily into the green pools of her eyes. He hugged her and pressed his cheek against hers. Standing there, they swayed gently. It felt good to hold her again, feel her warmth against him, feel her move with him, draw in her smell.

"How I've missed you," he whispered into her hair and a wave of tenderness swept through him. He cleared his throat and blinked back the sting in his eyes. It must have been the wind. She pulled back her head.

"You took so long, you beast," she said into his eyes and squeezed his neck.

He brushed her cheek, not daring to say anything. It would have been so easy to say the wrong thing then.

"That deal. Do I get a sample?" She fisted him in the ribs and he winced.

"Beast!"

"Just a little one?"

Her laugh a pleasant tinkle. "Well…"

A muted rumble rolled over the hills and soft rain began to fall. Her face turned up, eyes bright, sparkling like diamond pools. He slowly brought his mouth down on hers. They touched fleetingly, then her lips parted, soft and hot, her tongue a silky caress. Things faded a bit then and he had to break off to come up for air.

"Wow! I don't think I'm in shape for the full course."

She grinned contentedly and moved against him, making soft purring noises.

Lightning ripped the sky, followed immediately by a crash of thunder. Their shadows jumped. He picked her up and she rested her head on his shoulder. The door cycled shut behind him.

Down the corridor, heart beating quickly, he stepped on the cable-tube pad. It took them up to the main lounge. The transparent dome bubble overlooked the cliff and the hills beyond. It was dark inside, with only the faint green glow from the safety strip running along the bottom of the walls. The Wall showed a scene from some nameless city. He saw crowded streets, bustling traffic, and slender towers reaching toward a pale sky. Something out of a memory.

He put his arms around her waist and stared into her eyes. He ran his hands through her long hair, letting his fingers sink into the soft curls. Her chest rose and fell against him. A small pointed tongue teased her lips. Her eyes on him, she slowly opened the front of her robe. The swell of her breasts looked soft and ripe and he lowered his head to bite a dark nipple. She pushed against him and moaned.

"The sofa…" she mumbled.

Instead, he picked her up and carried her into the master bedroom, her head buried in his chest. He laid her down and her hips swayed seductively as she curled her legs back, her smile smoldering with dark passion. He ripped off his zip-jacket and sat on the edge of the bed. Her breasts were full and firm and the nipples hard. She groaned as he cupped them, his eyes boring into hers. He leaned over her and their lips met, her hard breasts yielding against him. Her arms went around him and she strained into him, tearing at his shirt.

Sometime later, his hand under his head, he stared at the black depths of the ceiling. Her head rested in the crook of his arm and her hair a veil over his chest. A moment stolen out of time meant to last forever, for he had no plans and wasn't going anywhere. She stirred beside him, her skin cool and smooth. He turned his head and gazed at her face, barely able to make out her features. Like everything around him, they hid in shadow. He brought up his hand, touched her lips with a finger and found her staring at him.

"You're not asleep," he told her accusingly.

"Good thing too. Taking advantage of me like that." She rolled over on her belly and rested her chin on his shoulder. Smiling mischievously, her fingers played with the hairs on his chest. He moved his hands down her back in slow strokes; pausing, lingering, moving gently over the swells lest a sudden gesture shatter the moment.

She shifted against him. With a low sigh of contentment, she nuzzled his naked arm.

"It's been a while, lover."

"What has?"

"Beast!"

"I thought you had a stud here every other night."

She lay against him and purred. "You're the only stud I need."

"And don't you forget it," he said grinning. Then his smile faded and he brushed her cheek. "I know it's been a while, Teena. Anabb—"

She pressed a finger against his lips. "I know. We'll talk about it later," she said playfully and bit his arm. "Shouldn't we be getting ready?"

"I would rather stay here."

"If we don't show up, Enllss will never forgive you." Her fingers walked across his chest, her nails sharp.

"Screw him."

She lifted her eyes and giggled. "Oh, Terr! What a terrible thing to say about your uncle."

"Rit! You know how I hate these formal straightjacketed

functions. You got to smile and pretend to be amused by stupid small talk. Bow to this or that asshole. Swapping inane banalities is not my idea of a rounded evening. I would rather be here with you."

She gave a tinkling laugh and shook her head. "You're beyond salvage. What about the debriefing?"

"I hate debriefings too," he growled.

"This Orieli visit, it's important, isn't it?"

He looked down at her. "What do you know about the Orieli?"

"When you didn't come back from your last job and Anabb disappeared, I knew something had come up. The whole analysis section talked of nothing else."

"Did you get your pretty hands on any of the comms?"

"Now, Terr—"

"You did, didn't you? The stuff is supposed to be classified."

She pouted. "I do have clearance."

"If you've already looked, then you know how important it is."

"But why are you involved?"

"Don't know," he admitted. "At any rate, it's over. After the debriefing, I'm all yours."

"Just in time too." She pulled herself up on her elbows. "I wish we could get away for a while," she said wistfully.

"I guess we could both use a break."

"Take me to Anar'on," she said suddenly and he looked at her in surprise.

"What made you say that? It's nothing but a windy, hot hell filled with sand."

"Not to you."

He stared at the blackness of the ceiling, thinking of rolling dunes and burnt rocks.

"No, I suppose not."

"After all the things you told me about that place, I want

86

to see it for myself. I want to see its amber skies and smell the burned sands. I want to see tarad grass and the spiny peelath. I want to hear the whisper of the dunes and see a painted sunset."

"Rit! Is that the way I really talk?"

"Uh-huh. It's creepy sometimes. I want to share the magic of that land with you, Sankri, my god of Death," she mumbled softly against him.

* * *

Low and gray the clouds drifted quickly, hugging the ground as they fled. The trees shivered and hissed with impatience. Muddy patches of blue showed through a torn sky. Sunshine would soon once again dry the tears from its land.

The landing apron warning beeped and Terr offered his arm. Teena took it, smiled and dropped a small curtsy, her dark green gown rustling. Shoulders bare, the gown swirling around her, she looked stunning. Nevertheless, hidden beneath her delightful exterior lay a cold professional. Not a field agent, but in its own way, her work was as important as his, perhaps more so.

She never served in the Fleet, being recruited to the Diplomatic Branch straight out of the Taltair Polytechnic. He'd already been with Anabb for two years and was attending one of those dull diplomatic functions when he literally stumbled into her. She smiled, ignoring his sudden awkwardness. He couldn't look away, totally captivated by her eyes. They seemed to grow, turning dark green as she regarded him with a touch of defiance. He asked Anabb to repeat something he'd said, totally consumed by those eyes. Anabb looked at him with tolerant amusement, but Terr was oblivious.

Then he was off after Kai Tanard again, then another assignment, wearing down her resistance between jobs. He could not believe they've been together for just over a year. Somehow it seemed much longer, so completely did she fill his life.

Standing beside her now, he didn't really feel like going anywhere. There were too many things he needed to talk to her about, to renew, but orders were orders. The thing was, he felt awkward in his parade whites, ribbons and medals. Anabb insisted, threatening to have him drive an M-2 shuttle on Cantor if he failed to show up properly attired. Well, it was only for the night.

The cable-tube took them down. The door cycled behind them and locked as the communal settled on the apron. Outside, the air felt cold and biting. The driver looked mean and didn't bother meeting them. Terr shrugged. Everyone was entitled to an off day. The door cycled open and the bubble became transparent. He waited for Teena to get in. He sank into the upholstery beside her and tried to make the best of it, flashing her an encouraging smile.

"The Center, right, sport?" The driver half turned, his eyes lingering on Teena. A crooked weed hung out of the corner of his mouth.

Terr touched the mike pad. "Right, and make it march."

The driver grunted and the soft purr of the plant changed to a persistent hiss.

They were high above the countryside before Terr turned and looked below, feeling moody. The house already lost among the hills.

"Got out on the wrong side of the bed, eh, sport?" The driver rubbernecking and feeling curious.

"Yeah."

"Know how ya feel," he said. "Bad day."

"Yeah."

"Things will pick up. You'll see."

"What's the idea with the open mike, pal?" Terr asked.

"Ah, got busted and haven't had time to get it fixed. And besides, I figure it saves the guys having to keep thumbing the pad all the time, see?" The driver sounded cheerful.

"Terr?" Teena touched his arm and pointed.

"You and the lady got something special going tonight?"

"Sort of," Terr said, taking a good look at the scenery around him, not liking what he saw. They should be heading west. "You sure we're going the right way, pal?" He sat up and looked at the city far on their starboard side.

"You betcha, sport," the driver said, his head bobbing.

"This doesn't look like the way to the Center to me."

"I wouldn't know about that, sport. Just relax." He chuckled and shifted the weed to the other corner of his mouth.

Whatever his idea, Terr wasn't planning to stay on for the encore. He slid his hand under his jacket and dragged out the small Service Special. Nothing fancy and left little fuss.

"Terr!" Teena looked at him in alarm.

He squeezed her arm and gave her a reassuring smile. He made a slight adjustment and pressed the operating end of the needler against the screen separating them from the drive compartment.

"Okay, pal. The gag's over," Terr said with plenty of snap. "You land this crate or get hurt—bad." No need to get excited and bungle it.

The driver didn't even bother acting surprised.

"You wouldn't shoot me, sport. Not this high up. Why, there wouldn't be enough left to stuff an envelope. Besides, you wouldn't want anything to happen to the little lady now, would ya?"

The guy had it all figured out, or someone figured it out for him.

"Someone must be awfully anxious to go to all this trouble. Your greasy pals paying you for this guided tour, maybe?"

"That's all high politics stuff, sport. Way over my head. Me, I gets a wad of dough for taking you on a little cruise. Nothin' violent, see?"

"I see you taking a long stretch on Cantor, *sport*!" Terr said and squeezed the contact.

The white beam sliced through the screen, the driver's left

ear, and the front bubble. Teena didn't even flinch. It must have stung like hell, for the driver screamed like he was dying. The combie sagged into a roll before the internal navigator compensated. The sound of air whistling through the hole in the bubble stopped abruptly as it sealed itself. The comedian up front rubbed his ear and stared at the blood on his hand.

"Oh, crappers," he whined. "Why'd you have to go and do that for, sport? I wasn't out to hurt ya."

"Just a free sample. In case you have some other funnies up your sleeve. I'm not in the mood for laughs right now."

"I'll have to get this fixed up. I'm bleeding," the driver spluttered and showed Terr his bloody hand.

"The Center, pal," Terr said, waving the gun around.

"Look, sport. This wasn't in the contract, okay? For the love of—"

"The Center!"

"Oh, crappers."

The incident cheered Terr up. He always preferred action to brooding. He sank back into the seat, smiled broadly at Teena and enjoyed the flight. His pal up front kept glancing at him from time to time, just to make sure he hadn't stepped out or something. Terr didn't disappoint him. All the while the driver kept muttering to himself. They were heading in the right direction, so Terr didn't mind.

The traffic began to get thick as they neared the cluster of towers around the Center. Terr's friend whimpered, coughed and wiped his forehead.

"Look, sport. I feel kinda sick, see?" he croaked, massaging his neck. "How about I let you off here and we part as friends. What'd you say, huh?"

"I would feel real bad if I let you go now, pal," Terr said, tsked and shook his head. "You know how it is."

"Yeah. I love you too, sport," the driver said miserably.

"Shouldn't you be getting into the control network?" Terr prompted him.

"Okay, okay. No rush."

The rocking length of the communal moved leisurely toward the main landing ramp of the Admin building. It crossed the entrance marker and followed one of the glowing yellow ribbons into the interior.

A security point barred the entrance to the parking lot. A beefy MP in parade grays, white gloves and boots, his worn phase rifle slung casually at port arms, stared at them suspiciously. Terr didn't particularly care for the way he stroked his rifle.

"Thanks for the flight, pal," he told the driver. "Unusual, but interesting." He didn't bother looking at the charge plate as the door opened. This one could be counted on the house. He waited until Teena climbed out before following. The MP stood there, calmly looking at them.

"You have clearance to enter this zone…sir?" he added as though it hurt him.

"First Scout Terrllss-rr."

"Oh, yeah?" The guard didn't look overawed. "How about an ID check, huh?"

"Lead on." Terr grinned cheerfully and turned to the communal driver. "Don't go away," he said and patted his shoulder. The driver nodded, looking sick.

The MP led Terr to an ID booth. Terr pressed his palm against the plate and waited until it cleared. The MP took one look and his face broke into an embarrassed grin. The rifle slid down his side and he stood to order.

"Ah, sorry, sir. You should see the cracks who try getting in here."

Terr chuckled and slapped him on the arm. "Glad to see you're on the job." He nodded at the communal. "I have a close friend there, but we had a falling out. Sad. He didn't feel like taking me where I wanted to go. See that the boys have a nice long chat with him about my detour. Refer it to Director Anabb Karr."

"Sir!" The MP grinned and brought up his rifle. He sure loved that weapon, Terr mused. He walked back to the communal and leaned against the open bubble frame.

"You don't have a thing to worry about, pal. I'll send you postcards to Cantor."

"Shoulda stayed at home," the driver muttered sourly. The MP hovered behind them.

"Does this kind of thing usually happen when you're around?" Teena demanded brightly as they waited for the cable-tube.

Terr laughed. "Only when you're with me, pet."

She made a face and fisted him in the ribs. "Beast! What will they do to him?"

"It all depends on what he has to say," Terr said comfortably and Teena gave him a sharp glance.

The cable-tube took them to the Admin executive level. Teena attracted admiring stares in her wake. Ariane, Anabb's personal aide, smiled warmly at her. The two had a hurried chat and a few giggles before Ariane ushered them into Anabb's office. The way Anabb paced around, he could not have been very happy.

"Start explaining, Agent Terr!" he demanded. "You should have been here twenty minutes ago."

"Explain what?" Terr said looking innocent. "All I know, this comedian in a hot communal decided to take us on a probable one-way health cruise in the country. But for him, the idea had a lot of appeal."

Anabb looked sharply at Terr. "Somebody tried to snatch you? Did you at least find out who sent him?"

"Well, the thought did cross my mind." Terr gave him a toothy grin. "But I was kind of rushed to get here."

"Enough with the cracks!"

Terr winced. "I don't know what he had in mind. I imagine the MPs downstairs will get the details out of him. Probably a small-time stickup artist cruising around for some action."

"And maybe not. All right. We'll talk about it later," Anabb said and turned to Teena. "My apologies. You look radiant, my dear."

The old bastard could actually be quite charming when he wanted to. Not that he had much time to practice it. Goes with the job, Terr guessed.

"Delighted, Mr. Director," Teena husked and curtsied to her boss. Decked out in full uniform with all his medals and orders, Anabb cut quite a figure.

"You'll have to be contented with me while your partner here keeps an appointment with the Commissioner. I'm sure it won't take too long."

"Your company is all any woman could hope for, sir," Teena said and smiled wickedly at Terr.

"You're flirting with me." Anabb laughed, offered her his arm and they headed for the doors.

"Hey, what about me?" Terr demanded in dismay.

"You wait," Anabb shot back without turning.

"Rit!"

He didn't have time to start feeling sorry for himself. The door panels opened and Enllss stood there.

"Terr, my boy!" he boomed and stormed in with Dhar in tow. "What a damned fine sight you cut. Those deck whites look good on you." His eyes raked over Terr, looking pleased at what he saw.

"Glad to see you fighting fit, Uncle." Terr grinned and nodded to his brother. Dhar seemed reserved and tense. Terr dismissed it as too much travel time.

Enllss comfortably patted the bulge around his middle.

"When Anabb picked you out of the Fleet and put you to work, I never figured you would last the distance."

"Neither did he. He's regretting it now and is trying his hardest to get me killed off in one of his bad deals," Terr said and they all had a good laugh.

They made themselves comfortable and spent time swapping lies and getting intimate. It pleased him to see Enllss still so active. Yet, he was just getting past his prime. Politics can take out more than it puts in, his uncle always told him. Terr knew Enllss yearned for a director's seat in the Executive Council. The coming elections would likely see that come about, if the internal squabbles between Sofam and the other Revisionist coalition partners didn't kill him first.

Enllss was the successful one of their family tree. Most of the other branches were either cut off through untimely demise, sought local posts on Kaplan, or taken service with the Fleet. Behind the polished smile and suave exterior lay a ruthless streak that first won him a seat in the General Assembly, followed by two terms as commissioner. His last stint was with the Bureau of Cultural Affairs, Serrll's intelligence arm, of all things. Maybe that is where he developed a love for intrigue.

Enllss looked old when Terr still crawled around as a Base Scout: young, idealistic and full of rights to end all wrongs. With youth went some of the other things too.

A moment of silence came between words, and both were lost in their own thoughts. Enllss wanted to know how Teena managed to put up with him and his secretive work. Terr told him it was pretty damned hard at times. Enllss nodded with an understanding smile.

"Must make for terrific reunions."

"Count on it."

"She is here, isn't she? Good. I want to talk to her later, make it up to her for snatching you away. By the way," Enllss said and gave Terr a bemused look. "Terchran will be at our exclusive blowout tonight. I thought it might be amusing for you to see the face of your political enemy."

"But he's a top cog in the Servatory Party wheel!" Terr protested. "What's he doing on Taltair?"

"Came with me for this Orieli debriefing with Anabb. Terchran may be a big mover in the Servatory Party wheel, but after hours, he wears a gracious and charming personality. Capital is a very exclusive and secular community, Terr. The secret of doing business is peaceful coexistence."

"And making sure you haven't been short-changed in the payoff," Terr said dryly.

Enllss did not smile. "The experience will do you good."

"If you say so. But if he should suddenly have an acute attack of terminal hangover tomorrow, don't blame it on me."

"Don't even *think* about it," Enllss said, all business. "Do you understand me?"

"Just kidding."

"Sure. If something were to happen to a Karkan maluran…Now, I didn't ask you over here simply to have a pleasant chat. We'll have that later. I have a Bureau to run and this Orieli visit is a complication I could easily have done without."

"That's what Anabb said."

"I bet he did." The window screen showed the Center's towers glittering in the gathering dusk. "I've been talking this over with Agent Dharaklin just before you got here. We didn't get far. My problem is this. Since your initial contact with the Orieli five years ago, the Executive Council had the Bureau of Central Planning and Development running models, exploring various future contact scenarios. Now, I don't know what Anabb told you about why you're here—"

"Something to do with worms," Terr said and didn't elaborate.

Enllss' shaggy gray eyebrows came together into a stormy line. "You have a pretty loose mouth for a First Scout, Mister," he snapped and thrust out his jaw.

Terr felt tired. "Let's get one thing straight, Mr. Commissioner. I'm here against my wishes because some bureaucrat in the Threats and Intentions Branch cannot count the number of fingers on his hand. We could have settled all this through a Wall conference on the way back from Salina, saving everybody a lot of time. There is nothing I can tell you that your bright-eyed geniuses haven't thought of already."

Enllss shook his head in resignation. "No wonder Anabb is trying to get you killed off. You haven't a drop of respect for your superiors."

"I can only put it down to blood in my ancestry, Uncle," Terr said stiffly.

"Impertinent bastard." Enllss laughed and folded his hands over the desk. "There are reasons why this had to be a personal contact, my boy. Now, as I was saying; my thumb-fingered staff, as you so colorfully put it, have dug up one of those models made by Central Planning and it has come back to haunt us. The implications are creepy if I'm to believe their findings. That's why both of you are here."

"You want me to hold your hand while we look at it, right?" Terr said with a straight face, trying to get some of his own back.

Enllss' eyes twinkled and he grinned. "Actually, it's all your fault. We made that model from some of the data you supplied to the Bureau of Cultural Affairs four years ago."

"Our second contact with the Orieli?"

"The very one. The model predicted that the Orieli would return to Earth, but Central Planning cannot understand how it arrived at the conclusion from data held in its knowledge base. Or they refused to accept the chain of arguments it used—which you supplied. That's why we rejected it in the first place. However, the Orieli *have* returned and I want you to corroborate the model."

"A tall order this time of day, and it's been a while."

"It's not something one is likely to forget," Enllss said dryly.

Terr pursed his lips, getting his thoughts together. "I can give you an extensional analysis. The way I see it, it boils down to empirical evidence. Look at our first contact with Karhide Zor-Ell. My mere presence would have alerted him to Serrll's existence. For one thing, he could tell that Earth didn't have the kind of technology needed to produce and support a subspace capable ship like an M-1 scout I used."

"Go on."

"Since my ship was alone, he would have deduced that I was a patrolling scout or currier. When he found the SMB, it would have automatically confirmed the existence of an interstellar power block such as the Serrll. And what did he do about it? Nothing. How does your model cope with that?"

"Apart from allowing us time to evaluate the impact of the contact, I remember that the Sol system happened to be the last item in his search pattern," Enllss reminded him.

"Come off it! Are you trying to tell me that after going through over three thousand light-years of survey, he would drop his investigation of us merely on the excuse that we were not in his terms of reference?"

"Karhide Arlon Dee mentioned contact with those Kran things. Zor-Ell could have been anxious to get back home and make his report."

"He could have, but I don't believe it. If I were him, I would have reported the presence of anything as hostile as the Krans at first contact, *then* continued on with my mission."

"Okay, you have me convinced on that point. Why didn't he prolong his contact with us?"

Terr gave him a nasty smile. "You should think of changing some of your advisors, Enllss. They've been driving desks for too long instead of ships."

"What do you mean?"

"We've covered this already, but…" Terr glanced at Dhar. "Tell him."

"In our case, Mr. Commissioner, when accidental contact is established with a new culture, SOP demands that we stand off for a specified period. There have not been any recent examples of such contact by the Serrll. Consequently, our evidence is historical. The last such event which comes to mind is the contact between the Sofam Confederacy and the Palean

Union."

"Culture shock, by damn." Enllss slapped his thigh. "The Orieli have simply been giving us time to evaluate the social implication of the contact."

"That's about the size of it, sir."

"You mentioned this when you first made your contact report. Mmm. Interesting." Enllss leaned back and his eyes studied Terr. "Maybe some of my advisors *should* spend more time conning ships. That still doesn't explain their interest in Earth, though."

"But it does, provided you accept my hypothesis," Terr said. "It's all there, Enllss. Your people simply refuse to see it."

"What are you getting at?"

"Consider my first encounter. Don't you think it's more than a little curious that the Orieli spent only two days nosing around Earth? Backward it might be, but it has its attractions. Still, after two days they just up and leave. Then twenty days later, they're back and shoot it out with Anatol Keller and his M-4s. Another day and they're gone again."

"So?"

"Almost a year later they show up for the third time. What brought them back?"

"That theory of yours about picking up an observer?" Enllss said and Terr nodded.

"The way I figure it, something went wrong with the first pickup attempt and it took them a while to work out the problem and mount a rescue mission."

Enllss cleared his throat and shook his head. "My Bureau did investigate the matter, you know. Your theory is shaky in the light of concrete evidence." Terr made to speak, but Enllss held up his hand. "Patience, my boy. Question. What does Earth have to warrant such detailed examination?"

"Anabb asked them the same thing."

"So he told me. If Earth does hide something, how come we never discovered it in millennia of continual observation?

And the clincher. What sort of an observer can remain effective and undetected for a whole year? A lot of contradictions, my boy."

"It doesn't signify."

"Oh? Okay bulging brains, tell me."

Terr looked smug. "I should make you sweat for it, but I'll let you off. Your questions, Enllss, are based on the capabilities and experience of Serrll's own operatives. Don't you see? All your reasoning is negative. We're dealing with a culture thousands of years our superiors. The extent of their capabilities and experience is unknown!"

Through the ensuing silence, Terr could almost hear Enllss chewing over what he'd said. Judging by his expression the taste wasn't altogether to his liking. Finally, Enllss winced and scratched his chin.

"That blasted model has predicted their return to Earth all too accurately. I cannot argue with you there. And the reason: resolve the anomaly they discovered during their first visit. It must be some burning problem for them to have gone to all this trouble. And because of Earth, they're willing to build a chain of observatories three thousand light-years long? Incredible."

"I don't think they're building them simply because of Earth," Terr said and Enllss sighed.

"Yeah. They might have landed the Serrll in a war with those Kran things and want to make sure we don't get splattered."

"By the way, what's the latest on their ultimatum?" Terr asked.

Enllss shrugged and waved his hand. "They've taken off, just as they said they would. I authorized Anabb to carry out limited negotiations with them until the Executive reaches its decision. Off the record, I expect the Orieli will get tentative approval with some strings attached before they reach the Moon; like including a Serrll team."

His eyes twinkled as he regarded Terr. "There is one good thing in all this. Our friend Terchran and the Servatory Party are running around in little circles trying to figure out what position to take."

"Keep him out of my way and I won't even vote," Terr promised.

Enllss stood up, concluding the meeting. "Tomorrow, I want you to see some people from Central Planning I brought with me. Be a good boy and go over that model with them, okay?"

"Have a heart, Enllss," Terr protested. "I've been running around in circles myself. I want to spend some time with Teena, not some screwballs from Central Planning."

"Tomorrow morning," Enllss said briskly. "Now, let's go and enjoy the party."

Rit!

Chapter Six

Terchran was pissed.

He wanted somebody's head, anybody's head. In particular, he wanted Dhar's head—preferably on a pike as a reminder to others, but not quite yet. That pleasure he meant to savor. The impudence of the young pup! He gave a small hiss of annoyance and tapped the desk with his knuckles.

He tried to stare down this silent enigmatic desert creature who stood so easily before him and failed. Those orange eyes…Something lurked in them which made him uncomfortable. Terchran did nothing to hide the displeasure he felt for the Wanderer. Fanatics, all of them, he decided—dangerous nonetheless and not to be underestimated. To the pit with them and their Discipline. Religious mud crud! The problem with double agents, he mused, lay in deciding which side they really worked for, if they *had* a side. It irked him intensely.

"You were supposed to neutralize him, not intimidate him!" he hissed with venomous disdain. His thin pointed tongue flicked across dry lips. "The kidnapping debacle has merely succeeded in alerting him. From his record, First Scout Terrllss-rr is extremely capable and one of Anabb's top operatives. He has cost us more than one cold body on a slab. Fa'sure, you don't use half-baked measures with someone of his measure. It's something which you of all people, should be aware of."

Behind his impassive features, Dhar felt pleased with the outcome of last afternoon's incident, even to the selection of the anonymous small-time amateur. For Terr, the attempt was hardly a problem, as Dhar expected.

Stefan Vučak

"I urged my cell leader not to take any precipitous action without clearing it through me, sir," Dhar said, his voice deep and steady, invoking images of vast openness. "The attempt would have worked. Her mistake—"

"Being a fool, fa'sure!" Terchran finished for him, his fishy black eyes bright. "I want you to terminate her."

Dhar felt a wave of consternation jolt through his body. He hoped his despair did not show on his face. He knew Terchran was ruthless, but this was an exercise in malice.

"Sir—"

"Spare me! She was incompetent and you were careless. I don't like either in the people I use." Terchran snapped his jaws with a finality that brooked no argument.

The glitter in Dhar's eyes wasn't exactly hate…

"What she does is my responsibility, sir. If she needs reprimanding, then I will do it, in private. Liquidating her because a hurried plan miscarried would be totally out of proportion. It would completely undermine the effectiveness of that cell, depriving you of a valuable source of intelligence. I respectfully decline to carry out your request."

Terchran hissed and stared hard at Dhar. His knuckles tapped against the desk. He admitted what the boy said made sense, but was it motivated by his loyalty to the Servatory Party or inner squeamishness?

"Very well. She has her life. Just see to it that your next attempt has at least a semblance of professionalism."

Dhar felt a surge of relief. So, even a maluran could be outfaced. He did not want to make a habit of it, though.

"I cannot move too openly, sir. Not now. It would only draw suspicion on me."

Terchran allowed himself a mirthless smile. "On the contrary, boy. Whatever suspicions Terr may or may not have, they certainly will not extend to you, fa'sure."

Dhar understood immediately. "Yes, with you here, suspicion will fall on your men."

"Exactly. I want that scout's head. See to it," Terchran snapped, his tongue flicking.

"If that is all, sir?" Dhar said, his face betraying nothing.

Terchran waited until Dhar walked out, then grunted as he pried himself out of the formchair. He turned and stared moodily at the sprawl of the Center spread before him. The city glittered beneath a muddy sky. Patchy clouds lay bunched low in the west, painted in browns and reds by the dying sun. It looked like rain later in the evening—*again*. Hiss!

He grabbed an opportunity to escape Captal's fickle weather, only to land in Taltair's. The thin rain here often cold, far removed from the warm torrents of his native Karkan. He longed to wade through steaming marshes where small waves from the shallow seas barely rippled as they slid up black, sandy beaches. He snorted at this moment of weakness.

Was he getting weary of it all? He shook his head and bit his scaled lip. After almost thirty years of playing Captal's games, he *was* getting weary. On Karkan, he would be a revered figure, able to enjoy the tranquility of retirement.

The thought appalled him.

Even being a maluran, a senior government policy maker, did little to stir his interest, not after shaping policy for the whole Serrll.

What really bothered him, he could not rid himself of a lingering headache from last night's function. Strangely, no amount of medication seemed to help. Hiss! He hated the idea of not being in total control. The admission came grudgingly, but Enllss had turned out a polished performance. He even contrived to bring him and that young pup Terr together, virtually bumping into each other. The boy apologized while his eyes cut and probed. The same kind of eyes, Terchran realized with shock, Dhar had. He had not enjoyed the experience. It spoiled the rest of his evening.

Thinking about it, his headaches started soon after his encounter with Terr. The door hissed open behind him. The footfalls were barely audible on the soft pile.

"I heard everything, sir," a shadowy voice rasped.

"Then you know what to do," Terchran hissed without turning. "When you get to the Moon, eliminate them. Eliminate them both!"

* * *

Terr sat back in the soothing comfort of the formchair, his eyes half closed. Sipping an iced drink, he glanced at the tall tumbler from time to time while playing with the crushed mess inside. Anabb talked like someone giving a sales pitch. Terr suppressed a yawn of boredom, forcing his eyes to remain open.

"Enllss wasn't happy with what you said to those Central Planning people," Anabb remarked casually.

"Tough," Terr said. "They should have done their homework better."

Anabb grinned. "Last night, what did you think of Terchran?"

"A cold fishy bastard. I hate to admit it, but Enllss could be right. It's useful to know the face of your enemy, and I always wanted to meet a real live Karkan maluran," Terr said with a mischievous grin.

"Enemies can be found in the most unexpected places." Anabb's oval eyes glittered secretively. "Like that communal driver."

"Now there was an enterprising operator. Did we get anything out of him?"

"Someone paid him to keep you in purdah for a while. That's all he knows."

"I'm inclined to believe him."

"The warehouse he was supposed to take you to was abandoned. Nothing there, and the communal stolen."

"Figures. He couldn't have dreamed up that gag all by himself, Anabb. It wasn't his style. Whoever set it up for him was in a hurry."

"You're not short of enemies."

"I've got one or two stashed around," Terr admitted. "But who would be mad enough at me right now to do something drastic about it?"

"What are you trying to say?"

"Terchran could have found out about my involvement on Trillian and wanted to get even. Unless, of course, you want to get rid of me yourself," Terr said, eyeing Anabb over the rim of his tumbler.

"Don't tempt me!" Anabb snapped. "Meeting that communal driver must have been a coincidence." He dismissed the matter with a wave of his hand.

"Never believe in coincidences. Didn't you say that once?"

"If I did, it's small of you to bring it up now. At any rate, I want to talk about something else," Anabb said and tapped the desk with a stubby finger. "A little negotiating I've been doing with Karhide Arlon Dee."

Terr drained his glass and twirled the crushed ice for a second. The tumbler made a loud click as he placed it on the tray.

"Sounds interesting," he said, not actually listening.

"It is. He agreed to include a complement of our men as part of his Moon base personnel. A payoff for letting him set up shop there. They've got it all worked out. Complete environmental assimilation: language, culture, biologicals, the works. Three months of undreamed of duty. Once in a lifetime opportunity!" Anabb stopped his passionate tirade and Terr stared at him with suspicion.

"You sound like a Wall ad," he said accusingly.

"We cannot very well allow them to prowl around the Moon all by themselves," Anabb said, wearing a beatific expression.

It took a while before the implication of Anabb's words

sank in. Terr's eyes snapped open and he was suddenly wide awake. He leaped out of the seat and shook his head, hands waving.

"Oh no! I know what you're thinking, you evil old bastard. No, not this time."

"There is no need to get excited."

"I'm not going!"

"Half the Fleet officers would jump at a chance like this."

"Then give it to them!"

"Such lack of gratitude." Anabb grinned and Terr's skin crawled. "Think of it, our first major alien contact in more than three and a half thousand years. You're getting a bargain."

"What I'm getting is a chance to have my ass shot off. No thanks!"

"Enough already!" Anabb snarled and slammed his fist against the desk. The burn on his cheek took on a purplish color and his eyes lost some of their charm. "You obey orders or I'll shoot off that ass myself."

Terr did not want any of it. "This time, you can rave all you want. I'm not going to be suckered again. I've got leave coming and I have plans—with Teena. You and the Orieli don't figure into them." He flopped into the formchair, crossed his arms across his chest and set his mouth into a defiant line.

After a while, glowering, Anabb picked up the decanter and poured them a drink. Terr raised his tumbler in a brief salute. They sipped in silence. It was a long drink and they got halfway through before Anabb spoke, picking his words with care.

"I know how tired you must be of lurking in gutters, climbing roofs for murky reasons, risking all," he said heavily. "All I can say, my boy, it's part of the job. You may think this a poor reward for what you did on Trillian, but I'm glad to see you back safe."

"So you can send me out again?" Terr said ungraciously before he could stop his mouth from flapping. Anabb was hurt and Terr didn't really mean it, but he didn't feel like apologizing.

"I'm sorry you feel that way," Anabb growled and folded his hands over the desk. Terr watched him, studying the battered old face as he went on, speaking softly, almost as if he were talking to himself.

"We have achieved much through a long history of struggle and hardship. By we, I mean the Serrll Combine. As Sofam's sphere of influence expanded to include those of the Karkan Federation and the Sargon Directorate, the struggle has become economic rather than military. The other interstellar power blocks have learned well and are now using our economic tactics against us to achieve their ends, not always in everyone's interest. You can see what Sargon tried to do to Pizgor, but you cannot blame them for that.

"The Orieli visit is a dubious blessing. As always, there are those who would turn this into personal gain. This time, it's still Sargon, pursing the Palean merger, but it could have been anyone. Nevertheless, we now have a chance to rise above parochial self-interest. What we do here might affect the Serrll for centuries to come. I'm not talking about personal careers, but matters on which the fate of worlds may depend." He took a sip and went on, his words soft yet penetrating.

"I'm telling you the way I see it. At least you deserve that much," Anabb growled and the burn on his cheek turned red. "You have never taken a lot of interest in the internal workings of the Legislature or the Executive. At this stage of your career, that's healthy enough. However, much of what you do is governed and controlled by unseen individuals in some closeted department on Captal. By supporting the Unified Independent Front, the Revisionists risk losing the governing majority in the Executive Council. That risk has been heightened by the intervention of the Orieli Technic Union. Their demand for access to the Moon has polarized the General Assembly and raked up old memories."

"You really think the threat of Kran incursion will play a part in Sargon's merger tactics with the Paleans?" Terr asked and Anabb smiled grimly.

"Don't you? Of course, you do. It gives a good argument to the Paleans, if nothing else, despite what happened at Lemos and Khiman-ra, in which you played no small part. If those two merge into a single power block, they'll assume dominance of the Servatory Party and we might very well see a return to military adventurism. Sofam doesn't care if the Servatory Party is destroyed in the process. It cares if Sargon's actions disrupt the stability of the Serrll. Until now, Sargon had two singular problems with their merger plan."

"The formation of the Unified Independent Front?" Terr said.

Anabb grinned wickedly. "That's one of them. The other was trying to persuade the Pizgor worlds to join Sargon's sphere of influence. Without those three systems, the merger would only be partially successful. Those systems were vital in the numbers game for Executive representation. They had another opportunity with the Rolan group, but that didn't work out. Both problems might be intractable. The appearance of the Orieli, however, coupled with the Kran threat, has been a gift from the gods. Instead of merely pursuing political advantage, Sargon now has legitimate security concerns."

"Is that why they opposed Orieli's access to the Moon? To garner sympathy?" Terr ventured and Anabb raised an eyebrow.

"You got it. As have the Paleans at Sargon's urging. This time they failed, but they haven't given up. They will try to undermine the Orieli again, and will do everything possible to see the Moon base operation fail. It must not fail, Terr!" Anabb cleared his throat. "I would regard it as a personal favor if you agreed to head this mission," he said gruffly.

Anabb was playing on Terr's sympathies and loyalty, and Terr hated him for that. Despite his insubordination and brave words about independence, he was a serving officer in the Serrll Scout Fleet, albeit detached while working for the Diplomatic

Branch. Anabb knew that, of course. He could make his request an order and Terr could refuse, and find himself driving an M-3 again, if he were lucky. Anabb preferred to apply subtlety, though. Why threaten when he could persuade.

Dirty, rotten, low, scheming bastard. Terr sighed in disgust.

"I must be the greatest sucker made for world-saving missions," he muttered and shook his head.

"Look at it this way." Anabb grinned and refilled their glasses. "It will keep you out of Terchran's way."

"Big deal. If he wants me on a slab, he'll get around to it. But if I'm to make the supreme sacrifice, I'm not going without Dhar," Terr said belligerently and shook a threatening finger.

"I wouldn't think of it," Anabb said soothingly, magnanimous in victory. "To show you that I'm not completely heartless, there is something in this for you."

"If I get back."

Anabb ignored that one. "On your return, elevation to the rank of Master Scout, third grade, and any medals you may fancy."

"You know what you can do with the medals," Terr growled, but Anabb ignored him.

"In addition, four full months of uninterrupted R and R to any place you care to name."

"Uninterrupted?"

"Uninterrupted."

"I don't believe you," Terr told him flatly.

"What do you want me to do?" Anabb exploded. "Give you my heart as collateral?"

Terr chuckled. Then he thought of something else and felt kind of sick. This may be a professional success, but it would be a personal disaster.

"What's the matter?" Anabb demanded.

"Teena," Terr said miserably.

"Rest assured, she'll be protected."

Terr didn't hear him. "What do I tell her? That I'll be away for three months?" He looked at Anabb in desperate panic. "She'll kill me!"

"No, she won't. She's a professional. She'll understand," Anabb spoke soothingly, but he didn't know Teena as well as Terr did.

"Understand? She'll understand that I'm a lying louse and she'll have at me with a cleaver! We were planning to get away," Terr groaned and buried his head between his hands.

Rit!

* * *

"You lousy son of a worm!" she screamed and Terr re-coiled.

He spread his hands and took a step toward her. "Now, Teena, my love. I can—"

"Don't you 'my love' me, you miserable hypocrite. For three lousy weeks, I don't know where you are or what you're doing, or if you'll ever come back. Then you're off to Salina without a word, leaving me with nothing but your empty promises."

"But Anabb said—"

"Anabb be cursed!" she raged, her fists clenching and un-clenching. "Now you stand there and have the gall to tell me you're going out again. This time, for three months. Three months!" Her cheeks were flushed and fire flashed in her eyes, always a bad sign. "Last night, everything you told me, just empty words and I was a fool to believe you." She swung her hand and slapped him hard. The sound exploded in his mind, the first time either of them touched the other in anger, and the pain cut deep.

He let her scream and rage as tears streamed down her stricken face. It all tumbled out: frustration, agony, anxiety, mis-ery, loneliness, and fear. He stood there and took it. She poured and he drank. It was a bitter brew.

"Enough, Teena," he whispered after a time. "Enough! Enough!"

Her head jerked, mouth open, eyes watery and glistening. Memories still shouted at each other in the sudden silence. His heart thudded painfully and his hands were cold and clammy.

"No more, Teena." He shook his head. "Please, no more."

Anger slowly ebbed from her eyes, leaving behind only the hurt.

"Oh, Terr." She sobbed helplessly and ran her hands through her hair. She covered her face in despair and wept. Hesitating, he reached for her and drew her to him. She flinched and her fists pounded against his chest. Then she sagged weakly against him and cried. Uncertain what to do, he held her.

"Don't cry, Teena, please don't cry," he whispered brokenly and stroked her hair. He kept saying things as she shook and sobbed and it tore him to see her like this. He cursed Anabb and his damned mission. He cursed the Orieli and the Serrll and near anybody else he could think of. If only it would make her smile again.

Tears smearing her face, she looked at him. "Damn you!" She wrenched herself from him and ran.

He heard her weeping in the other room and he didn't know how to take away her pain. No, that wasn't quite true. There was a way he could be with her always. It would also mean giving up what he was. For a time, they would pretend it was enough, but eventually it would destroy what they had together. He also knew something would have to change and soon or he would lose her. What tore at him, he didn't have any answers. Heart heavy, he went after her. She had thrown herself across the bed, her hair spilled around her. Every now and then, she shook and sniffled.

"Teena?" he whispered and sat beside her. The bed creaked and sagged. He touched her shoulder and she flinched. In despair, he sought the right words to say. "I'm nothing without you and I want to be with you forever. I know you worry when I'm gone, but as long as I know you need me, I can make it through anything. But...I can't be there for you all the time." Somehow, that didn't seem to come out right. He figured it was better if he didn't say anything more.

After a while, her sobs subsided. He reached for her and pulled her against him. Slowly, her arms came around his neck and her head rested against his shoulder. In the quiet room, her heart beat softly against his. The only light came from the green safety strip running along the bottom of the walls. In the darkness outside, the stars stared at them unwinking. The wind must have died down for he could not hear anything.

Gently, he traced slow patterns down her back. His hands moved over her, caressing her, hoping his touch would say the words he couldn't say. After a while, her sniffling subsided.

They talked then, the kind of things only said in the small hours of the night. Their voices were hushed and unhurried. Darkness was a protective cloak. He guessed it was difficult for both of them. They were two independent and proud people, afraid to bare the soft vulnerable interior; afraid of betrayal and hurt, afraid to voice their mutual need and dependence to be complete. But the words needed to be said and he talked, letting her glimpse something of his world and something of his soul.

After a moment of silence, warm against each other, she stirred.

"Terr?" she murmured.

"Mmm?"

"You haven't told me when."

"When what?"

"When you have to leave."

He wanted to say it didn't matter, that it wasn't important. In the end, he didn't say anything.

"Terr?"

"Yeah?"

"When?"

"Early," he told her.

"Terr?"

"Yeah?"

"How early?"

"Damn early...they'll pick me up at daybreak." He held his breath, waiting for her reaction.

"Why does it have to be you?" she asked softly, her voice full of misery. He stared into the darkness.

"I don't know. It's my job, I guess. It's what I do, Teena."

"Why now?" she demanded, knowing how unreasonable that sounded. She brushed back a rebellious lock of hair with a sweep of her hand. "You've been on two missions now without a break. We need to have some time alone. Soon, or what we have will die."

"I know, pet," he murmured. "I know."

He could have said something trite and stupid then. Something like, 'You knew what I was before we paired', or crap like that. Fortunately, he had enough sense to keep his mouth shut.

"I know this Orieli business is important, but it's so unfair," she said unreasonably. He had to agree there. "Afterward, will you take me to Anar'on?" she whispered into his shoulder.

"If you want me to. Anywhere," he said gently. "We'll have time for everything, then. I promise."

She shivered and looked at him, her eyes bright. Gently, like the fleeting touch of morning dew, her head sank to his chest.

"I'm sorry I struck you," she mumbled against him.

His throat tightened and he swallowed hard. "It's all right, pet," he said softly, holding her. "It's all right."

* * *

It was a lousy way to start a mission.

Tal Field was cold, wet, and miserable. No one gave a damn if one M-3 sweeper took off or not. Terr didn't particularly care either. The sky was dark and hard. Low in the east a watery sun tentatively poked its swollen red eye from behind bunched clouds, blinked, and vanished. The rain came down shyly, light and invisible, a soft cloak of gray blurring outlines and detail. The apron glistened with puddles in which oily rainbows danced to the whisper of falling rain.

Lurching around the interior of a smelly PC, on seats whose unsympathetic springs added nothing to their comfort, Terr glared at Anabb.

"You look pissed off," Anabb said brightly. The PC jumped and his grin faded a little.

"By all the ten gods. Coming out in a lousy PC. We could have taken a cable-tube at least," Terr said peevishly.

"I thought you were the one who didn't want any speeches, fanfares, crowds or pushy axe grinders." Anabb chuckled and grinned broadly. Terr snarled at him and stared at the deck.

The PC slowed and squatted with a crunch. Terr muttered something evil about insensitive drivers and rubbed his stern. Anabb stood up and opened the back door. The rain came slanting in, cold and biting. He cursed and jumped out. Terr followed him to the door and looked out. About what he could expect to see on a wet and miserable morning. He wiped the rain off his face and stepped on the glistening tarmac.

Squat, gray and ugly, towering over them, the M-3 stood poised and ready for flight. Uncoupled from all externals, only the landing ramp bound it to the ground.

"Damn eager to go," Terr muttered sourly and ran under the curve of the ship.

Anabb didn't waste any time with the preliminaries. He kept the introductions brief and to the point. Terr mumbled something polite to the First Scout commanding the heap, not really seeing him. However, he did appreciate Anabb's effort in giving him a personal sendoff, and saw Anabb off with a flourish.

They took off without stirring any excitement, just as

Anabb promised. On his way to quarters, Terr patted the bottle of prana water he had smuggled aboard. It was going to be a long flight to Salina and the Serrll Moon Base, and he planned to make the most of it.

During the late watch, Terr left the command deck and went to his cabin. Waiting for Dhar, he uncorked the bottle and filled two glasses with a finger of thick amber liquid that smelled of scorched desert sands and the spicy tang of peelath leaves.

The hatch slid away and Dhar stood there, tall and thin, his orange eyes bright.

"Come on in, don't just hang there." Terr waved him in and pointed at a formchair.

"On our way at last," Dhar said and nodded his thanks as Terr handed him the tumbler.

"Real stuff this time, not some of your cheap Captal imitation."

Dhar placed the tumbler on the palm of his left hand, turned it slowly with his right, then cupped the glass between both hands. Slowly, he brought it to his nose and inhaled the delicate bouquet of the liqueur. He gave a small nod, took a sip, and closed his eyes in appreciation. Terr watched his contemplation in silence, then performed the ritual himself.

Prana water was a strange mixture of desert spices and herbs. Sweet and dry, light and oily. It can only be obtained on Anar'on and nowhere else. There were substitutes, but even the most perfect synthetic imitation was only that, an imitation.

They sipped in silence, enjoying quiet contentment and an understanding that had no need of words. Terr sensed a tension in Dhar, a nagging worry.

"Nightwings," he said softly, looking deep into Dhar's serious eyes. "You are troubled. Let there be peace in your soul tonight, my brother."

Dhar expressed surprise at the depth of Terr's perception. Was his disquiet so transparent?

"I *am* troubled—"

"Then share your thoughts with me."

Dhar's mouth sagged. "This is something I must face alone, Sankri."

Terr frowned. He had sensed the turmoil in his Anar'on brother since their flight to Salina. If anything, it had intensified. He wanted to lighten Dhar's load, but some things one did have to face alone.

"Tah, the gods will tell," he murmured and raised his tumbler in a quiet salute.

They talked and drank long into the watch. When Dhar left, Terr stared moodily at the Wall. It didn't take long before he started feeling sorry for himself. Finally, he held up the bottle of prana water and took a long pull.

"What the hell," he said and waved the bottle around. "They can all go and screw themselves." He took another hefty swallow.

Well, one thing led to another. By the time the bottle got half-empty or half-full, depending on how one looked at these things, he was pretty well tanked up. He felt sad and lonely and he wanted Teena. He reached out with his right hand, the one holding the bottle, and her apparition appeared for him.

He broke into a huge smile and offered her a drink. She frowned and shook her head. He could see she didn't approve. He tried to pull himself together, but it was no use. He got all sentimental and mushy then. He told her how sorry he was to have left her alone again. She whispered that she understood and he believed her.

His head in her lap, she smiled down at him, stroking his forehead, murmuring it was all right. Terr remembered crying as he fell asleep.

Rit!

Some tough guy he turned out to be…

Chapter Seven

0835 Local. Eielson AFB, Alaska

Side by side the two F-16s lit off their afterburners and roared down the active runway. After an impossibly short runup, they rotated and waited for the gear to come up before pulling back sharply into a sixty degree climb. The air boomed after them as they disappeared into the deep blue of the winter sky.

Snowdrifts glittered in pale sunlight. Tendrils of white fog hugged the ground. Barely clearing the horizon, the sun gave off feeble warmth. This far north it would not get much higher. Nevertheless, after six days of dark skies and continuous snowfalls the sun a welcomed sight.

A KC-135B tanker spooled up its engines and moved ponderously down the approach ramp into takeoff position. Two red fire trucks clanked past the ready alert revetments. A giant Galaxy transport waited patiently beside an open hangar as cargo pellets were loaded into its cavernous belly. Trailing clouds of white vapor, jeeps and cars made their way along the swept taxiways.

The 354th Fighter Wing was again ready for business.

Rick 'Ticky' Broadman turned away from the window. This waiting, it always gave him the trots. He grunted under the awkward weight of his Nomex flight suit. His friend lay sprawled on a couch, feet stretched casually before a roaring fan heater, face buried in a book. Rick slowly shook his head.

"The hero get laid yet?"

"Twice," Captain Brad Evans deadpanned.

"Did you mark the spots for me?"

117

"Nope."

Rick looked disgusted. "Didn't I ask you to mark the spots?"

Evans kept reading.

"I heard you made the candidate's list for major," Rick said casually, picking up a battered copy of *Playboy* off the coffee table. He needed intellectual stimulation.

"Yep. Heard the same thing," Evans said without looking up from his murder thriller.

"Provided you don't screw the pooch before then." Rick grinned wickedly, leafing through the magazine admiring the displayed scenery.

"No way. The Air Force was simply a little slow in recognizing real talent."

"As was that Jap F-15 driver," Rick remarked fondly at the memory and Evans looked up grinning.

"The guy just shouldn't have lit off that Sidewinder. What could I do? But they won't come at us dumb next time. Besides, the Spratlys aren't an issue anymore."

"Yeah, but Japan hasn't withdrawn and I cannot see the Eighteenth being scaled back anytime soon," Rick said, referring to a contingent of F-15s added to the existing squadron of F-16s. Evans put down his novel and his eyes lit with an old fighter jock's killer gleam.

"If it comes to a shootout, I'll be just as happy kicking Jap butt as Chinese butt."

Rick had to agree, but it wasn't likely to happen—he hoped.

"Alert force! Active air scramble, active air scramble! Man your aircraft!"

Evans let out a yell of triumph when the klaxon blared.

"Shit hot!" they both said in unison and exchanged a high-five.

"Told you something would happen today," Evans said, punching his wingman on the shoulder.

118

With Shadow and Thunder

"Right with you, boss." Ticky grinned and threw the *Playboy* in the general direction of the magazine rack.

They were the only alert crew in the room and the sound of their running boots loud hitting the linoleum floor. The door slammed shut behind them and they were off at a run up the slanting concrete corridor.

A blast of refrigerated air hit Evans as he raced through the open door, making his ears and nose tingle. Snow glinted and sparkled from piled drifts around the base buildings. Evans looked up as he burst into watery sunshine and squinted.

Fleecy clouds nudged each other. The sharp air cut through his nose and throat, and smelled of snow. It was still, without a whisper of wind. The shadows were long and black where the gray ice waited for the touch of sun. Evans and Ticky scrambled into a waiting jeep. With a jerk, trailing white exhaust, they raced across the flight line toward the fighters already pre-prepped in the alert hangar.

The jeep squealed to a stop. Evans jumped out and waved at his crew chief fiddling around the single-seater variant of the F-15J Eagle the Japs flew. An old bird now, but still one of the most formidable all-weather capable fighters in the world. When he made major, he would be driving F-35s, real fighters, and that was all right with him.

"See you upstairs," he yelled at Ticky and scrambled up the access ladder of the large plane.

He put on his helmet as his ground chief helped strap him in. He quickly went through the pre-flight check. He plugged in his umbilical with a satisfying snick from the jack-plug, which connected him to the onboard computer and weapons system. Hands clipped on his oxygen supply, seat belt, G-suit, and the emergency oxygen hose. The anti-G device flexed the suit around his abdomen and legs, then relaxed.

After a last look around, Evans flipped the main power switch and watched the simulated gauges flicker into life on the LED screen. He set the fuel starter and cracked the throttle a

119

bit. There was a rapid whining as the sleek turbines built up. The Pratt and Whitney F119 engines bellowed into life and the fighter trembled beneath him. With one eye on the jet-pipe temperature, he opened the throttles until the RPM readout showed sixty percent, then cut back to idle. The canopy closed over him and he locked it manually. After a glance at his wingman, he released the brakes.

He checked the GPS setting and stirred the control stick. After glancing at the radio switches, he clicked on his microphone.

"Zulu Sierra flight, check."

"Copy," Ticky replied.

"Rammer ground, Zulu Sierra flight ready to taxi."

"Zulu Sierra flight, Rammer ground, cleared to taxi main runway, climb unrestricted."

As the two fighters skipped and began rolling, the chief on the apron snapped to and gave him a regulation salute. Evans returned it with a flourish and opened the throttles as instructions from the tower chirped in his helmet. When the aircraft lined up, he pushed the throttles against the stops to full military power and engaged the afterburners. With a surge that pressed him into the hard seat, the Eagle roared down the runway.

The markers flashed by and he felt the control surfaces beginning to bite. He eased back the stick. The Eagle stopped shuddering from the uneven runway surface and lifted, followed by a jolt as the wheels sagged in their wells. Evans retracted the gear, pulled back hard, and went into a sixty-degree climb.

Breaking through four thousand feet, he pulled the throttles out of afterburner and glanced back and left. The other Eagle right where it should be, below and behind him, covering his six. He quickly went through the after-takeoff checklist and scanned the instruments: RPM, temperature, fuel flow, hydraulics—no warning lights.

"Rammer ground, Zulu Sierra flight, breaking through five thousand."

"Zulu Sierra flight, radar contact. Turn right one-one seven for bogey. Range two-six-two miles. No IFF indicated. Climb and maintain flight level two-eight-zero."

"Copy that, Rammer," Evans replied and glanced at his wingman. "Two, got that?"

"Roger, lead."

Evans smiled into his mask and listened to the ECM, the Electronic Counter-Measures module. The module could detect transmissions from enemy radars while the fighter was still too far away to generate a usable return signature, effectively remaining invisible. Nothing. With the Eagle's radar absorption skin, it meant quite a distance. He took a long look at the deep blue of the sky and settled back to enjoy the flight. He only had a couple of chapters remaining in his book and hoped this wouldn't take long. Probably some commercial flight took a wrong turn and NORAD felt twitchy.

Although outwardly unconcerned about his coming promotion, Evans was very pleased with himself. Making major at twenty-six right in the groove of his projected career plan. Killing that Jap F-15 meant he would also have his choice of assignments. He would lose Rick, but those were the breaks.

On their wings, each Eagle mounted two advanced AIM-120 AMRAAM radar missiles and two AIM-9P heat-seeking Sidewinders. For close-in business the fighters mounted an internal rotary 20-millimeter cannon, at the moment switched off.

They reached twenty-eight thousand feet in a loose duce formation without any extraneous chatter on the radio. The flight perfectly smooth, Evans shifted his butt into a more comfortable position. Below him, the country lay spread in a sheet of white.

He tracked the green blip on his HSD, the Horizontal Situation Display, coming from the powerful APG-73/B radar.

"Two, got the return?" he announced on his digitally encrypted SSB, single sideband.

"Roger, lead. I got target acquisition. Contact bearing one-one-two. Range, six-eight miles."

The base prankster, Rick pulled some godawfull gags on the crews, not all of them appreciated. One of those practical gags on a light colonel back in Texas, who couldn't crap without referring to a procedures manual, landed Rick his present assignment. But in the air, Rick was all business. Being Evans' wingman during the recent furball with the Japanese Self Defense Force's fighters had not done Rick any harm either.

"Rammer ground, Zulu Sierra has radar contact on indicated bearings."

"Copy that. Make ID pass and verify."

"Zulu Sierra copies."

He activated the wide-field forward-looking infrared module and the television camera system in the nose of the fighter and got a clear return. It was two minutes to intercept. The computer-optimized picture showed a stationary indistinct sphere. Stationary? It could not be an aircraft then. A balloon? He hoped this wasn't going to turn into a wild goose chase.

The heads-up display target pipper started shifting in response to the search radar return and he switched mode to tactical. His electronic surveillance module threat receivers were silent, showing no IFF. The object, whatever it was, wasn't radiating any electronic transmissions.

It sure as hell wasn't behaving like no stray commercial liner, a MiG fighter or Bear reconnaissance bomber, or anything else, for that matter. However, he did not really expect to find a MiG or a Bear over Alaska.

Squinting, Evans could barely make out a speck of black against the blue as the F-15J closed at more than four hundred and sixty knots indicated. At six miles, he pulled back the throttles and bled off speed in a gentle climb, wanting to maintain an energy advantage over the target. As a situation, this did not look like a confrontation scenario. Still, no use taking chances. He flipped on the master arming switches. As the TCS panned the sky, the crosshairs on his HUD moved to cover the target. The AIM-120 growled eagerly in his earphones as it acquired. At three miles, he chopped power and his jaw sagged.

"Ticky, you getting this?" he said, not believing his eyes.

"Right with you, buddy. If this is some gag pulled by the Dreamland test center, I'll eat the thing."

"Shee-it!" Evans said as the two F-15s reefed around the glowing object. "Cameras rolling," he piped into his mike.

It was impossible not to recognize the object. A faint orange shimmer surrounded the craft in an envelope of some two hundred feet. The ship itself approximately sixty feet long, a smooth, flattened oval pebble with downward curving trailing edges, the surface light blue with blue-black and red markings. There were no visible exterior hardpoints or ports to break up the matte sheen of its surface.

It just hung there, waiting. Evans licked his lips and craned his neck as he maintained a steep left bank to keep the object in sight.

"Rammer, Zulu Sierra. Do you copy?" he grunted into his mask.

"Go ahead, Zulu Sierra."

"Unless someone is testing a new stealth fighter configuration I don't know about, bogey has been identified as an extraterrestrial vehicle, Rammer. Advise, over."

An uncomfortable silence lasted for a few seconds.

"Ah, repeat your last transmission, Zulu Sierra," came the choked voice from the controller.

"Repeat, Rammer. We have a visual on an object displaying no ballistic motion."

This time the silence stretched on for quite a while. Evans could only imagine the hornet's nest his message must have stirred. Then his mike crackled.

"Zulu Sierra flight, Rammer ground. Do you confirm sighting a UFO?"

Evans was caught in a bind. He knew of one F-22 driver who claimed he encountered a UFO during a high-altitude test flight. The guy had his cameras going, but the Air Force intelligence pukes crucified the poor bastard anyway. For all Evans knew, the shitter flew kites in Death Valley now.

The difference this time, he had Rick with him. He hardly hesitated.

"Affirmative, Rammer."

"Wait one, Zulu," a brisk new voice commanded. Then, "Establish contact if possible."

"Acknowledged." Evans shifted frequencies to Guard. "Unidentified aircraft, this is a United States Air Force fighter Zulu Sierra. Do you copy?"

The craft began to move.

* * *

1318 Local. Pentagon Command Center

"My God, Harry." Cannon stormed into the Tank waving the stump of a badly mauled cigar. The immaculately dressed marine guard closed the door after him. "Can't a guy have some peace around here, huh?" He stuck the cigar under Harry's nose. "I have a coffee and buns session with Moravik," he rasped, twisted his wrist and glanced at his watch. "In five minutes."

"I guess you'll be late, then." Harry Tarleton, a four-star admiral, smiled thinly.

"The Command Center is a shambles. Nobody wants to talk to me," Cannon said in outrage. He snorted and planted his hands on the large table occupying most of the room. "Somebody better the hell start telling me what's going on around here or I'll be kicking ass," Cannon growled, wearing a dark scowl.

Harry was used to Cannon's bantering and high-pressure tactics, and made appropriate allowances. As Chairman of the Joint Chiefs, Cannon's antics were famous and tolerated as a mild eccentricity. Cannon obviously did not give a short damn what people thought.

"Take it easy, Ray," Harry said bleakly. "That's why I called you here."

Cannon had a rare quality where his mere presence commanded attention. His six-foot-two stocky muscular frame, honed with regular exercise, wearing a stiff military bearing, demanded instant submission. The blond hair now faded somewhat, bristling on his head in traditional marine flat style. There was nothing faded about his close-set piercing brown eyes that darted like mapping radar. His large nose had been the butt of crude jokes for decades. A fleshy bulbous thing with veined nostrils, it looked like flared jet tailpipes.

The mouth demanded attention, wide with thin, pale lips. A perpetual cigar stub stood parked in one of the corners. His teeth were slightly uneven and stained after a lifetime of smoking. Despite rugged health, Cannon showed his age and no amount of exercise was going to remove the crow's feet around the eyes and mouth.

Cannon saw action in Desert Storm, the so-called hundred-hour war, and planned the blockading of Panama to counter Al Qaida attacks. His current problem was ensuring the United States had enough assets in place should China start mixing it up with Japan over the oil-rich Spratlys and making inroads into the South China Sea. God, what a political mess, that! Still, he relished the prospect of action, even if he would not be directly involved. It took him a while to convert his first lieutenant's bars to four stars. The sons of bitches who stood in his way were eliminated or now counted butterflies in the Aleutians. A hardnosed career professional, he had little time for deadheads, as many Pentagon staffers found to their permanent dismay.

As far as Cannon was concerned, wars were fought on many fronts, and not all of them faced a shooting enemy.

"Can't you give me a hint, damn it?" Cannon growled, chewing the end of his cigar. "Don't tell me you landed yourself a war!"

Harry grinned. "Nothing so simple."

The Tank was a medium-sized conference room situated on the second floor of the Pentagon building, close to the River Entrance. Here, Chiefs of Staff met twice a week to mull over important or urgent business. Being Vice Chairman of the Joint Chiefs, Harry chaired most of those meetings while also managing three-star operational deputies. A powerful post with wide-ranging powers far beyond those laid down in the strict interpretation of the regulations.

A recently upgraded active matrix organic electronic map, currently focused on Alaska, occupied the whole far wall. A repeater off the main screen in the Command Center down in the sub-basement. Colored symbols studded the map, denoting the disposition of all military and civilian assets in the area, friendly or otherwise. Cannon sank deep into one of the twelve contoured seats without taking his eyes off the map.

"Who else is coming?"

"Only the J-3 and the J-5," Harry said, referring to the chiefs of the Operations Directorate and the Strategic Plans and Policy Directorate. Cannon grunted.

"We'll start without 'em."

"They will bitch."

"Let them bitch. We'll brief them later. Or you can. Okay, what have you got?"

"See that red blip in grid twenty-four?"

"Yeah. Looks like it's stationary, judging by the two recon fighters milling around it," Cannon said. It took a few seconds for the impact of his words to get through to him. He opened his mouth, but Harry was already talking.

"That thing has been sitting out there since zero-eight-sixteen local. Just popped on the screen. When Space Command saw it, they alerted NORAD, who went ape and started leaning on buttons." Harry sighed heavily, referring to the North American Aerospace Defense Command. "They went through the usual checks. It could have been a satellite off course or something, but analysis suggested orbital insertion."

"Orbital insertion?" Cannon frowned.

"That's right. And it's not some booster shell suddenly deciding to come down either," Harry added.

"Go on. I just know I'm gonna love this."

"I doubt it. When the object remained unidentified, they sent out the alert Eagles from Eielson to take a closer look," Harry paused, uncertain how to go on.

"And?" Cannon grated impatiently.

"And they came into contact with a flying saucer, the genuine article," Harry said.

"The hell you say!" Cannon stared at him.

"We got a downlink from their TCS. It's the real thing."

"What's it doing now?"

Harry touched the controls and the map changed, showing the red blip inching its way southeast. He touched another control and a faint blue line indicated forward movement prediction.

Cannon clamped his teeth around the savaged end of his cigar as he regarded the plot.

"Shit!" he said at length.

That seemed to just about sum up the situation, Harry agreed.

* * *

The staff car leaned slightly as it took the Maine Avenue exit and headed along the waterfront. Cannon hardly glanced at the government buildings along Constitution Avenue. He preferred to drive from the Pentagon rather than clatter around in a helo. It gave him time to think things through. This latest development had certainly given him a lot to think about. He worried the stump of his cigar. Damned doctors, he fumed. They urged him to stop smoking, at least cut down, but he never felt completely dressed without a cigar. It wasn't lit anyway, damn them.

Beside him, Samuel T. Moravik, Secretary of Defense, wearing rimless glasses, stared vacantly at nothing in particular. Samuel hadn't said much as they drove down from the Pentagon. He'd been deep in thought ever since Cannon stemmed his torrent of vitriol for being late. A short, bookish man, Samuel was cold and calculating. A consummate Hill manipulator and a real son of a bitch to work for. But he was a professional, something that in his view sadly lacked in the previous Administration. An axe-wielding little turd when he took office, the wood he chopped was mostly dead or already rotten from within. He cut across a lot of the inter-service bullshit, streamlining and sharing development and procurement appropriations, which past Administrations only talked about doing. That episode wiped off a lot of other personal sins—and wasted dollars—as far as Cannon was concerned.

It didn't mean he liked the snotty bastard and wondered when some general or admiral somewhere would arrange a terminal mishap for Samuel.

A guard waved them through the western gate of the White House grounds. A marine guard saluted as they stepped out of the limo. Secret Service agents checked them in and accompanied them to the west wing entrance. Cannon scowled at them to Samuel's secret amusement.

All the National Security Council members were waiting for them in the Situation Room, a floor beneath the Oval Office. Subdued wood paneling lined the walls hiding the stressed concrete behind it. Screens and arrays of communications equipment took up the back wall. A long oak table stood in the center of the room on which pots of coffee, cream and sugar bowls stood. A lazy tendril of steam rose from one pot and Cannon breathed deeply of the refined brew.

Faces turned as they entered, the sound of conversation still lingering in the air. The president's chief of staff flickered her sharp eyes at Cannon. At the sight of her, Cannon almost winced. The Hill Bitch didn't waste time on him as she sat there, hands clasped firmly in her lap. It was chemistry. The two just plain detested one another. Cannon growled in resignation and went to his seat. Opposite him, the shriveled Vice President couldn't possibly have weighed his one hundred and forty-five pounds soaking wet. His health had been failing and it was unlikely he would last the term of this Administration, which was a pity, for Cannon rather liked the man.

He nodded briefly to the Secretary of State Swen and Dr. Doryel, who looked more like a prizefighter than a smooth, accomplished politician. Cannon held a grudging, but hostile respect for the National Security Advisor. At forty-two, Doryel was relatively young to hold the post. He knew almost as much about the tactical and strategic disposition of most of the world's armed forces as Cannon himself; no mean feat.

"Glad to see you, Sam...General," President Kurtland Hennery said briskly, his large pale-green eyes missing nothing. He waited until Cannon settled his bulk comfortably, then extended his hand down the table.

"Coffee?"

Cannon nodded. "Thank you, sir," he said and poured himself a cup. He took sugar, no cream.

"Very well, then." Hennery looked around the assembled faces before nodding at Moravik. "As you can see, Sam, we're all here, just as you requested. What have you got for me that's so burning urgent?"

Cannon smiled. The Old Man never wasted time. He would have made a first-grade field commander. Then again, in a way, he was, wasn't he? Cannon had never warmed to politicians. He saw enough of them come and go. There was something perverse about their life's priorities. However, Hennery's quiet and intense persistence at getting what he wanted won Cannon's unreserved admiration. It did not have the dash of a military assault, but it got results just the same. With barely over a year to go before the elections, he suspected that Hennery would be enjoying a shoo-in second term as a Republican president. No one in the Democrat opposition could touch him that he could see. They were still in the wilderness, seemingly losing their way after eight years with a president who smoked but never inhaled. With the exception of Harford, the subsequent two Administrations were all polish with little substance.

Of average height, Hennery's thin frame gave an impression of tallness. His face narrow, a long nose gave him an air of severe disapproval. Fighting Congress ass-lickers all the time and he would wear a severe expression too, Cannon mused.

His second two-year term as CJC would end in November and he planned to make the most of it. There were still things to be done. Both the Democrat and the Republican camps had put out feelers for him to enter Congress. The thought of mixing it with those screwballs in endless rounds of inane meetings and committee squabbles sent chills down his spine. He always admired Colin Powel, both as commander and a man, but a foolish one when he allowed himself to be drawn into the mire of power politics. The way Cannon looked at it, a soldier's destiny was to face his enemy in battle. Political intrigue had never been required reading at West Point, not officially anyway.

Moravik dragged down his glasses and rubbed the bridge of his nose. "I think I'll let Cannon tell it," he said, secretly amused.

"And what big secret is the military hiding now, General, that you couldn't tell us over the videophone or in the PDB?" The Secretary of State chuckled at some private joke. The PDB Swen referred to was the President's Daily Brief, containing the latest analysis of world issues the president should know about. Compiled by the CIA, it did not always contain information in the best interest of the United States. Swen saw to it that these days it did.

"If it's a secret now, sir, it won't be for long." Cannon's nostrils flared as he stared disapprovingly at the other man.

Swen wore a gaunt, dour, olive complexion face. Moist gray eyes stared vacantly beneath thin black eyebrows. He looked more like a Mafia Don than a politician. On the Hill, they called him the Undertaker. A mean bastard and someone to be always taken seriously. Swen played the bad guy to Hennery's good guy. So far the policy was working. Cannon suspected that Swen secretly enjoyed his hitman role.

"You have interrupted my meeting with the UK's Ambassador, General," Hennery admonished gently. "I've shot my morning's schedule to fit you in. Please come to the point."

"Sorry about that, sir." Cannon wasn't sorry at all, time for the politicians to do some real work. "Mr. President, I want your permission to bring Zone Interior to Defcon-3."

"What is this?" Swen frowned, glancing briefly at Moravik. "What are you trying to pull, Cannon?"

Cannon almost felt sorry for him, almost. "Mr. Secretary, at approximately fifteen-thirty hours today, EST, New York will have an extraterrestrial craft paying us a visit."

"Oh, Christ," somebody muttered. Hennery thought it was Doryel.

His shoulders sagged. In the current climate of European instability and realignment, with China and Japan ready to slug it out over the damned Spratlys, and the Midwest now more or less a desert, he did not need this. He closed his eyes and wished he were back in Texas, a simple state governor.

"You have a positive visual, General?" Dr. Doryel queried in a deep baritone voice, soft and cultured. Everything money and a Harvard degree implied.

A tall, elegant man, Doryel made his reputation at

Georgetown University's Center for Strategic and International Studies. Cannon did not consider him a friend. Nothing he could put his finger on, but Doryel's pinched, ferrety black eyes, set close together beneath pencil eyebrows, did not inspire trust. Maybe it was the suave cultured million-dollar creamy smile and the bright even teeth. Cannon heard that Doryel polished them every night before going to bed. Whether true or not, they certainly looked polished.

Cannon nodded, trying to keep his dislike from showing. Strictly speaking, Doryel should not even be at the NSC meeting.

"Yes, sir. There is no doubt about it. It or its destination. It started moving toward New York as soon as the alert fighters made their pass."

"So, it's finally happened," Hennery said thoughtfully. "What do we know about this thing, General?"

"The object is elliptical, sir, approximately sixty feet at its longest axis. The fighters reported the craft hovering, apparently waiting for them."

"They obviously wanted to give us enough time to get ready," Hennery commented dryly and turned to Moravik. "Sam, did we get anything on this from SIGMA or PLATO? If our friends have decided to make it official, they should have warned us."

Moravik shook his head. "Not a peep, Kurt."

"Maybe they want to see us run around in circles," Hennery mused.

"Mr. President," Cannon said urgently. "This craft is nothing like what we've seen before."

Hennery digested this piece of information. "A new contact?" he demanded and Cannon nodded. "Hell! Why not? Okay, let's pick at it. You mentioned our fighters found it hovering, General. Are we talking antigravity here, Dr. Doryel?"

"It is highly probable, Mr. President. Results from the MAJI Twelve group tend to concur. As you know, we have never been able to get the ones at Wright Field to fly. Not for long, anyway," he added wryly.

Hennery wondered whether that was actually true. He pursed his lips, uncomfortable about the whole thing. Ever since Truman, US policy toward UFO incidents had been one of denial and discreditation; publicly at least. He hated to think what exactly the MJ-12 group were doing with ships that have crashed or been shot down, or recovered alien bodies. Too late to worry about it now.

"Go on, Doctor," he prompted.

"Did the fighters report seeing any effects of an electro-magnetic field, General?"

"They saw an orange shimmer extending some two hundred feet from the craft. No external hardpoints, intakes or control surfaces. NORAD's analysis of its insertion track suggests it came from the Moon."

"The Moon?" Hennery looked startled.

Doryel smiled and nodded. "If it's our old friends, Mr. President, then it's only an inter-system scouting craft. Remember those pictures we got from that SIR-E survey bird NASA sent up?"

"That should never have been a live feed!" Moravik snapped. "A stupid oversight by JPL."

Hennery waved him into silence. "It was bound to come out sooner or later, Sam. Dr. Doryel, are you saying we have blown the Serrll Moon Base's cover and they have decided to say hello?"

"Something like that, sir."

"And if it's a new contact?"

Doryel shrugged. "Then it's new for everybody."

Hennery sighed. "You said, General, the thing is heading for New York?"

"That's right, Mr. President."

"The UN!" Swen stared at Hennery, his eyes bright with excitement. "Do you know what this means?"

133

"It means," Hennery replied coldly, "that our alien friends know a hell of a lot more about us than we do about them. Whoever they are." He frowned and looked at his chief of staff. "Kathy, I want you to cancel all my appointments for the day. Make my apologies to the UK Ambassador. Get the other cabinet members here in…forty minutes. I also want the FBI and the CIA directors. Arrange a hotline with Moscow and Beijing."

"Yes, Mr. President," her quiet, measured voice added a touch of calm to a rapidly overheating atmosphere.

Hennery nodded and leaned back in his chair. He looked at the faces around the table trying to gauge the impact Cannon's words had on his people. The VP was out of it, even if his health had not been failing. Hennery carried the man as payoff for political favors, but that was okay. Some debts must be paid. Swen looked determined and ready, as always—a coldhearted sonofabitch, but indispensable. No love lost there, only wary mutual respect that worked, which was enough. Moravik looked detached, belaying his close scrutiny of the situation. Hennery almost smiled.

He and Moravik went back a long time. He needed a real friend or two around when things got sticky. At any time, for that matter. Hennery suspected he would need that support before this episode finished. As for Doryel, he wasn't certain. Behind the polished Ivy League veneer lay a brittleness as though the clothes held up the man. Maybe he was wrong. This development may prove things one way or another. Then there was Kathy. She would be with him through thick or thin. Without her campaigning and organizational skills, he doubted he would have won the last elections. The relationship worked because neither tried to make it anything more than professional, despite the obvious attraction between the two.

"Before I see the others, I want your individual thoughts," Hennery demanded. "This puts a whole new slant on all our previous contacts. Swen?"

The SecState's gaunt face looked even longer as he weighed

up the electoral options.

"Bound to be social, religious, and cultural disorientation, Mr. President. Remember what happened five years ago when we dug up that Serrll saucer at Comalcalco? We almost went to war with China over that one. Fortunately for us, the work we did from the recent NASA probe has already laid some of the groundwork for public acceptance of an alien presence, however inadvertently. And as you know, we've spent the last twenty years conditioning the public for this moment. Still, it's hard to say what the international implications will be. We could speculate all day, but until we hear what the aliens have to say—"

"I agree. Sam?"

"Impossible to tell, Kurt," Moravik said. "Should they turn out to be hostile, my guess is that we'll be in trouble. You can be certain about one thing, though. You're talking about economic and financial impact, just for starters. Whether we like it or not, you'll be forced to reconsider the American position vis a vis the UN. Irrespective of what our alien visitors might know about Earth's governments, they have chosen to deal with the UN. That means dealing with Nikita Bandrik. And you know what *his* views are."

"Good point," Hennery nodded and glanced pointedly at Swen. He did not need to rub it in. It was something that Sec-State should have brought up. "I don't want to walk out of this with a policy, people. I just want hard ideas on the table when the others get here. Dr. Doryel?"

"Do we need General Cannon anymore?"

Hennery's pale-green eyes studied the general for a moment. The military would do what was necessary, effectively and without fuss. "Thank you, General," he said in dismissal. "I cannot say that you've made my day."

"What about Defcon-3, sir?" Cannon said.

"General, our visitors have not demonstrated any hostile intent," Hennery said coldly.

135

"But *we* have, sir, historically at least. It's only a precautionary measure and doesn't affect our international assets."

Hennery looked dubious. "Sam?"

The Secretary of Defense frowned and pulled at his chin. "Some sort of posture would be prudent, Kurt. We don't know what we're dealing with here. However, rather than a general internal alert, always expensive and likely to be misinterpreted, it would be more effective to bring some of our particle array platforms online. If it comes to an exchange, Brilliant Mirror might prove more effective against our visitor than an indiscriminate use of conventional munitions. There is always civilian collateral damage to consider. When you talk to the Russian president, you could advise him of our intentions. In case he gets anxious. Same with the Chinese."

"Good point. I want your brief on this after the meeting with the others. Work it out with Dr. Doryel," Hennery added, then turned to the Chairman of the Joint Chiefs. "Good enough for you, General?"

"It's an acceptable option, Mr. President," Cannon acknowledged grudgingly. "However—"

"General, has NORAD detected any other orbiting objects?"

"Well, no, sir."

"Until proven otherwise, I will assume our visitor's intentions are not belligerent. On the other hand, we don't want to be caught with our pants down. You're authorized to set up contingency options ready to be placed into effect on immediate notice. You can begin active tracking with our orbital assets. However, you're not authorized to go to Defcon-3. Keep this tight, General."

"Mr. President, are you intending to allow the alien to land on the UN building?" Cannon demanded, clearly dubious at the wisdom of the decision.

"I am."

There was a nervous moment of silence before Moravik

gave a polite cough.

"Kurt, our policy regarding extraterrestrials has been—"

"I know what our policy has been, Sam," Hennery cut him off. "What do you suggest? Shoot the thing down? Deny everything? Personally, I think the whole MAJI concept has been pushing us into an untenable and sometimes ridiculous position of denial. The aliens, whoever they are, have made an official contact. We cannot pretend anymore."

"All I'm saying, Kurt, this could have undesirable political repercussions."

"Sometimes you have to tell the truth Sam, and take your lumps," Hennery said firmly.

* * *

1532 Local. New York

Jake Morton sniffed the smog-tinged air, uncontaminated by any whiff of spring, and blew his nose. A prolonged blast that rivaled the sounds of traffic and earned him a dirty look from a dried-up spinster who looked like she wasn't getting any. He leered at her and walked on. Winter determined for a long stay, snow stood piled up in corners. The sun shone on the city with pale enthusiasm. He decided that New York in February was the pits.

As usual, traffic flowed heavily along First Avenue. Huddled figures in bulky overcoats hurried along the sidewalks, not glancing at anyone; absorbed with their own schemes or problems. There were sounds of car horns, the squeal of tires, cop's whistle, and the subdued background of pedestrian feet. Tendrils of fog twisted lazily over the East River.

Jake had an excellent view of the UN building. Resisting a strong temptation to walk off in search of a sensation, he picked a little cafe-cum-bar across the street, settled comfortably in his chair and caused dry martinis to disappear. This morning, he woke up cold, clearheaded and eager for action. His blood sang and he felt the gods were at last smiling down at him. Usually the thrill of waking left him bleary, stiff, sniffling and feeling the burden of the world on his shoulders, not to mention a hangover.

Being a freelance newshound for the *New York Times* was certainly not the most heavenly job on earth, but it did have its compensations. One of them left him before dawn, minus her stockings. He thought more than once about opening a second-hand store for used stockings. He had enough of them laying around in his apartment. Instead, he took another sip.

Jake twisted his right wrist and glanced at his ten-dollar platinum Oyster, still looking for the guy who sold it to him. It's been running for three months and he figured he still did okay from the investment. After sitting anywhere for an hour, he would have walked off in disgust. But that something which made scoops kept him practicing magic on martinis.

Jets howled overhead. Shadows slithered quickly across buildings and boulevards. People stopped and gaped at the awesome shapes of the three F-22 Raptor fighters brushing the tops of the skyscrapers. In wonder, the city watched the jets as they maneuvered above. No one minded the traffic jam, the snarl and the blaring of horns, the irate screaming of frustrated drivers, or the pedestrians standing on the wrong side of the flashing don't walk sign.

Jake had seen everything good and bad in man and the world he lived in. He made his buck writing about it. With a martini halfway to his mouth, his jaw sagged. What looked like a flying saucer, clad in an almost invisible orange halo, glided slowly toward the UN building. It hovered briefly, then sank to the roof. The F-22 fighters banked sharply and disappeared. Two NYPD helicopters circled overhead.

He wasn't even aware of the numerous fender benders and the blare of horns along the street as he ran out of the bar.

* * *

138

Nikita Bandrik, Secretary-General of the UN, and on the wrong side of the generation gap, gently placed his gold stylus on the desk and waited for the inevitable knock. He had heard the jets and seen the spaceship. He watched it now on his closed-circuit monitor. The thing just sat there, hovering some thirty centimeters above the roof. Security guards stood positioned around the object. Others covered the roof perimeter. The commander of that ship had shown a startling insight into human psychology by landing on the roof.

He would not care to step into a potentially unruly crowd himself, he thought at length. Which didn't say much for the human race, he mused.

Still in his early teens when the Next Generation Star Trek series splashed across the old television screens. Not what they subsequently called a *Trekky*, or a particularly hard sci-fi fan, but from that time on, he could never look at a star-filled sky without at least wondering what might be out there.

More than thirty years on, it was a hell of a way to have his questions answered or his hopes realized. He strongly felt the excitement of the moment, mixed with the inevitable tinge of uncertainty and a healthy dose of fear. No matter what happened today, business on Earth would never be the same again. They were all shocked when the archaeological team found the Comalcalco saucer, but this thing on the roof represented a quantum leap into the unknown.

Emotions in turmoil, he waited for the knock.

It sounded subdued when it came. Wide paneled doors swung toward him. Bandrik looked at his assistant with interest, but could not discern any emotion on the poker face. The poor man had lived with diplomacy far too long to get excited by anything.

"They're here, sir," his assistant announced sternly.

Bandrik suspected the coming of Judgment Day would have been announced with the same straight face and gravity.

"Very good, Monhabiq. Anyone in particular?"

"Thompson from Globe, Wilks from CNN…and Morton from the *Times*."

Bandrik's mouth twitched in a small smile. Monhabiq detested Morton and everything he wrote. "Show them in."

The media moved in with recorders slung across their shoulders, camera crews in tow. Dismissing the pomp and ceremony, they seated themselves and came right down to cases. Jake noted the flat monitor on the desk and didn't need a crystal ball to guess what the show was about.

"Gentlemen, let's try to keep it short and to the point," Bandrik declared. "I have a lot to do."

"On top of NASA's recent pictures, this is shaping into some kind of day, Mr. Secretary," Jake put in.

Bandrik smiled. "Almost inevitable, if you think about it."

"Mr. Secretary?" Thompson pushed himself before the mikes. "When were you informed about the alien ship?"

"I received my last call from the President over an hour ago. Obviously, the American military had the ship under observation longer than that. As far as he could, given the security implications, the President has kept me aware of developments as they took place. I have called a special General Assembly meeting for seven tonight, which should give most of the ambassadors, at least those in the country, enough time to get here."

"What about the F-22s, sir?"

Jake frowned at the stupid question and wondered how an experienced man like Thompson swayed with the mob.

Bandrik did not even hesitate. "As far as the fighters are concerned, Mr. Thompson, American national security is not my concern."

"Do you have any idea where the ship came from?" Wilks asked beside the thrust mike of his camera crew.

"The Moon, Mr. Wilks."

"A staging base?"

"You covered NASA's transmissions. It's unlikely our friends originate from within the Solar System. Recent speculation by your network suggests the aliens must have been observing Earth for quite some time. As to where they actually come from, we may find out tonight."

"You must feel flattered at being singled out like this, sir," Jake interjected quickly. "By coming to the UN, they clearly know a lot about us."

"Perhaps, but one thing stands out clearly." Bandrik looked at them. *Would they understand?* "Earth can no longer afford the luxury of divided interests, whether economic, political, or religious. There can be no better incentive for cooperation between the nations than the alien presence on our roof."

"A presence which you hope will at last fulfill the UN's charter to be the Earth's government?" Jake said quietly, aware of Bandrik's seemingly hopeless campaign.

"We shall see, Mr. Morton. The fact that our visitors are here, rather than at the White House, the Kremlin, or some other political center, speaks for itself."

"Speaking of the Kremlin, Mr. Secretary, what *about* the Russians and the Chinese?" a voice called from the back.

"What about them?"

"Have their ambassadors been in touch with you?"

"The President has been on the hotline with both leaders. I'm not aware of the content of those conversations. Invitations have been issued to all UN ambassadors as a matter of course."

"And the public, Mr. Secretary?" Jake asked. "What do we tell them? Is it war or peace with the aliens?"

"I don't know. I suggest you wait until the General Assembly has convened."

* * *

EXTRA! FLYING SAUCER LANDS ON UN BUILDING!
GENERAL ASSEMBLY TO NEGOTIATE PEACE OR WAR?

Stefan Vučak

LITTLE GREEN MEN TO BARGAIN FOR EARTH?
YOUR SOULS MAY BE WANTING, BUT GOD WILL PROTECT
THE RIGHTEOUS!
IS TOMORROW OUR DAY OF JUDGMENT?
ALIENS, GO HOME!

"Jack Willison reporting from the CNN center in New York. This afternoon, amidst gaping millions, an alien spaceship landed on top of the UN building. That simple gesture holds profound implications for Earth, a point not lost on Washington. Is this a response to NASA's recent Moon mission? This evening the General Assembly will meet the visitors in what might prove to be the most crucial talks since the Palestinian-Israeli deal. Will our religions and past beliefs be shattered by tomorrow? Will Americans and the world stare in terror at an alien invasion? By comparison, our existing problems pale into insignificance.

"Already, the event has caused a ripple of excitement, or consternation, depending on which side of the fence you happen to sit, among the scientific community. The deceptively innocent image of the alien ship hovering effortlessly a foot above the roof of the UN building has caused the equivalent of people jumping out of campus windows. I cannot imagine the theories that will have to be scrapped or papers written about the aliens and their ship. This far outstrips anything found with the Comalcalco saucer five years ago. Stay tuned for your ongoing coverage of this incredible event."

* * *

"Riots are flaring along First Avenue as opposing factions denounce what some claim to be an invasion, while others call a divine visitation. Traffic is a hopelessly tangled mess from Park Avenue all the way to the Franklin Roosevelt Drive. Motorists are urged to avoid the area; a futile request as, despite the cold temperatures, approaches to the UN are already clogged with teeming sightseers.

"Today, they quoted Archbishop Waller saying the foundations of the church will remain unshaken, come hell or high water. There is not much left to add to that, is there? This is Mark Rown for NBC news."

* * *

1855 Local. UN Building, New York

With the coming of night, the neon lights proclaimed their dominance. Color was a city that never slept. First Avenue blazed under hastily mounted polyarcs, intersecting with floodlights cast from ferries along the East River. The UN building stood out in unmatched glory. Noise like booming surf rose and fell from crowds packing the streets, boats on the river and surrounding office blocks; all waiting for a glimpse of the aliens. The networks hurriedly rolled out giant flat screens, pinning them to buildings to give the crowds continuous coverage of the history-breaking event.

On top of the UN tower, the elevator doors opened and Nikita Bandrik led out the Earth delegation. The TV crews were ready. Stomping from the cold, rubbing hands, they waited for the action to start. Just another live news coverage as far as they were concerned. Well, almost.

A technician brazenly stepped up to President Hennery and requested a voice test. Hennery looked startled, then with a smile, complied. Secret Service types, suspicious and grim, dressed in heavy overcoats, moved around unobtrusively.

A cold winter evening, and there was a smell of snow in the air. They all stood in a semicircle before the hovering spaceship, flanked by camera crews, floodlights, trailing cables, and snouts of hungry mikes.

It happened quickly before anyone had time to get ready.

143

A landing strip extruded out of the ship, formed an angled ramp and touched the roof. An excited murmur rippled from the assembled crowd among a few nervous titters. The hatch slid into the hull and spilled white light, revealing an opening of a square sunk on one of its corners.

Bandrik glanced at the president. They settled protocol quickly. New York might be United States soil, but the UN building belonged to Earth. Hennery acquiesced graciously. Stepping forward, Nikita wondered naively if the aliens knew English.

One by one the aliens stood outlined against the hatchway. Camera flashes flickered as the landing strip flowed, bringing them down to the roof. Bandrik swallowed nervously as the five aliens stood before him. The landing strip retracted and the hatch closed with a soft hiss.

"On behalf of all mankind, I welcome you to Earth," Bandrik said after a strained moment and extended his right hand.

"Thank you, Da Secretary-General," the red-haired, brown-skinned, six-and-a-half foot giant, spoke to him in flawless English, and took the proffered hand. Bandrik felt the steady pressure and the release, leaving him with a strange, but very soul-satisfying feeling.

Two civilizations met.

Bandrik turned and extended an open hand. "Sir, may I present Kurtland Hennery, President of the United States of America."

The alien nodded once, stepped easily beside Bandrik, and both faced the remaining visitors.

"Da Bandrik, Mr. President, may I introduce my associates: Da Terrllss-rr and Da Dharaklin, representing the Serrll Combine. And my officers: Tavac and Farly." Bandrik shook hands all around, starting to feel lightheaded and euphoric with the excitement of the situation.

With introductions concluded, the alien again faced him.

With Shadow and Thunder

"And I, Da, am Arlon Dee, representing the Orieli Technic Union."

Bandrik looked up into the red eyes and a glow of contentment spread through him.

"And I represent Earth," he said quietly.

* * *

The General Assembly hall was packed. Everyone who was anyone tried to get in, standing room only in the gallery, fast disappearing. The Sergeant-At-Arms had a tough time keeping order among enraged foreign dignitaries who resorted to physical violence to obtain one of the few visitor seats.

The aliens were seated behind the main podium. The huge emblem of the United Nations hung on the sloping wood paneling behind them. The hall sparkled with the constant flicker of camera flashes. It was hard to say who was more shocked, the aliens or the General Assembly. Neither side could possibly have experienced the events taking place.

Standing behind the smaller front lectern, Bandrik irritably glanced at his watch. Long past seven, he saw little point delaying things further. Those who could not make it would simply have to read about it. Finally, he banged his gavel. Gradually the vast theater settled into silence.

He did not waste time with elaborate introductions. The delegates wanted to hear from the aliens, not his pompous ramblings. Guarded applause came from the floor as Arlon Dee stepped down and solemnly shook Bandrik's hand. Arlon waited until the silence became pronounced, then began to speak in his flawless English. Many of his comments drew an excited and sometimes angry buzz from the floor.

"—home worlds of the Orieli lie in a giant globular cluster some 12,000 light-years above the galactic plane. Including the stars within the hub of this galactic arm, the Orieli occupy over 3,200 worlds.

"—does not seek military conquest. The Orieli is a loose association of many disparate societies and political blocks. Cohesion is upheld through economic, cultural, and technical exchange. We don't maintain formal governing institutions as you understand them. However, mechanisms do exist to support communication between systems, promote trade, exploration, development, ecoforming of new planets, and defense.

"—the observatory on the Moon is a recognized intrusion into your space. It is also an intrusion into your culture, although an unavoidable one. To put it simply, our purpose is to secure Earth and this whole sector from any possibility of Celi-Kran attack. Within our policy of strict non-interference, your affairs are your own."

"Then why did you bother coming at all?" a voice shouted from the floor, immediately followed by a wave of rising comment.

"Please address your questions to the Chair!" Bandrik snapped, banging his gavel as he glowered at the assembly. A sudden realization struck him and he turned to the bemused alien. "Karhide, will you permit us to ask questions, sir?"

Arlon looked up and smiled. "By all means. That's why we're here."

"Mr. Dee! What about—"

"Sir!" Bandrik rapped his gavel. "Unless you follow standard procedure the Sergeant-At-Arms will be ordered to clear the floor."

Angry protests rippled through the hall mixed with derisive laughter. Any attempt to clear the hall would have caused a riot and everyone knew it.

"Nirvan Skolski, Russian Federation." The barely accented voice of the Russian ambassador called out. "Karhide Dee, you have indicated a possible threat against Earth. Does that mean military involvement by the Orieli Technic Union? Is the ship on top of this building a military craft?"

An excited buzz ran through the assembly.

"Where is your mother ship, sir?" Skolski shouted and the floor erupted with noise.

Bandrik banged his gavel and relative silence descended. Arlon Dee looked grim as he gazed at the assembly.

"As I have stated before, Da Ambassador, the threat to this system is unlikely to eventuate in your lifetime. Hopefully, it never will for any of you. On the other hand, without military involvement, our protection would not be worth much, would it? As for my ship, it's on the Moon providing support for the construction of our base."

"Next question, please." Bandrik pointed his gavel at a gray-suited figure.

"Najim Ahmed Rumaithi, Kingdom of Saudi Arabia. Sir, what is the involvement of the Serrll Combine in this mission?"

Arlon turned and extended his hand toward Terr, who stood up. Terr had sneaked in a few stealthy landings on Earth during his tour of the Serrll Moon Base, but this was about as close as he wanted to come to a crowd of Earthmen. Their veneer of civility around him felt depressingly thin. And what of Serrll's? He didn't want to dwell too long on that one.

"Naturally, any potential threat against Earth is a threat against the Serrll Combine," he said, the microphone echoing his voice. "As a protectorate, Earth has been extended all the facilities at our disposal to ensure your security. However, our immediate objective is to evaluate the nature of the Kran threat and assess the implication of the Orieli's involvement in our space."

An excited ripple of comment swept through the assembly and Bandrik rapped sharply with his gavel.

"Order…Order! The Chair recognizes the representative of the United States of America."

"Opturkarh Terrllss-rr, can you please elaborate what it means exactly to be a protectorate of the Serrll Combine?"

Terr spent a moment arranging his thoughts.

"Simply put, sir, the Serrll maintains guardianship over developing societies which have not yet reached a cultural level enabling them to join the Serrll as an independent nonaligned system, or as a member of an established stellar political block."

"Where *is* your space, Opturkarh Terr?"

"What you call the Coal Sack, sir, in the region of the Southern Cross. All those stars belong to the Serrll."

"Thomas Bennett, United Kingdom. Mr. Terr, how long has Earth been what you call a protectorate?"

"As a protectorate, some four-and-a-half thousand years." A gasp and a ripple of murmuring greeted his response.

"And before that?"

Terr allowed himself a faint smile as he waited for the waves of excited comment to die down.

"Just another system far beyond the edge of what is now the Serrll Combine, sir."

"A question has been raised earlier, Da Bandrik," Arlon interjected smoothly. "You asked why we came. My response to this is a simple one. Once starships start to appear in your skies, it will be somewhat difficult to tell friend from enemy. Alerted, Earth can begin this perhaps unwanted, but necessary period of cultural adjustment. Adjustment to our presence and the presence of lifeforms whose motivation even we don't fully understand. This effort is not to be underestimated.

"I am not standing before you ignoring your religious, cultural or political institutions. I stand before you as an alien addressing all the people of Earth, not individual nations or men. However unpalatable, you will have to accept that Earth is not alone among the stars. The Serrll and the Orieli extend to you our hand in friendship. Whether you return the gesture or not is up to you."

After a moment of silence, the questions resumed. It was late into the night before the Assembly adjourned.

* * *

With Shadow and Thunder

READ ALL ABOUT IT! MOON TO BECOME A SPY STATION
EXTRA! EARTH SCRUTINIZED BY ALIEN PEEPING TOMS
WILL EARTH STAND IDLE AS INTERSTELLAR WAR
THREATENS?
ALIENS, GO HOME!

"Jack Willison reporting for CNN. In a special session this morning the Security Council met the so-called Orieli Technic Union to further discuss the implications raised by the presence of the aliens. Secretary-General Bandrik refused to make any comments after the conference. For the first time in history, the nations of Earth are considering setting up a planetary defense strategy, this from a reliable source. One thing is certain. Third-world countries are already bitterly protesting the non-interference clause. Confusion is running wild to the long-term effects of the alien visit."

* * *

"Archbishop Waller is once again embroiled in a controversy surrounding the purported historical landings on Earth by aliens, first postulated when we found the Comalcalco saucer five years ago. His position is unchanged and he openly condemned rumors of historical events that factions claim have been influenced by Serrll landings. Such rumors, he said, are baseless and only serve as a crutch for the morally depraved. Challenged to disprove the rumors by approaching the Serrll representatives, the Archbishop declined, saying the Church had nothing to disprove; faith will sustain the believers. However, telegrams dispatched to the Vatican may or may not cast doubt in the faithful. This is Mark Rown for NBC news."

Chapter Eight

Just a lousy proficiency training flight on a platform.

Leaning back in form-hugging couches, Terr and Taroptur Farly were following in a backup dart, cracking jokes and discovering the multiplicity of each other's cultures. The differences between them were enormous, but Terr felt he'd found a kindred spirit. Beneath his hard core of professionalism, Farly rebelled against authority and had a healthy cynicism not unlike Terr's own.

Both learned a lot.

In a moment of silence between chuckles, Terr locked his fingers behind his head and stared at the jagged peaks towering around them. Clad in harsh shadows the mountains moved with them as the dart glided above a dust-covered valley floor.

The Virtual Interface coupling made it seem as though he were out there. Terr *wished* for the interior view and the image in his mind changed to show him the contoured command consoles and the mainframe plot. The VI coupling made a real-time link with the dart housekeeping computer, and by extension, the Orieli cruiser's central net. A powerful facility whose application extended far beyond the ability to provide system thought control. It took Terr a while to get used to the giddy feeling of being able to experience and manage all the sensory data pouring into the Orieli ship's computer net.

The other thing unnerving about the Orieli ships was the almost complete absence of internal sounds. No unnecessary computer status chatter, the throb of the power pile, or even the background whisper of the life support system. Backup touch-sensitive contact pads glowed in colored arrays on the control panels, sometimes changing, briefly flickering. Nothing else. He would form a command in his mind and the computer would execute it.

The dart structural frame itself, they told him, was partially a grown, living entity, not a construct of machined parts. The ship had no internal wiring, the bulkhead composites forming an ever-changing variable circuit net. It would be difficult to disable such a craft, Terr mused.

"It's kind of pretty, don't you think?" Farly said quietly, watching the mountains march by.

Terr sifted through the words, realizing that Farly might be right. It had been a long time since he last stared at the stars like this and he missed the thrill. He missed the command and freedom of his own ship. Anabb, with his missions of intrigue and diplomacy, had poisoned him. Terr was no longer content with the simple or the routine. To be fair, he had chosen to walk this path willingly.

"It's the only place to be," he said after a while.

He canceled the VI link. Above the command consoles, status figures and full-dimensional images overlaid the mainframe plot. One image held steady, the TLM, telemetry, and position plots of the dart relative to the platform somewhere ahead of them.

Farly looked at him, his large brown eyes bright with intelligence. Terr knew Farly was physically young, but those eyes betrayed him. They belonged to someone old, wizened by decades of experience. The Zaronian's blue-green skin seemed to glow with life, black around the eyes and mouth.

"A change from your normal duties, then?" Farly commented wryly.

"What makes you say that?" Terr asked suspiciously and Farly chuckled.

"Attached to the *Diplomatic Branch*, aren't you?" Farly waited for Terr to think it through.

"Takes one to know one, right?" Terr said and chuckled.

"Something like that."

Terr didn't know whether to be annoyed or amused. It should have been obvious. The Orieli were just as curious about the Serrll as the Serrll were about them, and would have taken appropriate steps. That was the creepy thing about them. They seemed to understand and anticipate so well, something he found intensely disconcerting. He wondered what other special talents Farly had on call in his evaluation of him, and indirectly, of the Serrll. Then he broke into a grin and laughed.

"You find the situation amusing?" Farly asked in perfect Serrll interlingua, no doubt picked up from the data pack Terr transmitted to Zor-Ell during their encounter.

"Just curious about who's running the social experiment between us."

Farly's eyes glittered as he smiled. "This is only a training flight, Terr."

"Yeah, and I'm being taken for a ride."

"Medical alert," the computer announced. "Platform departing controlled flight parameters. Subject life signs critical. Operational override initiated."

In the mainframe plot, fleeting images appeared, showing the platform's environmental status and the occupant's vital signs.

"All life signs terminated. Platform no longer in controlled flight. Assumed neutral status." The plot displayed a full contour area map. A blinking topaz point indicated the platform's position.

"Provide diagnosis of bio-readouts," Farly commanded.

"Tentative analysis only. Pathogenic or physiological trauma dysfunction not indicated. Probable cause of death, neural disruption."

That set off faint alarms in the back of Terr's head.

It did not take them long to find the platform, a two-by-three katalan rectangular oval, its edges rounded, flowing down at the sides. It hovered a few tetalans above the dust, its shield net invisible. There were no seats on the craft, only contoured indentations for four occupants. Slumped beside the low curved control console the body lay a shapeless heap on the deck. Farly looked at Terr, his large eyes clear and penetrating. Terr shrugged. They lifted the platform into the cargo bay of the RV/4 dart and went down to the lower deck for a look.

The hatch opened slowly. Terr stood at the entrance and stared at the platform. Death brushed his face as it went. His hackles rose and he shivered. He knew the hand of Death. It came to collect him as he rode a smoking survival blister down to Anar'on. He walked away from that one, and he supposed it was a forgivable mistake to think he'd cheated Death.

To encounter it here, like this…Beside himself, only one other wielded the hand of Death. Why would Dhar be gunning for one of the Serrll crew?

Or was he?

"Terr?" Farly looked visibly concerned. "What is it?"

Could he have imagined it? Hardly. Terr could still feel the stiff hairs on the back of his neck.

"I thought I noticed something. Let's take a look at the body."

They walked around the platform, not touching anything. Terr crouched and peered at the Karkan. The face slack and the eyes glazed, the pupils mere points. The Death Messenger technique killed like that, inducing massive electrical disruption of the brain's neural transmitters. Depending on the timing trigger, death was inevitable.

"Looks like a stroke, or seizure," Terr muttered absently, trying to hide his disquiet.

"What makes you say that?" Farly said.

"Look at him, a boneless heap. I've seen it before."

Farly looked at him curiously. "You seem to be an expert on death."

"One of my specialties," Terr told him.

He had no doubts when they got the body off the platform.

153

He was dead, all right, and not a mark on him, but Terr knew that already. They flew back to *Tapal* in silence, each wrapped in his own thoughts. This was going to raise a stink with everyone. The Orieli cruiser hovered above the cluster of base surface buildings. Its nav screen almost fully retracted, barely flickering with incident discharges. Terr watched the black rectangular slab fill the sky as the dart moved up to meet it.

The huge outer Hangar Bay doors were open, yellow-white light streamed into space from the edge of the ship. The dart slipped through the force field into the cavernous bay. Terr relaxed as Cent Comp guided them to a landing point. Darts, platforms, and small two-man shuttles filled the bay. Repair and maintenance crews clustered around some of the craft.

The medical team waiting for them. Terr left Farly to take care of the body and the official details.

Using the PT, personal transport system, Terr materialized on the main officer's quarters deck. Living tissue matter transfer was something still beyond Serrll technology; problems with quark quantum stability at the matter/energy boundary, or some crap like that. Spontaneous creation of molecular groups also had something to do with it. During his contact with Karhide Zor-Ell, the Orieli had neatly sidestepped the whole problem of matter and information reconstitution by utilizing one of the dimensions postulated by the super-matrix symmetry string theory. The PT provided a literal dimensional doorway. It gave the Serrll scientists a lot to think about.

In his cabin, Dhar sat cross-legged on his bunk, staring at an empty bulkhead. Something like an aura surrounded him, an area of peace and tranquility that calmed. Terr sank into one of the couches and waited. After a while, he closed his eyes. It helped the waiting.

"You are far away, Sankri," Dhar murmured, voice like dying thunder rolling over low hills.

Terr opened his eyes and grinned. "Daydreaming."

"I too daydream sometimes. Of tall hooded figures and red

desert sands. Of clear running water, swaying peelath, the smell of tarad grass, and the treks of the Wanderers."

"You've been outside?"

"Walking?"

"It's not unlike the vastness of the dunes. Different surely, but it has the same quality of openness and peace. I tried it the other day."

"Sounds interesting."

"You should do it. Tends to bring things into perspective."

"Perhaps I will."

"I suppose you know why I'm here," Terr asked, wishing it were otherwise.

Dhar sat there, his eyes strangely dark.

"That crewman died at the hand of a Death Messenger, Nightwings," Terr said and felt the hand of Death settle unbidden on his shoulders. It happened sometimes and he could never do anything about it. He let it ride. "Could it have been aimed at me?"

"I see the cloak of power around you raised in anger, but we are brothers, Sankri," Dhar said and reached out with a long hand to touch Terr's arm. "That thought is unworthy of you."

"Unworthy or not—"

"Even without your aspect, the technique would not have worked on you," Dhar admonished gently.

Maybe not, but Terr had a nasty and suspicious nature—a talent. That part of him had gotten him out of more than one tight scrape and it didn't care if Dhar was a brother. It was a real pain to live with sometimes.

What did he know about the awesome heritage he had acquired on Anar'on? About the Wanderers and the means they were prepared to use to achieve their political ends? In the clean wind-swept sands of the deep Saffal, the Discipline and the *Saftara* litanies had a kind of purity of purpose easy to understand. Among the worlds of the Serrll, with its own shades of truth, could that purity have been subordinated? Subordinated

155

by a necessity when dealing with the Serrll on its terms?

"It's unreasonable, I know, but I get suspicious when someone tries to kill me. Like those accidents we've been having…that I've been having. Take that blowout in the new construction tunnel the other day, and me without a shield unit. Or the gag when a thirty seconds borer fuse went off after only five seconds. I had my shield then. The one I like best was being caught in a zero-gee training tank, remember? The problem I had, it had eight gravities when I was in it. Occupational hazards, I figured. Comes with the job, but the pace is picking up, isn't it? Now—"

"Sankri—"

"—we have a body! What's going on, Nightwings? Are you trying to get me out of the way?"

Dhar looked disappointed and Terr felt like a heel.

"I am saddened you should even think it, Sankri," Dhar said sternly.

"Right. Now you know how I feel," Terr snapped. Dhar unfolded his legs and sat back against the bulkhead. He crossed his arms before his chest and exhaled.

"Our footsteps have taken us in strange directions. It is unfortunate, my brother, that we now find ourselves on the same crossroad. Remember the piece of work you did on Trillian?"

About to deny the whole thing, but if Dhar knew to ask the question…

"What do you know about it?" Terr asked.

"I am somewhat involved," Dhar said awkwardly, intensely embarrassed.

Terr pondered that, not liking the flavor. "Are you saying Terchran is so sore at me for smearing Gashkarali, he sent that piece of Karkan shit after my hide?"

"He may have been after both of our hides."

"I don't buy it. Terchran plays in your face. If he wanted to get rid of me, I would be dead already."

Dhar almost winced. "By killing you himself? Hardly.

Sankri, believe me when I tell you that he wants you dead."

Terr shook his head and frowned. "All of a sudden, you seem to know a hell of a lot about my end of the business."

"I am not at liberty to say more," Dhar said heavily. "And I'm sorry about that."

"I'll bet, but I won't pry. However, if you suspected something, you should have told me. And why kill him? We could have interrogated him."

"And found what? I acted—"

"Prematurely," Terr said, angry and confused.

"—to save your life. I was in the platform bay when I learned you switched your training flight. It gave me a perfect opportunity to get rid of him. I barely had enough time to prime the Death Messenger before you took off with Taroptur Farly."

Terr looked hard at his alien brother. "Tell me. How did you manage to get onto him?"

Faced with the dread of inevitable certainty, Dhar nevertheless took that final step he knew could have only one conclusion.

"Sankri, I can understand your doubts and suspicions. I can see them in your eyes, but the bond we have is unto death. If you feel I have betrayed that bond, lay your hand on me now and let Death cleanse away my sins. I shall not resist."

His words rang in the ensuing silence and Terr felt his brother's pain. He wanted to kneel before Dhar and ask his forgiveness, but Dhar hadn't answered his question. The cynical part of him sneered and laughed at him.

In the platform bay, he had switched his training flight there and then. It was a spur-of-the-moment decision. He wanted Farly to show him some ground following instrument procedures in the dart and an opening to give the Karkan crewman a proficiency flight at the same time. Dhar could not have known of it beforehand. If he were telling the truth, he would have primed the Death Messenger *knowing* Terr would not be on that platform. What did that leave him with?

Was that crewman really a Servatory Party operative or simply someone damn unlucky to be in the wrong place at the wrong time? Thinking about it, he remembered that it took him a few minutes to change the training program and file a new flight plan with Primary Flight Control. In the rush, Dhar *could* have had enough time to set things up as he said.

My brother, what have you gotten yourself mixed up with? What have I gotten myself mixed up with?

Later, on the lounge deck, he brooded in the shadow of jagged moon peaks with the transparent hull curving back above him. The sky lay smeared with stars, thick in the sweep of The Arch. No one here disturbed the storm of his thoughts. Shaken, confused and angry, he found himself helpless, questioning everything he believed.

In the end, he could not escape the fact that Dhar was his brother. Dhar's very thoughts were his thoughts. They were one in soul. Dhar's hand raised against him? Impossible, and he didn't want to believe it. He couldn't!

Then again, he'd only seen Dhar a handful of times during the past year. Was Dhar the same person he knew as his first officer?

Terr told his cynical half to screw itself. Doubt Dhar? He would rather die.

Arlon pulled a meeting a couple of hours later to dissect the incident. They met in the senior officer's briefing room. Dhar looked troubled, his eyes pleading. Terr paused, touched his arm and smiled briefly, a smile that didn't come from the heart and they both knew it.

Being a professional, Arlon started with the easy ones.

"I'm sorry about your crewman, Terr. Medical has determined what killed him, but not why. That is puzzling. At any rate, Serrll Moon Base is making arrangements to pick up the body and affect a replacement.

"But before we get onto other matters, I feel I must clear the air regarding the incidents we've been having during the last two weeks. These have resulted in loss of time, materiel, and overall efficiency in the base construction program. I regret to say Terr, most of these incidents involved you. I shall say just one thing, Opturkarh. No more incidents. I will not tolerate any expression of Serrll politics in this base."

"That might be a tall order, Karhide," Terr said grimly.

"And why is that?"

"When an incident is a contrived accident, there isn't much I can do about it."

"Are you suggesting sabotage?"

"Let me tell you something about the Serrll, Karhide," Terr said with relish. "There are vested interests who would stop at nothing to see you out of this system. And it has nothing to do with Earth. That's only a convenient handle. The body you have on the slab in Medical was supposed to have been mine. A plan which misfired," he said and glanced at Dhar. "So you see, whoever is behind this won't give a damn about what you like or don't like."

"I could have you all returned to Salina," Arlon suggested mildly.

Terr laughed. "You could, but not until your scanner grid is operational."

"The scanner grid?" Arlon exchanged a glance with Opturkarh Tavac, his tongue making a quick circuit around his lips.

"Come, Karhide. You should credit me with some intelligence. Do you want me to explain?"

"By all means."

"Okay, then. Here you are, light-years from nearest friend, and let's face it, in potentially hostile space. You show up on Salina in your tiny little dart lander and demand to build a tracking station on one of our protectorates. You sought to keep us off balance with your steamroller tactics. To you, it might appear that those tactics have worked. And who knows, maybe they have. After all, you're here."

Terr was just warming up when he realized he felt unaccountably angry. Maybe he was used to the idea that the Serrll, with all its faults, deserved to run its own disasters. But that wasn't Arlon's fault.

"Since I've been attached to your crew, I have learned quite a lot about your procedures and the workings of your ship, Karhide. The display of firepower five years ago is a case in point. Opturkarh Karth could have stood off until Anatol Keller got tired of firing at him. But he didn't. He chose to return Anatol's fire. Was his response a normal one, brushing off an annoyance, or a premeditated act to show the Serrll who they were dealing with? In later contacts with us, that demonstration of power could be used as a psychological gambit to secure what you wanted, and when you wanted it. Getting the Moon must have seemed like easy pickings for you."

"You spin an interesting scenario, Opturkarh," Arlon said, his eyes predatory.

"And some of it might even be true. I'll leave that one to the bulging brains on Captal. We do have one or two around, you know. I would rather talk about your base here. It took me a while, but I'm sure I have it all," Terr went on more slowly. "Your whole setup doesn't make much tactical sense unless I take into account your first visit to Earth. Karhide Zor-Ell must have found something totally different to compel you to come back, supposedly concerned about Earth's safety. At the United Nations, you talked about protection, and that got me. Where was that protection going to come from? Your ship? You said you were pulling out as soon as the base is completed. Other ships? Just for Sol? I didn't think so. Where then?

"To you the Serrll may appear primitive and militaristic. Maybe we are. I'll not argue the point. However, paranoia can have its advantages when you're pursued. Only fools would believe that an operation such as this base wouldn't have at least defensive capability built into it. We're not fools Karhide, even if we sometimes act like it. When you assembled the scanner grid above the planetary plane, the pieces started falling into place. Sure, it's designed to be a tracking instrument, but there are a hell of a lot of energy arrays in that grid, supposedly serving a simple tracking sink. I would figure that once activated, the grid will draw almost unlimited power from Sol. Power the grid could channel through subspace and energize particle bursts capable of covering most of the inner system. That's what I would think the grid does if I had a suspicious nature. The Serrll will find out, Karhide. One way or another, it won't be pleasant."

Arlon was silent for quite some time. Digesting this new piece of information, Terr guessed. Arlon's tongue was getting a heavy workout and Terr wondered if Arlon had noticed.

"An impressive line of reasoning, Opturkarh," Arlon said at length, nodding. "I might have made an error in the approach I used with your government, but for the fact that I'm here as you said, and the base *is* being built. And you're perfectly correct regarding the scanner grid. Each element mounts a selective energy projector. However, I don't expect any repercussions from Captal. As I said before, we don't invade. I have been supplying Commissioner Enllss-rr with regular progress updates, supplementing the ones you've been submitting to the Diplomatic Branch. Your government knows exactly what I am doing here."

Terr gaped. "Captal knows?"

Was he venting his anger and frustration at the attempts on his life, reflecting his confusion with Dhar? Like the guy said, it was all high politics stuff. Maybe he should shut up and leave it all alone. He could go crazy trying to work out all the angles.

"What now, Karhide? You take over the system?"

Arlon laughed and shook his head. "All we're interested in is the safety of Earth and the Serrll Combine."

"Is that so? Tell me one thing. What did Karhide Zor-Ell find on Earth that makes it worth all this trouble?"

"I'm sorry, Terr. I cannot make that information available

to you."
Rit!

$* * *$

"They're M-4s, all right," Terr said, studying the mainframe plot through the VI coupling.

The three Serrll ships hovered above them in a standard triangle formation, their dark bellies covering the whole sky. Terr felt he could almost reach up and touch them. Nestled in the valley directly above the base, the Orieli ship could not even maneuver. Not a great tactical situation.

Eerily quiet, unlike the command deck pimples on top of Serrll outer hulls, exposed and vulnerable, *Tapal's* Primary Flight Control lay buried deep within the ship. To Terr, it made a lot of operational sense.

PFC was an ellipsoid area some six katalans high and fifteen katalans wide, split into two levels: Command and Operations. The command level stood out as a protruding platform curving along the long axis halfway up the chamber. A low-contoured console hugged the bulkhead. Swivel-couches faced the holoview repeater readouts from the main operations stations below, projected along the length of the platform's edge; a wall of images for those not hooked into the VI. One of the displays constantly showed a multicolored cutout of the ship's critical areas. Using voice commands or touch-recognition backup pads, provided authorized access to all ship's functions, but the Cent Comp VI coupling served as the primary thought control system.

That accounted for some of the eerie silence.

Operations was some three katalans below the command level. Like a bowl, its inner surface mounted one long backup contoured console, above which were projected three-katalan-high holoview images. They showed endlessly changing repeater displays from every part of the ship's internal and tactical operations.

Six form-hugging swivel-couches, separated by curving touch consoles, faced the center of the bowl. In it hung a variable image holoview sphere almost three katalans in diameter. Each operator controlled a specific area of ship's duties, such as tactical, engineering or sciences, feedback provided through the VI coupling, repeated in the holoview sphere and the command level displays. At the moment only two of the couches were manned.

Arlon leaned back and locked his fingers behind his head, a frown creasing his face. Beside him on his right, Opturkarh Tavac glanced at the tactical repeater plot. Apart from Terr and Arlon, no one else manned the command level.

"Well, at least they're not about to fire on us," Terr said moodily.

"It seems a rather excessive show of force just to pick up a body," Arlon muttered to no one in particular.

"Maybe they're lost," Terr suggested, sitting on Arlon's left, having relegated the engineering and sciences specialist to the ops level.

Arlon looked at Terr, not sure whether his leg was being pulled.

"It has been known to happen," Terr said with a straight face.

Arlon smiled faintly and touched a pad on the armrest of his command couch. Taroptur Farly once told Terr that even though the ship could be run from one's bed, certain things a man had to do in order to preserve his dignity. Fiddling with manual controls was one of them. Terr guessed that maybe the Serrll were not so backward after all, or the Orieli that omnipotent.

"Have they opened comms?" Arlon demanded.

"Coming through now, Karhide," replied the communications operator from the operations level below. The face repeated in the holoview before them.

In the mainframe plot, a window opened and an image formed. Terr groaned as he recognized the face.

"Master Scout Anatol Keller, Serrll Scout Fleet," he said harshly, his neck stiff. The full purple lips were set in an uncompromising line. "Karhide Arlon Dee?"

"And to what do I owe the honor of this visit, Master Scout?" Arlon asked pleasantly.

"It is no honor, Karhide," Anatol said ponderously. "I am instructed by the Bureau of Defense on Captal to carry out an inspection of your facilities."

"Your authority, Da?" Arlon asked mildly and his tongue went around his lips.

"Authority?" Anatol looked genuinely surprised. "The three ships above you, Karhide."

"Before I can allow you to start your, ah, inspection, Master Scout, I require a copy of your orders from the Bureau of Colonial and Protectorate Affairs."

"My word as an officer of the Serrll Scout Fleet should suffice."

"I'm afraid not."

"I caution you, sir. Your attitude is hardly one of cooperation, keeping in mind that you're here on the sufferance of the Serrll. If you persist, I have the power to change your mind."

"Come, Master Scout, all I request is verification of your orders."

"Out here, I represent all the verification that is necessary. You have one minute."

The image faded, showing the three ships drawing apart still in triangle formation, a standard attack pattern. Was Arlon aware the M-4s could tandem link their fire? Should he tell him? He wasn't sure about that one either.

Arlon glanced at Terr, disappointment all over his face. "Not much for small talk, is he?"

"You shouldn't judge all of us by his example, Karhide. Anatol is an asshole."

Arlon chuckled. "Are you always this forthright?"

"One of my less redeeming qualities," Terr agreed with a grin.

"Tactical caution. Serrll vessels extending secondary shield grid," the housekeeping computer announced immediately. "Increased power core emissions detected. Weapons systems being activated. Targeting emissions detected. Cent Comp status. Primary unit maintaining condition one under autonomous control. Primary interceptor net now at level two. Secondary shields on active standby. Tactical control in PFC. Status. Condition two on active standby."

"Well, hardly an auspicious start to our relations, wouldn't you say?" Arlon commented dryly.

"I know we get twitchy where Earth is concerned, but I cannot imagine why the Bureau of Defense would have issued such asinine orders. Sol falls under the jurisdiction of the BCPA."

"Mmm. Factional power politics, then?" Tavac pointed out.

"It's possible. We both seem to have a morbid fascination with the planet."

"Or a guilty conscience. Something the Serrll may have done in the past, perhaps?" Arlon's red eyes regarded Terr intently, his tongue going around the lips.

Terr wondered if the alien suspected, then decided not. The Serrll had ceased genetic engineering experiments over 2,500 years ago—as far as he knew, not that the thing was ever exactly a secret. Still, as he told Enllss, they did not know the extent of Orieli's capabilities. Could this be the source of their intense interest in Earth, figuring out the reason for the accelerated development of human technology?

Then again, where the hell would Arlon get the idea to ask such a question anyway?

"Hardly a guilty conscience, Karhide. Any sins we may have committed are now long behind us."

"Sins have a funny way of coming back to haunt you." Tavac grinned broadly.

"In the shape of an Orieli cruiser?" Terr asked and they all laughed.

"Sometimes Terr, an alien encounter is just that," Arlon commented.

Something that basically Farly said. Terr didn't believe this one either.

"I cannot pretend to understand why Anatol is here, but if he's looking for trouble, our tactical position sucks."

"I doubt that your Master Scout will press the issue. Still, Cent Comp copy?"

"Ready."

"Secure from condition one. Execute condition two."

The tactical plot image overlaid the mainframe plot, showing the three M-4s and their shield rings within a faintly glowing scaled grid.

"Condition two commencing," the computer said. "All decks at level two alert. Primary fire control on active standby. Secondary fire control to scanner grid on passive standby. Auxiliary Flight Control passive. Interceptor net now at level three. Secondary shields now at level one with level two on active standby. Tactical control in PFC. Status. Condition two active. Tactical profile: three M-4 6/A Serrll Scout Fleet units maintaining an equilateral triangle holding pattern. Firing lock activated. Presumed hostile."

Moments later an additional operator materialized and quietly took up his position at the operations level below. It was Dhar. A surge of emotion washed through Terr. He turned to find Arlon watching him.

"Karhide?" He managed a half-hearted chuckle. "If I didn't know better, I would say you were getting ready for a fight."

"You know better." Arlon grinned and showed a mouthful of even teeth.

"Come now, not all three! I have a healthy respect for your

ship, but an M-4 is no toy and things have changed in the five years since our last contest of strength."

"Is that so?" Arlon looked at Terr and raised an eyebrow.

Did he hear him right? He raised his left hand and stared at the sleeve of his uniform. Indigo and not the gray he wore all too seldom these days. Arlon caught him at it and their eyes met.

"My apologies, Karhide. Please forgive my impertinence," Terr said bitterly and clamped his mouth.

"When fired upon, my alien friend, it doesn't matter whether it is by an enemy or some political stooge. Either way, I have to protect my ship and our base."

Terr, an alien in an alien ship. To Arlon, Serrll politics were hardly consequential.

The plot cleared and Anatol looked at them, haughty and arrogant. Terr wished he could reach out and smear that smirk all over his black face. The stupid bastard, or some party-motivated hack on Captal, was about to screw up everything.

Could *Tapal*, without being able to maneuver, hold off the M-4s if Anatol pushed it that far? Surely Anatol could not have forgotten what happened five years ago. At any rate it looked like Terr was about to find out.

"Karhide Arlon, I order you to power down and stand to."

Terr winced and rubbed the scar above his left eyebrow, not daring to look at Arlon. He couldn't understand why Anatol appeared determined to deliberately bait the Orieli.

"Without verification of your orders, Master Scout, I cannot allow my position to be compromised," Arlon said, ignoring the threat.

"Destruction of your base would relieve you of such weighty problems, Karhide."

"Surely you're not suggesting a contest of power, Master Scout? What would that prove?"

"That I have the upper hand," Anatol snapped. He had a point there, Terr thought. Then again, he had three M-4s, which made up for a lot.

"Before you make a hasty decision, Master Scout—"

Anatol turned, apparently talking to someone. When he spoke again, his face worked with emotion.

"Karhide Arlon Dee. We have detected anomalous energy readings above the planetary plane. They're coming from your scanner grid! Have you mounted energy projectors on that thing? If you have, I will fire on you right now!"

"Master Scout, I believe that information has already been—"

"Answer me!" Anatol thundered.

"I was doing just that," Anatol said, his patience starting to wear thin. "The Bureau of Colonial and Protectorate Affairs has been advised of the purpose of the scanner grid—"

"I don't know anything about that. All I know is that you mounted an illegal energy array in this system."

"I have tried to be reasonable, working within the protocols set by your government. That doesn't appear to be sufficient. Before you do anything hasty, perhaps a little demonstration might be in order."

"Demonstration? What kind of demonstration?"

"Mars is visible to your instruments now. If you would please locate Phobos, I shall begin my demonstration. By the way, I wouldn't try approaching or interdicting the grid. You'll know why in a minute. Transmission ends."

Anatol did not get a chance to say anything as his image dissolved from the mainframe plot. The display reverted to tactical, showing a checkered grid converging quickly around a white dot hovering above the curve of Mars. Centered, the dot pulsed softly. Terr turned to Arlon and found that his mouth had gone dry.

"Cent Comp copy?" Arlon said briskly.

"Ready."

"Fire grid on predetermined coordinates."

"Targeting coordinates accepted and locked. Tactical caution. In present mode, verification authorization is required from the first officer before the secondary unit can be engaged."

Arlon glanced at Tavac who nodded. "Tactical order confirmed."

"Acknowledged. Engaging secondary unit."

Tactical cleared. For a few seconds the mainframe plot image seemed to rush toward the pale orange horn of Mars. A few stars stared coldly in the background. Terr knew what was coming.

Hugging the edge of the sun's photosphere, a web of force lines captured the streaming plasma and photon flux, channeling it into an artificial quantum point singularity. Collapsing, regenerating, the singularity-powered stream of energy, derived from the ripped plasma atoms, shot toward the central module of the scanner grid from the singularity's poles. Fed through the twelve projectors of the array, the energy bled into the surrounding shield layers. As each layer overloaded, cascading outward from grid to grid, a locus of instability formed on the outer layer. Energy surged into the sink and flowed along the precursor geometry lines, charging the distortion field torus.

Not daring to breathe, Terr waited. Then, like spokes in a wheel, violet tracks of ionization leakage ripped through space, following in the wake of energy surges fired through subspace. They converged on a point above the orange crescent of Mars. Something flared white and Terr put up his hand to shield his eyes. He could feel the blood drain from his face as he watched the growing sphere of incandescence.

The tracks faded slowly and a new sun now shone above Mars. To have such power…

When the plot shifted, Anatol's ships were gone.

* * *

EXTRA! MIGHT IS RIGHT, ORIELI DEMONSTRATE
A FALLING OUT BETWEEN ALLIES?
NASA SENDING A SPY MISSION TO THE MOON
SECURITY COUNCIL—AN IMPOTENT MOUTHPIECE?
ALIENS, GO HOME!

"Jack Willison reporting from the CNN center in New York. Are the Orieli muscle flexing, or giving someone a warning? According to NASA, Phobos completely vaporized, and scientists are at a loss to explain how an energy beam can instantly reach Mars from the sun. That might be very interesting for the boys at NASA and CalTech, but closer to home there is something more immediate to think about. Almost two hours ago, people again lined the streets, this time watching the enormous Orieli mother ship as it drifted slowly out of a cloudy New York sky. Almost nine hundred meters in length, it hovered above the United Nations building like a thundercloud. Watching it, I cannot help but wonder at the Orieli's version of non-interference."

* * *

"Archbishop Waller said today that God does not necessarily fight on the side with the most artillery. However, he is extremely interested to find out whether the Orieli hold Christian principles.

"The Leave Earth Alone society today marched before the UN building in protest at this latest alien appearance. The Vision of God sect marched in protest of the Leave Earth Alone protest. Police bundled both downtown. This is Mark Rown for NBC news."

* * *

"Muscle flexing, Da Skolski? That's a bit melodramatic,

isn't it?" Arlon remarked quietly.

"And what would you call it, sir?" The UN member for the Russian Federation spluttered in cultured American English.

"I would call it a system test, Da. We're not infallible."

"A somewhat extreme example, Karhide. Was it a necessary one?" Nikita Bandrik asked. An approving ripple of assent went around the table.

Bandrik tried to bring this meeting to the General Assembly floor. The six permanent members of the Security Council would have none of it. Unpalatable as the fact was, the Security Council still wielded the real power behind the UN. Most of the General Assembly members were outraged, of course, and understandably so. At least Bandrik managed to ensure they held the meeting under the glare of publicity. He hated to stoop to covert manipulation, but he did not hesitate to use this opportunity to achieve his ends.

This very meeting would strengthen his motion to make the Security Council subordinate to the General Assembly. Of course, while most of the UN funding continued to be provided by the permanent members, curtailing their power had its dangers. If it came to a crunch, could he count on India and the new South American blocks? Probably not. They may have the political will, but not the necessary economic and financial muscle. Still, precipitated by the alien visit, they made that small, but vital step.

"It was necessary, Da Secretary, to verify the operational status of the grid. The consequence of failure in case of Kran incursion would be catastrophic. In any event, no harm has been done to Earth."

"I disagree, sir," Dr. Doryel spoke sharply, sitting next to the American UN ambassador. "Harm has been done to Earth. Your very presence has caused harm." The pencil eyebrows arched as he looked around the table to a murmur of assent.

"In what way, Doctor?"

"I only have to look at Mars to see it. As for Earth, you

171

appear in your small shiny ship, and bald as brass, you tell us that we're now under the benevolent protection of the Orieli; sanctioned by the Serrll Combine, whatever that means. We're supposed to be suitably impressed and grateful not to ask too many awkward questions. Well, sir, when our social structure, our religions and our political institutions are disrupted, you tell us that no harm has been done. All this on some remote possibility of a hypothetical attack by an unknown enemy sometime in our future? It won't wash."

Arlon and Tavac exchanged glances. Terr knew what they were thinking. He thought the same thing. Here was one smart item who had put his finger right on the problem. If the Orieli were prepared to protect Earth under any circumstance, why the need to inform Earth and unnecessarily inflame the Serrll? Terr couldn't figure out why the Orieli were so anxious to advertise themselves.

Something that Dhar said during their briefing with Enllss kept bothering him. It had to do with alien contact procedures. No, there was something else. *Rit!* He just couldn't remember it.

"Very eloquent, Doctor. Please go on," Arlon prompted after a moment of silence.

"You claim non-interference. Yet, you go around our system turning Phobos into slag. What next? Another base? Another demonstration? Where is the cooperation we expect from an ally? You want us to spread the word to the rest of the world saying what nice guys you are. Well, we want tangible return for the right of allowing you to stay on the Moon."

An angry buzz went around the table, accompanied by a lot of nodding of heads and hostile glances directed at Arlon. The Australian Security Council president rapped his gavel and managed to reestablish order.

"And what would you have us do, Dr. Doryel?" Arlon asked at length. "Heal your sick? Feed your hungry? Educate your ignorant and pray for your dead? Unfortunately, gentle-men, this you will have to do yourself. The Solar System is yours, when you're in a position to take it. As far as our base is concerned, you have no rights."

Silence hung heavy in the room. A fly buzzed overhead and a faint sigh of air-conditioning filled the background. Arlon slowly stood up, placed both hands on the table and looked at the suddenly tense faces around him.

"You want tangible return?" he asked softly and his tongue ran quickly around his lips. "You get the freedom of Earth."

* * *

NON-INTERFERENCE, ALIEN POLICY
POOR OF THE WORLD UP IN ARMS
VATICAN DENOUNCES ALIENS AS DESTROYERS OF FAITH
DEMONSTRATIONS SWAMP THE WHITE HOUSE

"Jack Willison reporting for CNN. After a special closed session of the permanent Security Council members, faces were grim when the meeting with the aliens finally broke up. Rumors of attempted arm bending by the United States were fiercely denied. For once, the Russian ambassador declined to com-ment. Shortly after the meeting the huge Orieli ship lifted off, supposedly returning home, followed by hundreds of private aircraft as it glided slowly above New York. What will it bring the next time it comes?"

* * *

"Religious groups around town are making an exodus to the mountains, proclaiming the end of the world in thirty days. The chosen will await salvation as close to God as they can climb, while leaving their earthly wealth to the Church. Mean-while, business is booming for one-time artists peddling bibles, icons, rosaries and holy water to the salvation seekers. This is Mark Rown for NBC news."

Chapter Nine

When Terr tried to move his head, sharp lances of pain stabbed through his eyes. Sprawled face down on the deck, he dragged his arm from under his body. He grimaced as pins and needles produced a few seconds of exquisite torture. The damned thing had fallen asleep on him. His head throbbed. He clamped his teeth and gingerly moved his hand to the back of his head. Feeling the greasy mess, he didn't have to have it spelled out to know it was blood.

He propped himself up on one elbow, leaving a smear of dark blood on the deck, and looked around: empty couches, data displays, and repeater holoviews. The mainframe plot was a blank plate. He knew he was in a dart and probably in flight.

"Cent Comp copy?" he mumbled and winced as somebody screwed down the vice around his head.

"Ready."

"Report status."

"All systems nominal. Operating under quarter secondary boost. Tactical caution. Under the current unspecified flight plan, destination parameters are uncoordinated. Unchecked orbital insertion in three point-two minutes."

Unchecked insertion? That meant a long dive with no future at the bottom. His mouth went all cottony then, but he still managed to think furiously. He could not have been unconscious very long, then. What he wanted to know, with its autonomous shield net up, could an RV/4 dart survive a headlong smash into a planet? What about the backups and safety systems? He knew the central housekeeping computer at the Orieli base monitored all flights by its auxiliary units. Departure from normal flight parameters brought instant clamor and a raft of warning messages. He had seen it tested. Since the dart computer did not protest, he assumed the VI coupling was disabled, including some of the dart's own housekeeping functions…or were overwritten.

"Mainframe plot, tactical." His head throbbing, he hoped the computer could reestablish the personal VI link.

"Unable to comply. Command functions inactive."

"Abort current flight plan!"

"Unable to comply. Second-level override disabled."

"Emergency override! The ship is on a terminal flight path."

"Unable to comply. Command functions inactive."

"Rit!"

Well, that was that.

Dhar had gone to a lot of trouble to see to it that he arrived at the planned destination, the slimy son of a canal worm. Without the necessary command codes to unlock the computer, there wasn't a thing he could do to check the dart's flight, or the time to do it.

Thinking dark and evil thoughts, Terr clutched the edge of the couch. With nothing more than a stifled groan, he dragged himself up and sagged into its yielding form. He waited a few moments until the throbbing in his head subsided before opening his eyes, then scanned the main repeater plot. Almost full, Earth stood out blue-white and brilliant, moving closer even as he watched it.

What crapped him off, he made it so easy for Dhar. In frustration, he slammed his fist against the armrest.

No one could approach him with murderous intent without the shadow within which he walked rearing its head in warning. He could see Dhar even now, standing beside him while he preflighted the dart for a supposedly routine proficiency hop to check out that he had all his procedures down cold. Seems he couldn't even *die* without following procedures.

Some things remained the same no matter whose uniform one wore.

It was also his solo flight. Dhar and Farly came to wish him luck. He played it down, although excited as a kid with a new toy to take apart. Even the prospect of facing some of Farly's surprises during the flight, which just had to be there, didn't faze him. Dhar hung back, smiling, and Terr felt comforted by his brother's presence.

When Farly left, Dhar struck.

Why, my brother? I trusted you, damn you!

He swallowed, the lump going down hard, still not believing this it was happening. He didn't mind the hurt. That would heal—if he lived, unlikely as that seemed at the moment, but the pain he felt inside was a heaviness of Death itself.

The three minutes went awfully quick. The dart hurtled toward sunrise, already biting through the upper atmosphere. A sleeping village would perhaps hear the tortured scream of air before they died. It could be a city, still and waiting as the fireball grew, then the terrible rending shockwave.

"Tactical caution," the computer went on remorselessly. "Insertion point. Impact in four seconds."

The Pacific was all a shade of emerald greens and violet blues. The sun flared over the Sierras as they rushed up to meet him. He did not move. Whatever questions he had, he would now take with him. He stared at the holoview and waited. It was easy to die. He didn't know what those other hero types made such a fuss about.

The cliffs reached for him.

"I'm sorry, Teena," he whispered just before he augured in.

* * *

Aktalkul sat leaning against a boulder watching his goats. They looked contented grazing on the lush mountainside meadow. The sun had barely risen above the ridge, casting low, black shadows. The valley silent beneath its blanket of mist. The air tasted sharp and clean and he breathed deeply. It was going to be hot later, but now it was quiet and peaceful. Goats locking horns and bleating at the sky broke the peace.

The sound stole into his awareness, growing ominously louder. Puzzled, he cast his eyes across the heavens. Jets seldom ventured across the mountains. It came out of darkness shrouded in orange fire. He knew something about meteorites and saw many at night, but this was something different. With growing anxiety, he stood up and watched the growing fireball. The goats stopped feeding and were stomping nervously. The air stilled, hushed and waiting.

A rumble like dying thunder stole through his bones. Aktalkul crouched behind a boulder, anxiously watching the fireball as it plunged down. It hung there for an instant, then the heavens split. The flash glared naked against the mountain. Shadows jumped and the roar reached him with the shockwave. A painful grip squeezed his chest. When he opened his mouth to scream, nothing came. The mountain trembled. The air whistled and roared in anguish through the valleys. It plucked at his clothes and his body. Clouds of dust filled the air.

Able to breathe again, Aktalkul crossed himself and murmured a prayer. A mushroom cloud writhed and twisted as it climbed. Dust boiled within its expanding head. Sand, stones and pebbles rained around him as muted thunder rolled across the valleys. His goats were scattered over the plateau, huddled in twos and threes. He looked at the mushroom cloud and wondered.

* * *

Aktalkul picked his way among the boulders and stood at the lip of the crater. A dark cloud towered above him, angry at his intrusion. Flashes of lightning darted within its twisting head. He hesitated even then, wondering whether he dared

178

tempt the gods.

Everything in sight was dead, burnt, and blackened. Smoke curled slowly from charred trees and shrubs. It was very quiet, without a breath of wind. Below him lay the crater. It was huge, wide as a playing field, its bottom lost in smoke and dust. One side of the mountain was completely blown away exposing shining cliffs. The ground trembled beneath his feet, rumbling in protest. Slowly, he made his way down.

Nervous sweat beaded his forehead by the time he reached the bottom. He cursed the rashness that brought him here and he kept glancing over his shoulder to check on possible demons that might be following. He crossed himself, muttering an ancient litany. He also made a quick prayer to the saints. It couldn't hurt.

Light broke in sheets through the smoke, revealing fused rock and sand. He picked his way gingerly between the hot areas and walked toward the center. Then the dust lifted and he stopped in his tracks. Large, wide as a house, it lay partly buried. It gleamed dull blue and had blue-black and red markings.

He walked closer, staring openmouthed at the strange machine. Not far from the machine lay a body, one arm reaching out for something. Aktalkul felt fear deep in his stomach and he crossed himself quickly. What manner of creatures would rush out and descend on him? Pity overcame fear as he looked at the injured being. He walked uncertainly toward the body and wondered how anyone could survive such a crash. A low agonized moan came from the creature and he stopped and watched as the alien tried to raise himself. Pain twisted its drawn face and the eyes stared at Aktalkul.

"Please...help..." the creature whispered and sank back into the dust.

Aktalkul gingerly moved closer and knelt beside the alien. He removed the gourd from his shoulder and brought the water to the other's lips. Some went down. Most of it trickled over the indigo uniform. The alien coughed and opened his eyes,

179

then his head sagged into Aktalkul's lap.

* * *

Twin-tailed jets skimmed low over the mountain. Aktalkul watched uncertainly as they circled. Their wings glittered as they maneuvered above him. Following the jets, two green helicopters, their enormous blades clattering, swung around the mushroom cloud and sedately settled at the edge of the crater. The blades whooshed, raising more dust from which uniformed men began to pour. They stationed themselves around the helicopters, their rifles ready.

A group of officers, civilians and soldiers scrambled down and slowly walked to where Aktalkul stood. He looked at the streaking jets, the helicopters, the men with their well-oiled rifles, and wished he were back with his goats. The officer leading the group said something to a young lieutenant who saluted and moved briskly toward the alien machine. More soldiers with rifles held ready followed after the lieutenant.

The soldiers reached Aktalkul and formed a semicircle around him. The beribboned officer, a full bird colonel, looked at the alien and pointed at a captain who quickly walked closer and knelt beside the body, his medical bag beside him. Aktalkul watched with interest.

"Major?" the colonel barked at the assistant standing beside him.

"Sir!"

"Establish an exclusion perimeter a klick all around. Block all access roads. I don't want a bird getting through without you knowing about it. Maintain a CAP with the Apaches in case some nosy news helo thinks the restrictions don't apply to him. Copy that?"

"Sir!"

"Right, get on with it." The colonel nodded and frowned at the two ungainly UH-60 Blackhawk troop helicopters, their blades still turning slowly.

Just then, three AH-64 Apache gunships flew overhead. Heavily armored, carrying laser-guided Hellfire antitank missiles, unguided rockets, a 30mm cannon, and an array of sensors, it was a formidable all-weather day or night fighting platform.

Satisfied, he turned to Aktalkul.

"What is your name, senior?" the colonel inquired pleasantly, voice deep, used to command. His face craggy, ugly-handsome that women found appealing. That appeal cost him a marriage and maybe a set of stars to replace the eagles on his shoulders. He had become resigned to both.

"I just saw it come down, that is all. I do nothing," Aktalkul said and wrung his hands.

"What were you doing here?"

"Minding my goats. I do nothing!"

The officer raised his hand. "Okay, okay." He turned to one of the civilians looking around the crater. "Doctor Raydon? Do you want to question him?"

"Eh? Thanks, Colonel." The older man looked frankly at Aktalkul, drew a pipe from his vest pocket and proceeded to suck on it. He had a small pinched face and a balding head. His movements were short and precise as though measured by a calculator. For all that, he looked friendly.

"Now, amigo mio," he said soothingly. "You said you saw it come down, right? Care to tell me about it?" His pipe puffed into life and clouds of aromatic smoke hovered around him.

"Well, senor, I was looking after my goats, as I said," Aktalkul began haltingly, then warmed to his story. "Still early and the sun, she was just peeking over the mountain. There was a noise and a great fireball came from the west." He indicated with his hands and the civilian nodded. "There was an explosion and much wind. The ground trembled. After the wind go, I come to see. I find the strange machine and this man. I give him water and then you come."

"Now, let me get this straight. You found him like this? You didn't take him out of that machine?"

"No, senor." Aktalkul shook his head vehemently. "I find him here."

"What made you come here?"

Aktalkul shrugged, wishing he hadn't. "I only wanted to see, senor."

"Mmm. Thank you, amigo."

"You welcome. Can I go? My goats, see."

The colonel coughed and moved in. "You'll have to come with us, just for a while."

"Why?"

"You need to be checked out for radiation exposure. Just to be safe. We'll notify your family. Don't worry about it."

Aktalkul did not like it at all. What will happen to his goats?

"Colonel?" The medical man looked up from the body.

"What is it, Captain?"

"Doesn't look like he suffered anything major; contusions and abrasions mostly. Except for a cut and a lump back of his head. It could be a possible concussion. We should move him to the isolation facility right away."

"In a moment, Captain."

The young lieutenant walked up and saluted. "I checked it out, sir. The craft is completely intact. There aren't even any scratches on its underbelly. Given that it slid over some sharp rocks, there should have been *some* damage. No sign of an entrance either."

"Any residuals?"

"The place is clean," the lieutenant said, his eyes flickering to Aktalkul.

The colonel grunted and looked questioningly at the civilian puffing contentedly beside him.

"Any ideas, Doctor?"

The man sucked on his pipe and shook his head. "Frankly Colonel, I would only be guessing. Probably shielded by some sort of a force field, I would imagine. Judging by the size of the impact crater, the thing must have been going at a hell of a clip. Lucky for us it landed where it did. Think of the frightful mess if it plowed through a town. At any rate, we'll have to wait for him to fill us in," he said and pointed at the alien.

"Yeah," the colonel muttered, his eyes glued on the ship. "When can you begin your investigation, Doc?"

"Pretty much—"

"I want to see the inside of that thing."

"—right away. We have most of the necessary equipment with us."

"Then get started. If there is anyone or anything you need, let me know. Lieutenant, you look after the Doctor here."

"Sir!"

"Right." The colonel looked at the alien and pointed at the waiting stretcher-bearers. "Get him into the chopper. Come with me, senor."

* * *

SPACESHIP CRASHES IN THE SIERRAS!
EARTHQUAKES ALONG SAN-ANDREAS FAULT RESULT OF ALIEN CRASH?
WHERE ARE THE SURVIVORS?
ANOTHER ALIEN DEMONSTRATION?

"Jack Willison reporting for CNN. An impenetrable lid of security has been clamped around the New Mexico impact crater caused by the crashed alien spaceship. A cordon of grim-looking MPs are stopping everyone from approaching the crater. This is undoubtedly as much a measure to hold back the curiosity seekers, as not wishing to waste time in taking advantage of the opportunity that fell into NASA's lap, as it were, to look over the ship.

"The Russian Federation has filed an official protest with

Washington and the UN when their scientific team was refused permission to visit the site. The Russians and the Chinese are warning the US against unilateral exploitation of any technology that might be gained from the alien ship. Such an attempt they said, would lead to serious deterioration in relations between their countries. They went on to cite the incident with the Comalcalco saucer that brought China and the US close to the brink five years ago. Tongue in cheek the American ambassador to the UN announced that the US fully supports an international mission under UN auspices to properly investigate the crash site and the alien ship. Knowing how long these things take to organize, the US is clearly hoping to learn as much as it can during the confusion and before the Serrll or the Orieli mount a recovery mission."

* * *

"Archbishop Waller scathingly attacked publishing houses for flooding the market with books dealing with extraterrestrial visitations. He called this an open threat against the Church and Christianity, commanding the faithful to resist the profiteering motives of the publishers. Are the foundations of the Church so weak that they're unable to resist simple commercial opportunism?

"The Vision of God sect claims the Air Force shot down the alien ship and challenges the President to deny it. The President's press secretary flatly denied any military involvement with the crash. This was received with skeptical jeers from the sect organizers protesting outside the White House. Meanwhile the Leave Earth Alone society is making an exodus to the crash site, promising to destroy the alien ship, claiming, 'They will leave us alone after this'. This is Mark Rown for NBC news."

* * *

With Shadow and Thunder

Opturkarh Tavac sat with hands folded across his chest, eyes keenly appraising the figure standing rigidly before him. A shadowy moonscape outlined the silent form. The office had little in the way of decoration: a low-contoured desk, loose couches, and half-empty shelves. The VI coupling provided everything else.

Finally, Tavac placed his hands on the empty desk and stood up.

"Taroptur Dharaklin, I will not even attempt to understand or seek your justification for what you have done. You willfully placed the life of a fellow officer, presumably your friend, in grave danger. You also performed an act of sabotage, causing the possible loss of a valuable craft. I can understand that merely changing a uniform has not changed your loyalties to the Serrll, but you betrayed that as well. By indulging in your particular brand of gamesmanship, you allowed one of our darts to fall into Earth's hands, creating a potentially unstable situation. Da, if you were one of my own, I would have you in VI isolation for the next hundred years!"

Tavac stared at Dhar's impassive face, trying to find some emotion and saw none.

"I have advised Commissioner Enllss-rr of your actions. An M-4 will be here in five days to remove you from this base and affect your replacement, as well as replacement of Opturkarh Terrllss-rr. Do you have anything to say?"

Dhar had a lot to say. In the end, what *could* he say? He had betrayed Orieli's trust, as he knew he would have to from the very beginning—as Enllss had known, and probably Anabb as well. Worse still, he has betrayed Sankri's trust. *My brother, I had no choice.*

"No, sir. I have nothing to say," he said heavily.

Tavac nodded. "Cent Comp copy?"

"Ready."

"Log entry. Temporary status of Second Scout Dharaklin

as Taroptur in the Orieli Space Arm is revoked. Effective immediately. Level two access privileges only."

"Entry noted."

"Second Scout, until the arrival of Serrll authorities, you may stay here or elect to be repatriated to the Serrll Moon Base."

"With respect, sir, I wish to remain here," Dhar said, his voice husky.

"Very well. While here, you will wear your Scout Fleet uniform, Da. That is all."

It had been that simple.

Dharaklin stood in the darkness of the base's observation lounge. He stared at the profusion of stars arching above the jagged lunar peaks. He felt empty and drained, trying in vain to preserve some sense of perspective, unable to find any. Somewhere in the labyrinthine corridors of Captal, someone would plot his action into a computer, a small datum in the tactical struggle between the powers. Would that same person note the emotional down payment he'd had to make to compromise the teachings of his master and the Discipline? Somehow, he doubted it.

Heart heavy, he longed for the feel of hot sands running through his fingers and the sight of amber skies burning under a noon sun. In the cool of the evening, he wanted to smell the spicy tang of tarad grass and listen to the whisper of peelath leaves. The desert was a cleanser, stripping away the veneer of artificiality. He needed its purity now.

The image was there in his mind. All he needed to do was step through and he would have peace—more likely an escape. There would be no peace or escape for him until he faced Sankri. As he knew he must.

Reality shifted and he found himself in the shadow of Athal Than, beneath the desert stars of the Saffal. Above him, he beheld the bent image of Amulran the Damned holding up eternity. Behind him the Stalker stood frozen, waiting to loose the arrow of doom at his enemy that would topple everything into chaos.

Ending eternity seemed a small price to pay for betraying a friendship.

He understood the image all too well. Reality rippled again and he saw himself standing in a sterile room looking down at a still form lying on a medical bed. He waited a long time before reaching out with his arm. The aura surrounding the form changed subtly.

"Sankri, my brother," he whispered sadly, then recoiled in shock as Death reared its hand between them in the shape of coiled blue lightnings.

Terr moaned and shifted, his face contorted as in pain. Shaken, Dhar withdrew, the warning of the gods haunting his thoughts.

In the silence of the observation lounge, he allowed himself a long exhale. In performing his duty to Enllss, he might have damaged Serrll's relations with the Orieli, playing into Sargon's hands. Someone said that when fighting for freedom, you have to be prepared to pay any price, even your honor. He found scant comfort there, and he did not really believe that crap. Once lost, honor was merely a veneer of expediency. He had known that even as he started spying for Anar'on and the Unified Independent Front.

Right now, he cared little for the political fallout of his actions compared to the cost of having wounded the soul of his brother.

* * *

A fly buzzed somewhere overhead. It droned aimlessly, then stopped. Just as well. A sound of muffled footsteps came from outside, faintly echoing, hushed voices, and more footsteps. Terr opened his eyes. He blinked against the harsh light and ended up staring at an open window. Wide gauzy curtains swayed gently in the cool breeze. Two potted plants lined the wall beneath the windowsill. Beyond it, he saw a gray sky dotted with white fluff.

He allowed his gaze wander around the room: surf green walls, white ceiling with a pair of double fluorescent tubes, a small table and two chairs in one corner. A familiar smell of antiseptic lingered in the air. He knew that smell well. A telemetry board blinked solemnly beside the bed, tracing silent graph lines in the monitor.

He wore a white one-piece, short-sleeved gown fastened at the back. He was naked underneath. Raising the cotton sheet, he wriggled his toes. All there. Goosebumps ran down his arms and he wished someone had kept the window closed. He wondered how long he had been here.

Lying there, his mind slowly filled with rage, suspended between his yesterdays and the bleak emptiness of his tomorrows. He sighed and felt a weight in his chest that wouldn't go away.

Why, Nightwings, my brother?

Hands clasped behind his head, he summoned Dhar's image, taking in every line and every shade of his skin. He had opened himself to him without reservation. Dhar was closer to him than any other being. Teena was flesh of his flesh, but Dhar was soul of his soul. If Dhar said die for me, he wouldn't have even hesitated. Had Dhar not walked the corridors of his subconscious to bring him back from whatever hell he had been? His life was Dhar's for the taking, but not like this!

What could have compelled Dhar to raise his hand against him and violate the teachings of the Discipline? Ends and means? Wasn't that what they discussed on the way to Salina? Was all this about Gashkarali? Which would mean Dhar indeed worked for Terchran.

That stopped him for a moment. Terr simply could not see his brother stepping down into the gutter with the Servatory Party. Who then? Who would benefit if he suddenly faded out of sight? On the other hand, was this directed at him? Sargon wouldn't shed any tears if the Orieli and the Revisionists were embarrassed over this.

In the end, his suspicions didn't matter. All he knew, Dhar betrayed him; betrayed everything Terr believed could never happen, and the pain he felt wouldn't leave him.

He turned his head to one side and covered his eyes with his hand.

Something shifted within him then, like an awakening, cold and impersonal. The veneer of innocence cracked and fell away to expose the hard and cynical part of his other self whose heart was ice and the face stone.

In whatever hell we find one another, there will be a reckoning, my brother, Terr promised himself.

Sometime later, he tried to sit up and groaned as pain shot through his head. He sagged against the pillow. The door opened right on cue and the quacks walked in. They both wore white lab coats studded with pens. One had a shiny pink bald patch surrounded by a shock of white hair streaked with gray. He sported a chubby round face hung with steel spectacles on a fleshy red nose. The other was young with a touch of frost around the eyes. He had a thin severe mouth and a suspicious stare. Terr labeled him the executive type. All he needed was a briefcase.

"Awake, eh?" the older man boomed pleasantly. "I'm Doctor Wald, Opturkarh. Or is it Commander? No matter. I'm your mentor for the duration." He glanced at the telemetry board and grunted. "You'll live," he said indifferently.

"Was there any doubt?" Terr asked.

"Guess not. You seem ruggedly healthy, but then…"

"Yeah, you can never tell."

"Alien physiology was never my best subject. Give it another day or so and we'll have you up and about."

Another day or so? Terr began to wonder how badly hurt he really was. "Okay, Doc, give it to me straight."

"Well, apart from a nasty cut on your head, lacerations, and some superficial burns, you're okay."

"You don't know what a relief that is, Doc. I thought it was something serious."

Wald looked at Terr in surprise then laughed. "We had 'em worse, young feller. Now," he said, rubbing his hands with a rasp. "What do we feed you? You didn't leave a menu last time you called," he said accusingly. "We've been giving you glucose and water and stuff for the last two days. Not good."

"Two days?"

"Yep. You tell us what you want, young feller, and we'll do the rest. Suit you?"

"I guess so," Terr said and smiled at this strange friendly man. "You could start by closing that window over there and getting me another blanket."

"Eh?" Wald turned his head at the open window and glared at his assistant. The window got closed.

"Suit you? About the menu…"

"Let's see…citrus fruits and animal proteins are off the list. No chemical additives or colorings of any type. If you're think-ing of supplements, vitamins in small doses, excluding the vit-amin C group. As you might have gathered, excess in the C group will do frightful things to my body chemistry. I guess carbohydrates, fats, and most sugars are okay. I think that should about do it."

"Fine," Wald boomed and turned to his sidekick. "Got that?"

"Yes, Doctor."

"By the way?" Terr looked at them. "Where am I?"

"Why, the Johnson Space Center, Houston," Wald said. "We had you in the lunar isolation ward the first day. Running tests and stuff. I had them bring you here once the tests proved negative. It seems you've been immunized against just about everything we have. Remarkable. Well, if you had the guts to step out into New York's air unprotected, you must have been well prepared. Umm, there is a government stuffed shirt and some military big wheel outside anxious to see you if you feel up to it. I can tell them no, Commander."

"Might as well." Terr shrugged. "Thanks, anyway."

"Don't mention it. If they start getting obnoxious, press the button beside the bed. If it's still connected," Wald added and walked out chuckling.

Terr tried to figure it out, but wasn't given the chance. The two items had walked in. One a four-star general with a burnt-out cigar stuck in a corner of his mouth. His piercing brown eyes looked at Terr with predatory interest. The other a bouncer-type civilian who looked vaguely familiar wearing a polished smile and bright, even teeth. Terr had him pegged as a government flunkey. He looked the type.

"Opturkarh Terrllss-rr," said the marine formally. "Allow me to present Doctor Doryel, the president's National Security Advisor."

"The man with the awkward questions," Terr said, remembering him.

Doryel smiled thinly and nodded.

"And I am General Cannon, Chairman of the Joint Chiefs."

"I guess this is where we trot out the fancy speeches, General, but I'm fresh out." Terr had him pegged the minute he walked in. He knew what they wanted.

"No need for speeches, Commander. Just some answers."

"No promises."

"We shall see."

The battle lines were drawn.

"Opturkarh…that's quite a handle. May I call you Terr?" Doryel put his polished smile to best use. Terr nodded. "Our government would like to know how you came to crash. I trust you can appreciate our interest and concern."

Terr could certainly appreciate their interest. He figured their concern would only last until they managed to get inside the dart. On the other hand, the guy could be sincere. Miracles

191

happened all the time.

There was a moment of uncomfortable silence that he did nothing to shorten. How could he tell them it was through the hand of a brother? How could he tell them of treasured memories now shattered and gone? How could he tell them of the hurt that wouldn't go away?

"I was on a training flight," he told them truthfully. "I had a computer malfunction which locked my controls. There was nothing I could do."

"And your injuries?"

Terr shrugged. "Jumping into the crater, I suppose. I don't remember that part too well."

"I see." The two exchanged glances. "There *is* one thing that has been bothering me, Terr," Doryel said smoothly.

"And what's that, Doctor?"

"How is it your Orieli friends haven't come to pick you up? If this is some sort of test—"

"A good one, Doc, but unlikely. Maybe they don't know I'm missing?"

"This is a very serious matter, Commander," Cannon growled. "Don't treat it lightly."

This was getting more difficult than Terr had imagined. "Look, General, I appreciate you having me patched up and all. If you would only take me back to my ship—"

"You're not well enough to be moved." Cannon smiled by way of an apology.

"I see. Am I your prisoner then?"

"That's a very unpleasant way of putting it."

"Then how would you put it, sir?"

Cannon dragged out the stump of his cigar and pointed it at Terr. "Look, Commander, please don't misunderstand us. No one is threatening you."

Terr patted the covers and gave him a trusting smile. "General, just to make sure there is no misunderstanding, let me make it easy for you. At the UN, with the glare of the world press on us, everybody was nice and polite. Things are different now. You suddenly have an uninvited alien on your hands and you're not quite sure what to do with him. Letting him run around could be awkward. No telling what could happen. The best thing to do is to keep him away from any excitement and wait it out, see what develops with his Serrll and Orieli friends. Don't worry, General, I'm not annoyed. I would have done the same thing. Then there is this matter of my ship, isn't there? Now we have added another dimension to the problem."

"What the devil do you mean?" Cannon said, suddenly on guard.

"Come, General. I know what you want. You must also know that I cannot allow you access to the kind of technology that ship represents. It would create an unacceptable polarity in the Earth's balance of power. You cannot risk a possible confrontation with the other major Earth powers, and we certainly won't permit it. Remember Comalcalco five years ago?"

"*You* were the one who destroyed that ship?"

"If I hadn't, the United States was about to enter into a nuclear exchange with China."

"Rubbish!"

"Perhaps, but a possibility the Serrll needed to eliminate. After all, it *was* our ship."

"Which you carelessly left behind. Do you have any idea the industries that never got off the ground because of your meddling?"

"You're doing well enough, General, with the startups using data taken from the ship before I had it destroyed. And here we are, faced with the same problem all over again. Except that this time, the Serrll is prepared to intervene openly. As for the ship, it can take care of itself."

Cannon and Doryel looked at each other and Terr gave a hearty laugh. "You must have tried everything except blowing it up. Let me confirm your worst fears. Without me, you'll never get the ship open and I will never open it willingly. I'll let it rot

193

first, not that it ever would."

"We're not barbarians," Doryel allowed a touch of temper to creep into his voice.

"Precisely."

"You could show us, teach us."

Terr yawned and settled back into the pillows. "I'm tired. Oxygen-rich atmosphere, excitement, you know."

"You have your rest, Terr," Doryel said with a grin. "We shall talk again."

"I'm sure of it."

Cannon clamped his teeth on the cigar, saluted, and stomped out.

"I guess he doesn't like me." Terr managed to sound hurt.

"It's a complicated problem you dumped in our lap, Terr."

"Only if you make it so."

Doryel nodded and held out his hand. In his palm, he held a small brown sphere the size of a silver dollar. "Perhaps you could tell us what this is? We found it in your uniform pocket."

It was Terr's energy sphere. He cursed silently, unable to get his hands on it, not wanting to summon Death to get it. The Orieli issued each of the Serrll team with one of the things. A psionic device with a hundred-and-one uses: shield generator, energy weapon, light and heat source, and lots of other things. The catch, he had to be in physical contact with it to make it work. Terr would have given his right arm for it.

"That?" He looked at Doryel. "Never seen it in my life."

"I see. A curious thing to be carrying around. Feels warm to the touch," Doryel said, playing with the thing. "Do you have everything you need?"

"Doctor Wald is taking good care of me."

"I am pleased to hear it."

Terr propped himself up.

"Doc, before you go, please consider carefully the posture of your military. What happens to me is not important compared to Earth's future relations with the Serrll. Don't allow expediency to overrule what your political judgment must surely be telling you is an unwise course of action. When the Orieli come looking for me, and they will, what will you tell them?"

Doryel studied Terr for a long minute, weighing his words.

"You put your case eloquently, Commander. Nonetheless, the Orieli are not here and you are. If you will excuse me?"

"Of course," Terr said and smiled as Doryel walked out.

His smile faded as the door closed.

Rit!

* * *

"Incredible." Cannon stared in fascination as the sphere turned dull black under the fluorescent lamp.

Doctor Raydon switched off the lamp and smiled with satisfaction as the sphere turned brown again. His teeth clicked against the pipe stem as he shifted it to the other side of his mouth.

"Indeed."

"Does it absorb all EMR wavelengths, Doctor?" Cannon demanded, still staring at the sphere.

Raydon's eyebrows climbed and his eyes flickered at Doryel. "Very astute, General. Indeed it does. We put it in a black box once. With no energy input, the surface of the sphere turned into a perfect reflector, but it's selective. Damnedest thing I ever saw."

Cannon looked sharply at Raydon. "What do you mean, selective?"

"It's opaque in the visible spectrum, of course. Otherwise we wouldn't be able to see the thing."

"You tried lasing it?"

"We got nothing that made any sense. What you have here, General, is a device probably operated by nanometer-sized assemblies running molecular circuitry nets. I suspect the thing is half alive."

"Tell me, Doctor." Doryel picked up the sphere from the desk and fondled it. "If this thing absorbs energy, at some point it will reach overload. What then?"

Raydon shrugged. "I would imagine safety circuits exist to prevent that."

"But what does the thing *do*?"

"You got me there, General."

"Okay," Cannon said and raised both hands. "You can tinker with it later. What I really want to know is when are you gonna crack the lock on Terr's ship?"

Raydon sucked on his pipe. "Better be prepared for the worst, General. I'm beginning to suspect that Commander Terr might be right. Nothing we tried so far has worked."

"Impertinent whippersnapper! I will not be dictated to. What's holding things up? Can't you cut the hull? There is no substance invented that can stand up to a laser drill."

"We cannot cut it because we cannot get *at* it."

"What the hell are you talking about?"

"It's driving us wild. You see, every second or so there is a pulse of energy emitted from the hull. It's like three-sixty-degree radar, a spherical sensor blanket if you will. If anything starts moving toward the ship, the activation interval becomes shorter. When an object reaches a certain terminal speed a force field activates to protect the hull. We fired a laser at it. No effect."

"Crap!" Cannon said. "How can it beat a laser?"

Raydon smiled thinly. "I am postulating a faster-than-light reaction time, General."

Cannon stared at him. "You're shitting me. Instead of using something fancy, why don't you simply cut it with a torch, or drill through it?"

"We tried, believe me. We managed to burn away a layer or two of what looked like paint, but that was about it. The underlying hull didn't even get warm. A diamond scrape suggests the thing is constructed of some polymer matrix that's part ceramic, organic, and metallic. After a few seconds the surrounding material began to flow and the scrape healed itself. I think the ship is made of the same kind of stuff as that sphere."

Cannon growled, mauling his cigar. "What are we talking about here, Doctor?"

Raydon gave a small shrug. "General, Space Command reported that ship coming in at better than twenty-eight miles per second. Even then, I think it was only cruising. If that wasn't extraordinary enough, it crashes into a mountain without sustaining a scratch. Compared to that, you shouldn't be surprised that we haven't managed to pry it open. We're a bunch of savages standing around a tin can trying to invent the equivalent of a can opener."

"A can opener, eh? Crap!" Cannon snorted and turned to Doryel. "I want to talk to Commander Terr."

Chapter Ten

Hands clasped behind his back, Terr stared at the complex below, the sky streaked dirty gray. He could see dark lines slant toward the ground where it rained. There were few visitors along the sidewalks. The wind keened softly, a lost mournful sound that was somehow depressing. A squall moved in, blurring outlines and whipped branches into a frenzy. Large heavy drops struck the glass, smearing the world outside. He listened to the cry of the wind and waited.

He could see his reflection in the streaked glass. The eyes stared back at him, cold and hard, mouth a thin, grim line. The face drawn, devoid of humor. Not that he had a hell of a lot to chuckle about. The heaviness he felt, only a dull throb now, almost comforting. It fed the shadow of his other self, making it stronger. For what he intended, he would need that strength. He raised his right hand and stared at the sleeve of his uniform. Indigo blue and alien, not the familiar working gray. That is probably where he made his first mistake. He trusted the Orieli to protect him, forgetting the first rule of undercover work: you don't trust anyone.

As a consequence, the second mistake was even easier to make. He trusted Dhar, but it was hard to see how he could have avoided that one.

The lined face of his master wavered before him and he swept the image away. At this point, he didn't need a reminder to tell him the path on which he now trod was black and its purpose dark. He ground his teeth, his thoughts seething. He no longer tried to understand why his brother betrayed him.

Dhar had broken the faith and everything he believed impossible, as was the idea of Dhar attempting to kill him, he reminded himself.

He was alive and the answers would have to wait. First, he needed to get out of this gilded cage and reach the dart. He hoped that Opturkarh Tavac would have spared him the trouble. After three days of convalescence, it looked like he would have to do the job himself. Somewhere in the back of his head, it bothered him that the Orieli were apparently willing to write him off. It's not as though they didn't have another dart or something. They could have used their PT matter transporter just as easily. No, that wouldn't work. The PT system needed two polarizing plates, and the Orieli kind of forgot to leave one on Earth. They were probably using this incident for their own twisted ends, as were the Serrll.

No matter.

The hard lines of his mouth softened as another image appeared in the smeared glass. He did not try to look beyond her face. He drank in the curve of her chin, the smooth texture of her skin, and the green of her eyes. Gently, he reached with his hand and ran his finger down her cheek.

"Seems I have cheated Death yet again, my pet," he whispered. "Can't get rid of me that easily."

He imagined she smiled then.

Later, he didn't know when, a knock came on the door. He waited. He did not hear the door open, but he recognized the heavy footsteps of Dr. Wald.

"Up and about? Good, good."

Terr watched the rain fall. The silence became uncomfortable. "Are you afraid to die, Doctor?" he said, lost among the clouds and things.

"Well, young…" Wald said and faltered. Terr turned slowly and a shadow crossed Wald's face. "I…I guess not," Wald whispered hoarsely.

"I wanted to know, just in case."

"In case of what?"

"Are they here?" Terr asked and Wald nodded. "Please show them in."

Wald looked at him uncertainly, then opened the door wide and stepped aside. Terr caught a glimpse of a marine guard as Cannon and Dr. Doryel walked in. They exchanged glances when they saw Terr in uniform. The door closed behind them with a soft click.

"Thank you, Dr. Wald. You may go," Cannon said briskly.

"No." He looked at Terr. "I think I better stay."

"Didn't you hear me, Doctor? It wasn't a request."

"I asked him to stay, General," Terr said softly.

Cannon gave Terr the benefit of his court martial stare. "Very well, then."

"What is it you wanted to see us about, Commander?" Doryel asked smoothly, his little black eyes suddenly wary.

"To say goodbye, Doctor."

Doryel grinned slowly and broke into a condescending chuckle that didn't touch his eyes. Terr knew it would raise a laugh.

"What the hell is this?" Cannon bridled. Behind the baby brown eyes, Terr could clearly picture a small room with a single overhead light with him under it.

"I'm sorry, Commander, but I have to insist you stay," Doryel said affably, correct to the end.

"But I'm all packed. It would be most annoying if I had to go through it all again." Terr tilted his head. "Is that your final word?"

"For the present."

"Last chance...no? Okay, then. As a cabinet member of the United States government, I formally request that you return me to my ship."

Doryel looked hard at Terr, unsure where this was leading. "I'm afraid, I can't do that," he said slowly.

Terr nodded in disappointment. He hoped he wouldn't

have to go through this. Death had waited in his shadow and now they were one. It settled on his shoulders and he felt the keen thrill of its power. It made him strong and he pitied the weak mortals who stood in his way. Slowly, he reached out and caressed the broad green leaves of one of the potted plants.

"Beautiful," he said absently. He tore the leaf from its stem and held it in his hand. Small blue tongues of flame licked around the leaf. Gradually, starting from around its edges, the leaf turned black and began to curl in on itself. "But it's dead now. And if I should reach out and touch Doctor Wald…" Terr looked at the blackened leaf and closed his hand around it. It was startling to hear the sharp crumbling crackle in the deadly silence of the room. He opened his hand and twisted bits of leaf fell between his fingers.

Doryel went white. His polished diplomatic smile hung like a cheap rag. Cannon didn't even flinch, his eyes cold—a real hardcase. Cannon would not be easy to intimidate.

"A very impressive parlor trick, Commander," he growled and nodded at the pieces of broken leaf on the carpet. "But it will take more than that to get out of here."

"I never doubted it."

"You realize it's my duty to stop you."

"By all means, General. I wouldn't dream of interfering with your duty."

"What if we refuse?"

Terr turned and probed Doryel's resolve. "Then the United States loses a promising diplomat, a four-star general, and a space center."

"And you propose to do all that by yourself, Commander?"

"All by myself, General."

"I'm sorry things have turned out like this, Terr," Doryel said uncertainly. "We never meant it to go this far."

"Yeah. You keep repeating that to yourself, Doc. After a while, you'll even get to believe it."

Doryel stared at Terr, then grinned ruefully. "I deserve that,

I suppose."

Cannon reached into his pocket and dragged out a compact cellular phone. "Move in now," he barked.

A sudden rumble of trucks, the sound of hobnailed boots, and the barking of orders brought Terr to the window. He looked out, tsked and shook his head.

"A sendoff committee, General?" Cannon had anticipated Terr's restlessness and its cause.

A solitary jeep and two Humvees raced across the manicured lawns, leaving trails of dirt and mangled grass. Terr figured the caretaker wasn't going to be very impressed. Troops, decked out in jungle greens and black berets, stationed themselves around the vehicles. He pulled back from the window, his smile a bit strained.

"You really shouldn't have gone to all this trouble, General."

"No trouble at all. Just a precaution." A helicopter, all green and brown, clattered into view. It banked sharply and hovered above the lawn. There was a sudden grabbing of hats and movement of lips. The rain fell fine as mist and the wind wailed thinly. Terr was sure the boys were enjoying themselves hugely.

He shook his head and looked at Doryel. "Must we go through this?"

Maybe Doryel sensed something, Terr didn't know. For a bare moment the diplomat seemed unsure of himself, remembering who Terr was.

Becoming increasingly nervous, Doryel spread his hands. "This isn't what you think. The military is here for your protection."

Terr gave him a thin smile and nodded. "I think I've been protected enough, Doctor. You had your chance to do this peacefully, but you chose to harangue and hold me up for extortion. I'm sorry, but I cannot hang around playing your little games anymore."

When he locked eyes with Wald, the doctor stiffened, but

didn't flinch. Terr shrugged. A low rumble of thunder came from outside. Death rode in his hand and Wald paled as Terr reached for him. Blue sparks arced between his fingers. It took courage for the mortal to face him like that. Then he thought, why should this man die? For political expediency? Hardly worth it. He dropped his hand, grinned a death's grin, and took a step toward Doryel.

"My God, no!" Doryel screamed and scrambled back until he was hard against the wall. He looked wildly at Cannon. "Stop him, stop him!"

One glance from Terr and Cannon froze in his tracks. Maybe Terr could kill him by touching him, and maybe he couldn't. He obviously didn't want to take the chance. Terr's hand hovered above Doryel's shoulder, the crackle of blue sparks unnaturally loud.

"Things are a bit different now that you're on the receiving end, eh, Doc?" Just to show him he meant it, a bolt of blue light cracked against the wall above Doryel's head. The diplomat screamed and shrank back from Terr's hand, whimpering like a child.

"I want to live," he sobbed and collapsed to the floor in a cowering crouch.

The door flew open and the marine guard rushed in. His eyes scanned the scene even as he crouched, holding a handgun with both hands, pointed at Terr.

"Drop that weapon, soldier!" Cannon bellowed. The marine looked startled, his eyes flickering doubtfully from Terr to Cannon.

"Sir, I don't know if I can do that."

"You heard my order, Marine!"

Reluctantly the soldier straightened, clicked on the safety, and threw the automatic at Cannon's feet.

"Now get out! I'll call you if I need you," Cannon rasped and kicked away the weapon.

Unhappy, the soldier stood to attention, saluted, and

walked out. The door clicked shut after him.

Terr nodded in approval. "Very good, General. What now? I don't suppose the President would be pleased if Dr. Doryel met with an untimely death, do you?"

Cannon gave Doryel a brief scrutiny, obviously not liking what he saw. "Maybe you can kill all of us in this room, Commander, but that won't get you to your ship. My men are waiting outside."

"True. Then again, how many of those boys are you willing to sacrifice before one of them puts a bullet in me? I somehow doubt that killing me would be to your advantage either, or of your government. It wouldn't look good in the papers, you know. The Orieli wouldn't like it either."

Cannon appeared to digest that one. As much as he personally wanted to grind Terr beneath his feet, he still had to answer to his president.

"What do you want?" Cannon demanded at length.

"I'm sure your Air Force would be glad to loan us one of their Marine VTOL Harrier aircraft, General. You have military assets as part of this installation. Have an aircraft here in fifteen minutes," Terr said and pointed at the cell phone, then studied the golden wings on Cannon's chest. "As a marine pilot, you've flown a Harrier before. I'm sure you wouldn't mind taking a little refresher flight with me, would you?"

The muscles in Cannon's cheeks twitched as he goggled. "You're crazy! I haven't driven one of those crates in years."

"Well then, here is your chance for some practice."

"You'll only get us both killed!" Cannon grated, voice brittle, full of venom.

"I imagine you'll be careful, as will any stray fighter that might follow us with questionable intent."

Cannon's mouth was a tight line as he raised the handset. If Terr harbored any ambitions of making friends with him, he could forget them. Cannon punched in numbers and waited. It didn't take long, the conversation brief and to the point. He switched off and glared at Terr.

"In fifteen minutes, just as you asked."

"Fine. Oh, one other thing," Terr said and turned to Doctor Wald. "Please have the energy sphere brought to me."

Wald didn't say anything. He gave Terr a long look and walked out. Everyone so damned touchy! To hell with them.

Doryel picked himself up off the floor and the diplomatic mask fell back in place. He cleared his throat and looked at Cannon.

"I'm sorry, General." Cannon didn't say anything. What was that about petals and roses, Terr mused. Earth had some quaint sayings.

They waited.

After a while, a knock on the door caused heads to turn. It was Wald's assistant, the man with the frosty stare and the executive image. Terr was right about the icy stare as he watched the other close the door. The assistant reached beneath his lab coat and pulled out an ugly Service forty-five.

"Just stand perfectly still, you," he said and pointed the thing at Terr.

Unholy anger surged through Terr. Death in his eyes, he glared fixedly at Cannon.

"Tell him to drop it or he dies," he snarled, his voice trembling with fury.

"You can save your breath, Commander," the assistant said harshly, his eyes never leaving Terr. "I don't work for him."

A federal security agent? So be it. Terr stretched out his hand and reached for him.

"No!" Cannon yelled and made a grab for the gunman.

The shot rang out with a crash and something heavy slammed into Terr's left side. With the power in him, he hardly felt it. Lightning ripped from his fingers and Death walked in his shadow. A look of surprise and terror crossed the other's face even as he died, his body flung against the far wall. There was thunder and a smell of ozone and cordite. The glass in the window blew out and the wind howled into the room. The body on the floor was a charred, bloody mess with a large hole where his chest used to be. Terr raised his arms high and lightning crackled between them.

Doryel rolled up his eyes and crumpled.

A tearing crash, the hinges squealed, and the door burst open. Two black berets rushed in with silenced submachine guns held waist high. Terr roared and leveled his hands. Blue lightning lashed out and the two berets twisted and shriveled and screamed. Blood gushed from their charred bodies in hot, steamy spurts, staining the carpet. Terr shifted his hands and his voice was the voice of thunder. Wood splinters hissed around him and lightning danced.

When the dust settled, only a jagged hole remained where the door used to be. His wrath burned hot. When he leveled his arms, Cannon dropped to his knees and cowered in shock and astonishment.

"So you would provoke my anger, Earthman!" Terr thundered. "Then die!"

All Cannon had to do was blink, but even gods have compassion. Not that Terr did, but he needed the sonofabitch. He swore and shifted his hands. Again and again, lightning ripped down the corridor until, among the dust and falling masonry, silence descended, heavy and still.

As his rage cooled, Terr looked down at his side and winced. Only a flesh wound, but deep and stung like hell. Blood flowed freely down his uniform and he clamped his left hand against the wound. It didn't help any, but it made him feel better. He walked around the burnt remains of Wald's assistant and his nose wrinkled. He turned the body over with his foot.

"Forgive me, my master," he whispered as he bent over the body. "I'm not a worthy disciple of the Discipline." Worthy or not, he thanked the gods as he pulled the little brown sphere out of one of the pockets, snorting at the smell of charred flesh and clotting blood.

The sphere pulsed warm and he closed his hand around it gratefully. He activated the shield with a mental command. The whistling scream of a low-flying jet brought him quickly to the gaping hole left of the window. The sleek, fixed-wing Marine Harrier glided slowly overhead and hovered. It descended daintily, bounced once, hesitant, then squatted firmly, its jets throwing up grass and dirt. He watched with keen interest.

Doryel moaned and looked around him in a daze.

Terr's left side had gone numb and he thought briefly about having it treated. A couple of hours more wouldn't make much of a difference. By then, he would either have reached the dart or it wouldn't matter anymore. Death still lingered over him. To protect him from himself? He let it ride. All things considered, the burden wasn't that heavy.

Cannon shrank back as Terr walked up to him. Terr extended a hand toward the gaping doorway. "If you please, General."

Cannon licked his lips, and something like awe twisted his face as he staggered up.

"Who…" he croaked, looking down at Terr. "Who are you? *What* are you?"

Terr laughed, then chopped it off before it became hysterical. They stepped over the bodies. At the doorway, he paused and looked back.

"Goodbye, Dr. Doryel. Don't think that it's been fun, because it hasn't."

He and Cannon marched to the elevator in silence. He didn't feel like chatting and he guessed that Cannon had things on his mind. It took only a moment for the thing to come up. They stepped in and the elevator moved smoothly down. When the doors opened, he nudged Cannon to move ahead of him. As they walked out the rifles came up with a clatter.

The soldiers stood or crouched, shielded by armored Humvees. Terr could see shouldered missiles pointed his way. They even had two heavy machine guns trained on him. It may have been a bit extreme, but he could not fault their enthusiasm.

"General, I know all these GIs are anxious to have a look at me, but those weapons are making me nervous. An accident could happen. You might get shot and I lose a hostage. A bad deal all around."

Cannon gave him a glance, then waved at a crusty major decked out in full webbing and jungle greens. Cannon gave a curt order and the major saluted and began shouting at the men. Everyone lowered their hardware and stood to.

A wooden-faced MP walked beside them toward the waiting jet, its turbines spooling. Along the way, Terr staggered and the MP shot out his hand to steady him, flinching slightly at the contact with Terr's shield. Terr leaned heavily on his arm and looked up at the impassive, chiseled face.

"You should have that attended to, sir," the MP's voice rumbled, reminding Terr of another with a deep voice, burning eyes and a hand he also leaned against.

"It will keep." Terr nodded and they walked on.

They stopped beside the jet and Cannon motioned for the pilot to climb down. It was cold and Terr shivered. Browns, yellows and reds mottled the sky. Black clouds raced toward the sunset. The wind plucked gently at his uniform. After a glance around, Cannon quickly climbed into the front seat.

Terr reached for the access ladder when the pilot coughed discretely beside him.

"Ah, excuse me, sir. You'll need this." He held a small box in his hand. "Earplugs."

Terr nodded, switched off the shield, pocketed the box and climbed up. LED displays, flat screens, small levers, and rows of buttons crammed the rear cockpit. The pilot's head appeared beside him.

"You'll have to fasten your seatbelt, sir," he said apologetically. "Here, I'll show you."

He strapped Terr into the three-point restraint system and

tugged at the straps to make sure they were snug. Terr felt like a kid being taken for a ride by his mother. He put on the proffered helmet and plugged it in.

"No need to worry about oxygen, sir. You won't be going that high." The pilot withdrew and the canopy closed, locking with a click.

The engines howled and the jet shivered. Terr felt pressured into his seat and they were airborne. The earplugs helped, but not much. The aircraft swayed a bit and he grabbed the sides of the cockpit. Maybe trusting himself to Cannon's skill hadn't been such a brilliant idea after all. He issued a mental command and the shield came up again. It would protect him in case this didn't quite work out. The jet steadied and the complex fell away beneath them. The Harrier went into horizontal flight and headed for the cloud cover.

For a rusty marine puke, Cannon handled the aircraft well enough.

It took maybe ten minutes to leave the low-pressure area around Houston. After some initial turbulence, the flight steadied and became smooth. Even the engine noise had subsided to a contented purr. Terr checked the ground shadows to make sure they were heading in the right direction. Cannon didn't bother striking up a conversation. Terr was thankful for that. After the rush and excitement of getting away, reaction had set in. He was satisfied to sit there and let his thoughts wander.

After a time, he looked down.

Desert, bleak, hot and desolate, glared from below. Barren rock flowed in reds and browns against an orange sea of sand. Houston was nothing but a brown mushroom of pollution somewhere far in the east. Beyond it, Terr thought he could see the ocean glittering against the setting sun. It could have been heat reflection. Now, he only saw the desert. He looked at his side and pulled away his hand. It came away dark brown, caked with dried blood. He shrugged and clamped the hand back into place.

After a while, Cannon turned his head, wearing a triumphant grin. "Goodbye, Commander. We'll be seeing each other soon."

Terr heard Cannon's throaty laugh even as the canopy fell away and he was blasted into the air. The chute ruffled out, filled, and gave a sold jerk. Savage pain lanced through Terr's side. He followed the jet with his eyes as it circled, the sun glinting from its polished surfaces. It dipped its wings and faded into a black dot.

Terr kept swearing all the way to the bottom.

* * *

The two Orieli cruisers flew parallel courses, one slightly up and behind the other. The Earth-Moon system lay open ahead of them. The ships had broken out of subspace over an hour ago, gliding in slowly to give the Serrll time to react.

The M-4s lying in their path was not the reception Zor-Ell expected.

"They're standing off below the planetary plane, Karhide," Opturkarh Tremane said seriously. "Three of them, Serrll M-4s. Unless he's been replaced in the last twelve hours, Master Scout Anatol Keller is commanding."

Wearing a pained expression, Zor-Ell looked away from the tactical repeater plot. "It had to be him. Someone on Captal must hate us."

Tremane allowed himself a small grin. "I would not be at all surprised." His tongue flicked quickly around his lips. Zor-Ell sighed and shook his head.

"I hope he doesn't try any of that macho crap again. Can't we even visit without making a diplomatic incident out of it?" Zor-Ell demanded petulantly.

"You know how it is, Karhide. Push, shove, needle and see what we will do."

"Well, if he keeps pushing, he'll see what we'll do."

Tremane grinned, glad it wasn't his problem. Whatever armament they carried, the Serrll threat could be brushed aside. His karhide ordinarily did not put up with bullshit in any way, shape, or form. Still, no matter how personally satisfying, OSCOM, Orieli Space Command, on Zaron would frown on such a course of action. They all needed to keep the broader objectives of their mission in mind.

"How does it feel to be back here?" Tremane asked casually, looking at the blue and white of Earth in the mainframe holoview plot.

Zor-Ell's face tensed, betraying a rush of emotions within. How *did* he feel about this planet and its strange people? After four years, he would have thought the scars had scabbed over. He swiveled in his couch and looked hard at his Cetan first officer.

"Ask me some other time when I'm not busy," he said gruffly, surprised at his reaction.

"Karhide, we have open comms with LTN-12," Taroptur Coni announced from the operations level below, his face repeated in the holoview plot on the command platform.

Zor-Ell glanced at Tremane. "Status of Serrll units?"

"They're coming in with their shield grids extended. Tactical shows increased power core emissions—"

"Figures."

"—and our interceptor net is still at level one."

"Secondaries?"

"On active standby. My guess is, they'll wait another four minutes or so before committing themselves. Do you want to go tactical?"

"Negative. I want to keep Cent Comp in advisory mode for the moment. Increasing our level of readiness might be seen by the Serrll commander as an open invitation to start something he won't be able to finish. Regardless of his behavior, he *is* an instrument of the Serrll government."

"I hope he remembers that," Tremane said dryly and Zor-

Ell chuckled.

"I know. They seem to be a trigger-happy lot."

"We both postulated their profile, Karhide. Serrll behavior reflects a prolonged period of dominance with little or no opposition."

Zor-Ell nodded. "Yeah. I wonder, though, if we're observing standard Serrll doctrine or something that's been prepared especially for us? Advise Karhide Karth that *Seera* is to maintain relativity. Coni? Put me through to Opturkarh Tavac."

In the mainframe plot a window image opened showing Tavac in the LTN-12's Primary Control center.

"Someone in Sector Command must have been listening for a change," Tavac said with feigned surprise. "But I never expected the area commander himself." Tavac grinned broadly, although the brown eyes looked tired, and the black hair had lost some of its gloss.

"Take it from me, it's a dubious distinction," Zor-Ell said. "I have your relief crew, Opturkarh. Karhide Karth will convey you back to *Tapal* where Karhide Arlon Dee is waiting to take over the patrol area."

"I won't be sorry to leave this rock, Da."

"Look at it as an exercise in character building."

"So I've been told. When are you commencing direct transfer operations?"

"I'm not. This one will have to be a physical transfer deal. We have equipment that cannot be sent through the transport gateway, but we'll be sending you the smaller stuff shortly. Tavac, can you give me anything on our reception committee?"

"All phases of our contact with the Serrll have developed as predicted, Da. With two notable exceptions."

"I take it that one of them is Master Scout Anatol Keller?"

"Right. The other, of course, is Opturkarh Terrllss-rr."

"What's your assessment?"

"The second seems to be a case of inter-factional rivalry."

"I read you, Tavac. And the first?"

"If I didn't know better, Karhide, I would say that we were victims of a reverse case study."

"One that is obviously still running."

"As is ours."

Zor-Ell pondered Tavac's words. "It's possible. I will want a full analysis when I get down."

"I'm preparing the longwinded version now, Da."

"Observational caution," the housekeeping computer said. "Target vessels assuming standard triad configuration. Data links established. Vessels now under tandem control. Recommend increasing readiness status."

"I'll have to cut this short, Opturkarh. Our Serrll friends are getting restless and want to play."

"Karhide, Anatol Keller could be out to even the score for last time."

"This is a peaceful contact, Tavac," Zor-Ell admonished sternly, but a twinkle of amusement glittered in his eye.

"I am properly chastened and am looking forward to seeing you at LTN-12."

Zor-Ell smiled as the mainframe plot image faded. Tavac was a good officer, more than ready for his own command.

"The Serrll have opened a channel, Karhide," Tremane said and licked his lips.

"Relative stop. Comms? Let's see what they have to say."

When the VI image cleared, Anatol stared at them haughtily, his eyes taking in the Primary Flight Control.

"Karhide Zor-Ell, your advisory message has put me in a very awkward position. You're entering a protectorate area, sir. Accordingly, I must insist that you maintain present status."

"The agreement between our governments gives me unrestricted access to our base, Master Scout."

"By one ship only. You have two of them here in a position to threaten Serrll sovereignty."

"Come, Master. Surely you're not about to suggest—"

"I'm not suggesting anything, Karhide. It's up to you to

213

make the explanation for your presence here."

"Then permit me to do so. In addition to being a routine crew rotation and a resupply operation—"

"You don't need two ships for that."

"—it is also a diplomatic mission."

"A diplomatic mission?"

"Master Scout, you must be aware of the incident involving your personnel and one of our RV/4 darts that crashed on Earth. Before proceeding to Captal, I intend to resolve the matter."

"Captal? Why do you want—"

"I will explain the nature of my mission to your government. As for the other ship, it will depart as soon as the relief operation has been completed."

Anatol frowned, deep in thought. "I will need to advise Captal of this development, Karhide. In the meantime, you will hold your position, sir."

"The situation on Earth is very unstable, Master Scout. I urge you to expedite—"

"I sympathize, Karhide, but I must follow due form. The matter will have to be routed through the Bureau of Colonial and Protectorate Affairs. Normally, this is done through Salina. The BCPA have offices there. They in turn will have to dispatch a priority message to Captal, await its return and contact me. The mess could drag on for days. You see how it is, Karhide." Anatol smiled urbanely.

"You are making it perfectly clear, Master Scout," Zor-Ell said wearily, recalling that Keller used the same tactic against Karth during their first mission. "I have no intention of fossilizing here while your bureaucratic machinery moves a cog. However, in the interest of maintaining cordial relations, my ships will remain here. All I need is one dart to carry out my resupply."

"I cannot possibly permit that, Karhide. Same reasons."

"This is hardly a reasonable attitude to take toward a

friendly power," Zor-Ell pointed out calmly.

"I'm only following orders, sir."

Zor-Ell stared impassively at the image, damned if he was going to allow the alien to see him get exasperated.

"Master Scout, as per the protocol agreement between the Serrll Combine and the Orieli Technic Union, I have been following all due procedures laid out in that agreement. If those procedures have changed, I require formal notification from the Bureau of Colonial and Protectorate Affairs. Do you have a copy of any such amendments, Da?"

"I do not," Anatol blustered, momentarily thrown off track.

"According to that agreement, Da, I am able to approach our base. As I said before, for the sake of amity, I'm willing to stand down my ships—"

"A prudent decision, Karhide."

"—and await the result of your communication with Captal. Since this process, as you point out, might turn out to be a lengthy one, I nevertheless need to request your permission to begin relief operations using one of my auxiliary craft."

Anatol's look of triumph faded, replaced by an angry scowl. "For a moment, Karhide, I thought you were going to be reasonable. As I said before, until I have queried Captal, you will stand down."

Something cold glinted in Zor-Ell's eyes and he sat straighter on his command couch.

"Very well. To avoid an incident, I will stand down as requested. However, my relief operations will proceed."

"Negative! I'll regard such action as hostile and respond accordingly. Karhide, don't press the matter."

"Master Scout, I have tried to comply with your demands; demands which are clearly outside the articles of agreement between our respective governments. I'm not in a position to debate the finer points of that agreement. I have a relief operation to conduct, which I shall commence immediately."

"Karhide! I warn—"

"Da, if you feel that my action contravenes our agreement, you're free to file a formal protest with the BCPA. Transmission ends."

"Tactical caution. Power fluctuation detected in target vessels in preparatory firing phase," the housekeeping computer announced even as Anatol's image faded from the mainframe plot.

"Karhide! We've got to—"

"Very well, Tremane." Zor-Ell waved at his first officer in assent.

"Cent Comp? Enable autonomous control. Condition two on active standby."

"Comms?" Zor-Ell prompted. "Advise Karhide Karth to maintain position. He is not to engage."

"Cent Comp status. Primary unit maintaining condition one on tactical. Interceptor net now at level two. Secondary shield net on active standby. Tactical control in PFC. Status. Condition two on active standby."

"Karhide? Ship is ready," Tremane said.

"Very well," Zor-Ell confirmed, watching the mainframe plot. "I think...yep, here it comes."

The tactical plot showed the projector dome beneath each M-4 brighten as their shields flared. Three yellow lances stabbed out and merged into a cone that formed a contorted point of energy. A single enhanced beam, trailing white ionization, impacted the Orieli ship. The interceptor net around *Valon* scintillated in the visible spectrum, overloading under a massive 384 TeV discharge. Backsurges rippled along the shield force lines.

Before the M-4s could fire again *Valon* extended its secondary shield net. It took three more hits from the M-4s without any visible effect before the firing stopped.

Zor-Ell drummed his fingers on the armrest of his couch. In the tactical plot the intensity of the shield rings around the

Serrll ships had diminished. He admitted that Anatol's tandem fire control tactic caught him by surprise. It was obvious now why the Serrll prowled around in groups of three. An interesting maneuver and something that OSCOM might want to consider employing against the Krans.

"Cent Comp, ship status?"

"Level one damage to the secondary interceptor net array control matrix. Self-repair response initiated. Full integrity in two point-six minutes. Primary interceptor net at level two. Secondary net at level one. Maintaining condition one."

"They caught us napping, Karhide," Tremane remarked beside him. Zor-Ell nodded.

"That they did. I guess we both learned something today. Raise the Serrll ship."

Anatol had mastered his emotions by the time he faced Zor-Ell again. His face was still flushed with impotent rage. The fact that the Orieli ship did not respond was, if possible, even more humiliating. To have his fire ignored like that...he hoped the data gained was worth it. Damn Anabb and his orders!

In the main display plot, Zor-Ell did not look angry or agitated. Anatol found the cold glint in those large eyes very unsettling.

"Master Scout, I shall now begin my relief operations. Please do not interfere." The request was formal and polite, and sent chills down Anatol's spine.

"The Serrll shall not take this lightly, sir!"

"I hope not, Da."

"This is not the end of it, Karhide," Anatol snarled and cut contact.

In the end, Anatol decided he'd been lucky.

* * *

President Hennery pointed at the open page of one of the newspapers on his desk. His pale green eyes blazed as he stared at Cannon.

"Did you read the evening headlines, General? Armed forces holding open hunt for alien. Insane alien bent on destruction. Shoot to kill. Bah! You carry out policy, not make it, damn it all to hell!" he roared and slammed his fist against the old *Resolute* desk that many presidents before him had given a pounding. "What in blazes did you think you were doing in Houston? A one-man inquisition?"

Hennery snatched the paper and flung it against the wall, where it made an untidy pile on the carpet. Forcing himself to calm down, he stared coldly at the stiff form before him.

"Your irresponsible ill-conceived actions have caused intense embarrassment not only to me and my administration, but to this country. With your misguided vision of military security, you may have compromised Earth's relationship with the Serrll and the Orieli. I'm afraid, General, that your kind of vision is no longer relevant. You're relieved as Chairman of the Joint Chiefs. I will consider whether further disciplinary action is warranted."

Cannon was a proud and capable man. He didn't get his four stars by licking ass. As he stood on the presidential seal in the Oval Office, he stared at his commander-in-chief in bewilderment, shocked at the speed of events. Did he carry it too far?

"I was acting in the best interest of the United States, sir," he said at length. "If that's a crime, you can have my resignation."

"I determine what is in the best interest of this country," Hennery snapped testily. "You should have used judgment instead of zeal. Good intentions aren't worth a damn when you don't know what you're doing. Your resignation is accepted, effective as at end of month." He leaned back in his chair and pressed a button on the intercom board.

"Kathy? Send in the others."

"Yes, Mr. President."

Doryel led them in. He took one look at Cannon's stony face and shrugged philosophically. His own resignation already offered and accepted. How the mighty have fallen. He might go back to teaching. There were plenty of universities that would take him at his value. Dr. Raydon sucked on his pipe and chatted with the Secretary of State.

Hennery stood up and paced, waiting while they seated themselves. He stopped by the tall window and looked out. Pennsylvania Avenue was crowded with the usual throng of tourists and commuters. They were well into spring and the trees in Lafayette Square were lush and green. The evening sky deep purple and clear.

He walked to the head of the desk and spread his hands before him. "There is only one point on the agenda, gentlemen," he said and gave each one of them a brief look. "Opturkarh Terrllss-rr. And I don't mind telling you that I'm completely crapped off at the way the whole situation has been handled." Some of the Harvard veneer had scraped off during the day, letting through the Texas drawl. "An alien crashes, is injured, and we cement our relations by starting off with a cellar-and-light routine. My God! What were you people thinking? The papers have really gone to town on this one. You should read the *New York Times*! Congress is more than willing to make me the sacrificial lamb when the Serrll or the Orieli come looking for him.

"And when they come, and they will, what do I tell them? We have killed him because he refused to spill his guts? And all this supposedly done in the name of national security? God save me from good intentions. Okay. This is what I want done. Commander Terr is to be found and found alive. He is to be brought to me and nothing else. Nothing else! Do I make myself perfectly clear?"

"Take it easy, Kurt," the Secretary of State said smoothly. "We'll do it any way you want."

"You had better, Sweeny, my boy, or I'll have you on the

carpet. You and Dr. Doryel should never have allowed matters to go this far."

"Now, just a—" Swen blustered and started to rise out of his seat. Hennery pointed a finger at him.

"Sit down. Doryel has paid for his mistake. I wouldn't add to it if I were you. Just fill me in and don't leave anything out."

"Well," Swen glanced at Doryel and cleared his throat. "All we know is that he is somewhere in New Mexico. There is evidence to suggest that he might be trying to reach his ship."

"And can he? I understand that he's wounded."

Swen shrugged. "I don't know."

"Great," Hennery said in disgust. "Get to all the papers, television and radio and tell the people to calm down, before it's too late." He sat down and reached across the desk for the pitcher of iced water. He poured some into his glass and sipped. Twirling the tumbler between his fingers, he looked up at Raydon.

"Okay, Doctor, the surveillance tapes. Tell me what happened at Houston. I want to know what we're dealing with here."

* * *

Terr reluctantly became awake. He didn't want to open his eyes, not yet. The inside of his mouth tasted like the stuff birds ignore at the bottom of the cage and his face probably looked it. There was nothing cheering about the prospect of getting up. He felt nice and stiff and enjoying it, the sand beneath him packed hard. If he moved, it would only remind him of the breakfast he wasn't going to have, the hot shower he could only drool about, and the assortment of aches and pains that would start clamoring for attention.

It simply wasn't worth it.

He recalled his parachute landing. Fine as far as it went. He had walked away from worse. After unclipping the harness, he rummaged around the seat for survival equipment. There wasn't any. Why give a guy who is down a break? He gave the seat a savage kick and muttered an obscenity. In a way it helped. Dusting himself off, he looked around.

The ridges rose out of the sand, jagged and long, and he seemed to have fallen between two of them. Small dry scrub dotted the undulating plain. Dead trees stuck out of the sand. The sun, a dull orange ball, hung there and stared at him. A thin wind plucked at his uniform. Studying the terrain a hushed silence crept over the desert. Nothing stirred. A shadow reached out and touched him, and he remembered another crash, also in the desert. He supposed there was a moral in it somewhere if he cared to look for it.

According to his research, eight years ago, this landscape had rolling green farmlands. Clearly, Earth's climate in this part of the world had taken a massive hit. Compared to the shimmering sands of the Saffal, this stuff didn't look all that bad. He contemplated one ridge, then the other, and mentally tossed a coin. With shadows around him, he turned and began shuffling and sliding toward a black line of hills that seemed to go all the way to the horizon.

He didn't remember reaching the rocks, crawling under an overhang, or falling asleep. Sometime in the night, he thought he heard the whine of helicopter turbines. He wasn't sure.

That was yesterday. Now, it all seemed unreal somehow.

Blinking, he sat up and gasped. His side had stiffened up horribly and hurt like hell. A dull throb started there and spread evenly along his ribs. He guessed it was going to be one of those days. An absurd situation just to retain his freedom, but that's the way he was. During the night, huddled under a rocky overhang, with the mournful keening of the wind for company, he wondered why he bothered putting himself through such an ordeal. He should have stayed put and waited for the Orieli to show up. It would certainly have been more pleasant than prowling about the desert with a bullet wound. He took a lot of time thinking about that.

He crawled out of his upholstered cave and shivered. It was bitterly cold. Touched with fire the ridge looked like some scene out of hell, a place he shall probably have an opportunity to visit before long. Overhead in the deep violet sky, some stars still flickered shyly. In the east, he saw only blood. In the stillness, everything suddenly paled and the sun opened its eye. A sliver of orange brushed the stars and they were gone.

That was sunrise.

He groaned and cursed as he worked the stiffness out of his muscles, then began to walk.

It was still early morning when the helicopters came. Hidden between some rocks, he watched as every now and then, one would come clattering over the ridge. They always banked steeply, rotors almost scraping the sand. Hugging the terrain, they would be gone. A slow grin of satisfaction spread across Terr's face as he pictured Cannon pinning little colored flags into a wall map, getting puzzled and angry. The thought gave him intense pleasure.

He didn't linger. When the helicopters left, he moved out. With their array of IR sensors, radar, satellite imaging, and crap like that, he wasn't fooling himself that he could evade them for long. They'd obviously followed his trail from the parachute landing. What little cover the rocks offered was only illusory. He figured if he lasted the day, he'd be ahead. The interference pattern his shield emitted undoubtedly helped to scramble Earth's remote sensors, but it was delusive protection. Getting out of their space center in such spectacular fashion was bound to get talked about. He counted on that.

It didn't take long for the Humvees and the jeeps to come, thin creeping lines trailing ribbons of dust hanging lazily over the shimmering sand. Resting in the shade of a boulder, he tried tearing his uniform to make a bandage for his side, but the material was tougher than it looked. He guessed it would be the old hand-against-the-side trick again. Walking, he licked his lips trying to forget his growing thirst. This trek wasn't funny any-more, not that it ever was. If he wanted to get anywhere, he needed to get some transportation fast.

Making shade for a boulder, he looked up and squinted at the sun. Where it touched, it burned. There was a certain estab-lishment near Sal Field on Captal, admittedly of questionable reputation and favored by the seedier element of the citizenry. An even seedier character by a doubtful name of Kelso ran the place.

Anyway, this joint wasn't a place where Terr would be seen taking a polite lady-friend to, but it was on his list of visited establishments. Kelso served the longest, tallest, coldest refrig-erating fluid this side of Cantor. And he needed a shot now, bad. He worked his tongue around his lips imagining himself surrounded by tall, icy pitchers.

He sure could have used one of them.

With the sun high overhead, he began to regret his rash decision to park himself where he did. He had cover on three sides. When he got to it this morning, deep shadows sheltered the landscape. He could not know it would take the Humvees hours to cover four odd talans.

Rit!

If they didn't hurry up, he wasn't going to be worth finding.

He swallowed, but it wouldn't go down.

Just when he began to think that maybe he should start something or other, there came a snarl of labored engines. About time. He peered through a crack in his fortress, his shield on, and waited. Only one path ked into the gorge and he held it. They rounded a patch of boulders and roared into the pass, heads bobbing in the two jerking vehicles. They didn't even slow down. He tsked and shook his head. A helmeted figure with a mike stuck before his face sat in the leading jeep. An antenna mast whipped behind him.

Terr grew out of the rock and the helmeted face fell apart in astonishment. The driver jerked the wheel hard around. With

223

a shower of sand the jeep slid to a stop broadside on. Terr raised his hand and pointed. The pale orange beam, hardly visible in the harsh sunlight, lanced at the rock and sand in front of the jeep. Cold radiance scattered the shadows and the sand glowed, crackled and fused. The trailing jeep appeared and slid to a shuddering stop behind the first one.

In the ensuing silence, there was the pinging of hot metal, the smell of engine oil, dust, and burnt rock.

The nonplused lieutenant appeared to be making a mess of the gum in his mouth. He studied the molten slag, adjusted his tinted glasses and stood up.

"I guess that could have been me, right? What now, Opturkarh?"

"Everybody out and throw down your weapons. Them too." Terr pointed at the second jeep.

The lieutenant removed his glasses and spat into the sand. "I got orders to search and locate. I have done so, Mister. Unless you're planning to melt us all down with that fancy heater of yours, I guess your day's ruined."

He had guts, Terr admitted, but not much brains. "Look, pal. You're a real hero type, but just for once, can't we forget that crap?"

"Sorry, Opturkarh." The lieutenant shook his head. "General Cannon gave us specific orders."

"Wise up, Lieutenant! Cannon is sitting in a nice air-conditioned office playing soldier. It's you I got on the receiving end."

The lieutenant stared at Terr for a moment, then turned to his men and nodded. "Do as he says. Stack your weapons against them rocks."

Looking at Terr, they started climbing down and formed a loose group. With a reluctant glance at the lieutenant, they piled their hardware against the boulders.

One of the GIs shifted his M-16 slightly. The beam struck him full on the chest and he toppled over the side of the jeep like a crumpled sack. Terr had been hurried. Maybe the soldier was dead, and maybe he wasn't.

"That's not very smart, Lieutenant," Terr said wearily. "If you piss me off, I can make this real nasty."

The lieutenant thought about it and barked an order. "Gunny!"

"Sir!" An older, scarred man stepped forward, clearly a seasoned professional.

"I gave orders for the men to stack their weapons, Gunny. Did I say for them to do anything else?"

"No, sir!"

"If one of those motherfuckers tries something without orders, I will personally shove it where it will do the most good. Do you read me, top soldier?"

"Won't happen again, sir," the man said and glared at the others.

Mouth working on his gum the lieutenant nodded and climbed out of the jeep. With his left hand, he reached across his body and undid the flap of his holster. He dragged out the forty-five and tossed it into the sand. Muttering, the rest of the men stacked or threw down their remaining hardware. When the clatter subsided, Terr pointed with his hand. When the glow faded, only a pile of fused metal and sand remained.

"Okay, Opturkarh. What now?"

"Your comms gear," Terr said and pointed at the slag pile.

"They will want to know where we are. If I don't tell them, they'll come looking."

"Not for a while. By then, we'll be gone."

"We?"

"You and me. The radios, Lieutenant."

The way his eyes worked Terr over, the lieutenant would rather slug him one. But then, he had his men to worry about. The lieutenant turned and dragged the canvas-covered set out of the jeep. Terr indicated at the slag pile with his head and the lieutenant heaved the set in its general direction. If the fall

225

didn't bend it, the energy sphere beam certainly finished it.

"Now tell your men to line up against the cliff."

"So you can pick us off?"

"I could have done that at any time. Don't spoil it now."

Chewing furiously the lieutenant jerked his head at the men. They looked nervously at each other and moved back. One of them bent over their fallen comrade and turned him over.

"Hey, he's alive!"

The lieutenant glanced at Terr and jerked a thumb at the body. "Put him in the shade. I'll deal with him later. Okay, Opturkarh. Now that we're all nice and cozy, what've you got in mind?"

"Much as I like the company, Lieutenant, we're going to take a little tour of this desert. There are parts I haven't seen yet. Of course, your next sitrep will be a bit late, which might cause some raised eyebrows, but no panic. Not for a while. Meanwhile, we shall be enjoying the scenery."

"What about my men?"

"They have water, they'll be found. Speaking of water, I could use some."

The lieutenant licked his lips and nodded. "Yeah, I guess we could all use a break. Gunny?"

"Sir."

"Water for everybody. Have you had anything to eat today, Opturkarh?"

"I was kind of rushed."

"By the way," the lieutenant commented and grimaced. "That's a pretty long boner for a name…"

"Terr will do."

"Yeah. That wound. My medic should take a look at it. Okay, Gunny. Get the men under shade and call the medic over."

The men started unpacking their gear. The lieutenant and Terr picked some shade in the lee of a rock wall. Terr sat down on the hot sand. He stretched out his legs and leaned against the rock, also hot. The lieutenant sprawled beside him and yanked off his helmet, his dark blond hair wet, plastered against his head.

The sergeant walked up to them and offered Terr a green plastic canteen. "It's a bit warm, sir," he said apologetically.

"Set it down, please," Terr said and the sergeant complied. Terr nodded and reached for the canteen. Moving slowly, he brought it to his lips, his shield letting it through. The water was warm and tasted of plastic, but he drank eagerly and immediately felt better.

His shoulders sagged with contentment.

"Thank you, Gunnery Sergeant."

A smile twitched at the corner of the soldier's mouth. "Don't mention it, sir. I also got two packs of MREs. I know they're not fit for man or beast, but that's all we've got, sir."

"MREs?"

"Meals ready to eat," the lieutenant muttered beside him. "That's all, Gunny. Ah, Riley, see to the Opturkarh's side."

The sergeant gave Terr one last look and walked back to his men. The medic laid down his canvas bag and knelt.

"If you'll just lift your left arm, sir…You've got a nasty gash there. It'll need at least eight or ten stitches."

"Just put a patch over it," Terr said.

The medic glanced at the lieutenant, noticed the scowl, and hurriedly rummaged through the bag. Terr pulled up his shirt and watched with interest as the medic unpacked the gauze patch. The medic opened a bottle smelling of antiseptic and picked up a swab.

"I will need to clean this up, sir. Might sting a bit."

"Go ahead."

When the medic's hand came into contact with the shield, he gasped and snatched it back. "What the…"

"Apply slow, firm pressure," Terr told him. "Your hand will go through."

The stuff did sting, but the pressure patch made him feel better. He tucked in the bloody shirt, watching the lieutenant open the meal pack. The lieutenant glanced at him and pointed out the items laid out in their little preformed cubicles.

"Bread biscuit, water, cheese spread, chocolate, can of some stew, jam, fruit, and this stuff looks like dried meat."

Terr sure could have eaten something, but he would only be poisoning himself. "I'm afraid most of those things contain substances toxic to me."

"Terr, those things would be toxic to anyone," the lieutenant said dryly and pushed the pack away. "It's a covert scheme by the civilians to get rid of the Army."

Terr chuckled. It felt good resting in the shade, letting his thoughts wander. Still, he wasn't going to get anywhere parked on his butt.

"Much as I would love to set up housekeeping, Lieutenant, it's time we went," he said and pointed at his jeep. "If you please."

The lieutenant could not do much about it and knew it. He shrugged and grunted as he got to his feet.

"Gunny, see to the men." He walked briskly to the jeep and climbed in.

"Good luck, sir," the grizzled old sergeant said and saluted. The lieutenant nodded and started the engine.

"See ya, LT," the men chorused.

Terr slid into the seat beside the officer and winced at the touch of hot upholstery. "Get moving, Lieutenant. Southwest."

The jeep snarled into life. With a jerk, they raced into the desert.

Chapter Eleven

"You're sure about that, Master Scout?" Anabb demanded, trying to mask his dislike. Just chemistry, he decided in the end.

Anatol's eyes flickered nervously at the figure sitting silently at the far side of the table. Tapping the little rectangular data wafer against the palm of his hand, Enllss gave no indication he was paying attention, which amounted to a lot of crock, of course.

"My TLM and sensor data will confirm it, sir. Our fire would have collapsed their entire interceptor grid had we managed to get in another burst. An M-6 would have done the job."

The whisper of the life support system crept into the silence. Dark gray formchairs ringed the long black table. A full-dimensional floor-to-ceiling Wall display occupied the near wall. On the opposite side of the briefing room, the wall was transparent. Seemingly within touching distance, tall crater peaks thrust into a black sky. Surface buildings of the Serrll Moon Base radiated across the dusty plain, obscured by one of the two comms towers. An M-4 hovered some twenty katalans above a small landing apron, connected to the terminal by an access tube.

Anabb frowned. "But you didn't get in another burst. Not your fault. CAPFLTCOM will go over your data, Master Scout. A thankless and dangerous task, but you've done well."

Anatol fought to contain his surprise. Peering closely at Anabb, he looked for signs of condescension. These days, he viewed any kind of approval from civilian command with suspicion.

"Thank you, sir," he said guardedly.

Enllss looked up and spoke for the first time. "You're relieved of your command, Master Scout. Effective—"

"But, sir!" Anatol felt the blood drain from his face, his pallor hidden by his black skin.

"—immediately. Make all preparations necessary for handover of the Serrll Moon Base to your executive officer. By no later than seventeen hundred hours tomorrow, you will report to my ship where you'll be returning with us to Taltair for reassignment. Confirming orders from CAPFLTCOM are in your computer."

Anatol sat stunned, unable to believe…

"Sir, I have carried out—"

"Have I indicated any displeasure with your performance, Master Scout?"

"No, sir."

"Then I would advise you to suspend your indignation until you have all the facts. Do you know Prima Scout Tetran?"

"He is based on Talon and commands Fleet forces in the Deklan Republic, sir."

"You're now his operations officer. Fates have given you a singular chance to even out a mistake made five years ago, Master Scout. Don't waste it. That's all."

"I…I don't know what to say, sir." Operations officer meant certain promotion to prima scout rank within four years.

"No need," Enllss said gruffly.

Still dazed, Anatol rose, stood to, hesitated, then briskly walked out. The translucent doors closed behind him with a click. Anabb impatiently tapped at the inlaid pad on the table. The Wall filled with shifting, flowing color patterns.

"Cold son of a bitch," he grumbled sourly.

"A hard person to warm up to," Enllss agreed, stood up and walked to the transparent wall. Hands behind his back, he stared moodily at the bleak landscape. "Capable enough, though. What are we dealing with here, Anabb? Tell me what you're thinking!"

With Shadow and Thunder

Anabb shifted in his chair, the leather creaking. It wasn't often that Enllss allowed himself such a display of concern. On the other hand, there were probably few people in whom he could confide. Maybe more than anything, Enllss could be looking for candor. Anabb's relationship with the commissioner had never been personally close. Their respective positions did not allow it, but Enllss had always permitted Anabb to voice his views openly without fear of repercussions. They both gained something from it.

"You have advisors, Enllss, who can tell it better than I. One thing I do know. If the Serrll doesn't get its shit together, those Kran things will roll right over us."

Enllss snorted impatiently and turned. "When? In a decade? A century? It's all speculative."

"Why would the Orieli lie? You only have to look at their base and the logistical infrastructure necessary to maintain it. All that just for Earth?"

"They have us in a box, you know. Galling, isn't it? We're committed to a massive Fleet buildup whether we want to or not. We need M-6s and M-9s especially. It will take years to roll them out, though."

"You should be thankful that we *have* the years."

"Maybe. What the blazes do we do with them if the Krans don't show up? The government wouldn't survive the fiasco."

"Expand," Anabb said simply.

"Come again?"

"What is your exploration policy, Mr. Commissioner?"

Enllss stared thoughtfully at Anabb. "Are you saying that we've become insular?"

"You should ask the Bureau of Central Planning and Organization," Anabb said dryly.

"I will."

"If the Kran threat is real, we need a buffer of tactical staging outposts for advanced warning and operational sorties. Either way, the effort will generate economic growth, channeling the expansionist drives of Sargon and the Paleans, to name only two, outward where it is needed."

"A policy that could easily backfire on us," Enllss pointed out. "It could accelerate their merger."

"It's a risk, but our problem is more immediate. You must realize, Enllss, that should the Orieli grow tired of our antics, they could interdict the Sol system. Without heavy assets in the area like an M-9, we couldn't stop them."

"I know. What about their blasted scanner grid?"

"All the more reason for concern."

"I hear you, but it won't happen. They're not hostile and it doesn't fit with their behavioral profile."

"I'll keep it in mind next time we go pushing them around."

"Temper. Your orders to Anatol were to back off if the Orieli powered up. Since they didn't, I think it proves my point."

"Proves nothing. While we play our games, let's not forget who we're dealing with."

"We needed to find out," Enllss said in exasperation. "Now that we've got our intelligence, we can stop pushing our luck."

"I wonder if Karhide Zor-Ell will be as understanding next time."

"You know Anabb, you can be a real pain in the ass sometimes," Enllss remarked, openly irritated. "Terchran is milking Terr's crash for all it's worth and Sargon is stirring the Assembly over this nebulous Kran threat. Instead of supporting me, you're pissing in my face."

Anabb smiled broadly. "Just telling it the way it is, Enllss."

"Screw you."

"It's been tried," Anabb said affably, regarding Enllss with amusement. "Talking of Terr, I warned you that your elaborate scheme was going to get someone hurt, but you didn't listen. Terchran appears satisfied, but you may have set forces into motion neither of us understands or can control."

Enllss bridled and glared. "You forget yourself, Prima

Scout! If my methods don't meet with your approval, you can raise the matter with Sill-Anais. Until then, you will continue to obey my orders."

The burn on Anabb's cheek colored, but he held his temper. "My only concern was to get Terr off Earth, Mr. Commissioner."

After a moment, Enllss nodded. "So I gather. Sorry I snapped at you. I'm just somewhat miffed at our Orieli friends."

"By not rescuing Terr themselves?"

"Right the first time. They have the ships and could have yanked him off Earth, saving us no end of problems."

"Maybe, but why should they? Earth is our protectorate, not theirs."

"You're sidestepping the problem and you know it. Still, I hate to sound callous—"

"That has never stopped you before," Anabb said, eyes twinkling. Enllss glared at him.

"You're saying that we should have gone down for Terr ourselves? Terr is my nephew and I don't want to see him hurt, but Dhar has given us an unexpected opportunity to study Earth/Orieli reactions. It could be a valuable insight into both their psychologies."

"While you were caught up in grand strategy, don't forget that it's individuals who have to go out and risk their hides for us, not the unknown masses," Anabb said stiffly.

When the silence began to get heavy, Enllss nodded and sat down. "I have not forgotten. Even though you're impertinent to bring it up now. Is Dhar outside?"

"He's waiting for us."

"Then let's get it over with."

"I don't like this, Enllss, and you can take it any way you want," Anabb said and tapped the inlaid control pad. The doors hissed open and Dhar walked in, his eyes taking in everything. He waited for a moment, then stood to.

"Reporting as ordered, sir," he said heavily, staring fixedly at some point before him.

Anabb waved him to a seat with an impatient gesture. "Sit down, agent Dharaklin," he said and passed a hand through his hair. The veined burn on his cheek still held color.

Dhar moved to a vacant seat and slowly lowered his bulk, allowing the formchair to mold itself around him. He raised his eyebrows and waited. Enllss sat in silence, playing with his fingers. Two mottled red spots colored his cheeks, mouth set in a firm line. It was obvious to Dhar that an argument had just concluded.

And there could be another one.

"How have the Orieli been treating you?" Anabb ventured.

"Well enough, sir. I could not report earlier—"

Anabb raised his hand. "I know. You didn't have secure comms."

"Yes, sir. May I speak freely?"

"Spill it."

"My objective has been achieved, sir. Under the circumstances, I am formally tendering my resignation from the Diplomatic Branch and the Serrll Scout Fleet."

Enllss looked up and shook his head. Anabb had been expecting something like this and didn't even flinch.

"Care to tell me why?"

"For the sake of maintaining my cover with Terchran, I have lost my honor and jeopardized our relationship with the Orieli. That was the price for playing the game and I accept the consequences. However, I have taken the life of a fellow crewman and endangered and embittered the life of my brother. I have betrayed his trust and the teachings of the Discipline. That I cannot accept," Dhar said bleakly and stood up. "I shall return to Anar'on, sir, and await Sankri's vengeance."

"Quite a speech," Enllss mused, his eyes suddenly cold. "I'm touched, really. Seems to me, though, you didn't talk much about honor and the Discipline while spying on us for Anar'on and the Unified Independent Front. Son, you haven't even *begun* paying the price for playing the game."

"Mr. Commissioner, you have no right—"

"Sit down!" Enllss thundered. "As someone pointed out to me, individuals make things happen, not policy. If the struggle didn't cost something, it wouldn't be worth the effort. You're ready enough to enjoy the gains made through the sacrifice of others as long as you can conveniently ignore how it was done. Well, son, now you've seen how it's done. Instead of feeling sorry for yourself, I would suggest you take pride at being able to contribute! Your resignation is refused, Mister."

Wary, Dhar gingerly lowered himself into the seat. In the ringing silence, he fought hard to maintain his composure, feeling a flush of indignation suffuse his face. He could almost see the aura of anger radiating from Enllss. It was anger that came from conviction and a belief in a cause. The words could have been his master's. He struggled to resolve the currents of conflict threatening to tear him apart, his warm glow of moral outrage swept aside. The desert called to him then and he hungered for its solitude and peace.

Heart heavy, he looked at Enllss.

"Sir, there is truth in your words, but they give me little comfort," he said in a low trembling voice.

Anabb listened to the exchange without interfering, conscious of a similar exchange he'd had with Terr. Then, for his own ends, he did what he had to, as Enllss was doing now.

"Mr. Dharaklin, you're confused and hurt that Terr might be suffering. I may appear cold, but he'll be picked up. I am going down personally to see to it, but he hasn't made it easy for himself. We've been monitoring Earth's comms. Not content to sit and wait to be rescued, he goes charging about the desert in his high style trying to reach his damned dart. Thunderation! He caused more flap with their authorities than a war!" he said, his fists clenching and unclenching.

"You didn't expect him to simply sit there and wait, did

you, sir? Within a day, he would have realized that we and the Orieli were caught up in a game of political expediency where he hardly mattered," Dhar said bitterly. Anabb slammed his fist against the table.

"Did he believe that we would abandon him?"

"It probably looked that way to him."

"Mr. Dharaklin," Enllss interrupted. "We have another complication. The SP cell you're running on Taltair. They have gone and taken Teena."

Dhar gaped at such an impossibility. "How could that happen? Shadowing agents were supposed to be guarding her."

"It was done on my orders," Enllss said softly, his chin thrust out in defiance. "We leaked the information to your cell leader and she did the rest."

"With respect, sir, why? Terchran has no interest in Teena."

"Added insurance in case your efforts with Terr were not entirely successful. Your cell has been ordered to keep her on Taltair until you arrive. This happened before you engineered Terr's crash. By then the operation was already in motion. You'll return to Taltair with us, where you will instruct your cell leader to hand Teena over to you. You will then take her to Anar'on."

"Anar'on?" With slow dignity, Dhar stood up. "And Sankri? What happens when he returns to find her gone and me with her? How will you explain that?"

"I'm aware of the personal hurt he has felt and no doubt will feel when he finds both of you gone," Enllss said heavily.

"I don't understand why this is necessary, sir."

"I know that. I can tell you this much. In two months the Unified Independent Front will hold a plenary conference on Anar'on. All the independent General Assembly members will vote for the formal ratification of the UIF. Whether he is satisfied with your performance or not, Terchran will have his hands full lobbying the UIF for support. By taking Teena to Anar'on, drawing Terr after you, I'm hoping Terchran will forget his pique long enough for ongoing events to consume his attention."

"A dubious supposition to rest Sankri's life on, sir. And mine too, perhaps."

"Nevertheless, that's what you will do."

Dhar stared at Enllss, wondering how much of the truth he was being told. Whatever the truth really was.

"Mr. Commissioner, everything I have done has fueled Sankri's belief that I am his enemy. Taking Teena will only serve to confirm that belief. When he confronts me, and he will, the bond between us may not be enough to stay his hand."

"I know that," Enllss said harshly. "It's a price you pay for being a player."

* * *

Shadows stretched lazily across the baked ground. Dying fire from a bloated red sun tinged the dusty western sky. The breeze stirred restlessly from the desert and made the grass whisper. The cluster of houses looked worn and tired as the desert itself. A tumbleweed shuddered and rolled in an ungainly gait across a lonely street. Muddy-yellow light made round pools beneath cracked telephone poles. Somewhere a dog barked briefly, then subsided into muffled growls. A dust devil played with a spout of sand. The place seemed deserted.

Terr rolled his tongue across dry, cracked lips. Every joint in his body ached. The muscles in his legs twitched with fatigue. This was the end of the line. Not ready to give up exactly, but he needed time to rest and recover. Time he suspected the Earth authorities were not going to give him. He looked around and leaned against the battered fence. It creaked mournfully and sagged beneath him. His breathing a rasping wheeze in his ears as he waited for something to happen. He only heard the tired sigh of the desert.

Terr kicked at one of the cracked fence boards. Flakes of dirty paint gaped at him like hungry mouths. The board fell easily into the sand. He stooped under the top bar and slowly walked across the street. Sand lay piled against the curb. The neon light above the hamburger store flickered dull green. Half the letters were smashed and the tubing hung limp. Reedy music and loud voices came from somewhere up the street. Someone gunned an engine and there was a squeal of tires as the car roared away. Then the silence returned.

Covered by dust and streaked with rust, the blue and white police cruiser waited patiently beside the sidewalk. It too had seen better days. The stone building behind it could have been pretty once. Now it looked neglected and gloomy. Terr staggered up stone steps to the ancient carved door, feeling like his feet were set in cement. The hinges screeched as the door swung in.

"Shut it after you, Mac," said a voice from within. "Be with you in a minute."

Terr closed the door and leaned against it. It was cool inside the old building. The place smelled dusty and used. He felt himself starting to tremble. He stared at a wide back covered with a wrinkled khaki shirt. A dark stain ran down along the spine. Long legs rested on the table. The reading lamp sent a shaft of white light across it. Dog-eared wanted posters hung on a board behind the cop. A rack of polished Winchesters and shotguns stood fastened to the far wall. An open doorway led to the holding cells. Two naked yellow bulbs on the ceiling kept the shadows at bay.

Morrow dropped his feet to the floor with a crash that raised dust and swiveled in his seat.

"Now, Mac. What can I..." he started and his lantern jaw sagged, the wad of tobacco in his mouth forgotten.

The book he held thudded loudly against the gaping floorboards. His clear black eyes opened like holes. Burnt brown by the sun and wind, his skin wrinkled around the eyes and mouth.

A rebellious lock of black hair fell across a high, flat forehead.

Awfully quiet as they stared at each other, Terr worked his mouth to say something, but it was all too much bother. Morrow slowly raised his left hand and swept it across his untidy hair. As he tugged at the open collar, his right hand crept toward the holster.

"Don't do it," Terr croaked. Morrow looked startled and his hand froze. Then he chuckled and relaxed.

"Okay, Mac. What now?"

"Is there anyone else in here?"

"Why should I answer that?" Morrow said easily. "You gonna kill me anyway, Mac. I read the papers."

Terr felt buzzing somewhere in the back of his head and he slowly slid to the floor. Morrow reached for his gun and Terr flicked up his right wrist. The cop was quick, but he couldn't beat the orange beam as it struck the floor between his feet. A sharp crackle and smoke spurted around Morrow's legs. The smell of burnt wood hung heavy in the air.

Gun frozen halfway out of the holster, Morrow looked at the hole between his boots. Chuckling nervously, he slowly pulled his hand away from the gun. He crossed his arms in his lap and sat back in the chair. Mouth working on the tobacco, he turned his head and aimed at a spittoon.

"I can take a hint, Mac," he said, grinning as he wiped his mouth. "No need to scare the pee out of a feller."

Terr didn't hear him. He was trying to remember the last thing the cop said. If he could only let go and sleep. Brain fuzzy, full of desert images, he tried to concentrate.

"What papers?" Terr croaked and licked his lips.

"Well, now." Morrow brightened, looking like he was enjoying the whole thing. "It seems like you're quite a desperado, Mac. The whole darned Army is after you. No telling what death and destruction you're dealing out, but you don't look so hot lying on the floor there."

"It's the mileage," Terr said weakly and chuckled. "Your

deputies?"

"Gone for the day."

"Officer," Terr whispered. "Would you please give me some water?"

Morrow stared at Terr for a long time, then stood up and walked to the wall fridge. He took out a glass and a pitcher of iced water. Standing over the alien, he held out the glass. Terr looked into his eyes and switched off the shield.

He drank slowly, savoring every mouthful. When he finished, he gave back the glass and said thanks. Then he closed his eyes.

* * *

The hinges groaned in pain and Terr winced. An individual in black trousers and white shirt cautiously poked in his head and hurriedly closed the door.

"Sheriff," the man squeaked in a high-pitched trembling voice. "I demand to know what you're doing to meet this threat against God and Church. Hear?"

Morrow looked up from his book, his long legs on the desk, and stared at the fat preacher in astonishment. His mouth worked quickly on the wad. The preacher's collar was grimy and the sleeves were rolled up. Nervous little yellow eyes stared from folds of sagging flesh. His head was bald and glistened with sweat.

"What are you talking about, Reverend? What threat?"

"You don't know?" The clergyman looked dumbfounded, his eyes growing round. "It came over the radio hours ago." He mopped his face and sagging jowls with a dirty linen rag and inhaled deeply.

"What came, Mac—I mean, Reverend?"

"Why, that...that...creature!" The clergyman emphasized his meaning with some waving of hands. "They reported him

to be somewhere in this area. Something to do with an unconscious Army officer and a broken jeep they found some miles
from here. Well?"

"Frankly, the whole situation is a lot of hog, Reverend,"
Morrow said and nodded sagely. "There's no need to get riled."

The clergy paled and shook a well-manicured finger at the
law. "I will not allow the name of the Church to be bandied
about by some agent of Satan! I warn you—"

The jail door protested as Terr pulled it toward him. The
clergyman had his mouth open when his head jerked toward
the sound. His eyes bulged and his face drained like dirty dish-
water. He crossed himself quickly and started backing toward
the door.

"In league with the devil himself," he whispered and
glanced nervously at Morrow. "The people shall hear of this,
Sheriff," he said and fled, the door banging after him.

Morrow looked at Terr and shook his head in disgust.
"Well, Mac, now you've done it."

Terr looked at the door, then back to Morrow's disapproving scowl. "I gather that priest is liable to cause us trouble?"

"Heaps. I'll try and set you straight, Mac. That was Reverend Mario," he paused as though the name sufficed to explain
everything. "And he's no priest. Besides trying to save our
souls, he has some fool notion that you're working with the
devil to lead the people into damnation. You shoulda heard his
sermon, Mac, when the UN held that meeting with them Orieli.
Boy! Spouting fire and brimstone, he was." He chuckled fondly
at the memory. "I guess he don't like you guys much."

Morrow dropped his legs to the floor with a crash and
stood up. "The point is, he'll bring the town on you. No telling
what he'll get them to do. Mobs is ugly." The cop's eyes bored
into him. "What's that about some Army officer?"

"I had to commandeer a jeep to get out of their search area.
When the thing ran out of fuel, I sort of left him behind with
the jeep."

"He's hurt? If you've—"

"I didn't hurt him," Terr said truthfully. Stunning him would leave the lieutenant with a headache, but no permanent damage. Besides, the lieutenant hadn't been such a bad guy for an army type.

"Okay. I believe you. How did you slip past the helos, satellites and stuff?"

"It's a big desert, Sheriff."

"Yeah, and it's growing."

"And I probably haven't slipped past them anyway, judging from what the clergyman said."

"Mmm, a matter of time, eh? We've got to do something about getting you outta here. You may have fooled them for a time, but they'll come looking. And with Mario on the prowl—"

"You have a car. You could drive me."

"Hah! It ain't so easy. Where do I drive you before some other mob gets to you, eh? Besides, I gotta live in this here town. Not good."

Why did he bother? Morrow could just open the door and…and…Life was a bitch, Terr decided.

"Anyhow, you shouldn't be walking around. Not with that gash in your side. You sure you don't want Doc Gant to look at you, Mac? He's only a vet, mind you, but he can take—"

"I'm sure," Terr said, stopping the flood of Doc Gant's sterling qualities. Muffled voices and shouts grew outside. Something heavy struck the door.

"Well, he sure as hell didn't waste any time about it," Morrow grumbled sourly.

"Sheriff!" came a bull, throaty voice. "We know he's in there. We only want to do what's right. Don't try and stop us."

"You hear, Sheriff?"

"I better go and see what's on their minds, Mac," Morrow declared and walked to the gun rack. He picked out a shotgun pump and checked the breech. He walked to the door, paused and looked at Terr. "Don't go away," he said and walked out.

Angry shouts rose like a wave, Mario's high-pitched voice prominent among them. A shotgun blast broke the commotion, followed by hollow silence. While Morrow talked, catcalls and jeers kept interrupting him. When his voice began to get heated, Terr figured that maybe Morrow wasn't getting his message across. He shook his head and switched on his shield. He couldn't let Morrow get hurt because of him, now could he? And Morrow only had a shotgun anyway.

There were startled gasps when he walked out. Morrow glanced at Terr and nodded. Mario shook his fist and pointed a finger at Terr.

"I told you!" he screamed. "It's an abomination!" He faced the crowd and raised his arms. "Thou shalt not suffer an abomination to live!"

An angry murmur of assent swept through the crowd. Several citizens, brandishing axes and pitchforks, stepped forward, glancing back with every step to make sure of their support. Terr stood on the steps and stared down at them.

"For God and Church!" the clergyman screamed. Someone threw a brick at Terr. It slammed against the shield and fell at his feet.

He raised the intensity of the shield until it flared, surrounding himself in a shimmering golden cocoon. The crowd fell back and someone whimpered. He raised his hands, palms down and leveled them. A sheet of white light fanned over the crowd.

Shotguns, rifles, axes, and assorted hardware clattered on the street as the citizenry melted into the darkness. A child wailed somewhere in the shadows.

"Wait!" Mario shouted after the retreating figures. "His power cannot stand the word of God!"

"I ain't hanging around, Reverend. You never told us that a guy could get hisself killed," the citizen puffed self-righteously and disappeared into the gloom.

Mario muttered a quick prayer to sustain him in this, his hour of need, and looked at Morrow.

"It's never too late, Sheriff. You've been blinded by that creature of Satan. Do your duty."

Morrow lowered his shotgun and leaned on the barrel. "Look, Reverend. You're stirring up a heap of trouble for nothing. There is no evil involved here, just another godly creature hurting. If you persist in this stupidity, I guess I'll have to run you in."

"You wouldn't dare lay a hand on me!"

"I have to keep the peace in this town, Mac. The law doesn't recognize that having the black cloth gives you a license for lawlessness."

"We'll see what the Mayor has to say about this, Sheriff."

"Granpaw will probably agree with me." Morrow guffawed. Mario gave Terr a look of condemnation, then ran after the crowd. Terr didn't blame him. He'd seen it all before. The only difference lay in the garb they wore. He was just being moody.

Rit!

"I only want to get out of here," Terr said and looked at Morrow. "They can run their lives any way they want. Why don't they just leave me alone?"

Morrow shook his head. "You've got what we want, Mac. If we can't have it, we'll see to it that you don't neither." Terr stood beside him, listening. "Take us, for instance. For the last eight years, this land hasn't seen any rain that matters. What used to be the richest farmlands on earth have turned into sand and salt. Payback time I suppose for what we did to this stinking planet.

"The young have gone. This is nothing but a ghost town now, populated by ghosts and old relics like me. So, people have turned to men like Mario for salvation or something, but I figure men like him are already damned. We fear and hate you because you're different and because our problems don't mean nothing to you." He spat out tobacco juice on the street, picked up his gun and stalked to the door.

"Yeah, life is hell," Terr muttered.

Morrow placed his hand on the door handle and turned. "What now, Mac?"

"The clergyman is probably calling the authorities. I'm not anxious to be around when they get here."

"I don't blame you. And where did you figure on heading, eh? The desert? With everyone after you? You got a special hole you planning to crawl into? Besides, you're in no condition to go anywhere, Mac. You oughta be in a hospital."

"You want to drive or shall I?" Terr grinned at him.

"Plum crazy," Morrow muttered under his breath and walked into the police station.

* * *

COUNTRY IN UPROAR OVER ALIEN SCANDAL
WOUNDED ALIEN SLIPS THROUGH ARMY CORDON
THE UN CONDEMNS AMERICAN TERRORIST TACTICS
RUSSIANS OFFER SANCTUARY TO ALIEN

"Jack Willison reporting for CNN. Interesting new developments from the research vehicle that soft-landed on the Moon two days ago. After a series of low orbits, Prometheus-1 reported increased spaceship activity around the Serrll base. Although the vehicle failed to locate the Orieli base, NASA is pleased with the data coming in.

"Rumors have it that Earth will finally be held to account for the treatment Opturkarh Terrllss-rr received at the hands of US security forces. Still on the run, probably trying to reach his ship, the alien is understandably skeptical of the Administration's attempts to calm the situation. President Hennery is urging the people to cooperate with the authorities in locating the missing alien. Congress is in an uproar over the fiasco surrounding the alien and the Army's attempts to gain entry into the crashed ship. Under increasing international embarrassment, the United States may accelerate the process of allowing a UN team to the site."

* * *

"Vatican finally hands down its ruling on the so-called historical Serrll landings on Earth. All members of the clergy are warned that any connection with biblical writings and alien intervention will be severely dealt with. Excommunication was only one of the threats mentioned. Archbishop Waller urged the people to seek out the teachings of the Church. In these critical times, he claims, when the Church is undergoing it severest trial, faith must sustain the followers.

"Meanwhile, the Vision of God sect and the Leave Earth Alone society continue to clash over irreconcilable ideological differences. The single-minded fanaticism of both groups has led to a wave of protest from ordinary citizens caught up in spontaneous violence. Until either group actually kills someone, the authorities seem powerless or unwilling to stop the increasingly polarized attacks on innocent citizens and property. This is Mark Rown for NBC news."

* * *

The small M-1 scout drifted slowly toward the towering bulk of the Orieli ship. It paused before the gaping hangar bay in the sheer wall of the ship, then disappeared into the giant maw. The hangar doors closed behind it.

Transported directly to one of the briefing lounges, Zor-Ell waited for them, relaxed and smiling. Enllss and Anabb looked about them with undisguised interest. A low table stood near one side of the triangular room. Another wall was transparent. The stars stared back, harsh and white. Shrubs and broad leafy plants occupied the remaining wall. A lichen-covered boulder masked a miniature waterfall. The tinkle of bubbling water made a pleasant and soothing distraction. Subdued indirect lighting provided adequate illumination over the table, keeping the rest of the room discrete.

"Please make yourselves comfortable, gentlemen. I shall keep this as informal as circumstances permit," Zor-Ell said affably as he waited for his solemn-faced guests to settle in.

"Very impressive," Enllss muttered, nodding at the incredible room. "Reminds me…" he stopped, his suspicion growing. Was this setup for his benefit or simply decoration? He had taken pains to study the holoview record of the Salina conference, trying to get a handle on the Orieli. His analysis team corroborated Anabb's evaluation. The Orieli were not trying to be deliberately subtle. It was just that they seemed to understand things so well. Diplomacy without guile made him uncomfortable.

"It's relaxing, but its upkeep can make it an awkward distraction sometimes, Da Commissioner," Zor-Ell said after casting an approving glance at the greenery.

Enllss shifted in his seat trying to dig up a hidden meaning behind those words.

"Like this meeting, Karhide? There is no need to mince words. Your encounter with elements of our Fleet has been an embarrassment for the Serrll, but an isolated incident. I can only apologize. You have my government's assurance that it will not happen again."

"Focus on territorial integrity is always commendable, Da. Provided that in its zeal the effort does not overlook broader strategic threats."

Enllss fought hard to keep a straight face. This guy was beautiful, certain the Orieli have seen through the Serrll's attempts to gather operational intelligence while issuing a warning, of course. The Krans were more of a threat to the Serrll than the Orieli.

"It is not always possible to control what an individual commander will do," Enllss said dryly, willing to play along.

"To the lament of high command everywhere, Da Commissioner," Zor-Ell agreed and gave a faint smile. "Very well. I shall consider the incident with Master Scout Keller closed. Now, if you will permit me to explain something of my mission here—"

"Before you do that, Karhide. We have a more immediate problem," Anabb said, wishing that someone would stop these amateurish psychology games.

The atmosphere suddenly became cold. The silence grew into noticeable tension in the room.

"Since you choose to bring it up, Da Director," Zor-Ell began icily. "By all means, let us deal with it. I will say this. While the Serrll maintains a contingent at our base, we will *not* tolerate any expression of political dissent. Despite our warning, you continued to pursue your provocative policy."

"That is hardly fair," Anabb replied evenly, feeling very much ill at ease.

"I suggest Opturkarh Terrllss-rr would disagree, Da."

"What are you proposing to do, Karhide?" Enllss asked.

"I shall be making an immediate flight to Earth before the situation escalates beyond their capacity to control it. The Serrll can face up to the consequence of its actions, Earth cannot. With their fragmented and pluralistic regional ideologies the RV/4 dart is a dangerous and destabilizing variable, as is Terr's very presence."

"A variable which the Orieli have chosen to exploit for its own ends as well, Karhide. You could have made the recovery yourself already," Enllss replied testily, then kicked himself for his blunder.

"By violating our agreement? When we requested Serrll

Moon Base to recover Opturkarh Terr and the dart, it was denied. Under cover of opportunistic expediency to evaluate our reaction, you abrogated your responsibility to Earth. Do not speak to me of exploitation, Da Commissioner."

In the ensuing silence the gurgling of the waterfall seemed overly loud. Whether he liked it or not, and he didn't, Enllss admitted that Zor-Ell had a point.

"You're ready enough to take unilateral action now, Karhide," Anabb pointed out.

"Not unilateral. The presence of your M-4 is a mandatory requirement and will serve to drive the point home, Da Karr. Earth must not see us as divided interests."

"Indeed," Enllss mused. If they allowed Earth to intimidate them the situation could become an intolerable nuisance in any future incident. Only one thing remained unclear to him. Did the Orieli deliberately wait for him to show up before mounting this rescue? Possible, but he was disturbed by the psychological implication behind that declaration.

"Da Commissioner," Zor-Ell said, his expression stern. "The Orieli is very aware of the difficulty our presence has caused the Serrll. Let us not endanger the process by manipulating the situation."

Enllss bit his lip. The rebuke could not have been clearer.

"It has been a salutary lesson, Karhide," he said heavily and Zor-Ell nodded. It did nothing to dispel the tension in the room.

"Before we make preparations to get underway, I wish to clarify something of my presence," Zor-Ell said. "After my initial contact with Terrllss-rr five years ago, we have not made subsequent missions to Serrll space. Except for one a year later."

"Recovery of an observer, perhaps?" Enllss queried, studying the alien closely, but Zor-Ell refused to be drawn.

"We estimated that five years provided ample time for you

249

to evaluate the impact of that contact. Karhide Arlon Dee initiated what we call second-contact procedure."

"The Kran threat?" Anabb suggested and Zor-Ell shook his head.

"I have been warned not to underestimate you, Da. I do not. In turn, do not attribute to us a level of subtlety that might be illusory. Everything Karhide Arlon Dee stated concerning the Celi-Kran is fact. Fact I will prove to your General Assembly. The Orieli does not meddle, Da."

Enllss allowed himself a long grin. "May I suggest Karhide, with your base beneath us, the Orieli have a unique definition of what constitutes meddling."

"An understandable misconception. What I'm about to tell you, Da, is for Enllss-rr, not the Commissioner for the Bureau of Colonial and Protectorate Affairs."

Enllss nodded once. "Understood."

"Despite the Kran threat, my recommendation to the Orieli government clearly stated that we should mind our own business and allow you to mind yours. Please don't take this as an offense, Enllss. The Serrll Combine is not ready to share the stars with others until all who occupy them are *us*, not *they*. Be that as it may. We're faced with a mutual threat, you and all who occupy this part of the galaxy. Times dictate the means. We have no choice but to sit on your doorstep, so to speak. You might not like it, but you will like it even less once Kran ships appear in your early warning plates.

"I'm not here pretending to hand out judgment. Future relationships between us is not in my hands. I am merely stating points of incompatibility. Let us remain friends from a distance, rather than brothers in arms. My statements should not be construed as reflecting Orieli policy, only a personal observation."

Enllss gave a wry smile. If he believed that, then he was more gullible than he thought.

"Tell me, Karhide. What *is* Orieli policy? With the alleged

Kran threat, your presence in our space is more than just a simple contact."

"I agree, Da Commissioner. That, however, I will present to your General Assembly personally."

* * *

"There is a farmhouse ahead, Mac. Bath, hot food, a soft bed," Morrow drawled slowly and leered at Terr.

"Ah, you're cruel," Terr groaned and Morrow laughed.

Terr sat up and looked wearily out of the side window. Blackness lay all around them. He couldn't even see the stars. "Keep going. We cannot stop now. Just keep going."

He gasped as the car jerked, then looked down at his side. He pulled away his hand. Despite a new bandage, there was fresh blood on it. He sat back in the vinyl upholstery and closed his eyes.

"No way, Mac! You'll die on me like this. Want me to get stuck with a lousy murder rap? And me a cop. How would I explain you away? Why, they'd lock me up and throw away the key."

Morrow swung into the driveway and the old car lurched, tires crunching on gravel. He swore and slowed down. Hell, Terr didn't feel a thing.

They stopped before the looming shape of a two-story building. Morrow pulled on the handbrake, switched off the headlights, and opened the door. Terr staggered as he stepped out of the car. He leaned heavily against the dusty hood. It was cold and he breathed deeply of the crisp desert air.

Two silver rings crowned a quarter moon. In the white glare the stars were barely visible. They hung, a canopy of light, in a lazy arch across the heavens. The breeze whistled softly, carrying with it fine sand. It stung as it struck his face and hands.

Morrow slammed the door shut and his boots crunched as

he walked around the back of the car. He stopped beside Terr, shook his head and sighed.

"I'll say this for you, Mac. You don't give up."

Terr managed a dry cackle. "Give up? To whom?"

Morrow stared at him for a while and grunted. "Screwed if I know why I'm doing this anyhow. I'll probably lose my lousy pension over this anyway," he muttered sourly.

Tall poplars and old pines surrounded the ghostly outline of a dark house. They swayed gently to the muted sound of rushing surf. Terr had to lean a bit on Morrow's arm as they walked to the front porch. Loose boards creaked under their weight. A cat, its back arched, spat at them. Its yellow eyes flashed bright, then it was gone.

Morrow took a quick look around the yard and hammered on the door. From upstairs came a sound of grunting and a creak of bedsprings. A rectangle of yellow light splashed on the ground beside them. The window rattled as it opened, rasping as someone dragged it up.

"What's going on down there?" The voice sharp and no-nonsense. "Who's out there?"

Morrow stepped into the light and looked up. "Sheriff Morrow from Cott County. I've a badly injured man here."

"Pretty far from your territory, aren't you, Sheriff? Why didn't you holler for help?"

"My car radio is busted, is why," Morrow shouted back, glad the man had not asked him about his cell phone. "Now, are you gonna let us stand here or what?"

"Who is it, Mark?" A young woman clad in a thin nightdress leaned out. Mark pushed her inside and closed the window. A cricket ventured a few bars of his song, then decided against it. The porch light came on and a key rattled in the lock. The door swung in letting through a rifle barrel.

"You can't be too careful around here, Sheriff," Mark said apologetically, eyeing Morrow's uniform and badge. Thin, weather-burned and hungry looking, his black hair was disheveled, giving him a slightly mad appearance. He looked friendly enough, lips full and showed uneven teeth. He opened the door wide, looked around quickly and lowered the Winchester.

The barefooted woman stood shyly beside the door. Her long dark brown hair spilled across her shoulders. She might have been pretty once, but sun and hard work had added lines around her eyes and mouth beyond her years.

"Where's your man?" Mark demanded.

Terr stepped out of the shadows and stood beside Morrow. Mark turned pale and the Winchester quivered in his hands. The woman gasped and brought her knuckles hard against her mouth.

"No need to panic, folks," Morrow said. "No one is getting hurt."

"Please put your weapon away," Terr said, trying to stand straight. "All I need is a couple of minutes to pull myself together."

"Uh, you'd better get going, Sheriff," Mark said and licked his lips. "I watched the TV. I don't want no trouble."

"Mark Larkin!" the young woman gasped in surprise. "I'm right ashamed of you. I saw the news too. They said it was all a mistake. Where can they go this time 'o night, anyhow?" She stared openly at Terr as he tried hard not to tremble. On impulse, she stepped out on the porch and placed her hands around his waist.

"Sally!"

"Hush, Mark! Men," she declared with contempt. "We're not turning away the injured, no matter who they are. You're going to confession on Sunday, hear?"

She frowned, pulled away, and looked at Terr in surprise as she held out her hand. There was brown blood on it.

"Why, you're bleeding!"

"Ow, hell!" Mark lowered his rifle and opened the door wide. With a bit of help, Terr managed to steer himself through the door and into a huge warm den.

The high ceiling showed dark exposed beams. Worn un-painted stairs wound up. Railing protected the upper level. Loose rugs covered the polished wooden floor. Coats and sweaters hung on hooks beside the door. Stacked on the floor was an assortment of shoes and boots. Along one naked brick wall, four staggered shelves held books, cups, flowers and other odd things. Couches and loose cushions made a rough semicir-cle before the flat television receiver.

"Hey! It's the spaceman!" came an excited shout from up-stairs. "Wait till I tell the guys."

Terr looked up. Three kids stared down at him from be-hind the railing.

"Back to bed, all of you!" Mark snapped, "before I takes the cane to you all."

"Aw, Daddy." Wedged between her brothers the little girl looked down with large pleading eyes. "Just for a little while. Pretty please?"

"Out of the question!"

"Now, Mark…"

Mark looked at his wife and shrugged. "Well, okay," he grumbled, rewarded by shouts of happiness. "But only for a few minutes, hear?"

"Oh, boy!" The boys rushed down the stairs and crowded around Terr as Sally guided him to a couch. He sank into its softness with a grateful sigh.

"Can you tell us about your base on the Moon?" one of the boys chirped, his wide round eyes danced with glee. He had his father's teeth, uneven and with gaps.

"Yeah, neat. How does your spaceship work? You should have seen it hovering above the UN building. Man!" said the other and tilted his spread hands in imaginary flight.

"Nah, tell us about the Celi-Kran. Do they really have ray guns like Buck Rogers? Bzzz…Zap!" He swung around the room with both thumbs and forefingers blazing.

The little girl just stared at Terr. Clutching her brother's pajama leg, her large brown eyes stared at him in wonder and awe, round face shining with health and quiet serenity.

"I said you could watch." Mark glared at them. "Not run a quiz."

Terr raised his hand. "It's all right." He smiled, looking at each of them in turn. "About the base, you might even get to see it. I'll see what can be arranged."

If he got out of this in one piece, he reminded himself.

"Did you hear that, Paw?" one of the boys exclaimed, jumping up and down. "A trip to the Moon!"

"Now, boys," Mark spoke sternly. "I'm sure Commander Terrllss-rr has more important things to do than take you all to the Moon, for Crissake."

"The least I can do."

"See, Paw!"

"And my spaceship? Real antigravity, you know. It can go faster than light, too."

They just watched him, mouths around with wonder and eyes full of stars. His heart went out to them. The naive innocence of children!

"Bath is ready!" Sally called from somewhere down the corridor.

"Right," Mark growled kindly at the kids. "Off you go now, hear?"

"Ow, Paw."

"You've had your quiz. Now git."

"We'll see you tomorrow, won't we, Mister?" the little girl asked as she walked backward after her brothers.

"Sure." Terr nodded and smiled. "You'll see me tomorrow."

Her smile warm and happy as she ran squealing up the stairs. Terr closed his eyes and there was an all too familiar smell of antiseptic in the air.

Rit!

* * *

"Now, men!" Colonel Bradley snapped. His face shaved blue, his trousers were creased razors. He glared at the ranks before him, braided cap set at a rakish angle.

"If you want to draw your GI benefits, you keep those itchy fingers off them triggers." A half-hearted ripple of strained laughter came from the assembled shadows. "Whatever they want, the buckles from your belts or your favorite blue pix, it's your duty to hand it over with a grin."

The crater and the cliffs around them were clad in black. Stark polyarcs glared down from the poles. The eastern sky was a sheet of blood. The place would be a small hell once the sun staggered above the cliffs, but right now, the intense cold made him cringe. Drawn out of their tents by the clatter of weapons and heavy boots the civilian staff looked on with mild contempt at the frantic military.

"Colonel?" A tall burly figure dressed in jungle fatigues and black beret stood easily beside Bradley.

"What is it, Major?"

"Radar plot shows two large objects displaying non-ballistic motion heading our way, sir."

"ETA?"

"They're already here, Colonel." Bradley glanced sharply at the portly form as the civilian stepped out of the shadows. Casually, almost with indifference, the man drew a pipe from his pocket, clamped his teeth on the stem and looked up. Bradley followed his glance.

The massive shapes glided slowly, silently above them, their bellies shimmered a reflected brick red. One was a huge rectangular slab with downward curved flowing edges. The other ship dark, utilitarian, roughly triangular. Neither exhibited any lighted ports. There was hardly any sky left as they slowed. Then they just stopped, without any noise. Studying the smaller ship, Bradley did not doubt he looked at a machine of death.

The men glanced nervously at one another and shuffled their feet.

"Silence there!" Bradley growled, staring at the ships. Big bastards! Suddenly it seemed to get very warm.

They didn't keep him waiting long. White light lanced from the side of the larger rectangular ship as great hangar doors retracted. A tiny yellow-pulsing dot detached itself from the towering starship and began to sink. It came down very quickly. Bradley wondered why the Orieli didn't use their Star Trek transporter. Maybe they didn't want to startle anyone. Very considerate of them if true, he mused.

The flat platform shape stopped short some six inches above the glazed crater floor and hovered. The yellow shield surrounding the craft pulsed briefly, turned crimson, and died.

There were three of them, Zaronians, blue-skinned, eyes bleak and grim. Bradley recognized gold braid when he saw it, even when alien. His boots clicked together, toes at a forty-five-degree angle, shoulders square.

"Tan...hut!" he growled and the shadows around him came to with one clean smash of feet. Bradley executed a perfect salute.

One of the aliens stepped off the platform and brought the tips of his right hand to his forehead. "Karhide Zor-Ell, at your service, Colonel," he said in a soft Eastern accent.

Bradley wondered how the hell the guy could speak such flawless English. "Colonel Bradley, sir, United States Air Force." He relaxed and automatically extended his hand. The alien took a step toward him and grasped the hand firmly. Bradley smiled at the alien, wondering what to say.

Zor-Ell stood beside him and rubbed his hands. "Damn cold this time of morning, eh, Colonel?"

Bradley grinned hugely and looked up. Blood still streaked the sky, but there were blotches of orange on the eastern rim. "Not when the sun gets up, sir. Then it's a bitch."

Zor-Ell turned toward the platform and nodded. The yellow shield sprang up immediately and the platform lifted and moved slowly toward the fallen dart. It stopped before the ship and hovered. The two aliens climbed down. They stood before the dart and a hatch drew smoothly back, splashing the ground with a triangle of white light. The landing strip extruded out of the ship and the two aliens stepped on it. It retracted and the hatch closed behind them. Bradley glanced at Dr. Raydon. The civilian beside him smiled musingly and shrugged.

A few minutes later the shield around the dart glowed dull red, brightened and flared white. Bradley lifted his hand over his eyes and squinted. Abruptly, the shield dimmed and glowed crimson. The dart shifted, righted itself, rose a few feet, and hovered. The hatch opened and the landing strip slid out. One of the aliens walked down the strip and jumped. The landing strip retracted immediately. The dart began to rise, its shield hardly visible. It slowed to a hover beside the open hangar doors, hesitated, and moved into the starship. The platform glided back silently and stopped before the assembled men.

Zor-Ell faced Bradley. "Well, Colonel, that about wraps it up. I apologize for tying you down like this and I appreciate the service. You may dismiss your personnel, Da." He turned, climbed on the platform and they were gone.

Bradley stared after them as they disappeared into the hovering ship. The hangar doors closed and the two ships drifted off.

"Pity." Doctor Raydon shifted the pipe to the other side of his mouth. "We could have gotten the thing open if we only had a little bit more time."

"I suppose you want to go after them and say, 'Look, old chap. We're not quite finished, what? Would you mind terribly dropping in a bit later? That's a good fellow.' Well?" Bradley snarled with heavy sarcasm.

Raydon chuckled indulgently. Bradley took off his cap and wiped the sweatband.

"Major?" he rasped irritably.

A black figure materialized out of the gloom. "Sir?"

"What are we hanging around here for? Like the man said, start packing." The major disappeared among the shadows shouting orders. Bradley fiddled with his cap, in a way glad it was over. The place had begun to give him the creeps.

A piece of gold wedged itself above the jagged skyline. Sheets of light fanned into the crater. The pressing gloom disappeared and the sky smiled. Bradley snorted and flipped his cap into the tent behind him.

* * *

The leaves whispered and the breeze brushed Terr's face with a mild caress. A sparrow twittered on the window ledge. It fluttered away in alarm when he turned his head. He could smell the pines and the burnt sand of the desert. He stretched his arms and yawned. It was a big yawn and he was sorry when it finished. He tried another, but his heart wasn't in it.

He shrugged philosophically and locked his fingers behind his head. He wiggled his toes, watched the blanket move and chuckled, content to revel in the dreamy glow of the morning.

What was Teena doing now? His face softened and he stared at something far away. Teena…to touch your hair again, your face, to see you smile, to hear your laughter. He felt the longing deep within him and also an inexplicable sadness. Then he thought of Nightwings, the Wanderers and of shifting sands, and prana water, and his face clouded.

He cursed Anabb and crumpled the bedsheet in a clenched fist. If this is what it takes, he didn't want any part of it. He'd had enough. The smooth-talking bastard won't be pulling anymore world-saving missions for him. And he can shove his promotion up his ass.

A sound of relaxed voices came from downstairs. He sat

up and winced. His left side looked inflamed and felt very tender. He touched the bandages around the wound, feeling the warmth of his body. It could have been worse. His uniform lay neatly on the chair beside him, pressed and cleaned. The energy sphere made a small indentation on top of the trousers. Finally, he threw back the covers and swung his legs out of the bed. It didn't take long to wash up and dress.

He opened the door and stepped quietly into the corridor. The door behind him closed with a soft click. He walked toward the stairs and peered over the rail. He could not explain why he crept around like that, but his inner alarms were clanging. He knew the feeling too well to ignore it.

They were seated around a great wooden table. Mark and Morrow on one side and three characters dressed in various shades of gray worsted on the other. They all had that aware look about them of hitmen: blank, dry faced with no expression.

Coffee and toast lay before them. A thread of steam rose lazily from the pot. Fresh rolls surrounded slices of red ham on a chrome platter. Terr's mouth watered and he swallowed. He hadn't eaten since he left Houston. Sally appeared from the side door carrying jam and another plate of toast.

"We should let him sleep as long as possible," Morrow said and slurped at his coffee. "He's had a rough time."

"There is no hurry, Sheriff," one of the three spoke softly and smiled. Terr bet it hurt his face.

"He's wounded pretty bad, Inspector. You taking him to a hospital?" Mark ventured.

"Yeah. We'll take good care of him. Right, George?" The one with the ingratiating smile glanced at his sidekick.

The other looked coldly at Mark and nodded. "Right."

Terr switched on his shield and started down the stairs. He didn't know why he did that. One of the boards creaked and faces turned at the sound. The three strangers stood up, not too quickly, but ready for anything. He could smell a professional when he stumbled over one. And these three were grim under-taker types.

"Good morning, Opturkarh," said the one with the soft smile. He reminded Terr of the communal driver on Taltair, except for the eyes. "I trust you've slept well?"

"Well enough," Terr said cautiously.

"I'm glad to hear it."

"Terr?" Morrow looked uneasily at Terr like he'd pulled a fast one. "These men here are FBI agents."

Chapter Twelve

"The FBI? You can take it that I'm suitably impressed," Terr said.

"They've come looking for you, young feller," Morrow said gruffly.

"Indeed? That was quick. No need for IDs gentlemen. I'll just take your word for it."

Laughing boy smiled thinly and the other two sat down. "Sorry, Opturkarh. Iam Special Agent Arskin. My associates, Agents Farrow and Tanner." The two sidekicks didn't seem overawed by Terr's presence. They just sat there nursing their cups of coffee. "You've given us quite a chase," Arskin pointed out affably.

"The chase isn't over, Mr. Arskin."

"You must have read the papers, sir. Sheriff Morrow had a set in his office. Surely you realize there is no need to continue with this, ah…"

"Hunt?" Terr suggested.

Arskin frowned. "As you say."

"Well, I don't know anything of the kind, Mr. Arskin. Just pretty words in a second-rate rag."

"General Cannon had overstepped his authority and President Hennery only wishes to make amends. The whole thing has been a mistake."

"That's what the paper said, but if you have no objection, I'll continue on my way."

"Opturkarh, if you'll just come with us—"

"I want to hear it from your President," Terr said and pointed at the black telephone on the credenza.

"I sympathize with your skepticism, sir, but it's all over now. Why push it?"

"I want to hear it from your President," Terr repeated softly.

Arskin frowned and bit his lip. "If you would only come with us. Some reactionary might take things into his own hands and you could get hurt."

Terr touched his side and chuckled. Arskin had the grace to blush.

"Your concern is commendable, Mr. Arskin. It really is."

"I'm sorry that you're being difficult, Opturkarh," Arskin said and his eyes grew hard. "But I'm afraid I must insist." He reached beneath his jacket and Terr looked at the operating end of a snub-nosed revolver. "You leave me no choice."

The two sidekicks jumped up, held their feet slightly apart, hardware covering everyone. Morrow gaped at them.

"What the hell are you doing?"

"My job, Sheriff. Now, if you'll just ease that gun out of its holster," Arskin ordered.

"Be damned if I will!"

Arskin turned and pointed his gun at Morrow's head. "You've got about two seconds," he said softly and cocked his gun. The click sounded awfully loud.

Morrow clenched his fists and glared, then slowly eased out his gun. It thudded loudly as it struck the floorboards. Arskin looked up and his eyes bored into Terr's.

"End of the line, Opturkarh. Just to show you I mean it…Mrs. Larkin? Please be good enough and get your children in here."

"What are you going to do?" Her voice quivered, but she looked defiantly at Arskin.

"It all depends on our alien friend up there."

Mark stepped up to him with clenched fists. "You won't get away with this. There are laws to deal with mugs like you."

Arskin laughed and turned to his sidekick. "Did you hear

that, George? Laws, he said."

"Yeah, it's funny," George grunted, not taking his eyes off Morrow.

Arskin turned to Mark and looked at him with contempt. "I'll show you law," he snarled and swung the barrel of his gun against Mark's cheek. As Mark clutched his head, Arskin clubbed him on the back of the neck. Mark crashed to the floor and didn't move.

"Mark!" Sally screamed and rushed to her husband.

"Stand back!" Arskin growled, shifting his gun to cover her. She stared at it in terror and backed away.

The children slowly emerged out of the kitchen looking pale and frightened. Shuffling, they gathered around Sally's long skirts and waited round-eyed. Time seemed to freeze as Terr contemplated the scene before him. Arskin and his thugs appeared determined to get him at any cost. They sure as hell didn't act like any law enforcement agents.

"Hostages?" Terr tried to force a smile but he didn't think it quite came off.

"They don't have to be," Arskin said. "I would hate to see this fine family hurt because you chose to be uncooperative."

"Then what?"

"Then we leave."

"FBI agents my ass." Morrow looked disgusted. "You guys are more like the cheap hoods I sweep off the streets every day."

Arskin moved his gun and fired, the crack sharp and flat. Sally screamed and the children started crying. Morrow staggered back and stared in surprise at the blood welling from his chest. He shook his head and sagged to his knees. A trickle of blood oozed from his mouth and he toppled to the floor.

"I'll take the children next." Arskin glared hard at Terr.

"Please!" Sally sobbed clutching her kids. She looked imploringly at Terr, her cheeks wet with tears. "Don't let him hurt them."

Terr looked at Arskin, wanting to reach out and crush him. If this was the kind of government hospitality he could look forward to, he was better off in the desert. His gesture for freedom was not worth Morrow's life. Not any of their lives.

"Okay, you've made your point," he said harshly and took a step down the stairs.

Mark groaned, drew his knees under his body, and launched himself at Arskin's legs.

"No!" Sally screamed.

The shots rang out deafeningly. Sally shuddered, swayed, and fell even as her little girl screamed. The bullets smashed into Terr's shield and clattered down the steps. Terr raised his hand and the orange beam cut two of them in half. Blood splattered across the table as they fell, staining the cups and the toast. He swung his arm at Arskin. Stepping back, Arskin gave a wild cry, dropped his gun, and threw his hands before his face.

"Don't kill me!" he cried out in terror.

Terr did not feel anger. He didn't feel anything. He just stared at Arskin and issued a mental command. Arskin gave a muffled yell and his head dissolved in the beam. Blood gushed high from the raw stump of his neck. His body jerked in convulsion and fell in a heap. His fingers twitched, clawed at the floor and then they were still.

A thick cloud of cordite drifted toward the ceiling, the stink mixed with the cloying smell of blood, charred flesh, and bone.

The outside door banged open. Terr crouched and swiveled. The man looked middle-aged and well dressed. He had a cruel, thin mouth hardened by a life where death was a constant companion. Did Terr's mouth look like that? The man's eyes traveled across the room in one sweep, his face without expression. When those eyes looked up, Terr fired. The beam caught the man high on the chest and he crumpled to the floor. His hands had been empty.

Terr held his arm stiff before him, listening. The door slowly swung in and out as the breeze gusted. It creaked faintly as it moved. The silence hung heavy in the room. He surveyed the carnage around him and his shoulders sagged. He switched off the shield and bit his lip.

Blood dripped from a cut on Mark's cheek as he cradled Sally's head in his lap, rocking her slowly, crying softly. His left arm hung limp. A large red patch below his shoulder glistened wetly as it caught the light from the doorway. Terr walked slowly down the stairs. Mark looked up and gulped back tears.

"She's dead," he sobbed quietly. "God damn them to hell! Oh, Sally...why...why?"

Terr knew, but he could not really tell him.

He stepped over Morrow's body and knelt beside the children. He examined them quickly. A deep scar furrowed the little girl's forehead. She was pale and sweat glistened on her cold skin. Her breathing slow and even, and Terr turned to one of the boys—dead, shot through the stomach. The boy who asked about the base was unconscious. The bullet had scarred his chest and shattered the elbow of his left arm. Blood oozed steadily from the raw, jagged wound. Terr stared at him absently and stroked the boy's head. He swallowed hard and blinked.

He picked up the unconscious girl and carried her to the couch. He placed her brother beside her. The crude bandage he made for the boy stopped the bleeding. Terr lifted the bloody tablecloth and covered them, tucking in the corners. They needed expert medical attention, and not the kind that Earth authorities were able to provide. If he could get them to the Orieli base, at least part of the guilt he felt would be purged.

The man in the doorway groaned. Terr barely glanced at him. He walked over to the telephone and picked up the old-fashioned receiver...dead. He stared at it for a while, then gently put it back in its cradle. He turned and looked at Mark moaning softly as he stroked Sally's hair. Terr could do nothing for him.

He walked over and knelt beside him. "I'm sorry," he whispered, desperately searching Mark's eyes for something. Forgiveness maybe?

Mark looked up, his eyes accusing. "I wish I could say I didn't blame you, but I can't. I can't." His head sagged and he cried.

Something strange happened then. Death settled on Terr's shoulders and he clenched his hands. A moment of pain and Mark would have peace. He and his loved one would be together in whatever afterlife these people believed in. Terr clenched his teeth and looked up in anguish. Let it end! He wanted to scream, rend and tear. It would have been easy to blot it all out.

He stood up and walked to the man beside the door. The guy was having a good time moaning and twisting and Terr let him enjoy it. He switched on his shield, sat on a chair and waited. He knew him, or his type, which said the same thing. The guy spoiled it the minute he walked in. Only certain people look at things the way that man did. Terr ought to know, and that wasn't any fault of his own.

It took a while before the agent managed to stagger to his knees. Sensing Terr's presence, he stopped moving and opened his eyes. They were cold and black and deep as they ran over Terr. For an ordinary man those eyes would have been hard to face. Then again, Terr was not exactly a man, or ordinary.

"An impasse, Opturkarh," the agent said and a ghost of a smile touched the corners of his mouth.

Terr wanted to reach out and crush him. Something of his anger must have shown for the merest flicker of uncertainty touched the face before the mask snapped back into place. But that one moment of doubt had been enough. Terr owned him.

He let the silence hang for a while and he didn't know who needed it more.

"And how do you figure that?" he asked between clenched teeth.

The guy smiled, cool and intimidating. "I'm still alive."

"That can be corrected."

"I don't think so, Opturkarh." The agent looked with disdain at the bodies lying on the floor in a bloody mess. "They were fools and they paid for it."

"What about the Larkins? Why them?"

He shrugged indifferently. "They were a convenient way of achieving our objective. This is only a setback, you know. It doesn't change anything."

"You have it all figured out, right?"

The agent didn't even blink as he searched Terr's face. "It's all over, Mister. We know where you are and where you want to go. It's only a matter of time, and not much of that."

"By we, I would guess you're some sort of a Federal mouser. CIA perhaps?"

"Why pick on the CIA?"

"Never mind."

Pain stabbed through Terr's side and he gasped. He cradled the side with his left hand and massaged the tender spot. The damned thing had started to itch unbearably, but he was afraid to scratch.

He turned his head and looked at Mark, still weeping, his cheeks wet. The smell of fresh blood hung in the air, sharp and heavy. It was the smell of Death. The door groaned as it swung gently on the hinges.

Terr stood and Mark looked up. Their eyes met. Mark looked past Terr. "He's one of them, ain't he?"

Terr nodded. "Yes."

Apparently satisfied, Mark bowed over Sally's body again. Terr watched him with a profound feeling of helplessness. He should have let them take him. He should have…

Rit!

The agent was standing when Terr turned, his eyes ready. Too dangerous to live and too valuable to kill.

"I'm a very patient man Opturkarh, and you're a long way from your ship. When you make that mistake, and you will, I shall be there."

Terr pointed at the doorway and nodded. "After you."

The agent's eyes drilled into Terr, then he turned abruptly and walked out. Terr took one final look around the room. His footsteps sounded heavy and loud and Death still rode on his shoulder. The door clicked shut behind him and he swore. The agent waited for him on the porch. Terr glared and shook his head.

"Don't say it," he growled softly. "The way I'm feeling right now, it wouldn't do to strain our friendship."

The other chuckled. "If we're going to get along, the name is Treval."

"I shall keep it in mind."

The Lincoln in the driveway was a dark blue heavy with a high polish. The porch boards creaked as Terr walked past Treval. Gravel crunched underfoot as he strode to the car. He opened the driver's door and looked in. The thing had enough switches, dials, and plastic buttons to equip a starship. It also had a cell phone.

Treval reluctantly made the call. Terr sympathized with him. In the end, he saw the light of Terr's argument after he burned the man's left ear off.

* * *

A line of Australian blue gums stood guard on either side of the highway, making shadows dance on the windscreen. Clipping the treetops, the sun flashed and dazzled between the branches. The old pickup engine hummed to itself. Listening to the whisper of the tires, Terr stared absently at the broken yellow line in the center of the road. Ahead, the highway shimmered and twisted. It was still early morning but already uncomfortable in the rising heat. The crisp freshness of dawn gone, sucked into a steel sky.

Terr followed the telegraph poles as they slid by. The

269

Stefan Vučak

power wires sagging, rising, on and on. Relaxing and kind of hypnotic. How easy it was to let the mind wander, seeking escape and relief. Beyond the trees wild scrub dotted the desert sands. Through the blue haze, he stared into the wavering distance. His thoughts drifted to Teena. He reached for her and she was there, standing before him, smiling, arms outstretched. He longed to touch her, but he could not move. He just looked at her, his face hard against the glass. She faded slowly and there was only the scrub and sand left.

The tires whispered on the highway.

Mark's noisy old pickup smelled of gasoline, earth, and fertilizer. The upholstery was scratched and torn, and grit littered the floor. Maybe it had been a bad deal trading this can for the air-conditioned comfort of the Lincoln. What little traffic came their way looked all the same, outdoor type. Maybe he'll get lucky. Maybe.

Was it worth it? What could he do with a whole world against him? He'd burned his bridges when he declined Cannon's extended hospitality. He wasn't kidding himself. The only reason he made it this far, the massive search machinery Cannon had set into motion was ponderously slow to move. He had a sneaky suspicion he wasn't going to last the day.

He glanced at his sidekick and their eyes met. Treval's were cold and flat and Terr wanted to say something breezy, but he couldn't seem to find the words. Anyway, what difference did it make? Like the man said, life was hell. He turned his head and watched the wires rising, sagging, on and on.

They drove in silence.

"You'll never get away with it, you know," Treval said suddenly.

Terr turned and searched the man's hard face. Hard like his mouth. A face that had developed a callus against the pain and hurt of being alive.

"Get away with what?" Terr asked after he had a think.

Treval's mouth fixed itself into a slow grin. "You don't

have to be cagey with me, Mister."

"You did it all for me. I'm simply coming along for the ride." Treval frowned and Terr grinned. "You don't understand, do you?"

"What do you mean?"

"Order, counter-order, disorder. When you called off your dogs back there, they'd have packed up their marbles and left. No questions asked. I wanted the Larkins taken care of. Coming from you a request for an ambulance would look natural, all things considered. By the time they get reorganized…well, we shall see."

"Why do you want to go to Beeville?" Treval demanded. "There is nothing there. It's only a small farming town."

Terr looked at him, undecided whether to tell him. What he had in mind, Treval wasn't going to get a chance to use the information anyway.

"They might have light aircraft."

Treval stared at Terr in disbelief. "A crop duster? Is that it?"

"That's the general idea."

"You're mad! We have every grass strip from Texas to the Sierras covered."

"Don't let a little detail like that distract you. Just remember the ear."

Treval gave Terr a withering glance and his knuckles turned white against the wheel.

"Careful. You'll bend it."

Treval stiffened and his face drained. Terr laughed, thinking of his broken side, the hunger gnawing at his middle, the dull ache that he felt all over and wouldn't go away. He had a lot to laugh about.

They reached Beeville by mid-morning. A curve in the road and the town lay before them. It was a barren one-street place with a dozen houses, some stores, and a filling station. A Greyhound coach was pulling out, black smoke belching from its side. The stonework on the ancient town hall was smudged brown and caked with white streaks. Bird shit. The whole place had a weary, sleepy look of a man who had labored long and was now resting.

They drove on in silence. Terr had things on his mind and did not feel very talkative. At the edge of town a rifle-pitted speed sign, supported by a crooked steel pipe, said thirty-five. They slowed down.

Outside the drugstore a ragged group of Negroes and whites slouched around a trashcan. One held out a bottle wrapped in a brown paper bag. Another reached for it, tilted back his head and the Adam's apple bobbed. They didn't even give the pickup a cursory glance.

With the only set of traffic lights around, they turned red as the pickup approached. Treval brought the pickup to a rattling stop and the brakes squealed. Nobody got excited about that. A stooped old black lady wheeling a rickety pram loaded with groceries, shuffled painfully across the street. Treval casually took his left hand off the steering wheel and relaxed.

"Don't do it," Terr said and shook his head.

"Do what?" Treval flared, looking indignant as though Terr had made an improper suggestion.

"Open the door and make a break for it. I would get very upset and you could get hurt, bad."

"I don't know what the hell you're talking about."

"Never mind. Just don't go for any of those beginner's tricks. I've tried them all."

A car horn blared behind them and Treval jerked his head around.

"You waitin' for a special shade of green, Clyde?" snarled the smart ass in the hot convertible. Treval muttered something uncharitable and eased the ancient car into gear. As they clanked off, the convertible roared behind them. It flashed past with a scream of burning rubber. All Terr saw was long brown hair, steel-rimmed sunglasses and a glare of contempt behind

272

the upturned middle finger of a right hand.

"Punk!" Treval spat and glared after the sleek car.

The houses thinned out quickly and they were alone again. The tires whispered and the power lines sagged and rose and sagged. They almost missed the turnoff. The sign was a faded, cracked old board nailed to the side of a tree. It said half a mile. Treval shot Terr a glance, reversed, and they lurched and bumped along the track. A thick cloud of brown dust swirled behind them.

An old weather-beaten house stood beside the road. The red tin roof gaped, showing the blackened beams beneath. The windows had been smashed in long ago and now gawked, black and helpless. Tall weeds lapped beneath the windowsills. A twisted tower, rotting boards, and a toothless wheel remained of what used to be a wind pump.

"This is as good a place as any," Terr said. "Stop here."

He guessed Treval must have known what he had in mind, for his lips tightened as he brought the pickup into the overgrown driveway. The engine pinged as it cooled. The dust hid them briefly from the rest of the world.

"The end of the line?" Treval asked somewhat uneasily.

"That's about the size of it." Terr nodded and turned to face him.

"Are you going to kill me?" Treval tried to make his voice steady.

Terr saw the Larkin kids covered with blood and his hand twitched. Hot anger burned in his eyes. Treval saw it and stiffened.

"I won't kill you. That would be too easy. No, you'll live, but you won't enjoy it." Terr reached out with his right hand and Treval gave a little scream as the lightnings touched him.

* * *

273

Like the town, the three hangars looked worn and over-used. Sun, wind, and sand had stripped paint, cracked the timbers and warped the tin sheeting. Two single-engine aircraft waited negligently on the grass. Behind them, stacked in ragged rows, were drums of fuel. A low shed on the far side of the field, painted dirty yellow, held a mast aerial. There didn't seem to be anyone around. If Treval was right and someone guarded the place, they must have taken the day off.

Now that he was here, staring at the shed and the silent aircraft, he wondered what to do about it all. Simply walk up to one of the things, climb in and take off? The idea seemed to lose some of its appeal the longer he thought about it. He pulled back his head and leaned heavily against the hot tin of the hangar. He felt his legs fold like soggy newspaper and he slowly slid to the hard aground. He chuckled weakly and closed his eyes.

The noise came from some long, deep pit, its bottom a red point. The point grew and light flared bright and painful. He squeezed his eyes and buried his face in his hands. Red images danced and faded before him. He removed his hands and blinked hard. For an instant, his vision reeled and swam and he clutched the ground as it moved beneath him. Then he recognized the noise.

He didn't spot the aircraft until it banked sharply above the field and sank quickly into a final. It touched without bouncing and taxied toward the hangar. It was a neat professional landing. A man wearing khaki coveralls emerged out of the radio shed and started walking toward the hangar. He was an old geezer, his white hair fluttering in the propeller draft, but his steps were sure and strong. The monoplane coasted to a stop some thirty katalans away. The engine raced, then died. The propeller whooshed briefly then all was still. In the distance, the air swam and twisted in the heat. An insect buzzed near Terr, circled once, and wandered off.

The pilot pushed open the cockpit door and climbed out

on the wing. He looked around once and jumped down. Something military about his stance and Terr frowned, but it was too hot to worry about it.

"Hey, Joe?" shouted the man in the coveralls. "What kept you, man? I ain't got all day, you know."

"Simmer down, Pat," the pilot drawled easily as he peered around the engine. He lifted the cowling cover and looked inside. "The bitch started misfiring and I had to set her down and—"

"I told you about them plugs, Joe. One of these days—"

"Yeah, I'll run myself into the ground," Joe said and dragged the tinted glasses from his face. He slipped them into his breast pocket. "Let's skip the lecture, okay Pat?"

"Sure, sure, sonny." The other grinned and shook his head. "Wanna tank up?"

"Might as well." Joe slammed the cover shut and followed Pat to the hangar. They stopped beside a small side door and Pat fiddled with the lock. The hinges groaned and the door swung in. Joe waited as the main door rolled up with a rattle of chains.

Joe walked in and emerged pushing a forty-four-gallon drum on a two-wheeled trolley. He kept swearing all the way to the aircraft. He coupled the hose to the fuel connection on the wing and started cranking the hand pump.

That kept him pretty busy. Terr tried not to think about all those open spaces around him as he slipped along the hangar wall, making like he belonged there. He felt the edge of the doorway and took a peek inside. He could not see much in the gloom and there was no sign of Pat. He stepped over the threshold and leaned heavily against the tin. There were no shouts coming from outside. He wasn't too disappointed.

Things started to emerge out of shadow after a while. The inside looked big, bigger than it had any right to be. The sides were lined with greasy benches. Racks of assorted hardware hung along the walls. Something bulky lay in one corner and he could not see what it was. It looked like an engine under a tarp. The smell…his nose wrinkled and he exhaled with disgust. It came from the two drums beside him. He peered at the nearest one, saw an oily yellow liquid and gagged.

He didn't know where the hell the old guy came from. He just stood there, holding a heavy looking plastic bag and not too sure what to do about it. He grunted when the beam struck him and folded like a barman's rag. The bag made a soft thud as it fell on the concrete.

"Hey, Pat!" The silence shattered like cheap crystal. "Hurry up with that bloody spray!"

Terr trembled with reaction and waited for the sound of footsteps. No one came looking. Someone shouted and he held the sphere ready.

He could hear them talking, the voices pretty loud. He turned his head, shifted into a crouch and squinted through a tear in the tin sheeting. A tall man with ginger hair and faded jeans shook his head and pointed at Joe with a bony finger.

"I can't let you take off. Orders."

Joe kept the pump going and barely looked up. "Whatever it is Kike, save it. I got a job to do."

"Now, Joe, be reasonable. This is straight from the Civil—"

"They can go to hell! What do they expect me to do? Sit on my ass for a couple of days? Like hell! Sorry, Kike. As soon as I tank up, I'm off."

"It could mean your license," the ginger man said. "You fly them crates real good, but you've only been here two days."

Joe stopped pumping, straightened, and stared at Kike. "I've had a bellyful already. Now, why don't you just do a fade before I do something that you'll regret."

Kike opened his mouth then changed his mind. He shook his head and walked off. He stopped after several paces and turned.

"Which spread you doing today, Joe?"

"Tanner's, I think. Haven't got them sorted out yet," Joe growled, his right hand rippling with muscle as he pumped. After a while, he looked up, stared at the hangar and swore.

"Damned if I know what's taking him so long. Hey, Pat!" he bellowed. "What the hell are you doing anyway? Making the stuff?" Joe kicked the drum savagely and stomped toward the hangar. "Fucking bureaucrats. Sit on my butt while they look for some damned son of a bitch."

Of average height, Joe gave the impression of someone taller. Maybe it was the commanding voice or that military presence. Ruggedly handsome with clean features, he had a finely sculptured nose and a generous mouth that could laugh easily, but was now a scowl. His short brown hair looked blond in the harsh glare.

Joe walked through the main hangar door and stopped. He turned his head and his eyes locked with Terr's. He snorted, looked down, and spat.

"Shit!" he said like he meant it. "I guess you're the sorry son of a bitch everyone's been looking for."

"I guess I am," Terr said.

Joe took one look at Pat's slumped body. "What have you done to him?"

"Take it easy, Joe. He isn't hurt," Terr said and let him think about it.

"Now what?" Joe started, then raised his right hand. "Don't tell me, let me guess. You're tired of this bloody private hell you've landed yourself in and you want to head off for some cool beach, a tall iced drink, and a couple of grass-clad chicks to keep you from getting lonely. Right?"

"That sounds pretty good," Terr agreed, ignoring the sarcasm.

"And if I don't cooperate?"

The beam flicked delicately at his feet and white smoke spurted from the concrete. The pile of red slag crackled and steamed. Joe stared at the angry glow and shrugged.

"I never liked the crop dusting business anyway, but I've got to tell you. If you're expecting to just scoot out of here, the Feds have the skies all bottled up."

"So I've been told. Let's go."

Joe shrugged and abruptly started walking toward the aircraft. He climbed on the wing, opened the small side door and stepped in. Terr didn't waste any time with parting speeches. He walked to the other side and hauled himself up. Joe opened the door for him and Terr slid in beside him. He strapped in like he knew what he was doing.

The engine whined, coughed, and fired. Joe picked up the revs smoothly, eased back the throttle and the little plane bounced daintily over the grass. "Any special place you have in mind?" Joe glanced at Terr as he checked the elevators and the flaps.

"The Sierras," Terr said.

"Christ!" Joe stepped on the brakes and the plane rocked. "You planning to make for your ship? This bird doesn't carry that kind of juice!"

"We'll fill up on the way," Terr told him with a reassuring smile.

"Just slip up to any gas station, right?"

"Right."

"Mister, I've met some nutty guys in my time, but you're something special," Joe declared savagely, dragged dark glasses out of his pocket and slipped them on.

He cleared with the tower and gave Terr a long look. Shaking his head, muttering to himself, he opened her wide. The engine snarled. With a light skip, the plane rolled off. It was a bit bumpy as they raced along the grass strip, but Terr didn't mind. Then the nose lifted and the ground sagged beneath him.

Chapter Thirteen

Hennery stared at the CIA Deputy Director of Operations and ground his teeth. Hellfire and damnation! It was all falling apart around him even after he'd given specific instructions. He crumpled the telex message and ground the flimsy against the palm of his hand.

"There couldn't possibly be an error in this, could there, Floyd?" Hennery's voice rasped like drawn steel. He knew the truth when it stared at him, but he had to ask.

"No error, Mr. President," the wretched man said, standing stiffly at attention in the Oval Office.

"This…this Treval character. What the hell did he think he was doing?" Hennery demanded, willing himself not to send his fist slamming against the desk. "And who in hell gave you the authority to involve the CIA within the continental United States?" Hennery stared coldly at Floyd, unable to believe the turn of events. With the aliens waiting for him in the Roosevelt Room, he did not relish the encounter.

"The possibility was raised in your PDB yesterday, Mr. President."

"And action disallowed, damn it! But you went ahead anyway, didn't you?"

"An overzealous interpretation of one likely scenario, Mr. President," Floyd said, staring fixedly past the president's head, seeing his career in ashes. Shit runs downhill, he remembered someone telling him. Scant comfort now.

"Where is Opturkarh Terrllss-rr now?"

Floyd squirmed, looking miserable. "We don't know, sir."

"You don't know? What *do* you know?"

"We found Treval near a strip airfield outside Beeville, New Mexico, Mr. President. He is completely paralyzed. Despite our interdiction procedures, it's possible that Terr has commandeered an aircraft. By now, he could be anywhere. We're still working on the assumption that he's trying to reach his ship, which narrows down his options. But there is a lot of ground between him and the Sierras, and the alien has proven unusually resourceful."

"Wounded, starved, hunted, and he still manages to give everybody the slip." Hennery looked disgusted. "And the Larkins?"

"We have them at Houston, sir."

"Now we go and shoot up our own civilians. Get out of here, Floyd. And don't come back without Terr. When you do, I'll have your resignation. I'd also get a lawyer if I were you. Now, get out!"

Floyd clenched his teeth, turned, and quietly shuffled out, his thoughts on the situations vacant columns.

Hennery brooded and waited. When the intercom chimed, he leaned heavily across his desk and pressed a button. It was Kathy. They were waiting for him, waiting for their pound of flesh.

Damn, damn, damn!

* * *

"Where is Opturkarh Terrllss-rr, Da President?" Zor-Ell asked softly, his eyes frosty and unforgiving.

The echo drifted around the Roosevelt Room and died. The faces around the oak table were drawn and tense. They were all there, the ones who mattered, anyway. Hennery had seen to that. Cannon, Doryel, Wald, Moravik, Swen, the Vice President, and the FBI Director. Some of the cabinet secretaries bitched when they were left out, but he quelled them. One place stood empty—Harry Tarleton, his new Chairman of the

Joint Chiefs. Tarleton was out somewhere in the desert trying to locate the missing alien.

The silence stretched thick and heavy. Hennery sat alone at one end of the table studying the two aliens facing him from across the other end, his judges. One of them was short and stocky and had a ragged burn across one cheek. The taller stared back without blinking. The large brown eyes seemed to burn with inner fire, sharp and penetrating. His skin had a delicate greenish-blue hue that merged into black around the eyes and mouth. It was impossible to read emotion in that face.

Hennery wished to God that he were somewhere else. His shoulders sagged and he found the years on them heavy. He'd chopped and pruned, but he could read the signs. There would be no second term nomination for him, not after this fiasco. Strange thing was, he didn't feel too badly about it.

The alien watched and waited. What could Hennery tell him? They killed and maimed in the name of justice, home, honor and old apple pie? Damn Cannon, he fumed, dreading what was to come.

"I don't know, Karhide," he said and dropped his eyes.

The silence dragged on, painful and poignant. A chair scraped loudly and someone cleared his throat. Anabb looked steadily at the unfortunate man across the table.

"Mr. President, opportunistic exploitation of our person-nel, whatever the circumstance, is something we cannot con-done."

"Believe me, Mr. Director, I wish I could say something, but there isn't." He searched the alien face and wondered what thoughts flowed behind those eyes.

"Indeed, Da," Zor-Ell agreed, his voice heavy with irony. "But that doesn't answer my question."

"I will answer your question, Karhide," Cannon said, reaching automatically for the cigar in his breast pocket. Out of the corner of his eye, he noted the disapproving frown on Sec-retary Swen's face. He ignored it. With relish, he clamped his teeth around the savaged end.

"Go ahead, General." Zor-Ell leaned forward and crossed his hands above the table.

"He's trying to reach his ship, sir, but you probably figured that one out already." Cannon paused, chuckling at the grim humor of it. "Of course, he cannot know that it's already gone. As I was saying, the reason why we cannot find him is because he's probably dead somewhere in the desert from loss of blood, exhaustion, thirst, hunger, or any such combination. If that weren't enough, we gave him plenty of reasons why he shouldn't trust us." He plucked the cigar from the corner of his mouth and proceeded to study the mangled end.

"You mentioned blood, General."

"Yes, sir. Because he was shot!" The blatant words rang startlingly loud. Cannon met the brown eyes unflinchingly. What the hell! They couldn't do much more to him anyway. Politicians, screw them.

"When did all this take place?" Anabb demanded.

"Two days ago, sir."

"Two days," Zor-Ell repeated woodenly. "Thank you, General. Da President, I shall be brief. We offered our hand in friendship and you chose to exploit it. What happened here did not result from any action by one man, but from a culmination of policy set against a background of political expediency." His face grim with determination, he stood. He clasped his hands behind his back and looked directly at Hennery.

"Da President, if Opturkarh Terrllss-rr should die as a re-sult of actions by your security services, I shall close all Earth's spaceborne facilities—indefinitely. Do you understand?"

Hennery did not and caught Cannon's eye. "What he means, sir, he'll knock out every piece of hardware we've got in space. The consequences would be appalling! Our defense pos-ture would be so much hot air. I suppose it wouldn't do our economy much good either, or the world's," he added gener-ously.

A babble of stunned voices rose in waves of incredulous protest. There were hot cries of bitter condemnation and more than a hint of irresponsibility on the Orieli's part. No one wanted the aliens or what they represented. There was always the one about the innocent being made to suffer. The responses were irrational because they had no way to implement them. Zor-Ell remained silent and unresponsive.

Hennery nodded, searching the alien face for some sign of compassion perhaps, and not finding it. He did not really expect any. What now? Maybe even two years ago, he could have stopped it. How often it takes a stranger to point out the obvious. But the price…

"Is this really necessary?"

"Necessary, Da President? What would you suggest? That we file a strongly worded protest with the UN? And the next time?" Zor-Ell shook his head. "No, Da. There must not be a next time."

"I protest!" Swen stood up and pointed a hooked finger at Zor-Ell. "You're doing this without giving us a chance!"

"Chance?" Zor-Ell's eyes were hard. "We gave you your chance at the UN."

They sat in shocked silence, overwhelmed by the turn of events.

* * *

Funny how sand and fire always seemed to follow in the footsteps of his life. If Terr was inclined that way, he might have taken it to mean something or other. But he was a pragmatist. He did not believe in any woolly stuff that comes in oily drinks or evil-smelling weeds. His aspect? Well, that was different. A straight out death wish with delusions of godhood. Terr wasn't superstitious.

Hah!

Humming softly to himself, Joe studied the clipboard in his

lap. They were low, perhaps fourteen hundred katalans. That was all right. He could only see sand, bare scrub, and an odd cactus. Nothing to run into. Beyond the port wing, touching the sky, a brown smudge stretched lazily across the hot horizon. Joe caught Terr looking at it and nodded.

"Sierra foothills."

Terr saw his face reflected in Joe's glasses. Face of a stranger.

The engine droned and Terr waited. He had this half-cooked plan involving him in a hero outfit against them, the bad guys. It went like all his epics, a bust. There wasn't even a gratefully sensuous babe in distress to, well, *relieve* things. Anyway, he always figured the hero mold to be a tight fit.

He had a couple of items he wanted to gnaw over, but there wasn't time. He realized there hadn't been any time since the jokers in mufti picked him up at Tal Field. How long ago was that? It seemed like another lifetime.

A glint of metal teased his eye and his head turned automatically. He could only see the empty desert, bleak and hostile. The hair on the back of his neck started to rise and he looked down where the shadow of their aircraft followed silently. He had an evil and suspicious mind. He wasn't born with it, though. It was just plain hard work and a certain natural aptitude. He knew what he saw.

Joe grunted and muttered something. Terr turned and watched a frown crease his craggy face. Joe leaned deliberately over the wheel and tapped a gauge with a long bony finger.

"Of all the bloody places to get stuck without gas," he snarled acidly and glared at Terr. "Just drop down to any gas station, right?" He snorted in disgust and flung the clipboard off his lap.

The thought of spending another night in some rocky crag didn't amuse Terr. That kind of thing might sound romantic to some city masochist, but the guys who write the brochures weren't crazy enough to swallow their own propaganda.

"If you got any bright ideas, Mister, there will never be a better time to trot them out," Joe said.

"I thought you might tell me." Terr shrugged, not really caring.

Joe pursed his lips and shook his head. "Nope. I'm fresh out," he declared flatly.

"There, I knew I could count on you, Joe." Terr gave him a wan smile.

"Asshole!" Joe snarled.

There was that glint again. Terr wasn't mistaken this time. Broken power lines sagged mournfully, trailing in the sand. A solitary pole leaned wearily. Another storm would probably bring it down.

"Joe?"

"Yeah?"

"Over there." Terr nodded in the general direction. Joe leaned against him and recoiled slightly at the touch of the shield. He stared and chewed at his lower lip.

"I don't see anything," he declared at length.

"Rit! Ten o'clock. Didn't you say you used to fly in some war?"

"Used to."

"Now I can see why you don't anymore."

"A wise ass. Okay, so it's a road, or it used to be one." Joe settled back and searched for the map pad. After a while, he looked up and shook his head. "Not there, but it doesn't mean anything. The place used to be a nuclear proving ground decades ago. There must be abandoned government installations all over the place."

"And you're planning to find one?"

"You bet. Better to end up on a road like this, than somewhere in the open desert. And besides, if I cracked up and claimed, I don't think the insurance would believe me."

"I could come to understand their point of view," Terr told

him with a straight face. Joe gave him a withering look and muttered to himself.

He banked the aircraft and followed the intermittent patches of black showing through the sand. He tried his whistle but was off-key. After glancing at Terr, he thought better of it.

Terr knew this wasn't going to last long. He watched the scenery when the engine spluttered and surged. The little aircraft sagged and went mushy.

"Bitch!" Joe hissed between clenched teeth and reached out to cut the switches. "Better hold tight. It's gonna be bumpy."

Terr held tight. The scrub was only a blur on either side of the wings. With only a few hundred katalans to play with, it didn't take long. The power lines followed them for a while, then the little aircraft touched. The wheels plowed through the sand and threw up a swirling cloud. The aircraft bounced over a clear patch and slammed down hard. The tail lifted sickeningly, then fell back with a crash. Terr was glad he hadn't had any breakfast.

It was deadly quiet in the cockpit. The heat rolled off the desert. Tortured metal pinged and groaned in protest. Nothing stirred among the expanse of rolling dunes and stringy, olive-colored hard scrub standing stiff and unmoving. The bleached white sky glared with pitiless brightness.

"Well, it's certainly not one of my best," Joe declared in disgust and ripped the shades off his face. With a squint at the scenery, he tucked them into his pocket. "But like they say. If you can walk away from it, it's a good one." He tried the side door. When it wouldn't budge, he kicked it open. He leaned out and a trickle of sand came down his back. He brushed at it absently and climbed onto the wing. "Coming?" He glanced at Terr and jumped down.

While Joe walked around the aircraft, Terr opened the side door and pried himself off the upholstery. Then he was brave and did something stupid. He jumped off the wing. The landing rattled the fillings in his teeth and some pretty lights sparkled in his head as a lance went deep into his side. He whimpered once and folded like a soggy smile.

He heard hurried footsteps and Joe knelt beside him. He turned his head in time to see Joe reach for him. When Joe's hand touched the surface of the shield, he jerked it back with a startled oath. He stood there and stared, looking frightened and helpless.

"I'll be all right," Terr said, wheezing like a broken pot. He felt the warmth in his side grow and he closed his eyes. If it would only end. Why couldn't they simply leave him alone?

"Terr!" Joe shook him, sounding more than a little concerned.

Terr opened his eyes, clenched his teeth and reached into his pocket. The sphere felt a warm, pulsing weight in his hand. He cut off the shield and the desert moved in. He could smell the burning sand, feel it move as he listened to its whispers. He breathed deeply of the dry air, opened his hands and ran them through the sand. The power flowed through him and he shuddered. Sand trickled between his fingers. The energy sphere fell out of his hand and he watched it roll away.

Joe stared at him, no doubt wondering whether some of his marbles had not run into the sand as well.

"Don't worry, Joe." Terr smiled faintly. "I'm like your Bedouin. A creature of the desert."

Joe regarded him suspiciously. "You gave me a fright, I can tell you. You sure you're all right?"

"Yeah, sure." Terr started to struggle to his feet. Joe shot out a hand and helped him up. Terr stood up with hardly a groan. Joe's eyes searched his and dropped his hand. A gust of wind stirred the sand and whined around the aircraft. Terr bent down, picked up the sphere, and slipped it into his pocket.

Joe climbed back into the plane and emerged with a water bottle strapped to a webbing belt. He clipped the belt around his waist and pointed at Terr. "You're bleeding." He glared at

287

him accusingly.

Terr didn't look down. "I know."

"Christ!" Joe grabbed Terr's hand. "Come on. Might as well get on with it."

They started down the road with the sun burning their backs. The sand crunched beneath their feet. Terr was not eager, for somehow he knew what waited for him at its end.

* * *

Windswept sand brushed his face. Somewhere ahead, tin sheeting banged loosely. The smashed windows gaped vacantly from the rounded huts. The patched corrugated tin was streaked with rust. The huts stood clustered around what used to be small hangars once. His feet echoed hollow on the cracked, warped concrete. Wiry green shoots stood stiffly between the cracks. Dust devils skipped over the dunes and sand swirled about his feet.

The place smelled of death and Terr's skin prickled. "I don't like this, Joe." When the safety catch clicked, he knew why. His shoulders sagged and he turned slowly, keeping his hands loose. Joe's face showed no emotion as he held the gun in a steady hand.

"I'm sorry, Terr," he said gruffly. "There wasn't any other way."

Rit!

It had ended, but not exactly the way Terr planned. His hand shook as he wiped sweat off his face. He stared at the dunes not thinking about anything, watching the dancing heat patterns. When he looked up, Joe's lips were drawn in a thin line, the grim resolve still there. He could blot out this creature with ease, but where would that get him? It didn't seem worth the effort.

"Why, Joe?"

"I had a job to do and I did it, damn it!"

Terr cackled, a dry rasping sound that shook him like a rag. He winced at the pain in his side and coughed.

"Neat, very neat." He smiled ruefully and nodded. "It was all a big snow job. Beeville, the empty street, the crop dusting routine. And I walked into it like an amateur."

"You never had a chance. We simply didn't want any innocent bystanders getting hurt."

"Like the Larkins. Tell me one thing? Why did your guys hang around after Treval made his call? The place should have been deserted."

"Treval?" Joe squinted at him. "What call?"

Terr stared at him in confusion. Then it dawned on him. He laughed a hollow rattle. Rasping spasms gripped his chest and he cradled his side. After a while the chuckles left him.

"A CIA team tried to pick me up this morning," he said with heavy irony.

Joe snorted and spat into the sand. "Crooks!"

Terr remembered the Larkins, and it was only this morning. "Something like that," he said and their eyes locked. Joe backed a step and shook his head.

"Don't do anything noble, Terr," Joe said quickly. "I didn't bring you all the way out here just so you can be a hero. You don't have to prove a thing to me. I mean you no harm. No one does. General Cannon has been relieved and there is no need to run anymore. Please believe me."

Terr shook his head. "I can't do that, Joe. You know I can't," he said and glanced meaningfully at the gun in his hand.

Thus they stared at each other as the jeeps roared from behind the huts, sending up a swirling blanket of dust. When it settled the soldiers were standing beside their machines, waiting. Terr could not see any weapons, but that didn't prove anything.

"You had better go and tell them how it is, Joe," Terr said quietly, ready to face them. Joe lowered the gun and reached out as if to touch him. Then he swore and shook his head. Terr watched him walk toward the waiting jeeps.

The sun hot on Terr's back, his shadow stretched before him, black and sharp. The air twisted and shriveled where it touched the sands. He looked up at the blue of the sky, perhaps for the last time. He slowly raised his arms and began to chant.

"And I shall walk in the shadow of Death. And it shall be with me all the days of my life. With shadow shall I smite my enemies and with thunder shall I purge their land!" The words from the *Saftara* rang loud. He felt the power grow in him and his voice deepened. "And all who stand with me in the shadow of Death shall know my power, and be comforted. With shadow and thunder shall I walk their land!" Lightings crackled between his fingers and a peel of thunder rolled over the dunes.

Teena!

He leveled his arms and roared out his anger. "Leave me alone!" A sheet of blue lightning coiled from his hands. Sand and concrete fused and spat where he touched it. He could feel his eyes smoldering and Death trembled in his arms.

A bolt of bright light lanced at the jeep and it glowed and twisted. The fuel tank exploded with a roaring whoosh and the concussion rocked the concrete. The soldiers scattered then. An automatic weapon chattered briefly and something plucked at his shoulder.

There was shouting, an angry buzzing he ignored. The puny humans would stand in his way? He shifted his arms. Death walked and the gun was suddenly quiet.

"Fools!" he thundered. The fires were hot in his soul and burned in his eyes.

A shadow moved behind him and he swiveled. Lightning crashed and the corner of the shed dissolved into a twisted tangle of melted tin. He clenched his fist and shook it at the wall of the shed. There was a clap of thunder and the shed flashed into a pile of slag. His anger faded. Looking about him at the ruins, he reached up and waited for the hand of Death to touch him. Thunder bellowed out his anguish. Again and again, lightning ripped the sky and the air was heavy with the smell of ozone.

Suddenly, everything became quiet. Oily smoke twisted from the burning wrecks. Fire crackled and snapped around him. The rumble of dying thunder echoed over the dunes and dust drifted lazily above the sheds. Slowly, the soldiers emerged and moved to surround him; silent, wary and waiting. Terr held his arms leveled, trembling with frustrated anger.

"Why can't you leave me alone?" he cried in dry sobs. "Just leave me alone!" He lowered his hands, with Death crackling between them.

A figure moved away from the others. With sand crunching beneath his feet, he started walking deliberately toward Terr. The stars on his shoulders glinted as they caught the sun. He looked old. Not in years maybe, but Terr could tell. The naval officer stopped just out of reach and his pale steel eyes did not waver as they searched Terr's. He clenched his jaw and tiny muscles jumped on his cheeks. The dying flames of the burning jeep flickered in his shadow.

"I'm Admiral Tarleton," the officer stated heavily.

"Another summit meeting, Admiral?" Terr said, not caring. A bullet would have been a welcome release then.

Tarleton flinched and shook his head. "None of this is necessary, Opturkarh," he said gravely.

"Necessary?" Terr's guts knotted and he clenched his fists to keep himself from trembling. He reached across his body and touched his right shoulder. When he held out his hand, it was covered with blood.

"This says different," he said hoarsely. His hand shook with anger and blue sparks crackled between his fingers. "You had me shot up and hunted down like some animal. Did you really think I would fold up and fall at your feet with gratitude? Well, I'm not through yet."

"Opturkarh, please!"

Terr was tempted; tempted to send him into oblivion. Despite the momentary satisfaction he would have gotten, it wouldn't have achieved anything. He actually didn't give a damn right then. Death rode in his hand as he thrust it out, palm up. He felt a pressure squeeze his chest and he blinked rapidly.

"Your hand, Admiral," he demanded roughly, watching the officer. "You want me to trust you. Prove it!"

Blue light crawled over his arm. Tiny sparks jumped and crackled at the tips of his fingers. Tarleton stared at the arm in disbelief, his mouth open, hanging like a door on a loose hinge. Beads of sweat dotted his forehead and his face turned a mottled white. Briefed, he knew what it meant to touch the alien. Was this a test of faith? He sensed the tense faces around him. No one moved. Tarleton looked at the alien and his tongue ran lightly over his lips.

Slowly, he raised his arm. He hesitated for an instant before clasping the proffered hand. Blue fire slithered from Terr's hand and stopped at Tarleton's elbow. He felt a cold, prickling sensation, and he shook as he waited for death. Then his clasp firmed and Terr returned it.

It seemed an eternity before the alien released him.

"Okay, Admiral," Terr whispered, his voice quivering. His whole body cried with pain and he couldn't run anymore. He dropped his arm and it hung limp at his side. Tarleton exhaled one long shudder and his hand shook as he wiped his face.

"God!" he said and seemed to sag a little.

Terr turned and walked slowly toward the desert. The one thing that always changed, yet remained the same. The ranks parted and awed faces turned after him as he strode past them.

He stopped and stared at the sands. The wind plucked gently at his clothes. He reached down and cupped a handful of warm sand. Foolish creature. The ancient voice echoed in his mind. The sand whispered as it ran between his fingers. Bent and broken, he searched the dunes for…what? Pity? That was for losers.

His eyes stung and he felt them filling. Bitter tears slid down his cheeks and the desert blurred. He tried hard to keep himself from swaying, but it was too much effort. He guessed it was pride that kept him standing; and his stiff, swollen side.

* * *

EXTRA! ALIEN FOUND IN DESERT
IS THERE A COVERUP OVER ALIEN FIASCO?
WHAT IS THE PRICE, PEOPLE ASK
GOD AND RIGHTEOUSNESS TRIUMPHS OVER EVIL
ALIENS, GO HOME!

"Jack Willison reporting for CNN. Rumors of CIA hoodlum tactics in searching for the escaped alien are flying thick and fast around the Hill today. Revealed exclusively by a reliable source, it is alleged that a senior CIA official has been instrumental in having a family in New Mexico executed for harboring the alien. Asked to comment, the CIA were strangely silent. They were also silent when asked by what authority did they operate within the confines of the United States. Someone will have some hard questions to answer down at Langley today.

"Minutes ago, under the shadow of the incredible Orieli and Serrll starships hovering above the White House, two small craft were seen streaking south. According to sources the craft were heading for New Mexico where Admiral Tarleton is holding the missing alien. Washington is thick with tension and I would not be in President Hennery's boots right now for all the jade in China. Stay tuned to our coverage of this incredible saga."

* * *

"Archbishop Waller was caught today in an invidious position of offering thanks for the apparent safety of the escaped alien, while condemning the extraterrestrial visitors for the growing unrest within the Church. When questioned, Cardinal Waller refused to be drawn into specifics. It's an embarrassing fact that the unrest he claims to be growing is not against the basic tenets of the faith, but against the Church's opulence and the discrepancies between what it teaches and what it practices.

"The Vision of God sect has proclaimed a Day of Judgment, sending chanting, wild-eyed unemployed youth picketing Pennsylvania Avenue, clashing violently with the Leave Earth Alone society. A sense of growing bewilderment seems to be pervading the community. Who can you trust? This is Mark Rown for NBC news."

* * *

Overhead, smeared with rust, the shadows slowly settled across the sky. The breeze tugged mischievously at Terr's hair, then went skipping across the flats. The air had lost some of its heaviness. He could almost hear the silent hiss as the brush waited for the night's cold embrace. The little death.

The hollow footsteps behind him sent hard, flat echoes bouncing off the concrete. They slowed and stopped beside him. He did not turn. He knew that walk. He watched the shadows and waited. There was no need to hurry anymore. They did not play him with largess, which was something at least. A stony-faced medic dressed his shoulder and side, then balked when Terr refused to have them sewn up. Tarleton met his eye and the medic left. He would get over it.

They left him alone afterward. He supposed he was grateful. Anyway, he did not feel very talkative. He didn't mind the grim master sergeant tagging after him. It kept the curious out of his way and he had a lot to think about.

"Well, Joe?" Terr said without turning. Dusk was reaching

out with a mauve hand, slowly closing over the brooding shadows.

"They'll be here shortly, Opturkarh," Joe said, his voice strained and stiff.

It couldn't have been easy for him. Terr turned and looked at him. Gold oak leaves gleamed on Joe's shirt collar. The cap was level, hiding the eyes.

"And now, Joe? Back to the crop dusting business?" he said, making small talk.

The grin slowly spread across Joe's face and he shook his head. "I don't think so, Terr. They haven't said." His eyes were penetrating and Terr didn't avoid them. "And you?"

The question echoed in his mind and he had no answer. He thought that by now, he'd have them all. He extended an open hand.

"We shall meet again, Major. Count on it."

Joe looked down at the hand and slowly clasped it in his. "I regret that you had to go through all this."

"Yeah."

Behind them came the sharp snarl of jeeps mixed with the heavy clatter of steel-shod boots. Someone cut in the floodlights hastily mounted on top of the huts, and startled shadows danced around them. Terr didn't have long to wait.

The darts glided silently against the backdrop of a blistered sky, two flat shapes clothed in faint orange fire, something he never expected to see again. In the space between the huts, the men formed two long lines some four katalans apart. Flanked by gold braid, he waited at one end. The darts stopped above them, but there was no rubbernecking from the ranks as one came down slowly and settled daintily at the head of the columns.

After a moment the hatch cracked and the landing strip slid out. Zor-Ell came out alone. He paused at the bottom of the landing strip and his eyes swept the stiff ranks. Terr could see him taking in the crumpled remains of the jeeps and the twisted sheds before he started walking, his footfalls soundless. It had been a long time between visits, Terr decided. He guessed that time had been playing with both of them.

Zor-Ell stopped a couple of paces before Tarleton and his eyes flickered over Terr's external scars. Meetings like these were always awkward and uncomfortable. This one was no exception. The introductions were formal and stilted. Terr should have been excited and eager, but he wasn't. He watched the proceedings with detachment, like the whole thing had been acted out before and he was sitting in on a dull rerun.

The alien turned and walked toward him. They exchanged thoughtful looks and Terr realized what was happening. The aura of confidence and power that awed him before still there, but he had gone through too much. They were on equal terms now.

Zor-Ell recognized the change, nodded and smiled. "Hello, Terr. It's good to see you again," he said in Serrll interlingua.

"You don't know how good, Karhide," Terr agreed softly, trying to tell it all with his eyes. He glanced over Zor-Ell's shoulder at the empty landing strip. He didn't know what he expected. To see Nightwings walk down, to explain it all? After all that had happened, he still hoped.

Zor-Ell studied him, sadness and regret in his eyes. "I'm sorry, my friend," he said gently.

Terr grinned feebly and nodded. He was about to ask Zor-Ell something, then changed his mind. No hurry. Everything was going to be all right. He turned to Tarleton standing beside them. The naval officer looked tightlipped and uncomfortable. Terr did not bother saluting.

"Admiral." He didn't care too much for going away parties and he'd had a bellyful already. With a last look at Zor-Ell, he hobbled stiffly toward the waiting dart.

Chapter Fourteen

READ ALL ABOUT IT! PRESIDENT MAKES PUBLIC APOLOGY
TO THE ORIELI.
CHURCHES LOSING THEIR IDENTITY?
EXTRA! WHO GETS AXED IN ADMINISTRATION SHAKEUP?
ALIENS, GO HOME!

"Jack Willison reporting from the CNN center in New York. For President Hennery, last night's events must have been more harrowing than any election eve. This morning on the south lawn of the White House, with thousands packing the Ellipse and the surrounds, looking old and battered, the President made his historic apology beneath the unknown might of the hovering Orieli starship, the Serrll cruiser having already left during the night.

"They say if you stand on the Theodore Roosevelt Memorial Bridge, you can see the chopped heads floating down the Potomac. Embittered and spent, Kurtland Hennery did not wait for the acrimony of Congress or his own party. Even as the huge starship slowly drifted eastward, he tendered his resignation from the office of the presidency. Given the Vice President's ill health, will Congress accept it? It's an interesting dilemma."

* * *

"Church is big business and the rewards are substantial. The operation is simple. To receive salvation, you have to have your checkbook ready. The Sunday sermon is a reading of the current balance sheet, and the flock are reminded that reaching heaven can only be accomplished by bleeding from the pocket. Hypocrisy like this may finally be getting the Vatican to ask itself the all-searching question. Could the Church go through the eye of the needle? This is Mark Rown for NBC news."

* * *

It started with the damned uniform.

Still half asleep, eyes gummy and mouth with that lived-in feeling, Terr did not feel crisp and bouncy, or about to leap tall buildings. He had plenty of stiff, squeaky muscles and he reveled in decadent self-pity. Groaning unashamedly, he staggered out of the bunk muttering silent curses. He stumbled into the shower, gasping as it worked him over. Then he began to dress.

It was an ordinary set of working grays.

He had the business finished and about to pull up his zip-shirt when he caught himself in the mirror. The face looked hard and the lines were etched deeper. The eyes glared at him with scornful cynicism, certainly not an innocent face. He took in the uniform and started cursing again.

Not the metallic indigo with its yellow Cluster-and-Circle on the chest. A thin red stripe ran down the seam of the trouser leg. On his left breast lay a gold-bordered blue oval filled with little colored pins and stars—fruit salad. A red bar beneath it showed the insignia of a Master Scout, third grade.

Rit!

His thirty pieces of silver? Oh, that evil old bastard. The low calculated craftiness of that twisted mind. First, Anabb maneuvered him into taking on this lousy mission. Then he had him playing second string to Dhar's sabotage antics. And this was the payoff? This time, though, all the smooth talk in the world wasn't going to help. Even a canal worm would take so much before it coils and strikes back.

He raged, giving the bulkhead a hearty kick, which did it no good, but gave him intense satisfaction. He could feel the hot flush of fury prickling his skin. The medic told him not to get excited and Terr damned his impertinence.

He knew what bothered him. He wasn't born yesterday, even if he acted like it. His pride, that's what hurt. To be treated like a minor pawn, shifted and maneuvered at will, molded. He found it maddening, infuriating!

Pride and humiliation, two bitches.

Damn him, damn him.

He collapsed weakly on the crumpled bunk, shuddering with nervous exhaustion. The weariness of utter disillusionment descended on him and his shoulders sagged. He buried his head between his hands and rubbed his eyes. A lot of things suddenly fell into place. Things that perhaps he would rather not have known, like waking up in Medical Bay. It seemed like an eternity now, but it was only a few hours ago.

He did not remember waking. There was a stabbing light and he winced, blinking back smarting tears. A face hovered above him. He heard muted sounds and smelled antiseptic. He knew those sounds and smells intimately. He seemed to have developed a habit of waking up in hospitals. A metallic taste in his mouth made him wince, and he tried to tell the face he was thirsty. A hand appeared carrying a bubble with a drinking straw. Terr sucked eagerly and followed the hand to the face.

"Thank you, Karhide," he mumbled and Zor-Ell nodded. Terr's head cleared up fast. After some grunting and groaning, he propped himself against the pillows. He pulled up the sheet and peered at his side. Baby smooth skin, not even a scar. His shoulder seemed to work okay and no back twinge. Still a little stiff and sore, but it was all there.

Zor-Ell grinned while Terr went through the checklist. "All in order?" he asked, mouth full of small sharp teeth.

"The paintwork doesn't have the right gloss, but that's okay," Terr said briskly, then took some deep, tentative breaths. "I'll take it anyway. Send the bill to the Serrll Diplomatic

Branch." He waved his hand expansively. "And don't forget to add the zeros. They're loaded," he said with a gush of generosity.

"I am pleased to see you well," Zor-Ell said. Terr remembered another using similar words and his face fell. Zor-Ell saw it and frowned.

"It's all right," Terr said. "Birth pains."

He knew what was coming, but he didn't want it to start. They spent some minutes in idle chatter, then there was nothing more to say. They looked at each other and the silence stretched on, becoming tense and uncomfortable.

"I'm sorry, Terr," Zor-Ell said briskly. "They're not here. Director Anabb Karr had an urgent mission on Taltair and Second Scout Dharaklin went with him."

About to play dumb, Terr figured who the hell was he trying to fool? He turned his head and stared at nothing. Even now, if Dhar walked in, he would have greeted him like a brother. He would have trusted him. Trust! Such a dirty word.

Life was hell.

"Tell me about it," he asked flatly.

"It can wait."

Terr looked at him and their eyes locked. "Until when, sir?"

"All right." Zor-Ell told it without injecting emotion. "We know that your friend Dharaklin is responsible for your accident. Commissioner Enllss-rr assumed authority over the matter and I didn't press the point."

"Enllss?" Somehow that didn't come as a total surprise. "And the sabotage incidents?"

Zor-Ell allowed himself a faint smile. "You can work that one out for yourself."

"Yeah," Terr said glumly and nodded.

"There is more to this, of course," Zor-Ell said evenly. "You rest now. We'll talk about it later."

"This is as good a time as any, Karhide."

Zor-Ell looked at him for a moment, deciding things.

"Later."

He left then. There was little Terr could do except lie there, thinking it through. Too much thinking can lead to headaches, especially if the thoughts held dark and murky suspicions.

* * *

He found Mark Larkin in the base observation lounge. Mark stood with his hands folded before him, his eyes wandering among the shadows. Terr walked up to him and stood beside him. He was used to waiting and there was no hurry.

The landscape was a place of silence and cold. Only the stars, brittle and indifferent, dared invade the shadows. A place of never-ending night haunted by its minions. Darkness lay heavy all about like a clammy cloak draped over the ragged, torn terrain. The stillness, waiting for the dawn that would never rise, humbled and subdued.

He had no idea how long they stood there, lost somewhere in their memories. He needed time to restore himself, to replenish something that had drained away. He felt old and broken, beaten to his knees. He longed to feel the flow of hot sand beneath his feet and gaze at pale amber skies, streaked with the rust of a waning day. He yearned for the simple peace of living each day as it came, without want, without need.

The years lay heavy on his shoulders. Had the experience been worth the price? He suspected the price had been somewhat excessive. He felt his face crease into a wry grin as memories intruded. He and Dhar used to sit in front of the mud huts, sipping fermented peelath berry juice, letting the embers of a dying fire warm their souls as the desert wind keened softly in their ears. Shadows would dance high all around them and their voices were lusty and free.

Terr remembered the talks that found them greeting a scarlet dawn, huddled around a smoldering ring of ash. Without a thought, they would gather a few essentials and set out into the

301

desert to follow the sun. It did not matter where. They were together and that was enough. Their favorite haunt was the oasis of Katai Than, where a still pool of green water, lined by tall peelath, draped with drooping taklan moss, waited for them.

The memories would not give him peace.

Rit!

"They're sending us down tomorrow," Mark said, the words coming out slow and measured.

"I know," Terr said.

Mark looked at him and a faint smile touched his face. "You know something? I always wanted to know what them astronauts found in space travel. I'm not a learned man, but I can appreciate the need now. Never expected to find out like this, though." His laugh hollow and Terr felt his pain.

"What are you going to do now, Mr. Larkin?"

Mark shrugged. "I don't rightly know. Might move out to Houston. I don't think I can go back to the farm. Without Sally, well, you know. It would never be the same."

"I understand. The kids will be happier in a large city."

"Yeah. They'll need proper schooling. The government is talking of compensation. If that comes through, I'll have enough to make sure they're taken care of."

They stood in each other's presence, awkward and tense. Then Mark turned and faced him fully.

"I can talk to you, Commander. You know how I feel. You've suffered much at the hands of my people and I understand some things better. Right now, without her, I feel dead inside. That will pass, I guess." Slowly, he held out his hand. "I'm not blaming you for what happened, Terr. If that means anything to you."

Terr took the hand and held it firmly. He kept looking at Mark because it took him a while to find the words.

"Thank you. It means a great deal." He had trouble clearing his throat then. "I will probably not see you again, Mr. Larkin. If there is anything I can ever do…"

With Shadow and Thunder

Mark shook his head. "You've healed two of my children. I'm grateful for that."

* * *

They sat on the platform, just another shadow brushing the night of space. Colored triangles blinked on the control board. The patterns shifted and small noises intruded in the silence as they drifted through the blackness.

Tommy sat beside Terr while Jenny knelt behind them, one tiny hand on each of their shoulders. The children chattered incessantly, all the while tacitly avoiding any mention of their dead brother. Like a secret, they were determined to share it alone.

Terr took this chance to have a break. He foolishly offered to take them on a tour of Zor-Ell's ship and the LTN base. The kids wanted to see *everything*! The experience left him haggard.

Tommy stared at the studded sky, his mouth gaping with undisguised wonder. "Look at all them stars. There must be millions of them."

"More than a hundred times hundred?" Jenny chirped delightedly. "There are, aren't there, Terr? Aren't there?" She tugged at his shoulder and he looked up. They were smeared above them in careless profusion that made a jagged, brilliant arch.

"More than a hundred times hundred, honey," he agreed. "More than a thousand."

"Oh." She was silent for a second, then tugged his shoulder again. "Will you take me there, Terr?" Her voice shy and uncertain.

"Hey, me too!" Tommy declared firmly.

"Sure. We'll steal a Kran starship and roam the stars." They grinned at each other in a shared conspiracy. Jenny bent down and their cheeks touched.

"I like you," she declared in a stage whisper.

"I like you too, honey," Terr said, amused.

"Where do the Orieli come from?" Tommy wiggled with excitement. "Did you see their ship above the White House?" Then he looked at Terr soberly and touched his hand. "Not that your M-4s aren't super, you know."

Terr nodded, trying hard not to laugh. "See that thick patch of stars?" He pointed at Sagittarius. "There, that's where they come from. You cannot see their stars because they're hidden behind giant gas clouds."

"I thought they came from a globular cluster." Tommy looked at him suspiciously.

"They do, but the Milky Way is their home also."

"What about your stars?" Jenny asked. "Where are they?"

He pointed at the Coal Sack. "All those stars, my princess. They belong to the Serrll."

"All of them?" she whispered in awe. "And there are bug-eyed green monsters and pirates and bad people? Are there?"

Terr thought of Terchran and smiled. Maybe not bug-eyed, but definitely green. "I guess there are."

"And you take care of 'em, right?" Tommy declared and with pointed fingers blasted away at the scenery.

"Yeah," Terr muttered. "I take care of them."

The terminator crept up on them, casting black sheets of shadow. On their left, hugging the horizon, the stars paled as a splash of muddy-red light grew and blossomed. The corona flared into a hard orange hemisphere. The kids stared open-mouthed as Terr pointed at the horizon on their left. They were so intent on watching the sun, they missed the real reason why he brought them here.

They faced a thin blue sickle. Behind it, a round black hole blotted out the stars. Almost invisible, bright blue pins winked and shimmered in the blackness. Pale phosphorescence flickered where the oceans hugged the equator.

"Earth," Terr said moodily.

"It's beautiful!" Jenny cried and clapped her hands with

glee.

"Golly, you can almost reach out and touch it," Tommy declared, then looked at Terr with a worried expression. "It looks so small," he said uncertainly and Terr laughed.

While the children gaped at their world, he stopped the platform. He gathered Jenny in his lap and cleared his throat. "I will tell you a short story, but you must keep it a secret, okay? This is only between the three of us." They nodded, eyes round and bright.

"Once upon a time, a stranger came visiting from a far planet. He meets two very special people and he loves them very much. They have a lot of growing up to do and this stranger makes them a promise. One day, soon, a starship will come for them and take them to his home world. Remember," he said looking at them. "It's our secret."

"We won't tell anyone." Jenny wriggled and snuggled against him.

"You can count on us, Terr," Tommy declared solemnly.

"Soon," Terr said and stroked Jenny's hair.

* * *

Terr breezed into the cabin wearing a thin smile only skin deep. Zor-Ell sat sprawled behind a milky slab, looking relaxed and comfortable, studying Kran cursive in the holoview. An amused twinkle lit his eyes when he looked up.

"I've been expecting you, Master Scout," he said, his words laughing. Terr glanced down at his uniform and shrugged.

"Not a bad fit, is it," he said, joining in the game.

"It suits you. You wear your power well."

"It has that effect when you don't give a damn."

"And you don't give a damn?" Zor-Ell asked and smiled broadly. "Care to sit down, or is the problem too weighty?"

Terr laughed then. He couldn't help it. "You're very much

305

like him, Karhide," he said after making himself passably comfortable.

"Like?"

"Anabb."

"Indeed?" Zor-Ell tilted his head slightly and his eyebrows climbed.

"Take it from me. Both of you have black and devious ways of doing what you do."

"I'm not sure whether that was a compliment or an insult."

"A problem, isn't it? Anyway, you want to hear a story?" Terr asked and Zor-Ell nodded. "Good. It's a bit unusual, but I'm in the mood."

"You have my undivided attention."

His eyes sparkled, amused, tolerant, waiting for Terr to catch up with the obvious. Maybe it *was* obvious, but Terr wanted to hang it out in the open anyway.

"It goes something like this. We've got this place, see. The people get along tolerably well. One guy…by the way, any resemblance to living persons is purely coincidental."

"Of course," Zor-Ell said with a straight face.

"As I was saying. This guy had it pretty good; interesting job, plenty of excitement. Then one day we get this joker dropping in, making waves. Bare-faced gall, if you asked me. Well, our innocent trusting soul gets talked into doing something noble, but nothing to get choked up about. Full of enthusiasm, our hero goes on this mission. Unfortunately, he isn't told everything and things start to go wrong. Incidents hazardous to our hero's health, things like that. I'm not boring you, am I?"

"Not at all. This is fascinating."

"I'm relieved. One day, our guy has an accident, a practical gag by a friend. Things get to be pretty tough then. He manages to live through his mishap with one or two suspicions, which are not particularly noble. He has a very suspicious nature, you know," Terr said seriously.

"I feel for him." Zor-Ell grinned.

"Yeah. Well, as I said, our hero is out to get some answers. Just to reassure himself that what he went through was noble after all. You see, he has this wild idea the whole pointless thing was staged. Two cultures engaged in a mutual evaluation exercise with our hero in the middle, used by both sides. Absurd, he thought. Ha ha." They both had a good chuckle. When it ended the silence rang with their laughter.

"He couldn't be right by any chance? Could he?" Terr asked softly.

Zor-Ell did not say anything. Terr figured that maybe he didn't have to. His hands went clammy and his heart hammered with the dread of certainty. He stood up and his face twisted with pain, disappointment, and frustrated rage.

"Why?" he demanded bitterly.

"You know the answer already," Zor-Ell said wearily.

"Don't tell me; political expediency, right? Why should you guys be any different? But you know what really gets under my skin? Your damn arrogance, that's what!" he roared and slammed his fist against the desk. "You knew, all this time. And we made it so easy for you. Just point us in the right direction and we were off, stumbling along like the fools we must have—"

"Terr—"

"—appeared. But you don't have to explain it to me, Karhide. When it comes to world-savers, I've had it done by one of the best. You know something?" His hand shook as he pointed a finger at Zor-Ell. "Your uniform. I would have done anything for it. I would have *died* for it. And you know why? Because I saw in you a dignity of conviction and an honesty of justice. I should have known better. It's only a rag like any other. The only thing that makes us different, Karhide, you were more practiced at it." Terr raged at him with the fury of hate. Death tingled in his hands and the power surged through him. He was tempted.

Zor-Ell's face turned hard, his eyes uncompromising. He

307

stood and clasped his hands behind his back.

"I couldn't have stopped it, Terr," he said harshly, "even if I wanted to. Which we didn't."

"You bastards! It was all a social experiment. An exercise in applied alien psychology and first contact procedures."

"You cannot pretend that you didn't know, or suspect."

"And that makes it all right?"

"We played by the rules you set, Master Scout."

There wasn't any sympathy in Zor-Ell's eyes, only hard duty. If Anabb used him, Terr got paid, and paid in full. He had his medals and his promotion. What else did he expect? Speeches, hero worship? He had nothing to bitch about. The knocks came with the territory, right?

He chuckled and shook his head. "I guess in the end we both did what we had to," he said bleakly. "When counting the stakes, one person's feelings hardly matter, do they?"

"You judge yourself too harshly. An individual always matters."

"You sure fooled me," Terr said and sneered. He no longer cared for reasons or explanations. He saw Teena before him and he longed for her touch. "What now, Karhide?"

"The BCPA is sending a replacement mission. It will take them a few days before they get around to it. Meanwhile, you have the freedom of my ship and the base."

Terr searched his face. "And you?"

"Complete my job," Zor-Ell said and shrugged.

"I suppose you're going to Captal? What a waste."

The starship commander faded and in Zor-Ell's eyes came understanding. "I know a little of what you went through, Terr. At the hand of a friend, it came harder."

"Yeah." When Terr reached the doorway, something made him turn. "What happened during that year while you were on Earth?" he asked on impulse. Zor-Ell didn't try to look away. Terr wished he could have read those emotions.

"We have this procedure," Zor-Ell began slowly, reluctantly. Terr listened closely. "It involves superimposing a brain pattern of a specially trained observer over the subject's memory matrix. The recipient is unaware he is carrying another personality. After twenty days the observer is retrieved and debriefed, the subject none the wiser. It's an infallible way of gaining information without having to reveal yourself to the natives.

"When we approached Earth, we had run out of observers and I was qualified. Something went wrong with the initial transfer, but at the time, we didn't know that we had a problem. At any rate, my first officer failed to have me retrieved after the twenty days expired. While they sought a solution back on Zaron, I remained stuck for almost a local year in another mind, not knowing whether I would ever again see the stars of home."

It was quiet in the cabin without any of the small ship noises. Terr understood, trying to imagine how Zor-Ell must have felt. Trapped more completely than Terr ever was.

"They obviously found what caused the retrieval failure."

"They did. And you can guess what it was," Zor-Ell said quietly.

"I don't have to guess," Terr said wryly. "The neuron matrix in the Earthman's frontal lobes has artificially created layers to enhance density and capacity."

"That's right, and there is only one way for it to have happened—genetic engineering. The species simply could not have evolved into their present form from available paleontological evidence. I became trapped when my memories leaked across the matrix boundary. Although of personal interest, we have another and more pressing reason for our presence here, as Karhide Arlon Dee explained. Earth forms a last link in a barrier that protects your flank against the Krans. We're interested in expanding our relations with the Serrll, but we need to tread carefully."

"And your contact with us so far has not been without incidents."

"It was revealing."

"Yeah. Everything you told me is highly confidential, isn't it?"

Zor-Ell looked steadily at him. "Of course."

"Don't worry, Karhide, I shall keep my mouth shut."

"I know, Terr."

The doorway closed behind him and Terr leaned against it. The corridor was empty. He stood there for a moment before walking off. He fancied he could hear the echo of his footsteps.

Looking back on it all, it seemed to be such a colossal waste.

* * *

Salina hung there like a rusty emerald shot through with smeared patches of orange and brown. Terr watched with mixed feelings as it filled the VI plot around him.

Once, a long time ago, as a kid, he used to spend his summers in the wilds of the family estate. He remembered his grandfather, wrinkled and bent. To Terr, he appeared old as time itself. His grandfather accepted his presence with amused tolerance. Away from house discipline, Terr was a reign of terror.

Recognition is a matter of contrast. He learned that when he returned to the estate years later. He remembered vividly the secret excitement growing in him, making him restless, watching the hills roll away and the slim tower of the old residence emerge out of the summer haze. Somehow, it was not the same. He could not recapture the carefree joys of his boyhood. Like the tide, time had receded, leaving him on a deserted shore.

He hadn't been back since. That is how he felt now.

The shadowing M-4s dropped out as the Orieli ship maneuvered into a parking orbit. Even as it took up its new station a swarm of local craft crowded around the cruiser. A squadron of three M-1s and a shuttle appeared over the terminator. They matched speed and waited. Zor-Ell stared at them with detached curiosity, then turned and blinked at Terr.

"I guess our presence has caused quite a stir."

"It's not every day that we make contact with an alien species," Terr pointed out.

"Alien species? Wait until you meet the Krans," Zor-Ell said and Terr's skin prickled.

They brought the Salina shuttle into one of the cavernous hangar bays. Zor-Ell and Terr went down to meet the delegation. A squint-eyed little First Secretary was Chief of Mission. He had sad eyes and a moist hand. He gave Zor-Ell the benefit of his myopic stare as he introduced the Assistant for Protocol and an Undersecretary for Alien Liaison. All very exciting.

They were told that Controller of Salina and Prime Director of the Rolan group was anxious to welcome back the Orieli. Zor-Ell made all haste. It would not do to keep Trianon waiting. Cel Field looked wilted and parched beneath the cool red sun. The ships littering the field swam in the twisting heat, their command bubbles glaring with polarized reflection. Salina was frigid and wet during winter, but summers tended to be very dry. They touched down at the military terminus and the access tube snaked out to meet them.

They were bundled into a cable-tube and ended up in a brightly lit hall at the Center, where they were supposed to meet some of the blue-chip citizenry. Trianon had the podium all to himself where he waxed lucid.

That's when Terr found he was a hero. He'd been a hero before. It wasn't all it was cracked up to be. The sob writers ate it up and maybe the hero angle could be used for something. He glanced down at the red bar on his chest and chuckled.

They all made speeches, telling each other what great guys they were. It would make great viewing on the early, late news. The grubs would sigh in blissful contentment, assured the government would not deflate their beds while they were asleep.

Terr knew he was being cynical. He had seen the grease

behind the machinery and his hands were kind of dirty.

When the thing broke up, he said his goodbyes to Zor-Ell, promising to look him up on Captal, and took a cable-tube to Trianon's offices. He had a small detail to clear up and Trianon might forget to see him. Terr hummed to himself as he walked to the reception desk, admiring some of the stuff hanging on the walls. There was one item, a rug. It looked like the guy who made it had spilled paint all over it and set it on fire even before he got started. He shook his head.

The dour-faced individual buffering the offices did not look relieved at the sight of Terr's face, and him being a hero and all.

"Can I help you, sir?" the individual managed to bring the words out in a sour mumble. It must have hurt him to say it.

"You can inform the Controller that Master Scout Terrllss-rr is waiting to see him."

Did Terr want to see the Controller *now*?

Terr did.

Did Terr have an appointment?

No appointment.

The other's eyes positively glowed with happiness. He was most apologetic, but without an appointment, Terr could not see Trianon. Terr had met his kind before. Small busybodies whose sole reason for existence was to pour sand into the gears of government machinery. He reached across the desk and grabbed the individual below the meaty neck and pulled. The eyes bulged in astonishment. He shook him a little and the skeleton rattled.

"Now you listen to me, you pompous little fart," he growled and squeezed. The other's mouth gaped like a landed fish. "The Controller wants to see me, pal. In fact, he is *most* anxious to see me. I can bounce you around a bit, but I would hate to get my hands dirty. I just washed them. Get the picture?" He pushed and the guy fell back with a flurry of arms and legs. Sounds came from him, little fluttery squeaks of indignation.

Terr glanced at the door panels and waited. "They're not open."

The other glared and his hand touched something on the console pad. The doors creaked and began to slide apart.

Terr grinned and patted his cheek. "Now, wasn't that easy?"

He guessed the other couldn't find words fitting enough to describe him. So he lost another hero worshiper. He'd get over it.

Trianon was making some calls and his eyes widened when Terr walked in. He waved at the formchairs in front of his desk and Terr made himself comfortable. It didn't take long.

Finally, Trianon closed down the Wall and slapped the desk with both hands. "Well, Master Scout?" he inquired, eyes cold. "Weren't you supposed to be on your way to Captal with our Orieli friends?"

Terr did not bother with the formalities. "Afraid not, sir. There has been a change in the itinerary."

Trianon stared. "I don't understand," he said and Terr believed him.

"I'm taking a detour to Taltair. I want to see my partner, among other things." Trianon's face could have been a carved slab of wood for all the expression it had. "I also wanted to check that my M-1 was flown over here from Taltair. I called your office from the Serrll Moon Base, remember?"

"Oh, yes, yes. The least we could do for one of our heroes. Heh, heh."

"By the way, Mr. Controller, have you seen anything of Anatol Keller?"

The smile sagged and the eyes turned muddy. "I'm not accustomed to following the movements of every Fleet officer, Master Scout," Trianon said smoothly.

Terr nodded. "Sure, I can understand that, but if he was

returning from the SMB with Commissioner Enllss-rr, he would have to clear through Salina, right? And Anatol is a guy you cannot forget in a hurry."

Trianon's smile faded and his fingers tapped the table. "I haven't asked for any courtesies, Mister, and I damned sure haven't gotten any. You call me 'sir'! You read that, Mister?" His voice grated like tearing steel. If he didn't watch it, he would ruin it.

"We just finished the ceremonies, Mr. Controller, and I would like to keep this friendly. I'm only interested in Anatol," Terr said easily.

"You insolent worm!" Trianon screamed and pointed a shaking finger at the door. "Get out! Get out before I have you thrown out!"

"Not before I get some answers."

"I'll see you on Cantor for this."

"I'm a hero, remember? You said so yourself. It wouldn't look good for Salina to intern a real live hero, now would it?"

"Get out!" Trianon roared, shaking with rage. Terr stood up and took a step toward the desk. Something must have shown in his eyes, for Trianon suddenly looked wary and uncomfortable. Terr wasn't in the mood for guessing games.

"I can find out from the Field Dispatcher…sir."

Trianon's mouth worked but nothing came out. Then he gave a strangled grunt and nodded.

"He is on Taltair, waiting for reassignment," he said, looking hollow and old.

"Taltair?" That was very interesting. Terr rubbed his chin trying to puzzle it out. Why would Anatol be waiting for reassignment on Taltair, of all places? It was only a Bureau of Cultural Affairs division. Then his eyes lit up and he grinned. The Diplomatic Branch was on Taltair, and Anabb was on Taltair.

Terr straightened and stood to. "Thank you for your time, sir," he said and held up his hand. "Don't bother, sir. I'll let myself out."

He took the cable-tube to the military terminus. There were no gun handlers with butterfly nets waiting for him. Just as well. His ship stood berthed at the far end of the Field and he took a sled-pad to get to it. At least it was there. He had a moment of panic in Trianon's office thinking the SMB hadn't relayed his message to Taltair.

The sled glided toward the ship and he hummed happily. As he drew nearer, he studied the familiar lines with fondness. *Sheeva* was a lovely ship, but the Fleet insisted in ruining it with an ugly gray color finish. It looked like a civilian heap. He really ought to do something about that finish one of these days.

It did not take long to preflight. He cleared with SC&C and took off, ripping through the atmosphere. *Valon* flashed by below him and he felt slightly sorry for Zor-Ell, but not so sorry that he wanted to stay behind.

Some six days to Taltair, it gave him plenty of time to think about things.

Chapter Fifteen

The sky had a green steely tinge, making it look harsh and ominous. Low clouds raced toward the night. In the west a haunting pattern of beaten copper and gold painted the dying day. Thunder rolled ponderously over the city. Rain fell, soft and invisible. The wind howled mournfully and Terr pulled up his collar, cursing silently.

He stopped before the entrance, shook out the collar and pushed his way through. There was no attendant, the place cool and quiet. Heads turned briefly to look him over, suspicious and hostile. The pairs ring stood empty. Too early for that kind of action.

He walked to the bar and Razzo looked up in surprise. "Well, if it isn't the hero." He wiped his hands against the apron and chuckled. "What'll you have, hero? On the house," he added generously.

"An item called Anatol Keller," Terr said. "Seen him cruising around?"

"No drink?" Razzo looked disappointed.

"No drink."

"Ah, now you've gone and hurt my feelings. After I tried to be nice to you and all, you being a hero." Razzo tried to look sad and almost made it.

"I'm about to burst into tears. And you never had any feelings. Now, about that item."

Razzo jerked his head toward the pairs ring and hooked a twisted finger under Terr's nose. "I'd hate to have to clean up the place again, hero. It'd spoil our relationship, see."

"I'll be neat," Terr assured him and turned into the gloom.

With Shadow and Thunder

There were enough occupied tables that Terr did not see him at once. Anatol was nursing a tall tumbler, staring absently at the contents. Guilty conscience? Terr strode to the table and sat down. Anatol looked up and his mouth fell. His black face was easier to read than a Wall ad. Surprise, then fear, melting into a mask of low cunning. Terr almost laughed.

"I'm looking up old friends. Never expected to see you here, Anatol. In a place like this, I mean," Terr said amiably and glanced around.

"You…ah…when…"

"Your conversation is sparkling." Terr chuckled and gave him a nasty smile. "I won't bother you for long, you being busy and all. All I want is a few simple answers. When I saw you, I said to myself, now there's a guy who can straighten me out."

Anatol had gotten over his excitement at seeing him and started to look his old, mean self.

"I've got nothing to say to you," he mumbled drunkenly.

"Now, is that some way to treat an old buddy? After all we've been through?"

"If you don't stop bothering me, Mister, I'll call the MPs."

Terr tsked and shook his head. He picked up Anatol's tumbler and poured the mess into his lap. Anatol yelped and sprang out of his seat. Terr was waiting for him. His fist connected with a satisfying thump and Anatol went spinning toward the pairs ring. Razzo let out a scream, but Terr had no time for him.

Anatol looked shaken, but he was game and in top shape. However, Terr was more enthusiastic. He eased up to Anatol, not trying to be fancy or anything. He had to slam him around a bit. Unfortunately, some of the furniture wasn't up to it. Terr held him around the neck and was about to make him eat the rug when Anatol coughed and shook his head. Torn between business and pleasure, Terr let go and Anatol dropped heavily. To show him he was really a nice guy, he even propped Anatol into a chair and dusted him off.

"About those answers. Care to try it again?"

Anatol wiped blood trickling out of the corner of his mouth and glared. One of his eyes was puffed and he would have a headache pretty soon.

"Finished your debrief?" Terr asked and Anatol barely nodded. "Anabb?" He nodded again. "Seen Dhar?" Anatol shook his head. Terr glanced at the broken furniture.

"I haven't seen him," Anatol mumbled, his tongue poking at the inside of his cheek. "I don't even know who he is."

Terr asked him one or two other questions, just to keep the conversation going. At the end, he grinned amiably and patted Anatol's shoulder.

"There, that wasn't too hard. We could have settled the whole thing over a drink. Now you owe Razzo some change for the furniture." Terr stood up and looked down. "If I don't see you again, I'll understand."

He almost got to the entrance when Razzo planted himself before him, slapping a meat cleaver against the palm of his left hand.

"You said you'd be neat."

Terr grinned sourly and pointed at his pal with the shiner. "My friend had a guilty conscience, Razzo. Had an urge to confess. Try him," he said and pushed past him. "I'll look you up sometime."

"Don't!" Razzo called after him.

A swell guy.

* * *

Terr knew how it felt when he had to do something unpleasant and disagreeable. His feet dragged, his shoulders stooped and there is a fluttery feeling where the stomach is supposed to be.

Well, right then, he felt none of those things.

The cable-tube took him up to Admin. The doors slid away and he gathered in the old sights and smells. The place had changed a bit and he wasn't sure he liked it. The curved reception desk was still the same, angled slightly toward the window screens.

Ariane looked up in surprise and her dark eyes smiled at him. "Welcome home, Terr," she husked.

He spent a moment looking at her. She had delicate high cheekbones, full lips and a long neck. Her narrow, oval head had no hair, and she was gorgeous. He simply could not figure what made her put up with a crusty old fart like Anabb.

"It's good to be back."

She leaned toward him and winked. "He's been pacing all morning waiting for you."

"He needs the exercise," Terr said ungraciously.

"Ariane, when he's through propositioning," Anabb's rusty growl came through the comms, "ask him if he will condescend to make a brief appearance, okay?"

Her smile faded and she hurriedly touched controls on her console.

"Agent Terrllss-rr is on his way in, sir," she said sternly as the translucent panels began to slide away.

Terr smiled at her and followed the beaten trail leading to the door. They closed behind him with a soft hiss. Anabb stood beside the desk, his back to Terr, looking out the window screen. Terr could see the towers of the Center fading into low cloud. Anabb turned and the window faded to dull gray.

The months have not made him any younger. His face looked hard and weather-worn, and it could not hide the lines. A cold face used to command and tough decisions. The burn on his cheek had faded a little. Lack of use, Terr guessed. The shoulders were not quite square, but then they never were.

Anabb sized the boy up and he gave a stillborn smile.

"Hello, son," he growled. "Good to see you again."

"It comes better from Ariane," Terr said easily, returning the gaze without blinking.

Anabb smiled broadly. "I don't doubt it. How was your

flight in?"

"Gave me time to think. Perhaps too much time."

Anabb nodded and waved at the formchair. As his boss poured them a drink, Terr made himself comfortable. Anabb handed him the tumbler. After twirling the mess inside, he raised the glass in a salute.

"To a successful mission," Anabb said and sipped.

"Hell, it's only a drink," Terr said and took a pull. It wasn't bad. Must have been the stock Anabb used to polish Captal legislators. He tried not to let that spoil it.

"Tell me, my boy. Was it rough?"

Terr remembered the pain, fire, blood, and other things. "You weren't there when I got back," he said evenly and chewed a bit of ice.

Anabb took it lightly, but some of the fire went out of his eyes and his shoulders sagged even more. "I wanted to be there, boy. You have questions, I'm sure."

"One or two." Terr laid the tumbler on the glass-topped tray.

Anabb eyed the pickled salad on Terr's chest and smiled. "Doesn't look bad on you."

"You're the second to tell me that."

"And who was the first?"

"Zor-Ell. We had a nice long chat after he got me patched up." He let Anabb think it through.

"You're feeling bitter and blaming me, but I also follow orders."

Terr chuckled and shook his head. "Don't try that one on me. I know how you operate. The whole deal has your smell. You get to remember it after a while."

"Give me a for-instance."

"All right. We'll start with the easy ones. About Anatol. That was a dirty trick to play on a sucker like him. Provoking the Orieli just to see how they would react."

"Who told you?"

"Zor-Ell talked and I bumped into Anatol on my way here. How did you get him to do it?"

"I told him, if he didn't obey orders and I found out, I would have him shot." Anabb smiled his evil grin and Terr chuckled in appreciation.

"Yeah. Even Anatol could follow a simple order like that. Tell me, what did you get out of it?"

"We needed to know if their weapons capability had changed in the last five years."

"If it did, it wouldn't have degraded, but never mind."

Anabb's features twisted, becoming cold and businesslike. "As for your next question, the incidents Dhar engineered, they were part of our evaluation program."

"Engineered to kill me?"

"Getting a bit paranoid, aren't you?"

"You're an evil old bastard, Anabb," Terr said with relish. "Organizing a bit of sabotage on an alien base just to see what they would do was okay. Good clean fun. Gives the boys something to talk about. I would have done it myself. The one I like best was being slammed around a bit, then sent on a one-way down trip in a dart. You must have heard about it. I had a few good chuckles over that one."

"You're cutting it a bit strong. Sure, I gave him a free hand to set up an incident or two. Mutual exchange of data, if you like. But why would Dhar want to kill you? As I understand it, he's your brother."

"*Was* my brother. I think he may be trying to even the score for Gashkarali."

"Your Trillian mission? It would mean that he's working for Terchran and the Servatory Party."

"That's right."

"Absurd!"

"That might be. I just want to know where he is, that's all."

"On a mission. I cannot tell you anything more."

"Never mind, I'll find him. Just one more thing while I'm

still in the mood. On my way from Salina, I had a lot of time to think things through. You shouldn't let your agents think, Anabb. Bad for them. In the end, it catches up with all of us. Call it an occupational disease. In my case, I realized how much I hated what you made me do through all the time I've been working for you as a paid killer. I walked in wide-eyed, granted, but you used me. You played on my needs. All your deals and schemes, it all sucks. A hell of a way to get what you want, or for a government to get what it wants. I blame myself partly, but I was naïve. You, on the other hand, you knew exactly what you were doing when you put me to work.

"What gets me, and I told Karhide Zor-Ell the same thing, is your damned arrogance at picking the rights and the wrongs. You would use anyone around you without a shred of emotion to achieve your ends. Maybe that's part of the job. I wouldn't know. Well, you can take your job and shove it. I'm through with your twisted ideas of honor. From now on, I'll be working things out without your help. If I bungle it, it's my ass."

In the sudden quiet, the only thing Terr heard was his ragged breathing. Anabb faced him, looking old, wrinkled, and alone. To hell with it.

"I'm sorry you feel like that about it, my boy."

"Yeah, I bet you are," Terr said, too late to take it back. It had been too late for quite a while. Anabb nodded and cleared his throat.

"As you said, it comes with the job. There are no easy ways around it," he said regretfully.

"Perhaps, but you can tell it to some other trusting sucker. I'm going on leave. Four months, wasn't it? I still have that, don't I?"

"Yes, you still have that."

"My report is in the channels, sir. Thanks for the drink," Terr said breezily, stood up and made for the doors.

"Terr!" Something urgent in Anabb's voice made Terr stop in his tracks. He heard more throat-clearing noises. "It's

Teena."

He reflected on the stooping shoulders and the fluttery stomach. He knew something bad was about to happen. Maybe if he pretended…He turned slowly and looked at Anabb standing behind his desk.

"They have her. Sorry, boy," Anabb said, looking tense and uncomfortable.

The bottom fell out of his world and he gazed into a dark chasm. It would only take a small step to plunge himself into it. Something in him withered and died. There must have been a lot there, for he felt all hollow.

Then it hit him. "You sent Dhar after her, didn't you?"

"Terr—"

"Don't say it. You would only spoil it." He felt his anger straining within him. "Haven't you taken enough from me?" He wanted to reach out and crush everything around him.

Teena!

Death settled on his shoulders and he clenched his fists. "You took away my pride and honor. I didn't mind. To play the power game, I sold my honor cheaply. You told me that before, but why her?" he thundered in anguished frustration and helplessness. Lightning crackled between his fingers and he took a step forward. Real fear in Anabb's eyes now, he stood his ground.

"You had to take from me the only thing I ever loved and cared for; the only thing which meant anything. And you took Dhar from me also." He leveled his arms and roared out his anger. A flash of light and a clap of thunder shook the office and the wind screamed around them. Between them, a blackened pit smoked where the rug stood. The shelving behind Anabb collapsed, sending the memorabilia crashing to the floor.

He shifted his hands and bellowed again. With shadow and thunder, Death walked with him and the power flowed through his arms. He felt pain deep within him and he wanted it to end.

323

He wanted peace, but it wouldn't come. He could only roar out his anguish and anger.

When it stopped, they stood in an empty shell. Pale twisted fingers of smoke curled above the charred remnants of furniture. Thunder still echoed in the silence. He looked at Anabb and pointed his hand at him.

"It would be so easy," he said harshly and his voice was the voice of Death. "You would hardly have time to scream, but that wouldn't solve anything. I want you to think about it, at night, when you try to sleep."

Anabb looked at the wreckage of his office, his evil grin mocking.

"I take it this means you're leaving the Branch?"

"You can take it any way you like." Terr turned and lightning flashed. The translucent panels splintered and collapsed. He walked through without looking back. For him there were no yesterdays. Ariane sat there, shaking like a leaf, one small fist pressed white against her mouth. He hardly noticed her.

* * *

Shadows stretched their long fingers and touched the gently rolling hills. Somewhere behind him lightning flashed. Thunder followed, a low distant rumble that set the air trembling.

He was far away, lost in memories. A dull ache throbbed deep in his chest. He felt a heaviness on his shoulders and realized with grim shock that it had been with him always—at least it felt like it. The communal made a gentle sweep and he looked down. The house lay nestled against the hillside. It stood in shadow, dark and empty. Lights showed in some of the nearby houses.

The communal hovered, then settled gently on the landing apron. For a moment, he thought she would come running out like she always did, but there was no one. The bubble opened and the driver held the door open for him. He sighed heavily and climbed out.

"Good night, sir," he heard the driver say. When Terr turned the communal was gone.

Inside, he walked through empty rooms, feeling and remembering. He lingered, touching things, hearing her laughter. He felt her presence everywhere. He heard echoing footsteps and stopped. They were his. In the Play Room, her long scarf lay in a loose bundle on the rug. He stared at it, then bent down and picked it up. He brought it to his face and drew a deep breath of her smell. He shared her sorrows, tasted her tears and bathed in her smiles. He buried his face in it and fought back the sobs.

Outside, he leaned against the ramp railing and smelled the wind and the wetness in the air. The rain fell, misty soft and caressing. He stood there and did not feel it. There was only hollow emptiness beneath black clouds.

"Teena!" he cried in agony and lightning crashed around him. Arms raised, he reached toward a turbulent sky.

About the author

Stefan Vučak has written twenty-one novels, which include eight SF books in the Shadow Gods Saga. His *Cry of Eagles* won the coveted Readers' Favorite silver medal award, and his *All the Evils* was the prestigious Eric Hoffer contest finalist and Readers' Favorite silver medal winner. *Strike for Honor* won the gold medal.

Stefan leveraged a successful career in the Information Technology industry, which took him to the Middle East working on cellphone systems. Writing has been a road of discovery, helping him broaden his horizons. He also spends time as an editor and book reviewer. Stefan lives in Melbourne, Australia.

To learn more about Stefan Vučak, visit his:
Website: www.stefanvucak.com
Facebook: www.facebook.com/StefanVucakAuthor
Twitter: @stefanvucak

More Books by Stefan Vučak

https://www.stefanvucak.com/Books/

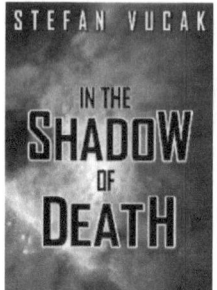  

  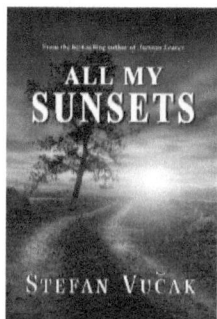